"We're safe now, Meggie."

Royce reined his mount near a still pond and dropped the reins as he set Megan away from him and slipped from the saddle. He held up his arms to her and she came into them, eagerly.

"Meggie," Richard murmured, his tone reflecting the wonder Megan felt as he gazed down into eyes darkened with desire. Slowly, he lowered his mouth to hers in a gently, questing kiss.

Instinctively Megan responded to Royce's heady touch. Her breathing grew rapid as the kiss deepened, and she could feel her insides quiver as Royce moved his hand down her back and pressed her closer. An unexplainable yearning burst into life at the very core of her being. . . .

DESIRE
AND
DECEIVE

Cordia Byers

FAWCETT GOLD MEDAL · NEW YORK

A Fawcett Gold Medal Book
Published by Ballantine Books
Copyright © 1989 by Cordia Byers

Library of Congress Catalog Card Number: 89-91403

ISBN 0-449-14580-8

Manufactured in the United States of America

First Edition: February 1990

With love to my wonderful daughter, Michelle,
and new son-in-law, Bobby.

Chapter 1

The spring of 1337 had been unusually warm, yet as the grey light of dawn gave way to another sunny day, the early morning chill still held reign in the stone corridors of the keep of Dragon's Lair. Megan shivered as she stripped off the rough woolen chausses and tossed them into the pile of discarded clothing at the foot of her bed. She quickly slipped on her tattered robe and tied the frayed cord belt about her waist. With a careless toss of her head and a quick sweep of her hand beneath the heavy mane of raven hair, she freed it from the neckline of the garment. Thinking no more about her tousled appearance, she strode across the chamber to the fireplace and sank down on the low wooden stool in front of the hearth.

A pensive frown marked her smooth forehead, and her brows knit with tiny creases over the bridge of her slender nose, as she held out her hands to the fire. The warmth began to seep into her chilled flesh while she gazed into the fiery orange and blue flames licking greedily about the logs. She paid little attention to the leaping tentacles that devoured the wood to give off the warmth her aching body craved after the long, cold night spent in the saddle. Her mind was preoccupied with far more serious matters than her own physical discomfort at the moment.

Megan gave a snort of disgust and shook her head. The previous night had garnered her little for her efforts, and if things did not improve soon, the people of Dragon's Lair would end up starving through the coming winter months. Leaning closer to the fire's warmth, Megan hugged her waist. Her frown deepened as her thoughts turned toward Mallory O'Roarke. Her lips thinned with distaste for the man who had left her in such dire straits. Her half brother and guardian to her father's estate of Dragon's Lair until she married, he had pauperized the estate before his death. His wenching, gaming, and extravagant living at court had taken everything her father had left her as well as the inheritance Mallory had received upon their mother's death.

Although Dragon's Lair's coffers were now empty, and only a small herd of sheep remained as a means to make her own living, Megan had a much heavier burden to bear than seeing to her own welfare. As the last of her line, she was responsible for the people of Dragon's Lair, who depended upon her family for their livelihood, especially to provide them with the seeds to sow their fields. This responsibility had become one of Megan's major problems. After the heavy rains ruined the crops last year, souring the seeds for the spring planting, it was her duty to buy or barter for the new seeds they needed. However, due to Mallory's selfish indulgences, she had no means of fulfilling that obligation to her people.

Her thoughts on her brother, Megan's expression hardened. Her indigo eyes flashed with loathing and she pressed her delicately shaped lips into a thin line. She didn't like to think ill of the dead, but she could honestly say she didn't regret that Mallory was gone. There had never been any love lost between her half brother and herself. He had been a cruel little boy and had grown into a vicious, selfish man. She had tried to love him because they possessed the same mother, but that had proved an impossibility even when they were children. If he thought she was getting more attention from their mother than he had received, he'd make her life miserable. There had been times when Megan had even feared for her life. When Mallory imagined he'd suffered an injury or insult at her hand, he'd go to any length to get revenge. He'd lie, steal, or do some other vicious thing in order to extract his due for the offense.

Megan could have forgiven him for his cruelty during their youth if his actions had been only those of a spoilt little boy. However Mallory had not changed when he reached manhood. With the power of Dragon's Lair's wealth behind him and the fact that he had become her guardian after her parents' death, he became even more detestable.

Mallory had found cruel pleasure in abusing Megan, despite the fact that she'd never cowered down to him. She'd inherited her father's indomitable spirit and she had refused to allow Mallory the satisfaction of seeing her conquered, no matter how abusive he became. She'd fought him, trying to give as good as she got, but due to his size and strength, she had always come away battered and bruised when he decided to beat her for an imagined wrong. Mallory's cruelty had not stopped with physical punishment. He'd also tormented her mentally. He'd flaunted the fact that she'd never be free of him because he'd gambled away her dower lands, relegating her to spinsterhood for life. To add to her suffering, he'd refused her the company of her own class, with the exception of her cousin, Faith. Megan was not allowed to go to court as was her right as the heir to Dragon's Lair, and he'd kept her secluded away, forbidding her to join him and his friends when they came to the country to hunt.

Much to Megan's regret and in spite of his threats to her well-being, she'd openly defied her brother on only one occasion. She'd joined him and his friends during one of his brief visits to Dragon's Lair. She'd dressed in her finest gown and had come downstairs, confident that Mallory would not embarrass her or himself by ordering her to leave. She had been right to a certain extent. He hadn't ordered her to leave, but she had soon fled from the party of her own accord. She had managed to endure the embarrassment created by his crude remarks about her appearance, but a few minutes later he had humiliated her even more. Mallory had offered Megan for sale to the highest bidder, with one stipulation— whoever purchased her had to guarantee that she be used as a servant.

Megan felt the heat rise in her cheeks at the memory. Even after all this time, she could not stop herself from blushing with shame.

No. Life had not been easy when Mallory was alive, nor had it been made better by his death, Megan reflected cynically. All that had changed was the fact she didn't have to endure his constant harassment and his ridicule. The people of Dragon's Lair were still her responsibility, as they had been for the past four years. Before his untimely death, Mallory had unofficially delegated them to her when she'd complained he was not seeing to their welfare, as was his duty. He'd turned Dragon's Lair over to her to oversee in his absences and did not complain as long as he had money to pay for his vices.

Megan came to her feet and strode across the chamber to the narrow, cross-slit window. She rubbed at her chilled arms as she glanced down into the courtyard below. Seeing only her cousin, Faith, feeding the geese from the castle steps, she lifted her gaze to the distant fields where her people labored. Though still early, the villeins of Dragon's Lair were already busy at their day's work of clearing the land for the spring planting.

"A planting that may never come to pass if things don't improve," Megan grumbled aloud, disgusted with her nightly excursions into the countryside. With Sandy's help, she had gained only a few pieces of gold from the travelers they had managed to waylay on the road to London. Since there were only two of them, they couldn't even attempt to rob the richer, well-guarded travelers who carried the gold they desperately needed to keep her people from starving in the cold months ahead.

Megan's attention was drawn back to the courtyard by the sound of horse's hooves upon the cobblestones and the loud squawk of geese alerting the inhabitants of the castle of the intruder's presence. She watched with interest when a lone rider reined his horse to a halt in front of her cousin and swept off his plumed hat in greeting. Without dismounting, he handed a scroll to Faith and then bowed once more from the saddle before turning his horse about and riding away. Puzzled by the man's actions, Megan watched him canter through the gates and turn his mount south, in the direction of London. It was unusual for any traveler to come to the castle without partaking of its hospitality, and she wondered who had sent him on so urgent an errand that he hadn't stopped for a refreshing drink of water. From her vantage point she couldn't make out the colors, nor could she fathom what reason he had for coming to Dragon's Lair.

A few moments later when the rider crested the distant hill, the breeze unfurled his standard and the morning sun illuminated the three golden lions of Edward III's crest.

"My God, 'tis the king's messenger," she whispered, and paled visibly. Megan leaned her forehead against the cool stone window facing and closed her eyes to shut out the sight. She felt a sinking sensation in the pit of her belly at the thought of what the message contained. She did not doubt that King Edward had decided to collect on Mallory's debts by confiscating Dragon's Lair. It was his right.

"Damn you, Mallory, for bringing this upon us," Megan cursed, pushing herself away from the window. She raised her chin and squared her shoulders, readying herself to face the worst when a knock sounded upon the door. Already knowing who was on the other side of the iron-bound portal, she bade Faith to enter.

"You have a message," Faith said, moving gracefully across the room to her cousin's side.

Megan nodded and held out her hand for the scroll. "I saw the rider from the window."

"It was the king's man, Megan. Do you think 'tis good news?" Faith asked, her large, doelike eyes shining with expectation.

"I seriously doubt 'tis good news, Faith. We've sorely been lacking on it in the past months, and I doubt anything has changed," Megan answered, and gave Faith a weary smile. She unrolled the parchment. A muscle began to twitch in her cheek as she scanned the document several times, unable to believe what King Edward had written. After several long minutes, she threw it onto the floor and, much like a little girl having a fit of temper, stamped on it with both feet.

Her eyes sparkled with fury when she looked once more at her cousin. "If our good King Edward thinks I'll be used by another man, be he king or kin, then he's sadly mistaken. I'll never let myself be dominated again."

"Oh, Meggie," Faith said. "The king isn't going to take our home, is he?"

"If only it was that simple," Megan spat, and began to pace the chamber like a caged animal.

Faith frowned. "If the king isn't going to confiscate Dragon's Lair, then why are you so upset?"

"That," Megan said, and pointed to the crumpled message on the floor.

Faith rolled her eyes heavenward as if seeking divine guidance in dealing with her hot-tempered relative before she bent and picked up the parchment. As she read, her expression grew pensive and she worried her lower lip with even white teeth. When she raised her eyes, they held a look of sympathy for her cousin. "Megan, it's the king's order. You can't go against him."

Megan flashed Faith an angry look through narrowed lashes. "I want no part of this, Faith. I've suffered enough."

"But, Meggie, it could be the answer to your prayers. The king knows the financial state of Dragon's Lair. I'm sure he would not have chosen anyone who could not afford the up-keep of the estate. Your problems will be solved."

"Solved? How can you say such a thing, Faith? If I obey the king, my problems will have only begun. I'll be little more than a chattel in my own home."

"It might not be so bad, Meggie. You could end your nightly excursions before you are caught and hanged. And you could begin to think about raising a family," Faith said in an effort to find a silver lining in even the darkest cloud.

"Give me strength" was Megan's exasperated plea as she held her hands up in supplication.

"I was only trying to put things into better light," Faith said, hurt by her cousin's behavior.

Contrite, Megan crossed to Faith and placed a comforting arm about her shoulders. She had no right to take out her frustrations on Faith. Her cousin was too kindhearted and had been only trying to make a difficult situation better.

"Forgive me, Faith. I know you were only trying to help. It's just that I don't want to be dominated by another man for as long as I live. I've tasted freedom since Mallory's death, and I have no intention of losing it again. If I marry the king's man, I would be relegated once more to the shadows of life."

"I understand your feelings, Meggie, but that does not change things. The king has commanded that you marry. How can you disobey him without suffering for your disobe-dience? He will surely take Dragon's Lair if you go against his wishes."

Megan considered her cousin for a long, thoughtful moment and then shrugged. "I will think of something before the time comes."

"Then you must think fast, Meggie. The king's man will be here within the week."

"What do you mean?" Megan asked, eyeing her cousin sharply.

"The date was at the bottom of the message, Meggie."

In one graceful sweep of a slender arm, Megan took up the trampled parchment and reread it. To her dismay, she had overlooked the final words, which stated her future husband would arrive at Dragon's Lair within the fortnight. The message had been dated five days earlier.

The parchment once more fell to the roughhewn floor. With an angry kick from Megan, it sailed into the air and slowly floated into the fireplace, to be consumed by the flames. Megan watched the parchment curl and crumble into black ash before she glanced at Faith and gave her a rueful smile. "If only I could rid myself of the king's man that easily."

"Meggie, please reconsider your decision. Edward can force you to marry, no matter how you feel."

A cunning light entered Megan's eyes. "True, he can force me to marry because women have no rights under the law. However, should his chosen courtier decide against this marriage, then perhaps the king would also reconsider his decision."

"But why would he decide against the marriage? He will gain Dragon's Lair and a beautiful wife."

"When he arrives I doubt he will want this marriage any more than I do."

"Megan," Faith asked, her voice grave. "What wild scheme are you brewing up in that head of yours?"

"You'll just have to wait and see," Megan answered smugly.

"Will it get us hanged?" Faith asked, seeing the devilment twinkling in her cousin's eyes.

"All I'll tell you for now is that when my future husband arrives, I will be more than glad to meet him. I'll even do my best to make him feel welcome at Dragon's Lair."

"Your words do little to ease my feelings, Cousin," Faith said, and laughed. Megan Wakefield did not have a timid bone in her body, and if there was a way to best the king, Faith did not doubt that she would find it.

"He'll have to hang me first!" To emphasize his words, Richard St. Claire slammed his large fist down on the rough-hewn table. The vibration from the blow rattled the wooden trenchers and tumbled several of the tankards that had been set out for the evening meal. It also served to make the hounds waiting beneath the table for the dinner scraps tuck their tails and scurry to safer ground.

"Edward will do exactly that if you don't carry out his wishes. He still hasn't forgotten all the trouble you gave him with your reaving, nor has he forgiven any of us for Anne's disappearance," Justin snapped, irritated with his stubborn brother.

"I won't have it. King or serf, I won't allow Edward to dictate my life. His lords may simper and fawn over him to stay at court and gain his favor, but I'm not going to bow to him."

"Then what will you do, Richard? Will you become Royce again and go back to reaving, with a price on your head as a criminal?" Justin's patience had come to an end. Richard had lived his life outside of society's boundaries for so long, the man thought he could do as he pleased without anyone to say him yea or nay.

"If I must," Richard answered belligerently. He turned and strode across the hall to the huge stone fireplace. With hands folded behind his back, he stared down into the jumping flames. The firelight emphasized the beauty of his scarred face as well as the angry tilt of his smooth-shaven chin.

"Damn it, Brother. Have you no feeling for your family or obligation to your duty as a St. Claire?"

Richard's features hardened at his brother's accusation. He glanced over his shoulder at Justin and pinned him with his angry glare. "You speak to me of family obligation. If memory serves me, I'm not the only one who did not wish to accept Edward's dictates."

Justin's swarthy complexion deepened in hue at the memory of his own objections to marrying Jamelyn. "I didn't want to marry, but I did my duty. And as you can see, I have no regrets that I chose to obey my king."

"Damn it, Justin. If Edward were bidding me to marry someone like Jamelyn, then I wouldn't have any qualms about it either," Richard grumbled.

"How can you be so certain that the Lady Megan of Dragon's Lair is not if you don't at least go and meet her?"

"I don't have to meet her to know exactly what she is like. You will recall, I met her brother at court last winter, and if he is any example of what the O'Roarkes are like, I have no need for further acquaintance. The only good thing I can say about Mallory is that he is dead." Richard gave Justin a wry grin.

Justin chuckled, yet Richard's humor did not sway him from his determination to see his brother obey Edward's wishes. "Surely you can't blame the girl for Mallory's shortcomings?"

"Shortcomings! Mallory O'Roarke!" Richard exploded. "The man was a vicious, lying coward and deserved far more than he received. He should have been hanged and quartered instead of being allowed to die with dignity on the jousting field."

"But O'Roarke's sister had nothing to do with the way her brother acted. She hasn't even been to court," Justin cajoled, trying to make his brother see reason. If Richard didn't obey Edward, then the St. Claires would once more be separated. He would have to flee into the highlands to escape the king's wrath. And after all the years they had been denied each other because of Richard's loss of memory, Justin had no desire to lose his brother again. He wanted his family together, especially since Jamelyn had given him Kathryn, his green-eyed, raven-haired daughter. Now more than ever he needed everyone he loved close to him.

"I've heard enough about the girl without her coming to court, Justin. Mallory tried to barter her away one night when he'd had too much wine. He said he'd never be rid of her any other way because she was too ugly. The bastard had laughed and added that they kept her hidden away when guests visited Dragon's Lair because they didn't want to frighten them."

"Surely you can't believe such tripe?" Justin asked.

"What else am I supposed to believe? The man was her brother. He should at least have enough sense to know what she looks like."

"Didn't you just call him a liar? I seriously doubt the girl is so abhorrent to look upon. O'Roarke wasn't such an ugly fellow. As I recall, the women at court seemed to think him quite handsome. And if that doesn't ease your mind, I gather from Edward's letter, the Lady Megan is only his half sister. She was sired by Lord Wakefield."

"Damn it, Justin. Can't you understand the girl's looks are only a portion of the reason I don't want this marriage? I want nothing to do with the O'Roarke bloodline even if she is only half-O'Roarke, as you say. What I can't tolerate is being forced to do anything, especially marry."

"I think it's time you realized you're not the only member of this family who will suffer if you don't obey Edward's wishes. Do you care so little about our welfare?"

Richard flinched as if his brother had struck him. He loved Jamelyn and his niece far more than Justin would ever realize. That was one of the main reasons he objected to Edward's power play with his life. Until he found a woman like his sister-in-law, he doubted he would ever love again. Richard sighed inwardly. He would give everything he possessed to have the love that Justin and Jamelyn shared. But it would never be. There was only one Jamelyn in this world, and she belonged to his brother.

"You know my answer to your question, brother. I would never intentionally do anything to harm either Jamelyn or little Kat."

"If you don't do as Edward bids, you will. Our monarch has a long memory, and though it's been four years, he still hasn't forgiven Jamelyn completely for going against him. His friendship with me is the only thing which kept her from being tried for treason and you from being hung for your crimes as a reaver. If you go against him now, he will dredge up all of his past grievances with our family, and those you love will suffer."

" 'Tis not fair, Justin. Edward deems this marriage for punishment. Though he speaks of friendship and his need of your service because of the troubles with France, he means to make me suffer for my crimes."

" 'Tis true to a certain extent, but you will gain Dragon's Lair," Justin argued.

"Dragon's Lair and its hag of a mistress. Neither of which is of any value. O'Roarke gambled away all the wealth from the estate long before his death. That is why the king is so anxious to get it off his hands. He sees two things he can accomplish by forcing me to marry O'Roarke's ugly sister: our family's wealth will provide for the upkeep of Dragon's Lair, and he'll not have to worry about offending one of his favored courtiers by making him marry the O'Roarke dragon."

" 'Tis unfair," Jamelyn said upon hearing Richard's assessment of the girl when she entered the hall. She crossed to the two men and eyed her brother-in-law with displeasure. " 'Tis unlike you to be so unjust, Richard. Till you have seen the girl, how can you be so certain of your own feelings?"

Justin smiled down at his wife and draped a loving arm about her shoulders. If anyone could make Richard see his mistake, then it was Jamelyn. The bond that existed between the two when they had conspired to outwit the king still remained strong. At times Justin found himself envious of it, and his brother. However, he firmly reminded himself that Jamelyn loved him, and her feelings toward Richard were only those of friendship.

As far as understanding his brother's feelings for the Lady St. Claire, Justin didn't know how deep they went. He only knew he couldn't let himself delve into his wife's past or he might find things there that would tear his family and happiness apart. He was satisfied as things stood. He loved and trusted Richard, and he owed his brother more than he could ever repay for protecting Jamelyn during the times when he himself had turned his back on her. Yes, the past was now over, and they all had to look toward the future. Justin had to convince Richard to acquiesce or his brother would have no future in England or Scotland.

"Will you not listen to Jamelyn?" Justin asked.

"You say I'm being unfair? What I see as unfair is the two of you banding together against me. From your own experience, I would think you would at least have some sympathy for my plight."

Jamelyn draped her arms about her husband's lean waist and rested her cheek against his chest. Her green eyes twinkled with mirth as she smiled lovingly up at Justin before looking once more at Richard. "Why should we feel any sympathy for you? At the beginning neither of us ever thought our marriage could be happy, yet look how things have turned out. We now have a beautiful daughter as proof of our union and love.''

"Will you not even try to understand what I'm going through?'' Richard beseeched.

"Oh, Richard. I understand,'' Jamelyn said, crossing to him and hugging him affectionately. ''You are so much like your brother, you can't see the forest for the trees. Justin was sure he could never come to love me because I was a skinny Scotswoman, and now you're doing the same thing because of Lady Megan's brother.''

Justin cleared his throat and glanced uneasily away from his wife. She spoke the truth, but he was pained to remember the misery he had put her through with his arrogance and prejudice against all of the Scottish people. He had come close to losing her because of his own callous behavior. Jamelyn was right in her assumption that he couldn't see the forest for the trees. His love for her had been there far longer than he had been willing to admit it, even to himself. His stubborn pride had nearly cost him his wife and child.

"Don't try your wiles on me, Jamelyn of Cregan. I am not Justin, nor am I going to marry the toad of Dragon's Lair,'' Richard said, jerking Justin from his reveries. Knowing Jamelyn's power of persuasion, Richard set his sister-in-law away from him and strode a safe distance from her.

Jamelyn set her chin at a pugnacious angle and braced her hands on her hips. She eyed her brother-in-law as if she were his mother, and he her recalcitrant child. Her Scottish brogue was more pronounced when she said, ''I'm nay asking you to marry the girl. I only ask that you be fair and at least go to Dragon's Lair and meet her. If she is the hag that you suppose from her brother's description, then I'll say no more on the matter. I will leave it to you and Justin to work it out with your king.''

Jamelyn did not say ''our'' king. After the duplicity Edward had shown in dealing with her at court, she could feel no friendship toward England's monarch. She held her own council on the matter, visited court with her husband, and dutifully acted the proper wife for his sake, yet Edward III would never be her king.

"Will you agree with your wife, Justin?" Richard asked, eyeing his brother.

"I would if it was as simple as that. However, it isn't. There is far more at stake here than just your happiness."

Richard threw up his hands in exasperation. "I will agree to visit Dragon's Lair, but I'll not swear to marry the chit, if that's what you are expecting."

"It's all we can ask for now," Jamelyn said, and cast an anxious glance at her husband. "Perhaps after you have visited the Lady Megan and have come to know her, then you will have a change of heart. Don't you agree, Justin?"

Justin released a long breath and nodded. Jamelyn knew that he was not satisfied with the way things stood at the moment, but he would not force the issue further for the time being. Richard would visit Dragon's Lair and see his bride to be, but when he returned to Raven's Keep, he'd better be prepared to do as Edward bid or face his brother's wrath. Justin would not let Richard's stubbornness jeopardize his family.

"Good," Jamelyn said, and bestowed a loving smile upon her husband before she glanced back to her brother-in-law. "Perhaps you could persuade Anthony to ride with you to Dragon's Lair. He could act as your intermediary if things go as you suspect they will."

"Aye, that isn't such a bad idea," Richard said, and quickly looked away from Jamelyn before she could see the cunning expression that flickered across his face. He would ask Anthony Godfrey to go with him to Dragon's Lair, and if things went as he planned, he would meet the Lady Megan and be gone from the place without her ever realizing he was Richard St. Claire.

"I'm sure everything will work out for the best since you're willing to meet the girl," Jamelyn said. Her natural optimism was evident in her exuberant smile. She wanted her brother-in-law to find the same happiness she had found with Justin. Richard deserved to have someone of his own instead of bestowing all of his love upon his brother's family. She was not blind to Richard's devotion, and, she suspected, neither was Justin. Her husband had never asked about the relationship between Richard and herself during the time they worked together to outwit the king, but she sensed he knew there was a bond that went deeper than ordinary friendship. And until Richard had a wife and family to love, Jamelyn could not break the ties that kept them close. He had befriended her in her darkest moments, and had she not already loved Justin, she could have easily given her heart to Royce.

"Don't get your hopes too high, Jamie. I've only agreed to meet the girl, not to marry her," Richard added.

"Oh, Royce," Jamelyn laughed, forgetting in that moment to use his Christian name. "Stubbornness runs thick in the St. Claire blood. I'll argue no more with you. 'Tis your decision what to do with your life."

"I agree," Richard said, and flashed his brother a triumphant look.

Justin shook his head in disgust and turned away. He'd said enough for the moment. Now all he could do was hope that the Lady Megan was not the hag his brother thought her to be, or else things wouldn't go as smoothly as Jamelyn seemed to believe.

Chapter 2

A raised hand from Richard brought the troop of riders to a halt in the copse of trees below the craggy outcropping of rock where the keep of Dragon's Lair sat commandingly. The rattle of armor and the squeak of leather filtered through the quiet wood as the men relaxed and waited for their orders, fully confident in the judgment of the younger St. Claire. He, like his brother, Justin, now had their loyalty without question, and they would die for him if he ordered it.

Anthony Godfrey removed his gauntlet and wiped away the sweat the hot day had beaded upon his brow. He glanced at his young friend and marveled at the respect the hardened soldiers now gave to Justin's brother. It had not been that way at first, he mused. It had taken Lord St. Claire's men a long time to acknowledge the younger brother. After learning of Richard's past endeavors, they had been skeptical about Lord St. Claire's decision to place his brother in command of his troops. They had also been unwilling to allow themselves to believe that Richard St. Claire was no longer the reaver, Royce, until he had proven himself a true St. Claire in battle.

Anthony smiled to himself at the change the past four years had wrought in the younger man. The wild reaver whom

Justin had nearly hanged had been replaced by an elegant gentleman who was at home in the presence of his warriors as well as England's monarch. Only those who knew him well ever suspected that the reaver still lurked just beneath the surface, ready to spring back to the forefront if ever needed.

Anthony let his gaze sweep over his friend. Richard matched his brother in size and build as well as disposition, but there was something more about the younger man which intrigued males and females alike. His scarred features, now in profile as he rested his folded arms over the saddle's pommel and stared thoughtfully up at the grey stone walls of Dragon's Lair, seemed to draw the ladies like flies to honey. Yet it wasn't his intriguing looks that drew men to his side, but the sense of power he exuded. He was like a hawk in all its splendor—fierce and strong—his strength commanding men's admiration and respect and often their fear.

Unaware of his friend's perusal, Richard observed Dragon's Lair's defenses with the eye of a battle-hardened warrior. The castle, built on the highest point in the surrounding area, had been strategically placed to make it nearly impossible for an enemy to take. Resting on granite formations that resembled a beast's claws shooting up out of the ground, Dragon's Lair keep seemed impregnable from Richard's vantage point. A cynical smile tugged up the corners of his shapely lips and he narrowed his sapphire gaze speculatively as he considered the motives behind Edward's sudden decision to see him married to the O'Roarke dragon lady.

"Punish and protect," he muttered in disgust. Dragon's Lair needed the St. Claire wealth to sustain it in order to protect Edward's wool route from reavers. In this time of crisis, when every piece of gold was needed to go toward his war against France, Edward had found a way to protect his valuable property as well as punish the St. Claires. Richard's annoyance with his king was reflected by the frown deepening across his scarred face.

"Richard, you look as if you're preparing for battle instead of going to inspect your future bride," Anthony jested, easing his horse alongside his friend's.

Richard flashed Anthony an irritated look. "I had rather face Philip's entire army than ride into the witch's lair."

"You may be surprised. The girl may not be as ugly as you believe."

A muscle twitched in Richard's smooth-shaven cheek. "She could be a beauty and I would still feel the same way. I want nothing to do with Mallory O'Roarke's kin. I've only come here to satisfy Justin and Jamelyn."

"I wasn't at court last year when you had the encounter with O'Roarke, and never truly understood what transpired between the two of you to make you hate the man with such an intensity. I know he was a cheating little weasel, but that doesn't seem enough to justify your enmity toward his entire bloodline."

"It was enough for me," Richard said. He glanced away from Anthony and back to the stone walls of Dragon's Lair. He couldn't tell Anthony that while in a drunken stupor one night, he'd rambled on and on about his feelings for Jamelyn, and Mallory O'Roarke had overheard. The bastard then seized upon the opportunity given him by the intimate knowledge of Richard's devotion. He had threatened to go to Justin with tales that he'd overheard Richard admit to cuckolding his brother with Jamelyn if Richard didn't agree to forget about the gambling debts Mallory owed him. Though what Mallory O'Roarke threatened was nothing but lies, Richard couldn't chance Justin even suspecting his feelings for Jamelyn. Such knowledge could destroy the bond that had grown between them during the past four years. Nothing could come of his love for his brother's wife except the destruction of the family he held so dear to his heart, and he'd not allow any man, much less a swine like Mallory O'Roarke, to ruin something he treasured. Blinded by fury, Richard could recall little of what transpired next; his attack upon O'Roarke was only a vague memory. He didn't remember pummeling the man with his fists until he'd nearly beaten Mallory to death with his bare hands. Richard had then been forcibly dragged off the man by several of his friends who had heard the fracas in the hallway beyond the ballroom.

The fight had been the beginning of bad blood between the two men. A coward, Mallory never confronted Richard again. He studiously avoided any situation where he would have to encounter his enemy face-to-face. However, that did not stop him from seeking his revenge in other ways. He'd spread nasty rumors about Richard's past with the hope that King Edward would blame the younger St. Claire for the robberies that had taken place near Nottingham. Fortunately, Mallory's own reputation hindered his malicious intentions. Of those who knew the two men, his lies were taken for what they were and did no harm to Richard. However, Richard's hatred for the man grew until it was like a living thing within him. And he knew if Mallory had not died that day at the tournament, he would have killed him.

Anthony shrugged. Richard's short answer did little to explain the reason for his animosity, but for now he'd let it rest. When Richard wanted to tell him, he would.

"Shall we send a messenger to notify them of our arrival?"

Richard glanced at Anthony, and a wry grin curled up the corners of his sensuous lips. "I can see Edward's reason for wanting us here if the inhabitants of Dragon's Lair have to be told of the presence of a troop of men at the foot of their walls."

Anthony chuckled and looked at the imposing walls. "Our good king does nothing without a reason. He inherited none of his father's indecisiveness, and that's what makes him a formidable monarch.''

"Are you hinting that I should forget my plan and meekly obey Edward's orders, Anthony?" Richard lifted a brow quizzically at his friend.

Anthony shook his head. "Far be it from me to give you any advice concerning your future, especially when you've set your mind to something. I know my limits of persuasion, and I wouldn't waste a breath in trying to make you see reason."

"I'm glad to hear it, because it would be useless. I won't change my mind."

Anthony drew on his gauntlets and glanced once more at the walls of Dragon's Lair. "Then shall we set this foolishness into motion? I'm hungry and thirsty. Hopefully the fair lady of the keep will at least have adequate provisions even if she doesn't have enough men to protect the walls."

"I dare say Jamelyn has insured our comfort with all the gifts she's sent to welcome the Lady Megan into the St. Claire family."

The leather saddle squeaked beneath Anthony when he looked back at the line of pack animals. Richard was right. Jamelyn, suspecting the dire circumstances at Dragon's Lair, had used the guise of the betrothal to send enough food and wine to provision their troops as well as anyone else in the O'Roarke household. She'd also included several bolts of velvet and damask to make sure the food and wine would not be misconstrued as charity.

"Jamelyn has a kind heart, Richard."

"Aye," Richard said, and nodded cynically. "So kind that she's willing to see me sacrificed to protect Edward's wool route."

"That's unjust, Richard. Jamelyn would never do anything to harm you."

Richard had the courtesy to flush. "I'm sorry. I know

Jamelyn was only trying to spare the Lady Megan's feelings and see we did not go without. It's just that I'm anxious to get this over with so I can put it behind me.''

''What if you like what you see? Will you then obey Edward and marry the Lady Megan?'' Anthony asked.

Richard shrugged. ''I'll decide that when the time comes. Now, it's time you visited Dragon's Lair, and please render my apologies for my absence. I shall join you there in a short while.''

''Then I'll bid you adieu,'' Anthony said, and touched two fingers to his brow before motioning the men forward.

Richard watched from the shade of the trees as the troop wound its way along the narrow, hard-packed road to the gates of Dragon's Lair. He heard his friend call out greetings and identify himself and then heard a loud squealing groan from the gate as it was raised. The rusty sound only served to further impress upon Richard the reason he'd been chosen to marry the mistress of the keep. He'd not even entered the bailey to see how badly things had fared since Mallory's death, but he already knew the dire straits that existed at Dragon's Lair.

The metallic rattle of Richard's armor disturbed the still glade as he dismounted and reached into the saddlebag to withdraw a drab brown hooded mantle, leather jerkin, and coarse wool chausses. It was a difficult task in the absence of his squire, but he finally managed to strip off his armor and chain mail. The broad planes of his sinewy back gleamed with sweat as he carefully packed the armor away in an oiled bag to keep the evening dew from dampening the polished steel and turning it to rust.

Satisfied he'd taken every precaution to protect the precious steel plates, which had saved his life in several fierce battles, he donned the coarse wool chausses and slipped the leather jerkin over his head.

Feeling suddenly freed of the bonds that society had placed

upon him during the past four years, Royce emerged from the depths where Richard had kept him secreted away. A roguish expression flickered across his scarred features as he braced his hands on his lean hips, a cunning smile spreading his shapely lips. He threw back his head and laughed from the pure joy of the moment. It felt good to know he was free to do and say exactly as he pleased without worry of repercussions.

He admitted that being Richard St. Claire had its merits, but a nobleman's life was far more restricted than a reaver's. A knight might have wealth and power, but he was also a prisoner in his own society. He had to obey the rules or be condemned and lose all that he held dear. Whereas a reaver might be poor and hunted, he was freer in many ways than the rich and powerful. He answered to no one except himself and his God. His life was in his own hands and he lived it as he saw fit.

Having completely shed Richard's elegant manners, he reached into the leather bag strapped behind his saddle and withdrew a lute. He ran his fingers over the taut strings and smiled at the sweet sound that filled the glade. With visitors at Dragon's Lair, a minstrel would have no trouble finding a meal for his services. Draping the lute strap over one shoulder, Royce tossed the mantle about his tall frame and raised the hood to shadow his features. Tonight he would play for his supper, and while his friends dined in the great hall, he'd inspect the woman Edward had chosen for him to wed.

"They're here," Faith cried breathlessly as she rushed into Megan's chambers and saw her cousin staring out the narrow, cross-slit window. "Your future husband has arrived. He and his men are at the gates now."

"I know," Megan answered without looking at her flustered cousin. "I saw them when they left the wood."

"Then shouldn't you go down to greet them?" Faith asked, pausing at Megan's side.

"No, I don't think that will be necessary at the moment. I want things to be just right before I greet our guests."

Faith frowned and glanced at her cousin. "Everything is in order. I've had the servants busy for the past week preparing for Sir Richard's visit."

"I know you have, and I appreciate all you've done," Megan said, reaching out to squeeze her cousin's hand reassuringly. "But there are a few things I need to attend to before I meet our guests."

"What kinds of things?" Faith asked worriedly.

"Just a few matters that only I can see to. It's nothing for you to be concerned about."

"Megan, I hope you're not still thinking of doing something to try to prevent this marriage. It's the king's will."

Megan glanced down at the courtyard as the St. Claire troops rode through the gates. "True, Edward has dictated I should marry, and I'll not say a word against the arrangement."

Unappeased by her cousin's answer, Faith frowned more deeply. "Oddly enough, I don't find your answer reassuring."

Megan chuckled and turned away from the window. Her steps were light as she crossed the bedchamber and looked at her cousin's reflection in the polished steel mirror. She smiled at the worried expression on Faith's lovely face. "I told you I would welcome the man Edward has chosen for me, and I'll not go back on my word. And should he decide to go through with the marriage once we've met, then I will meekly obey my king's wishes."

Faith bit down on her lower lip and studied her cousin suspiciously. Megan had never done anything in her life meekly, and she knew her cousin would not do so now. Concern knit her dark golden brows across the bridge of her slender nose. "Megan, please reconsider whatever wild scheme you have in mind. You are the king's ward and must obey his wishes. Think about the consequences of your actions for all concerned. You'll lose Dragon's Lair, and then what will happen to your people?"

Megan spun about, the smile gone from her lips. "That's unfair of you, Faith. When have I done anything but think of my people? Do you think I enjoy what I've had to do to survive these past months and years?"

Contrite, Faith lowered her eyes to the floor and flushed. "I'm sorry, Meggie. I shouldn't have said that. I know how you've suffered, and I shouldn't interfere. You've done well by us all since you've been responsible for Dragon's Lair. I know if it wasn't for you, we'd have starved."

"I'm sorry, too, Faith," Megan said, crossing to her cousin and draping a comforting arm about her slender shoulders. "I shouldn't have snapped at you. I'm just upset by the prospect of meeting Richard St. Claire. And I promise that what I do will have no ill effects upon anyone at Dragon's Lair, so you need not worry."

"I know you've always put us before your own happiness, and I've been selfish for asking you to do so again. Whatever you do, just know that you have my support," Faith said, giving Megan a hug. "I'll be damned if I'll let anyone harm you," she added with a show of spirit, totally unlike her usual self-effacing demeanor.

Megan returned the hug and laughed. "And if we stick together, not even Edward can conquer us."

Faith drew in a deep breath and raised her chin in the air. "I think I will go and greet our guests."

"Please extend my apologies for not coming down, and tell them I will join them at dinner. That will give me all the time I need to complete my plans," Megan said, a cunning smile curving the corners of her mouth.

At the look of mischief on her cousin's face, Faith felt a

chill of foreboding streak down her spine, yet she forced herself to ignore it. She would trust Megan to do the right thing. Her judgment had seen them through many bad times in the past, and Faith prayed it would continue to do so in the future.

After casting one last, skeptical look at the other woman, Faith closed the thick wooden door behind her and made her way down the winding stairway to the hall, where she could already hear the clamor of deep male voices. The sound sent a shiver of apprehension along every nerve in her body. It reminded her of the times when Mallory returned from court with his friends.

The horror of the memory made Faith pause, and she squeezed her eyes tightly shut to close out the past. She didn't want to remember the times Mallory had used her like a London whore. Nor did she want to think of the tiny life he'd forced upon her and then heartlessly and brutally made her lose.

A shudder shook her slender frame and she clenched her teeth. Mallory O'Roarke had been evil incarnate, and she was glad he was dead. Her only regret was that she hadn't had the nerve to kill him herself. If she had, Megan would have been spared the misery that she'd suffered at her brother's hand. Fortunately Megan had had the inner strength to overcome much of his abuse, but Faith hadn't been so lucky. Mallory's cruelty had left her with unhealed wounds, and she doubted if she would ever be able to trust any man again. In her opinion they were all beasts with nothing in mind except bedding the first female to cross their paths. She hated them, one and all; and she would never allow herself to be brutalized in such a manner again.

With that thought paramount in her mind, Faith descended the stairs. The glint of battle flickered in her pale blue eyes as she entered the great hall to meet their guests.

"My lady," Anthony Godfrey said as he strode forward

to introduce himself. Bowing, he continued, "I'm Sir Anthony Godfrey, a friend of Sir Richard St. Claire and Lord Justin St. Claire."

Giving Anthony an imperious look, Faith extended her hand to him and smiled coldly. "Welcome to Dragon's Lair, Sir Godfrey; I am Lady Faith Wakefield, Lady Megan's cousin."

"It is my pleasure to meet you, my lady," Anthony said, and gave Faith one of his most charming smiles as he took her hand within his own, intending to place a gentlemanly kiss upon it.

Faith withdrew her hand before his lips could touch her, and managed to control the shudder that rippled up her spine from the contact of his flesh with hers. "Lady Megan has bid me to extend her apologies for not being here to greet you but said for you and your men to avail yourselves of Dragon Lair's hospitality. She will join us at dinner."

Anthony stiffened at Faith's tone and demeanor. Rebuffed, he momentarily wondered what he'd done to affront the lady, then he felt his own bristles rise at her apparent and unjustified dislike. He was unused to such treatment from the fairer sex, and it took another moment before the full impact of the insult registered. She'd acted as if he were a leper and the mere touch of his hand might contaminate her precious skin. Anthony's temper began to simmer. He'd done nothing to inspire such a reaction. He'd behaved as a gentleman, and he'd be damned if he'd feel guilty for her attitude.

"I, too, have an apology to extend, my lady" was Anthony's gruff reply. "Sir Richard has been unavoidably detained and begs Lady Megan's forgiveness."

"I will relay Sir Richard's apologies to my cousin, Sir Godfrey. Please avail yourself of refreshments while I instruct the servants to take your things to your quarters. Your men may lodge in the stables."

At the woman's high-handed manner, a flash of annoyance

crossed Anthony's usually amicable features. He'd not had anyone speak to him in such a manner since he'd been on his nurse's knee. His less than friendly tone reflected his feelings when he spoke. "As you wish, my lady."

Faith nodded and turned away, leaving Anthony staring after her, dumbfounded and fuming silently.

"Shrew," he muttered, and ran a hand through his tousled blond hair, a gesture of complete exasperation. For the first time in his life his charm and boyish good looks had not held him in good stead with the opposite sex. The Lady Faith seemed to have disliked him on sight, and that in itself was an odd occurrence for a man who, since he'd reached manhood, had always had women falling at his feet.

"I just hope the Lady Megan isn't a shrew like her cousin or all is lost," Anthony grumbled as he crossed the hall and accepted a tankard of cool ale from a servant. If Lady Megan resembled her cousin in appearance, all would go well. However, if her temperament was anything like Lady Faith's, then nothing on God's good earth could force Richard to marry her.

Anthony lifted the tankard to his lips and downed the foamy dark brew. As his gaze swept over the great hall, moving from the vaulted, heavy oak-beamed ceiling to the flagged floor at his feet, he wondered why it was his fate in life to always become enmeshed in the St. Claire brothers' schemes when it came to women.

It's either my charming manner or my stupidity. And I vow it's the latter, Anthony mused to himself. A boyish grin lifted the corners of his sensuous lips and his spirit lightened considerably as he considered his involvement. If given the chance, he'd not change a thing. He'd enjoyed too many amusing hours watching from the sidelines as Justin fought a losing battle with the minx he'd married. Anthony glanced toward the stairs and his smile faded. He feared poor Richard wasn't destined for the same happy fate as his brother. If the

Lady Faith was any indication of what lay in the younger St. Claire's future, Anthony knew his friend would not find his married life half as pleasant as his brother's.

A frown creased Anthony's smooth brow. For the first time since Richard had concocted his wild plot, he was beginning to see its merits. Forewarned is forearmed, he mused, his mind lingering once more upon the ice maiden he'd met a few minutes earlier.

Richard leaned a wide shoulder nonchalantly against the doorframe and smiled down into the lovely pale blue eyes. He'd been told at the gate to ask for Lady Megan's cousin, Lady Faith, and now looking at her, he wondered if the mistress of the keep resembled this golden beauty. If she did, then he might reconsider disobeying Edward's order.

"My lady, an evening's entertainment for your guests in exchange for my supper, 'tis all I ask," Richard cajoled, using Royce's most persuasive tone.

Faith tapped her small foot against the uneven stone floor as she considered the minstrel's suggestion. With a million and one things on her mind, she didn't really have time for such minor details at the moment. Cook still had to be told how many to expect for the evening meal. Provisions were in short supply along with everything else at Dragon's Lair, and every morsel had to stretch as far as possible. They also had to make things look like all was well at Dragon's Lair. It would be too humiliating if their guests ever learned the true extent of their penury.

Faith glanced toward the roaring fire, where the cook was basting the haunch of venison that Megan had killed the previous day. Besides having to see everything prepared for their guests, Faith also had to send Megan a pot of lard from the pantry and have one of the girls scrape the chimney for soot. For what reason her cousin needed lard and soot, especially when she should be preparing herself to greet their guests,

Faith didn't know. But as usual, she would do as Megan bid her. Sooner or later she'd know what wild scheme her cousin was brewing.

"My lady," Royce urged gently, pressing his point when he noticed her distraction. "Please be generous to a poor minstrel who has fallen on hard times and needs a few scraps of food to keep himself from starving."

"All right," Faith said at last, her tone reflecting her exasperation. She wanted to put this business behind her and get on with more important matters. "Another mouth tonight will make no difference." Turning to a nearby servant, she continued. "Mary, see that he's fed, and then show him to the great hall. He will entertain our guests tonight."

"Thank you, my lady. May the saints bless you for your kindness," Royce said, making a perfect leg and bowing extravagantly from the waist.

Faith gave him an absent nod and turned away, her mind already on her own duties. Had she been less occupied, she might have wondered at the graceful execution of the visitor's bow, and his cultured speech. But her mind was already far away from the traveling minstrel with the patch over one of his keen sapphire blue eyes.

"Mary, my girl, show me to food and ale, and the first song I play tonight will be about your sweet lips and rosy cheeks," Royce said, giving the serving maid one of his most charming smiles.

Mary couldn't suppress a heady giggle of excitement, and her cheeks grew crimson as she led the roguish minstrel across the kitchen and heaped a bread trencher full of stew. Casting a wary glance in the direction of the cook's rotund figure at the fireplace, Mary furtively filled a tankard with ale and served it to Royce. His smile of appreciation and a conspiratorial wink made the girl's heart take wings, fluttering wildly within her breast until she stood tongue-tied, watching each morsel pass his shapely lips.

When he'd satisfied his appetite, Royce leaned back and smiled up at the watchful Mary, fully aware of the effect he was having upon the girl. " 'Tis filled to the brim that I am, lass. Now will you show me to the great hall so I may repay your mistress for my sumptuous feast?"

Mary bobbed her head rapidly up and down.

" 'Tis a good lass you are, little Mary. If I were a marrying man, I'd set my cap for you," Royce said, uncoiling his lean frame from the roughhewn bench.

"Ye be a-jesting with me," Mary giggled.

"Ye be a rare one indeed, bonny Mary, for you're as wise as ye are pretty," Royce laughed, and tweaked one of her rosy cheeks, his speech and manner changing as he slipped completely into his role as minstrel.

Leaning against the table, he propped a booted foot on the bench and lifted the lute. He ran his long fingers across the strings and arched a brow at the young girl. His deep voice stilled all movement in the kitchen as he began to improvise a song for the maid. "Me bonny Mary is wise and true, she knows not to listen to the roué. He cajols and pretends to bear his soul to woo the fair maiden. Me bonny Mary is wise and true, she knows not to listen to the roué. Wary and pure of heart, the lass sees the darkness in his heart."

Royce flashed the girl a wide grin as he concluded the short verse but continued to play. The amusement and delight of those who had gathered around him for the unexpected performance was apparent as he filled the hot kitchen with the jaunty tune. The music's effect could be seen in the exuberant grins of their work-worn faces. When Royce finished, he gave them a gracious bow, and they awarded him a resounding round of applause before going back to work with lightened spirits, their aching muscles momentarily forgotten under the minstrel's spell.

"Now, friends, I bid you farewell. 'Tis time to work for

me dinner.'' Glancing once more at Mary, he said, "If the fair Mary will show me the way.''

Blushing profusely and once more tongue-tied from his lyrics, Mary gave Royce a shy smile and led him along the stone corridor connecting the kitchen with the main structure of the keep.

The sound of laughter filled the great hall as Royce stepped from behind the tapestry, pausing to survey his surroundings. Turning his attention to the sound of merriment, he immediately spotted Anthony standing among his men on the far side of the hall. With tankards of ale in hand, his friends seemed to be enjoying Dragon's Lair's hospitality to the fullest. Pleased that all seemed to be going well, Royce bade Mary farewell with a lusty smack upon the lips and a gentle pat to the rear as she turned once more to the servants' entrance. She flashed him an embarrassed look before scurrying back in the direction of the kitchen with a wide, happy smile upon her lips.

Settling himself comfortably in the shadowy corner near the exit Mary had taken, Royce sat back and quietly watched his friends. His presence had gone unnoticed, and for the moment he was satisfied to have everyone, including Anthony, believe that he had not as yet arrived at Dragon's Lair.

From his vantage point he saw the servants spread the long table with linen and then light the candles in preparation of the evening meal. A short time later he saw Lady Faith descend the stairs at the end of the great hall, crossing to greet her guests. To his dismay, he saw Anthony's smile fade at the lady's approach and wondered what had transpired between the two to cause such a reaction in his friend.

She was gowned in an ungirdled pale blue velvet cyclas with a soft linen undergown of the same color. Her fair hair was parted in the center, braided and coiled into a chignon on each side of her head, and then covered in gold cauls to emphasize her lovely features. The Lady Faith was stunning.

Royce frowned as he glanced away from the woman and looked once more at his friend's less than amicable expression. It was totally out of character for Anthony to react in such a manner to any beautiful woman. He was a man who knew he had the power to warm the coldest maid's heart, and he felt it his duty to mankind to charm every woman who came into his presence. However, Anthony's dislike for the Lady Faith could be felt even from Royce's vantage point. He was courteous but cool as he spoke with her.

Puzzling over his friend's reaction to the Lady Faith, Royce didn't at first see the woman at the top of the stair landing. It was not until she had made her way down, and Anthony and Faith turned to greet her, that his attention was drawn to the diminutive figure in the stained cyclas. His heart leaped into his throat and his eyes widened in disbelief as the figure shuffled across the great hall. It took him a moment to realize she wasn't as tiny as he'd first surmised, but her back was bent and misshapen.

Royce frowned in distaste as she extended her hand to Anthony and smiled up at him through greasy, dark tendrils of lank hair falling over her face like stringy worms. Her idiot's smile was blackened with decay, and her high-pitched giggle could be heard from across the chamber when Anthony took her hand into his and bravely bent over it. She simpered up at Anthony and twisted her other hand into the worn fabric of her cyclas.

Royce felt his stomach lurch. At that moment he knew he was looking at the woman Edward had bid him to marry. Bile rose in his throat at the thought and he quietly slipped out of the great hall, making his way back to the kitchen. He'd seen what he had come for, and now it was time to get as far away from Dragon's Lair as possible. For the first time in his life, that bastard O'Roarke had not lied. His sister was as ugly as he'd boasted.

Royce spotted Mary paring vegetables at the long table

and quickly crossed to her. He pressed a silver coin into her hand and said, "Give this to your mistress and tell her I'm grateful for her generosity."

Without further adieu, he turned and swiftly made his way out of Dragon's Lair, then back to the copse of trees where his destrier was tethered. Breathing a sigh of relief at his escape, he shed his disguise and donned his armor once more. He mounted the huge black war-horse, urging the beast south toward the road that would take him to London and then to Windsor to face his King.

Anthony momentarily found himself speechless as Lady Faith introduced her cousin, the mistress of Dragon's Lair—Megan Wakefield. It was with a supreme effort that he managed to collect himself enough to take the dirty-nailed hand she extended to him and place a perfunctory kiss upon it. The hair at the nape of his neck stood on end when her high-pitched giggle pierced the air. He had to steel himself not to flinch in disgust when he looked once more into her simpering idiot's face with its black-toothed grin.

"My lady, it is a pleasure to meet you. I'm sorry Sir Richard was not able to join us, but 'tis his misfortune," Anthony said, outwardly exerting charm to compensate for his thoughts of murdering Richard. Justin and his young sibling had put him in many difficult situations, but none had been as untenable as this one.

Instead of answering Anthony's polite attempt at conversation, and much to his chagrin, the Lady of Dragon's Lair bent and whispered in her cousin's ear while giving him her crossed-eyed stare.

"Sir Godfrey," Faith stuttered, her own expression ashen. "My cousin asks if you will be kind enough to sit at her right tonight in Sir Richard's absence."

Anthony drew in a deep breath to shore up his courage,

cleared his throat, and then proffered Megan his arm. "I would be honored, my lady."

Again Megan whispered into Faith's ear before giggling and accepting Anthony's arm. She gave him a watery grin as she shuffled along at his side to the extensive linen-covered table.

Megan's hurriedly whispered comment about their guest and his ancestral bloodline made Faith flush scarlet with embarrassment. In an effort to hide her discomfiture from Sir Godfrey and regain her composure, she lagged behind the couple. She knew Megan had meant the remark about Sir Godfrey's unmarried, four-legged mother in jest, but Faith found little humor in the entire ludicrous situation. She had still to recover completely from Megan's changed appearance. Seeing her descend the stairs as a rotten-toothed hag had nearly put Faith into shock.

It had taken every ounce of willpower she possessed to act with a semblance of decorum when she introduced Megan to her guest. Faith still didn't know how she'd manage to get through the rest of the evening if Megan continued to use her to relay messages to Sir Godfrey. At the present moment all she wanted was to hide from her willful cousin and her wild schemes.

Megan let Sir Godfrey seat her at the head of the table but didn't wait for him to take his seat before she turned her attention to displaying enough bad manners to completely convince her guest that he should save his friend from marrying such a disgusting creature as herself. Grabbing a crust of bread, she gnawed off a large piece and then proceeded to wash it down with her wine. A moment later she slammed the tankard back down on the table and gave a loud belch as evidence she had downed the entire contents of the vessel.

Using the back of her hand, she wiped away a dribble of wine that had escaped down her chin, and glanced at Anthony. She had to control the bubble of laughter that tickled her throat at the look of sheer revulsion reflected upon his handsome features. Satisfied things were going as she had planned, Megan picked up her tankard and banged it on the table.

"More wine, Agnes," she called to the serving girl across the chamber.

Agnes's lips twisted suspiciously when she hurried across the chamber to do her mistress's bidding. She refilled Megan's tankard and then made her escape to the kitchen, where she could let loose her mirth.

All eyes in the great hall were trained on the handsome knight and the humpbacked crone seated next to him. Dragon's Lair's servants watched the pair curiously, wondering what mischief their mistress was up to with the disguise of soot and grease. Sensing the conspiracy directed against the newcomers, they managed to control their amusement while they served the evening meal. But like Agnes, they couldn't suppress it once they reached the kitchens.

"Gor! Did ye see the look on the young sir's face when the mistress came downstairs?" Agnes asked, sinking down on the bench across the table from her friend Mary. She brushed a stray strand of mousy brown hair away from her brow and giggled again at the scene she'd just left in the great hall. "He looked as if he'd suddenly swallowed a lump of dung."

Mary glanced toward the heavyset man who sat quietly at the end of the table, drinking a large tankard of ale and staring moodily off into the distance. Being so close to Sandy McTavis, Dragon's Lair's bailiff, made her slightly uneasy, but for Mary it would have been far easier for her to cut out her tongue than to stop her next remark. She wasn't compared to a magpie for nothing. "Could ye blame him? With all that goo smeared all over, no wonder he looked disgusted. I didn't know grease and soot was the latest thing for ladies."

The girls' laughter filled the kitchen as both gave in to their mirth once more.

" 'Tis enough out of the two of ye," Sandy McTavis growled. Setting his tankard down, he eyed both girls sternly. "Lady Megan has her reasons for what she does, and it's not our place to make jest about them."

"We didn't mean anything by it, Sandy," Mary said, sobering with an effort. "It's just that the young sir looked as if he wanted to sink into the floor when he bent over her hand. And I thought he'd jump out of his skin when the mistress give that high-pitched laugh." Mary fought to suppress another giggle.

"Ye've more to do than to sit here and gossip about yer betters," Sandy said, hefting himself to his feet.

"Don't be angry with us, Sandy. Ye know we wouldn't do anything to harm Lady Megan," Mary said, coming to her feet and peering up into the ruddy features of Dragon's Lair's bailiff.

"That's not the way it sounds. Yer silly gossip could ruin everything if one of St. Claire's men was to hear ye," Sandy said, and walked out of the kitchen.

The maid's apology did little to lighten his mood, and a frown of worry creased Sandy's brow as the bailiff made his way up the winding stone stairway to the turret overlooking the village. Leaning against the cool stone merlons, he gazed out over the thatch-covered cottages lining the narrow road before looking to the newly plowed fields in the distance. Black stripes in the twilight, the furrows lay waiting for the seeds of the new season. Sandy glanced up toward the darkening sky and rubbed his hand across his beard-stubbled chin.

It was planting time, but Megan had only half the money she needed to buy the seeds, Sandy reflected sadly. As he turned toward the east, he saw the first hint of a full moon rising over the treetops. Tonight would have been the perfect

night for another excursion into the countryside. The moonlight would have allowed them to waylay some unwary traveler and relieve him of his purse before making good their
own escape. Yet with Sir Godfrey and St. Claire's men at
Dragon's Lair, there would be no coins to add to the seed
money by dawn. Megan's attention was centered upon one
thing: convincing Richard St. Claire's envoy that it was his
duty to save his friend from a fate worst than death—marriage
to a simpering, ugly hag.

A rueful grin touched Sandy's full lips. Megan had told
him of her plans, but he'd not realized the true extent of them
until he had watched from his vantage point behind the tapestry. Her disguise had been completely effective, if Sir Godfrey's expression was any reflection of the man's feelings.
Sandy seriously doubted that anyone could force Richard St.
Claire to go through with the marriage once his friend re-
ported what he'd found at Dragon's Lair. Even the minstrel
had fled like a hare from the fox upon seeing the hag.

At the thought of the minstrel, Sandy's smile faded. When
he'd first seen the scar-faced man pleading for his supper,
something had made Sandy think he wasn't the ordinary traveling minstrel. The man's speech and the way he'd held himself had roused Sandy's suspicions. After listening to the man
jest with little Mary, he'd begun to believe his imagination
had been playing a trick on him where the minstrel was concerned. However, after the man's hurried departure, Sandy
knew his instincts had been right. The visitor had left a piece
of silver to pay for his meal, and no minstrel, especially one
who pleaded poverty, would possess a few pence, much less
any silver.

Still pondering the mystery of the traveling minstrel, Sandy
didn't hear the soft footsteps behind him. Nor was he prepared for the sight of an old crone standing so close at hand.
When he finally realized he was no longer alone, Sandy
jumped with a start, his expression mirroring his revulsion.

Megan's sweet laughter flowed softly into the night as she smiled smugly up at her friend. "If my appearance causes such a strong reaction in you, I know I don't have anything to worry about from Richard St. Claire once Sir Godfrey returns to Raven's Keep."

"Megan, you took me by surprise, 'tis all," Sandy lied, not wanting to raise her hopes before they knew for certain her plan had succeeded.

Megan folded her arms over the time-smoothed granite of the turret and, much like Sandy had done earlier, peered out over the village. "It's a perfect night."

"Aye, but it will do us no good."

Megan arched a brow at Sandy. "I don't intend to let Sir Godfrey's presence hinder our plans. We don't have the time to wait until he sees fit to finish his business here. For he's been instructed by Richard St. Claire to go over the estate books and see that everything is in order before my future husband comes to take everything I possess."

"Meggie, 'tis folly to even consider taking to the roads this night. And I won't be a party to getting you hanged. Should Sir Godfrey or any of his men see us or learn of what we've done, then you'd lose everything, including yer life."

"Then I'll go alone. We have only a short time before it's too late to plant the winter crops, and I can't chance that happening. As my bailiff, you already know we don't have enough stores to last another winter if we don't have a good harvest this season."

"Aye, but I fear for ye, Meggie," Sandy said, and draped a companionable arm about her slender shoulders. "I've watched ye grow up from a thin little stick to a beautiful young sapling, and I don't want to see ye cut down before yer prime. We've been lucky so far, but I've a bad feeling in me gut about our future on the roads."

"As you well know, I don't have any choice, Sandy. I have to risk it or we'll all starve. I love you for your concern, but it still doesn't change anything. We ride tonight,'' Megan said, and turned away.

''But what about Sir Godfrey? What if he sees us leave?''

Megan paused and looked back at Sandy. She gave him a soot-blackened grin. ''He'd just think the simpering idiot had escaped her wardens to cry at the moon like all who are struck with lunacy.''

''What am I going to do with you, Meggie?'' Sandy asked. Shaking his head in bewilderment, he smiled fondly down at her.

''Just the same as you've done since I was a child and you were the big boy who protected me from Mallory's viciousness.''

Sandy's smile faded. The unpleasant memory of the times he'd been unable to save Megan from her brother's beatings rose afresh in his mind, and he felt his blood begin to simmer.

When they were children he'd been able to bully Mallory enough to keep him from hurting her. However, as the years passed and Mallory realized his power over the people of Dragon's Lair, the bastard had taken great pleasure in hurting Megan just to spite Sandy. Given a choice, Mallory would have gladly rid himself and Dragon's Lair of Sandy. However, before he died, Lord Wakefield had stated in his will that Sandy should inherit his father's position as bailiff for life. Lord Wakefield's request was heeded, yet Mallory's hate for his old childhood enemy had made him find all kinds of ways to torture Sandy. His favorite was at Megan's expense.

Seeing the agonized look in Sandy's brown eyes, Megan instantly regretted any reference to their past. She knew the guilt Sandy still felt for not being able to help her, and her heart went out to him in understanding. She placed a comforting hand on his arm. ''That's all in the past now. He's dead and I don't have anything more to fear.''

"Aye," Sandy replied gruffly. "But I promise you no one will ever hurt you again as long as I'm alive."

"Oh, Sandy," Megan said, hugging him close. "You're more of a brother to me than Mallory ever was, and I don't know what I'd do without you."

"Probably get into much more trouble," Sandy chuckled at last. He picked up a strand of greasy hair and grimaced. "Now 'tis time to rid yerself of this mess; the night is growing late."

Megan smiled up at her friend and conspirator in crime. "I'll meet you in the copse of trees in an hour." With that she turned and hurried back in the direction of her apartments.

Sandy scratched his head as he watched her go. He loved Megan, but oddly enough, his feelings matched hers. She was a beautiful woman, but to Sandy, she was his precious sister, to love and protect. He intended to do that very thing until the last breath passed from his body. He smiled ruefully. He expected Megan would need him to keep his vow through all her wild schemes.

With a chuckle, another shake of his light brown head, Sandy turned and made his way toward the Judas gate near the kitchens. He'd retrieve their horses from the cave where he kept their reavers' mounts hidden. Then he'd meet Megan in the woods as he'd promised.

Chapter 3

"I don't believe I heard you correctly, Richard," Edward said, his heightened color belying his quietly spoken words.

" 'Tis true, Sire. I will do anything that you bid of me except marry the mistress of Dragon's Lair," Richard said, his heartbeat increasing at the dull flush of annoyance deepening Edward's usually pale countenance.

The king tapped his long, bejeweled fingers against the dark, gleaming wood of the massive chair where he sat, splendidly robed in a ruby velvet surcoat heavily embroidered with gold thread about the neckline and sleeves as well as its jagged-edged hem. Soft burgundy leather boots, decorated about the ankles with tiny gold chains studded with diamonds, encased his feet and legs, and a circlet of gold graced his regal head. Edward III looked every inch the powerful monarch he was as he regarded Richard through narrowed, sparkling eyes. He studied his knight with undisguised ire.

"I suggest you rethink your position in this matter, Richard. I have reason to see you wed to Lady Wakefield."

The scar that marked Richard's features from beneath the black leather patch to his jawline whitened. "Sire, bid me to fight and die for you, but do not bid me to do something I cannot.''

Edward came to his feet, towering above Richard on the step leading up to the dias of the throne. ''How dare you disobey me. I have given you a command and expect it to be carried out or you will regret the act to your dying breath.''

Richard did not retreat. He stood his ground, facing his monarch with an air of determination. ''Sire, I already regret I can't do as you bid me.''

''Damn me, Richard. I'll have you thrown into Newgate, and then, after you've enjoyed its hospitality for a while, we'll see how willing you will be for matrimony.'' Edward raged.

''If that is your wish, Sire, then I will obey,'' Richard said, unshaken from his resolve by the king's threats.

A look of exasperation crossing his handsome features, Edward raised both hands in the air and gazed heavenward as if seeking divine guidance with his recalcitrant subject. Though he'd only known Richard St. Claire for less than four years, he had to admit, the man was more stubborn than any he'd ever met. Edward had once thought the older of the two brothers was headstrong, but that was before he'd encountered Justin's sibling.

God, how he wished he could go through with his threat to lock the man in Newgate and throw away the key. It would serve St. Claire right for daring to disobey his commands. However, Edward was a far wiser monarch than his father, and he knew when it was best to retreat. Richard would have to marry the Lady Wakefield in order to protect the wool route, yet Edward also needed Justin's forces to fight France. War was now a surety since he'd renewed his interest in the French crown, claiming primogeniture through his mother, Queen Isabella. The French assembly had denied Edward's right to the crown, and Philip IV had seized his holdings in

France. Now he had no choice but to fight to reclaim his land as well as the throne.

"Richard, I understand your qualms about this match. Your brother also had similar feelings when I bid him to marry. However, as I see it, things have worked out between Justin and his wife," Edward said, changing his tactics and using his well-known charm.

"Aye, things have gone well for Justin, Sire. Yet I am not my brother, nor is Lady Wakefield Jamelyn."

"That has little to do with my need of your services," Edward snapped, his patience with the younger St. Claire wearing thin. "I need your assistance to reman Dragon's Lair. It's located at an auspicious point directly along the wool route near Nottingham, and I need you there to protect the pack trains from the reavers who have seen fit to steal my wool."

"I will gladly serve as your lieutenant, Sire. My men and I will guard the wool route from York; however, I see no need to sacrifice myself in marriage in order to secure your wool route."

"Blast it, Richard, you will do as I bid. I have need of your services, and it is your obligation to obey," Edward ground out, his temper overshadowing his charm. "And I will hear no more of it. Do you understand?"

"Sire, I have not changed my mind," Richard said, preparing himself for Edward's next outburst of rage. However, it did not come as he expected. Edward settled himself once more into the large chair and eyed him coldly, thoughtfully, for a long, tense moment.

"Then consider your marriage to Lady Wakefield postponed for now, and if you succeed in the mission I have planned for you, perhaps there will be no wedding in your future," Edward said, relaxing back into his chair without the least trace of warmth or emotion in his voice. He would teach the younger St. Claire a lesson, yet he would do so in such a manner it would not insult his older brother.

Relief washed over Richard and he smiled. "Anything you bid of me, I will do, Sire."

"That's exactly what I wanted to hear. For if you fail in this quest, then I warn you, there are those you love who will suffer for misdeeds in their past. I have a long memory, Richard, and it serves me well."

A chill rippled along Richard's spine. If he failed in this unknown mission, then Jamelyn and little Kat would be the ones to suffer. Edward had subtly reminded Richard that he hadn't forgotten the knight's part in stealing the grain the king had ordered Jamelyn to send back to England from Raven's Keep.

Richard gave a low, graceful bow. "I am at your service, Sire."

"Good," Edward said. "Then you will not mind returning to your old profession in the service of your king and country."

"Sire?" Richard asked, puzzled.

"You don't seem to understand I have need for you to return to the days when you were the famous Royce the Reaver, who stole from my pack trains."

"I still don't understand what need you have of my services in that capacity, Sire," Richard said.

"I want you to infiltrate the band of thieves who are stealing my wool and smuggling it to Flanders. Cloth merchants are growing rich off my embargo against the lowlands."

Edward smiled at Richard, well knowing the aversion the younger man would have to turning into a spy against the very element he'd led only a few short years before.

"Once you've accomplished the task, then you will try to learn the identity of the man who is the ringleader behind the scheme. If my suspicions are correct, it is someone here at court. But to this date, no one has been able to capture a single blessed reaver alive to get the information I need to prove my suspicions.''

Richard swallowed back his growing anger. He didn't like what Edward was asking, but he knew it would do neither him nor Jamelyn any good if he refused to do as the king bid. Edward was known to be as mercilessly cruel and hardhearted to those who opposed him as he was warm and generous to his friends. Edward was now extracting punishment by making Richard choose between friends he'd made in the past and the family he treasured at the present.

"I will do as you bid, Sire."

"A wise choice, Richard. I am also sending your brother to Flanders to ferret out any information from that side of the channel. He'll also have to convince the cloth merchants their livelihoods demand they ally themselves to England against France."

It also conveniently leaves Jamelyn and Raven's Keep without protection if I should fail to find the culprits behind the stolen wool, Richard mused as he again swept a low bow to his monarch and turned to leave.

"Richard," Edward said when St. Claire's hand touched the gold door latch. "I have the utmost faith in your ability to find those responsible, and I will expect to hear from you soon. Your mission is to remain a secret between us. No one, not even your brother, is to know what has transpired here today. Understood?"

"As you wish, Sire," Richard said, and quietly closed the intricately carved door behind him. He paused and drew in a deep breath in an effort to calm the rage that had been mounting since Edward's threats toward Jamelyn. He could take whatever the king saw fit to mete out, yet he couldn't endanger Jamelyn. At the young age of twenty-five, Edward was a cunning monarch who knew how to play the power game well. He'd learned it from his mother, Queen Isabella, and her lover, Roger Mortimer. Their scheming had succeeded in dethroning Edward II and having him killed, though no charges for the crime had ever been brought against them for the barbarous act.

His mind in turmoil, Richard strode from the palace without acknowledging those who greeted him as he passed through Windsor's stone corridors and made his way to the stables. He mounted the black horse, and without a glance back at the elaborate castle that Edward's masons, carpenters, and craftsmen were creating for England's monarch, he went back in the direction of Nottingham.

From his vantage point in Windsor's upper ward, Edward watched the lone rider speed out of sight into Windsor forest. Conflicting emotions warred within him. He liked Richard St. Claire and had not wanted to threaten to get the man to obey his commands. Yet Edward couldn't afford to let Richard escape unscathed for his disobedience. The monarch would not allow any weakness on his part to show or he might fall into the same trap that his father had with his noblemen. He was king of England, and his subjects would obey his commands.

Edward turned away from the leaded window and crossed to the large table with legs intricately carved to resemble curling vines. Across the front of the gleaming dark wood, the artist had inlaid bunches of grapes with gold. The metal caught the sunlight streaming in through the window and dappled it across the royal blue Turkish carpet at Edward's feet.

Edward lifted a scroll and unrolled it. A frown etched a path across his handsome face as he perused the document. More money was needed if he wanted to finance his war with France. His scowl deepened as he considered his last few options. He'd already raised a special tax by using threats of Philip's plan to send six thousand troops to Scotland. He'd also borrowed from the Florence money houses of Bardi, Frescobaldi, and Peruzzi, guaranteeing them payment from another tax he'd placed on each bag of wool. Edward had already defaulted on the loan since the major wool trains had been robbed of their precious cargo. That meant no more loans from the lenders and thus no place to gain the money he needed for his troubles with France.

"Damn," Edward swore, startling his attendants from their quiet conversation across the chamber. He crumpled up the parchment and threw it to the floor. Richard St. Claire was his only hope of salvaging the next shipment of wool. Should it not reach its destination, then the English weavers would be out of work, and he would be without money to finance his war.

Edward settled his lean frame in a gilded chair and picked up a quill. He dipped it into the gold inkwell and began to write. He didn't like having to force Richard to do his bidding, but he was wise enough to know he had to use every opportunity available to secure the wool route to Norwich. He would also use Justin's abilities to accomplish his aims in Flanders. He was confident that between the two St. Claire brothers, he would find out who was behind the theft of the wool. Then, when his financial difficulties were settled, he would be able to proceed with more important matters— namely, his quarrel with Philip IV of France.

Chapter 4

*Garbed in a monk's robe, Sandy peered at Megan from be-
neath* the woolen cowl. A furrow dug its way across his
forehead, and he shook his head. "Meggie, 'tis too dangerous to take them while it's still daylight."

"Sandy, we won't have anything to worry about if you
will only do as I ask," Megan said as she tied the peasant's
coif beneath her chin and firmly tucked her hair beneath it
before raising the hood of her cape. She was dressed in rough
woolen chausses, leather jerkin, and cape, a disguise that
effectively hid her gender. Upon observing the slender youth,
few would have known that she was a female, and none
would have recognized her as the mistress of Dragon's Lair.

Sandy glanced about their shady hiding place overlooking
the glade where several travelers had stopped to refresh themselves. "I don't like it. I feel something is not quite right
here. It seems far too easy. From the looks of 'em, they
should be carrying a goodly sum in their purses. Yet if they're
so wealthy, then why don't they have outriders for protection?"

"You're just anxious because you're in the guise of a
priest," Megan said, a mischievous grin curving the corners
of her shapely mouth, a twinkle of devilment in her indigo

49

eyes. "I wonder what Father Reynard would say if he knew exactly what use you have for his robe?"

"The good friar would probably have a seizure, and then I'd be accused of murder," Sandy grumbled, fidgeting with the coarse woolen garment draping his sturdy frame.

"Then we'd best get this done with so you can get the good friar's robe back to him," Megan said, turning her attention once more to the small group of travelers.

"Why can't we just ride in as usual? I don't like the thought of us separating. It's too risky."

"With only the two of us, it's best you're there to see how well they're armed before I arrive. Then you can disarm them before they know exactly what's going on."

"I still don't like it, Meggie. I understand your reasoning, but in the daylight 'tis going to be hard for us to make good our escape."

"It'll be dusk soon, so it will be dark enough to cover our tracks if anyone should follow," Megan said, glancing up at the greying sky.

Realizing Megan was intent on going through with the robbery, Sandy released a long breath and stood. He made sure his own weapon was secure beneath the folds of wool. He then lifted a length of rope and draped it like a belt around his middle. The rope would do to tie up their victims. Picking up a long stick to use as his staff, he looked once more at Megan. "Let's get it over with. Father McTavis wants to retire from the priesthood as soon as possible. He prefers to be just an ordinary reaver. It's far more honest."

Megan's lips twitched and she looked up at Sandy with eyes glittering from the rush of excitement coursing through her veins. This robbery was a challenge—their first without the shield of darkness to aid them. It was also the first time they had come upon any wealthy travelers who were not heavily guarded.

Megan could nearly feel the gold coins in her hand and

see the crops growing green and healthy in the fields. That thought alone was enough incentive for the bravado they were displaying today with their daylight robbery, yet another reason lay at the back of her mind. If they could gain enough gold to pay for the seeds from this robbery, she would be able to give up her nightly excursions into the countryside. The thought goaded her into action.

"Then, Father McTavis, it's now up to you. When you're certain you have everything in control, give the sign of the cross and I'll ride in to relieve our wealthy friends of their purses." She gave Sandy's arm a reassuring squeeze, then turned and crept back to where they had tethered their horses.

Sandy watched Megan disappear into the woods and shook his head at her irreverence. Mentally making the sign of the cross as a peace offering to the higher authority, he prayed God would understand that Megan meant nothing by her actions and would see fit to overlook her impious behavior. Though her faith had sorely been tested in the past, Sandy knew she still believed in God and His mercy. Even after all the times her prayers had gone unanswered about her brother, she never lost her belief in the goodness of God and man.

Shaking his head in wonder at Megan's indomitable spirit, Sandy made his way quietly through the woods. Certain he was far enough away from the travelers, he stepped out onto the road, and with staff in hand, he turned back in the direction of the clearing where they rested, completely unaware that soon they would loose their purses.

Their hooves silenced by the rags Sandy had tied about them earlier, the horses were quiet as Megan urged them to an observation point and waited for her bailiff to make his appearance. When he came trudging up the road, huffing and puffing, Megan smiled. Had she not known better herself, she would have believed he was a priest. Father Reynard's robe completely disguised Sandy's robust, work-hardened body beneath its woolen folds. The staff he carried added to the effect of a poor friar making some holy mission.

"Father," a well-dressed gentleman said, respectfully coming to his feet when Sandy entered the glade. "What brings you so far from your church?"

Sandy gave the man a peaceful smile. "My son, I have been called to give the last rights to a poor soul in the village of Southwell."

"But, Father, you've taken the wrong turn in the road. You're going toward Nottingham, not Southwell. You should have taken the road along the Witham," the man's companion said, also coming to his feet.

Seeing no sign of the men's weapons, Sandy released a long breath and feigned weariness as he assessed the strength of the two well-dressed men and their silent companion, who sat beneath a large oak. He shook his head sadly. "Fool that I am, I fear now I won't make it in time to assure the poor soul of a peaceful death."

"Father," the third man said from his place under the tall tree. "I find it odd you took the wrong road when it is so well marked."

Sandy raised his hands in a helpless gesture, though the hair on the nape of his neck rose in warning. "My son, I fear I was too concerned with praying for the man's soul to notice I was going in the wrong direction."

" 'Tis strange a friar from a nearby abbey should not know the area better," the man said. His gaze swept over Sandy from head to toe before he glanced about the clearing as if aware of a presence in the surrounding woods.

"I have only been at the abbey of Darley for a short while. I came from the South and fear I have as yet to learn my way about. I pray my ignorance will be forgiven by those I serve." Though his every instinct warned him that these men were not ordinary travelers, he ignored his feeling and made the sign of the cross to signal Megan.

A moment later when Megan rode into the clearing swinging her sword and demanding the travelers relinquish their purses, Sandy had no time to consider anything else. He moved to take the man nearest him, but before he could bring his own weapon from beneath the folds of the woolen robe, the woods came alive about them.

A loud whistle from the traveler who still sat nonchalantly beneath the oak brought a detachment of archers into the clearing, their arrows directed at Megan and Sandy.

Momentarily stunned by their unforeseen capture, Sandy stared at Megan as she was dragged roughly from the saddle by a burly man-at-arms. He knocked the sword from her hand, and it fell to the ground at her horse's hooves.

The third man rose gracefully, seemingly without a care in the world, and walked over to where Sandy stood with hands raised in the air. An amicable smile briefly touched his full lips before a snarl replaced it. Giving Sandy no time to prepare, the man drew back a gloved hand and slapped him across the face. Sandy's head snapped back and he tasted the sweetness of his own blood upon his lips.

Megan cried out in protest, drawing the man's attention to her. "Such loyalty among thieves," he chided, his voice silky with menace.

"Coward," Megan said, twisting and struggling against the strong hands that held her bound. "You hit an unarmed man who can't defend himself."

"I do not fight with vermin or thieves. I squash them beneath the heel of my boot or see them hanged as they deserve," the man answered, eyeing her contemptuously for a long moment before ordering, "Hang these two and leave their bodies for the vultures. That should give warning to any who think to trespass upon my land again."

"Aye, Lord Ashby," the sergeant answered. He motioned for several of the archers to lay down their weapons and take the two thieves to the small cart that had been quickly emptied of the gentlemen's luggage.

Knowing she and Sandy could not escape death, Megan determined it would be far better to die fighting than by the slow agony of strangulation. Waiting for the right moment to make her move, she feigned defeat, and hung her head. She allowed her guards to lead her toward the cart, which had been pulled beneath the limb of the large oak, where a noose swayed gently in the evening breeze.

Her moment came when the guards tried to hoist her up into the cart. Taking advantage of their loosened grips, she lunged sideways, kicking out at the same time and coming into contact with one man's groin while knocking the other off balance. Freed, she turned and dived for the sword, which lay only a few feet away. Rolling to one side, she came to her feet like a cat, agile and poised and ready to do battle.

Lord Ashby, hearing the commotion behind him, swung around to come face-to-face with the young boy standing with sword in hand and pointed directly at his heart. Daring not to chance the use of his archers in such close proximity to himself, he rapidly motioned them to lay down their weapons, and stood regarding the youth cynically. "Am I to believe you think you can take me with your sword? Surely you know you're only prolonging the inevitable. Even if you should kill me, you will be dead before I fall."

"Perhaps you are right, but I will take you with me," Megan said. "Now loose my friend or die."

Robert Ashby shook his russet-colored head. "I'm afraid I don't have time for this. Edward expects me at court by the end of the week, and I've already taken too much time in my efforts to catch the reavers who have been stealing his wool."

Megan cast a quick, wary glance about her before she said, "Then you have captured the wrong thieves, my lord."

"It truly doesn't matter—thieves are thieves. The news of your hanging will more than please the king and confirm my loyalty to Edward in every way since I'm one of the few protecting his interest in this area.''

''I fear the king will have to hear of your loyalty from your men if you do not release my friend,'' Megan said, moving closer to press the sword against Lord Ashby's chest and completely unaware of the stealthy movement of his hand toward the dirk strapped at his waist.

Robert Ashby calmly smiled at her, shaking his head. ''I fear not.''

Before the words were completely out of his mouth, Megan saw the glint of shining metal out of the corner of her eye. He struck so swiftly, she had only a split second to avoid the keen point of the dagger aimed at her stomach. She jumped back, her reflexes reacting instinctively to evade the dagger's blade. However, Megan was unable to save herself completely. The dirk missed her stomach by only a few inches, yet the downward thrust sent it slicing through the air and into her upper thigh. The sharp blade hewed open her flesh, the searing agony rendering her immobile long enough for Ashby to seize the advantage and strip her of her weapon. With a growl of displeasure and a blow from the back of his hand, he sent her tumbling into the dust at his feet.

As he towered over her, Ashby's handsome features showed no compassion as he pricked her beneath the chin with the tip of her own sword. Nor did the sinister smile curling his lips ease her feelings as she looked up into his cold green eyes.

''I should dispatch your soul to hell for that little trick, but I'll leave something to entertain my men,'' he said before thrusting the sword at the sergeant-at-arms. ''See he doesn't escape again or you'll stand beside him on the gallows.''

Without another word Ashby turned and stalked across the clearing to where his two companions sat mounted and ready to ride. Untethering his horse, he hoisted himself into the saddle and cast one last glance at the reavers before viciously spurring his mount in the side and setting him into a gallop down the road toward London. His companions followed in his wake.

Lord Robert Ashby smiled to himself, enjoying the feel of the wind in his face. His plan had succeeded well. Though he had told the young reaver he wanted to catch the thieves who had stolen the wool from the pack trains bound for Norwich, in truth his trap had been meant for any thief who chose to fall into it. He had waited days for it to happen, and today he had finally succeeded in snaring his quarry and earning the king's gratitude. This day's work would also insure that things continued to go as planned.

The regiment of archers soon followed in Lord Ashby's wake, leaving only the sergeant and two men-at-arms to execute his orders to hang the reavers.

Weak and trembling from pain, Megan staggered to the cart, where Sandy stood with a noose about his neck. Their gazes met momentarily before she was roughly thrust up beside him. Her hands were bound behind her back before a rope was placed around her throat.

"Better make yer peace with yer God, vermin. 'Tis the last ye'll see of this life," the sergeant chuckled.

"Forgive me, Meggie, I should have known it was a trap," Sandy whispered, his voice hoarse from the tension of the hemp about his neck.

" 'Tis not your fault, old friend. 'Tis mine, and I must ask your forgiveness for not heeding your advice," Megan said over the lump of dread forming in her throat.

She cast one last glance at Sandy and then closed her eyes. Her softly spoken words were the only sound in the quiet glade. "Holy Mary, Mother of God, pray for us sinners now at the hour of our death."

Chapter 5

Twilight was blending into night when Richard heard voices coming from beyond the bend in the road. Always alert to danger, he eased his mount into the woods and quietly maneuvered the stallion toward the source of the sound. In the fading light he could see the cart and its two occupants beneath the gnarl-branched oak. He recognized the Ashby colors on the three men-at-arms who were tormenting their victims with ribald comments as they readied the pair for death.

"Ye reavers won't be stealing any more of our good king's wool," the sergeant said as he raised his hand to signal the man-at-arms to pull the cart from beneath their feet.

At the man's words, all of Richard's senses came alert. The man in the monk's robe and the boy would be part of the band of thieves Edward wanted him to infiltrate. Seeing a quick means to put an end to the king's scheme, Richard seized upon the unexpected opportunity to join the reavers by saving their lives. He unsheathed his sword and gave his mount a sharp kick. His wild highland yell rent the still evening as he and his horse burst through the underbrush and into the clearing.

Taken off guard, the startled men-at-arms fell back under

the onslaught of the wild rider and his huge black stallion. Their momentary confusion gave Richard the time he needed to help the reavers escape. He maneuvered his mount behind the cart and swiftly cut the ropes binding their wrists. With one clean slice, he then severed the thick hemp just above their heads, leaving the nooses dangling from their necks.

"Get gone," he cried, turning his full attention upon the three men who had regained enough of their composure to regroup and launch an assault. Metal clashed against metal, ringing eerily through the still evening air as Richard held the guards at bay to give the reavers time to reach the safety of the dark woods.

"The saints be praised, Meggie. We've been saved," Sandy said, jerking the ropes from about his wrists and tossing them away. Taking no time to loosen the noose from about his neck, he jumped down from the cart and turned to help Megan.

"Escape, Sandy," Megan whispered, hobbling to the edge of the cart. Her wound prevented her from moving faster, and the white line about her lips reflected the excruciating pain she suffered.

"I'm not leaving you," Sandy said as he lifted her down from the cart. Megan gasped and shook her head. She gritted her teeth against the searing agony that raced up her right side.

"Obey me, Sandy. I can't travel in this condition. It's left to you to see that Faith gets the money to buy the seed for the crops."

"I ain't leaving ye, Meggie," Sandy said again with conviction, and made to gather her into his arms.

"No," Megan gasped, pushing him away. "I'll only slow you down. One of us has to make it safely back or everyone will suffer. We are the only people who know where the money for the crops is hidden. Now, heed my command and go," she cried, and gave him a shove toward the shadowy underbrush. Using the last of her waning strength, she turned, and without a backward glance at her bailiff and friend, she began to hobble in the opposite direction, hoping to draw any pursuit with her.

"Megan," Sandy said in a heart-wrenching whisper as he struggled against himself before turning and fleeing into the protective embrace of the night. He knew that Megan was right. It was best for at least one of them to escape. However, his love for Megan soon overran his better judgment. Sandy ventured only far enough into the woods to obscure his presence. From his vantage point he watched the battle rage between the men-at-arms and the stranger. He felt Megan's agony as his own as he glimpsed her crossing the clearing toward the safety of the darkened woods beyond.

Taut and pale, her face reflected the supreme effort it took for her to walk. Yet Sandy had begun to believe she, too, might make good her own escape until the sergeant-at-arms blocked her path. The bailiff's heart seemed to stop within his breast. Weaponless, Megan bravely faced the man, staring down the length of his shining metal sword. She looked resigned to the fact that she would not leave the clearing alive.

From the corner of his eye, Richard saw the young reaver's precarious situation and realized the unarmed boy was no match for the sergeant. With only a flick of the man's arm, he could end the boy's life. Calling forth all of his own skill and experience from battle, Richard swiftly disarmed the two other men and sent them fleeing into the woods. Guiding his well-trained steed with only the pressure of his knees, Richard urged the stallion directly at the sergeant-at-arms. The huge animal's wide chest slammed into the man before the sergeant could fulfill his intentions to skewer the youth. The force of the impact sent the sergeant flying through the air. He landed against the trunk of the large oak, and his helm cracked against the thick bole, staggering his senses. He sank slowly to the ground to stare blankly at the tips of his boots.

Richard took no time to consider the damage to the sergeant-at-arms. In one graceful, fluid motion he leaned from the saddle and scooped the young reaver up into his arms. Without a backward glance, he settled his light burden in front of him and urged his mount into the woods, the darkness covering their escape. Richard didn't see the second reaver come bursting through the underbrush, monk's robe riding up around his waist as he jumped over fallen limbs and other objects, waving his arms in an effort to stop Richard's exit.

"Lad, 'tis best to stay alert until we're sure we're not being followed," Richard said when he felt the young reaver suddenly relax against him.

He received no response from the youth.

Puzzled by the deathly stillness of his silent companion, Richard gently tipped up the youth's chin and peered down into his shadowy features. He frowned with concern as the boy's head lolled limply back against his shoulder.

"Damn," he grumbled, scanning the young reaver for any sign of injury. Spying the blood-streaked chausses, Richard released a long breath. The scene in the clearing had happened so quickly, he hadn't noticed the wound in the boy's thigh until that moment.

Richard's frown deepened and he tightened his grip on the reins. At the moment the boy was his only link to the wool thieves, and if he hoped to infiltrate them quickly and without suspicion, he'd have to use his rescue of the lad. From his own experience, he knew how the minds of the thieves worked. Loyalty to one another was the one thing that bound each group together. By saving the youth's life, he could gain their trust much sooner than if he attempted to join the band on his own.

"I'm not going to let you die, young one," Richard said, urging his horse deeper into the woods.

By the time Richard reined his mount to a halt in the mossy glade, the moon had crept over the horizon to bathe the woods in its pale light. A short distance away, a stream, like a silver ribbon lying serpentine upon black velvet, wound its way through the dark forest. Richard sat still and quiet, listening for any sound that might indicate pursuit. Hearing nothing but the gentle gurgle of water, he relaxed, confident he had managed to elude anyone who had attempted to follow.

Turning his attention to the youth who lay slumped in his arms, Richard dismounted and eased the still figure from the saddle. He marveled at the weightlessness of his unconscious burden as he crossed the small clearing and laid the young reaver upon a soft bed of moss that blanketed the earth like an emerald green carpet. Knowing there was nothing he could do until he made camp and built a fire, Richard turned his attention to their immediate need.

Finding enough dry wood, he quickly had a fire blazing. It chased away the shadows of the night and illuminated the clearing so that Richard could treat the young reaver's wound. Ripping away a strip of his own undertunic, he withdrew his dirk and began to saw through the woolen material of the youth's chausses. Experienced in dealing with wounds from years on the battlefield, Richard knew he had to cleanse the gash and then stop the bleeding with a strip of white linen or else the youth would die. Yet when he pulled back the bloody material to reveal the wound, which ran from the base of the right hip downward across the upper thigh, Richard momentarily forgot what he'd set out to do. His nostrils flared as he drew in a sharp breath, and his mouth suddenly went dry. His knuckles whitened about the bone handle of his dirk as he gaped down at the essence of femininity he'd exposed beneath the soft linen smallclothes.

"Damn!" Richard muttered, dumbfounded to discover far

more than he ever imagined beneath the coarse woolen chausses. The young reaver he'd thought a small man had turned out to be a girl.

Richard felt a chill of premonition. On another night such as this he'd encountered a spirited youth whom he'd also mistakenly believed to be a young man. She had turned out to be his sister-in-law, Jamelyn. That fateful meeting had turned his life upside down, and it had as yet to set itself to rights.

Running a long-fingered hand through his tousled raven curls, Richard absently shook his head in disbelief as he turned his attention to the immediate need of trying to prevent the girl from bleeding to death. He was relieved to find the wound was not as deep as he'd first thought, but it still bled, and that was his main concern. Later, when all was done, he could wonder at her reasons for being dressed like a man.

Richard worked swiftly and efficiently. After he'd finished binding the gash, he tugged up the fray-edged cloth in an effort to preserve what little modesty was left her by the tattered clothing. However, there was little he could do about the large seam his dirk had rent in the woolen material. Her lower hip and thigh were left exposed to view.

Otherwise satisfied he'd done all he could, Richard settled down to wait until the girl regained consciousness. If the wound did not become inflamed and fester, she would be nearly back to normal when she awoke. Leaning back against the bole of a large birch, the loose bark crackling beneath his wide back as he shifted into a comfortable position, Richard tilted his head to stare up at the star-studded sky. His thoughts turned once more to his brother's wife.

"Jamelyn, ah, my wild, sweet Jamelyn," he mused softly into the night. His love for her was still as strong as it had been when they had connived to cheat King Edward out of ᐧaven's Keep's grain. Although he knew she belonged to

Justin in all ways, heart and soul, he couldn't rid his own heart of the love he felt. His feelings had been born on a night much like this one. A night filled with stars and a young woman dressed in men's clothing. It was a love he feared he'd never be able to rid himself of completely. And it was this need to protect the woman he loved that brought him to this place in time to do Edward's bidding.

For a long, thoughtful moment Richard looked at the silent figure near the campfire. How different his life would have turned out if he hadn't met Jamelyn of Raven's Keep. He wouldn't now be in league with the king to capture the band of wool thieves. In all probability he would have been the man Edward sought.

Richard smiled and once more lay his head back against the tree. He closed his eyes and folded his arms over his chest. It was time to get some rest and stop wondering about the twists and turns in his life. For now he had one mission: to protect Jamelyn and her family.

Megan stirred and raised a hand to shield her eyes from the blinding sunlight that spilled through the leaves overhead. A frown deepened across her brow as she squinted up through her fingers, wondering why she was not in her bedchamber at Dragon's Lair. Still disoriented, she made to raise herself upon her elbows to better observe the surroundings when a searing pain shot up her side, quickly bringing to mind her wound. An involuntary cry escaped her lips before she clamped them firmly together to avoid another outburst.

"Good morning," a deep, masculine voice said. Realizing she wasn't alone, Megan snapped completely alert, the events of the previous night rushing back. She slowly turned to look at the one-eyed man who had saved her from hanging.

Drawing in a steadying breath, she prepared herself for the pain she knew would follow any movement and pushed herself upright. Striving to keep at bay the agony knifing through her, she gave her rescuer a wobbly little smile and said, "I fear in my present state it doesn't seem much like a very good morning to me."

"I would think it is far better than the one planned for you last eve," Richard said, and gave the girl a wry grin. Getting to his feet, he stretched his arms over his head and rolled his head from side to side to ease the stiffness his awkward sleeping position had created. From the way his muscles felt, he didn't believe he'd moved all night.

Megan nodded, sufficiently chastened. "Aye, 'tis much better. And you have my gratitude for seeing it didn't come to pass, Sir . . . ?"

"Royce McFarland," Richard supplied as he hunkered down beside the smoldering campfire. He tossed several sticks onto the grey ash and waited for them to flame before looking once more at the girl. " 'Tis fortunate you didn't bleed to death before I had a chance to bind your wound. Does it pain you greatly?"

Megan shook her head as she glanced down at the binding on her exposed hip and leg. Her pallor faded beneath the flush that suffused her skin when she realized her rescuer had handled her intimately and knew her secret.

"Then you know?" was all she could say over the lump of embarrassment filling her throat. She stared blindly down at the strip of white linen tied across her wound.

"Aye. I know the lad I rescued turned out to be a lass." Richard watched the blush rise to tint the girl's cheeks a lovely rose and realized for the first time she might be a comely wench if she took a few pains with her appearance and gowned herself properly.

Her embarrassment heightening, Megan strove to retain some semblance of composure. No one, except her maid, Mary, had ever seen her unclothed. She fidgeted nervously with the frayed cloth, unconsciously attempting to stretch it further over her skin.

"I fear there is little fabric left to do much good, lass," Richard supplied.

Megan flashed Richard an agonized look and then nodded with resignation. Finally she raised one shoulder in an offhand shrug and gave him a weak smile. " 'Tis like locking the gate after the cow has escaped. You can't see any more than you already have."

Richard chuckled, her jest making him even more aware of her loveliness. A sense of humor was rare in those who led hard lives. To those whose long days were filled with drudgery, it seemed a sin to laugh even if they had the energy. Richard suspected the girl's desperate life-style had driven her to the roads.

"No need to worry, lass. I saw only your wound," Richard said to ease her discomfort. "I was far too concerned with trying to save your life to worry about anything else."

"I fear I owe you far more than I can ever repay," Megan said, relieved by his answer.

"I ask no payment, only an answer to a question."

Puzzled, Megan looked at her one-eyed rescuer. "If I can answer it, I will gladly do so."

"I would know the name of the lass I saved," Richard said, and watched a flicker of uncertainty pass over the girl's pale features.

"I'm—I'm Meggie," Megan stuttered after a long pause. She couldn't tell even the man who saved her from certain death her real name. It would be folly to give anyone that knowledge, no matter what he had done for her. If the truth came out about her nightly excursions into the countryside, she would lose too much, including Dragon's Lair and possibly her life.

"Now, tell me, Meggie, what has brought you to this pass? In all my years on the roads, making my living in a similar manner to your own"—Richard gave Megan one of his most charming and roguish smiles before he continued—"you're the first female reaver I've come across."

Megan's mouth went dry. She didn't know how to answer his question without giving away the truth about herself. Moistening her lips, she finally managed to say, " 'Tis a far better living on the roads than starving in the service of some rich and mighty lord. My family—" Megan paused, calling to mind her villeins readying the fields for the seeds that she was supposed to purchase for the spring planting "—will die without the few coins I manage to lift from unwary travelers."

Richard nodded his understanding. Her reasons were just as he'd assumed; however, she was acting as if robbing a few travelers was all she'd ever done.

"Now, Meggie," Richard said, eyeing her suspiciously. "You must think me a fool if you want me to believe you've only taken a few meager purses. From what I heard your guards say last eve, your crimes are far worse."

" 'Tis your choice to believe as you wish. I'm telling you the truth, just as I told Lord Ashby when he sentenced me to die for stealing the king's wool."

Richard regarded Megan for a long, thoughtful moment, weighing her sincerity. He didn't think she was lying, yet he knew reavers were skilled at deceptions of all kinds. Wasn't his ruse at Dragon's Lair only the previous week proof of his own culpability? "Then you don't belong to the band of reavers who've attacked the wool pack trains from York?"

Again Megan shook her head. "Nay, I know nothing of them."

Richard frowned and turned his attention to putting several sticks on the fire. If the girl told the truth, then he was no closer to the wool thieves than he'd been last eve before making his daring rescue.

Wondering at the odd look flickering over the stranger's

face, Megan suddenly grew suspicious. "I am curious to know why you're interested in my dealings."

Richard jerked his thoughts back to the present. "Lass, as I've said, I'm of your profession and I'm looking to join up with a few good men interested in making a profitable living by taking far more than a few purses. From the situation in which I found you, I thought you might be able to aid me in my quest."

Megan nervously glanced away from Richard's keen, assessing gaze. "I fear I can be of little service. I know of no such men."

"Then you and the monk acted alone?" Richard asked, attempting to draw out any information of value.

"Aye" was Megan's morose answer.

Although the girl piqued Richard's curiosity, he refrained from asking further questions. For now he'd content himself with what he'd already learned about her. Settling comfortably once more beneath the birch, he leaned back and braced his hands behind his head. He peered up at the clear sky and thoughtfully considered his next course of action.

From what Meggie had said, he suspected her endeavors upon the road had earned her little. However, if he joined them, he could use his experience to change their fortunes. And that could lead him to those he sought.

Richard smiled to himself, liking the idea more by the minute. Perhaps Meggie and her monk were not the culprits behind the wool robberies, yet they were part of a chain that linked all thieves together in certain quarters. It was their survival system, their means of communicating with one another and those who acted as middlemen for the goods they stole. Without such chains, none would survive long. And he would use that system to lead him to the information he needed to solve Edward's problems as well as his own.

"I think we may be of use to each other, Meggie," Richard said, and bestowed upon her another charming smile.

A twig snapping nearby drew Richard's attention before Megan could ask what he meant. He sat up, tense and alert, his hand automatically reaching for the hilt of his sword.

Megan also heard the sound. Unable to do more, she sat warily surveying the surrounding wood for any sign of danger. Another twig snapped and she saw a flicker of movement in the bushes near Royce's back. Fearing they had been followed by Ashby's men, she called a warning, yet before the words were completely out of her mouth, Royce was already on his feet, sword in hand, to face the intruder.

"Show yourself or be prepared to meet your God," Richard ordered.

The bushes rattled, and a berobed figure eased from his hiding place with hands raised above his head.

"Ah, the monk has finally seen fit to show himself after all the danger is past," Royce chided, lowering his sword.

Sandy's insides recoiled from the stranger's censure, but his features reflected none of the chagrin he felt at having to face the man who had saved Megan's life when that responsibility was his own.

"Sandy," Megan said, breathing a sigh of relief.

"Are ye all right, Meggie?" Sandy asked, crossing to her and kneeling at her side.

"Aye, thanks to Royce. He saved my life."

Sandy flushed and glanced once more at the man Megan had called Royce. "Then ye have me gratitude."

Richard gave Sandy a contemptuous smile. "Any man would have done the same."

The reaver's cowardice was a raw spot with Richard. This monk's careless actions had nearly cost Meggie her life last night. It wasn't easy for Richard to forget the monk's retreat, no matter how much he wanted to gain information about the wool thieves.

"I'm no coward, if that's what you're insinuating," Sandy growled. Coming to his feet, fists clenched at his side, features flushing a deep red, he faced Richard. He didn't like the man's condescending attitude. He'd only done as he'd been bid.

Seeing the confrontation building between the two men and knowing she had to stop it before it was too late, Megan spoke without thinking of the consequences. "Royce, 'twas not Sandy's fault, but mine, that he didn't come to our aid. He was following my orders."

Richard turned his sapphire gaze upon Megan and eyed her dubiously. "A reaver following the orders of a wench? Surely you don't expect me to believe that? 'Tis more likely he fled to save his own skin and you're just trying to keep me from skewering him for the coward he is."

"Nay, I'm telling you the truth," Megan said, glancing nervously at Sandy. She could see the strain he was under to keep himself from throttling Royce, and she knew it couldn't last much longer. " 'Tis I who lead, not Sandy."

Richard glanced back at the berobed man. He arched a quizzical brow at Sandy and saw him nod an affirmation of Megan's statement. Slowly he shook his head in wonder. "I've seen many things in my life, but the two of you are the strangest pair I've encountered." Again Richard shook his head and chuckled. "A monk led by a girl barely old enough to be out of the nursery. 'Tis strange indeed."

"I see nothing strange about it," Megan said, slightly annoyed by Royce's amusement. "We have bellies that want to be filled just like anyone else."

"Which brings me back to what I wanted to say before your monk interrupted us."

"I'm no monk, and I'm called Sandy," Sandy growled, still glowering at Royce.

"Then, Sandy, if you're wise, you will listen well to what I have to say, for I can make you rich."

Sandy regarded Royce skeptically and, for the first time since he'd seen the rider come charging through the underbrush to rescue them from the hangman's noose, realized there was something oddly familiar about the man. He searched his memory to place where and when he'd seen the one-eyed stranger. It took only a moment to recall that it had been at Dragon's Lair when Royce had been disguised as a traveling minstrel.

"Your words aren't as convincing as your music, Sir Minstrel," Sandy said. "We don't need your help to make us rich."

"My music?" Richard said, startled.

"Aye, like yerself, I was at the castle known as Dragon's Lair, begging for a meal from its fair mistress. But unlike you, I didn't flee like a frightened hare before I managed to gain a nobleman's purse."

"Monk, I doubt you even saw the insides of the castle if you thought its mistress was fair. She was a toad with blackened stubs for teeth, and eyes that looked in two directions at once."

Megan managed with some difficulty to keep from laughing aloud. If her disguise had made such an impression upon a rogue like Royce, who had seen a much harsher side of life, then what impression had she left upon Richard St. Claire's envoy?

Hopefully by the time her wound healed enough for her to return to Dragon's Lair, Sir Godfrey would have satisfied himself upon all the estate records and would have returned to report to Richard St. Claire. After what Royce had just said, she didn't doubt for a moment that when her future husband heard Sir Godfrey's description of the Lady of Dragon's Lair, she would not be called upon to marry anyone in the near future.

"But the Lady—" Sandy began before Megan broke into the conversation, silencing him.

"Aye, Royce is right, Sandy. I saw the wench he speaks of. She was an ugly old crone." Megan flashed Sandy an annoyed look before she looked up at Royce and winked conspiratorially. "Methinks Sandy was too busy eyeing the serving wenches to notice the old toad with the stringy hair."

Sandy immediately realized the mistake he'd nearly made. He grinned. "At least I didn't come away with empty pockets."

"Aye, 'twas your good fortune I was frightened away by the hag or you'd have come away with only air in your pockets and nothing to buy bread and wine to fill your empty bellies. Feel proud, monk. Few people can boast they plucked a pigeon that got away from Royce McFarland."

"And you would have us believe you will make us rich? From what I've heard, you need us far more than we need you. At least we don't let crones frighten us away from our quarry," Megan said, her eyes glittering with mirth, her lips quivering from the smile she fought to contain.

Richard ran a long-fingered hand across his beard-stubbled chin. Now was the time to convince Meggie it would be best for both parties involved to join forces. "Aye, I'll make you rich if we work together. Alone, neither of us can succeed because we are too few. We can't waylay the travelers who have full purses and outriders for protection. However, if we join forces, everything will change."

Reflecting upon the last excursions she and Sandy had made and the few coins they'd gained from their efforts, Megan could see the logic of such a union. It would be the answer to her prayers and a means to end this horrendous life-style as a reaver. After last night, she didn't know how much more she could take. She had been so close to death that even now a chill of fear raced up her spine at the thought. Megan glanced over at Sandy to see his reaction to Royce's suggestion. Surprisingly, she saw him smiling his approval.

"All right, Royce McFarland. We agree to let you ride with us. However, I warn you now. It will cost you your life if you try to cheat us of what is rightly ours."

"Then 'tis settled; we work together," Richard said.

"Aye, 'tis settled," Megan added, feeling suddenly optimistic about her future and that of Dragon's Lair.

Chapter 6

The firelight cast its warmth over the solar where Faith sat,
staring aimlessly into the leaping flames. The golden glow
of the fire highlighted her smooth brow and high cheek-
bones, yet the shadows cast by her dark lashes hid the expression in her crystalline eyes. Her graceful, long-fingered
hands lay limp in her lap and she absently worried her softly
full lower lip with even white teeth. Distracted from her embroidery—a piece of work that depicted scenes from actual
events in Dragon's Lair's past and had taken up her evenings
for the past two years—Faith's thoughts rested with her
cousin, who had failed to return the previous night from her
excursion into the countryside.

"Oh, Megan. What has become of you?" she murmured
softly to herself, and swallowed back the lump of fear that
rose to choke her.

Coming upon the scene and taking unexpected pleasure
from witnessing Lady Faith relaxed and without the cold
expression she usually wore when she knew of his presence,
Anthony stood silent and unobserved in the doorway to the
solar. As his gaze feasted upon the golden beauty emphasized by the halo of firelight, he had to admit she was by far
the most beautiful woman he had ever seen. Sitting serene

and lovely with her pale hair mantling her shoulders in luminous curls, she looked angelical.

Anthony felt his senses stir. The breath caught in his throat, his heart began to drum against his ribs as blood wildly raced through his veins. For one brief moment, his thoughts flickered to the fiery, auburn-haired beauty at Raven's Keep, and he remembered a time when he'd thought he'd never see a woman to compare to Jamelyn. However, since meeting Lady Faith, he found himself likening the two women. Both were beautiful, but where Jamelyn was silk and steel, Faith was down and roses and as elusive as the clouds.

Anthony drew in a deep breath in an effort to cool his mounting ardor and bring himself back to reality. He was waxing poetic about a woman who loathed the very sight of him. Lady Faith had made her feeling very clear every time he came near her. He had tried unsuccessfully over the past two weeks to get over the barrier she had erected, but no matter what he said or did, she regarded him as if he had just crawled out of a slimy moat.

Anthony frowned. For the life of him, he couldn't understand the reason behind her irascible behavior. He had gone out of his way to accommodate everyone at Dragon's Lair, including its eccentric mistress, but nothing had changed Lady Faith's opinion of him. Wondering futilely if he would ever earn the lady's respect, Anthony gave a mental shrug and once more turned his thoughts to the rotten-toothed hag whom he had seen only once since his arrival at Dragon's Lair. She was the reason he'd sought out the beautiful Faith. He needed the lady to convince her cousin to come out of seclusion long enough to explain some of the discrepancies he'd found in the estate books as well as in the granary and storerooms.

If the books were right, he couldn't understand how everyone on the estate hadn't already starved to death. Dragon's Lair was in a much worse financial state than even Richard had surmised, and due to that fact, Justin might be able to intercede with the king on his brother's behalf. By pleading a lack of funds to reman the estate as Edward wished, he might save Richard from marrying the idiot the king had chosen for him.

"My lady," Anthony said. "May I intrude upon your time for just a few moments?"

Still bemused with worry over Megan, Faith turned to look at the man standing in the doorway. It took her a moment to collect her thoughts and remember who he was and why he was there. "How may I be of service, Sir Godfrey?"

"I've come across several things in the estate books that puzzle me and need your assistance," he said, crossing the chamber to stand before the fire.

"I'm afraid I can be of little assistance, sir. I know nothing of the books. My duties extend no further than seeing to the household. My cousin is the true chatelaine of Dragon's Lair."

Standing relaxed with feet wide and hands clasped behind his back, Anthony gazed down at Faith, marveling again at the pure lines of her flawless features as well as the wonderful color of her blue topaz eyes.

"I—ah—understand your position at Dragon's Lair, my lady," he stuttered, drawing his thoughts back to their conversation and away from Lady Faith's beauty. "I would not impose upon you if anyone else might be of assistance; however, I fear you are the only person who can convince your cousin to come out of seclusion and discuss the estate business with me."

Faith rapidly shook her head and came to her feet. "Sir, I'm afraid you greatly exaggerate my influence here. My cousin will come out of seclusion only when she sees fit. Now, if you will excuse me, the hour grows late and I have several things needing my attention before I retire. Good night, Sir Godfrey.'' Faith turned to leave, but Anthony's hand upon her arm stopped her.

"Lady Faith, I assure you it is necessary that I see your cousin. Could you not make an exception and talk to her for me?''

An agonized look flickered in Faith's crystalline eyes. How could she convince Megan to see Sir Godfrey when she didn't even know if her cousin was still alive? Yet, she reminded herself, it was her duty to protect Megan's secret until she knew for certain something had happened to her. Resigning herself, she looked up at Anthony. "All right. I will speak with her, but I make no promises. My cousin makes her own decisions.''

"That's all I can ask of you, my lady.'' Anthony smiled down at Faith, enjoying their close proximity. The sweet scent of lilacs rose to tantalize his senses and he drew in a long breath, savoring the heady odor. Anthony's moment of pleasure came to an abrupt end a moment later.

"Sir, if you would be good enough to release me, I will take your message to my cousin,'' Faith said, regarding Anthony as if he were a slug.

Anthony's pride rebelled at the unspoken insult and he tightened his fingers about Faith's arm, drawing her toward him. He could feel her resistance, yet it did not dissuade him from his purpose. He would know the taste of the haughty Lady Faith's lips tonight, with or without her permission.

"Why are you in such a rush to take your leave, my lady?'' was his softly spoken question, his gaze roaming over her lovely face and coming to rest upon her luscious mouth. Again he felt his blood begin to stir hot and fast in his veins.

"Sir Godfrey, you are taking liberties and imposing upon my cousin's hospitality,'' Faith ground out. Straining against the hand about her arm, she paled visibly. Her heart pounded erratically against her ribs and her breath grew uneven as images of Mallory transferred themselves upon Anthony's features. She fought to control the panic the memories created. It had been well over a year since her cousin had abused her, yet Anthony's touch brought back all the horror she'd suffered at Mallory's hand.

"My lady, I mean no harm. Is it too much for me to ask to have a few moments of your company?" Anthony said, seeing her stricken expression.

"Aye, when I have no wish for yours," Faith managed to say over the lump of fear in her throat.

Anthony let his hand fall to his side and shook his head in regret. In the past he'd experienced many reactions from women, but Lady Faith was the first to look as if she'd faint from his touch.

"I'm sorry, Lady Faith," Anthony said at last. "I've done everything in my power to overcome your dislike of me, but I see now I'm doomed to failure. Forgive my rudeness a moment ago and please accept my assurance it will never happen again."

Baffled by the strange turn of events yet still wary against his attack should he be using his apology as a ploy to make her relax her guard, Faith absently rubbed her arm as she gazed up at him. "I accept your apologies, Sir Godfrey, though I find it puzzling you should think I dislike you."

Anthony arched one blond brow and eyed Faith in disbelief. "After the way you've acted toward me since my arrival, I find it even more puzzling you should act so bewildered by my mention of your very obvious feelings about me."

"Then, sir, I fear we are two perplexed people, who don't really know what to think of each other," Faith said, feeling the tension ease from her body. There was something about Sir Godfrey that made her relax. Perhaps it was the honest expression in his pale blue eyes or the hurt little boy look that crossed his handsome face when he spoke of her dislike. She couldn't be certain exactly what it was, but suddenly she didn't feel threatened in his presence. And she didn't want to question it. For the first time in years she felt safe enough to converse with a man without thinking he would miscon- strue her actions or expect far more than she was willing to give. A tiny glimmer of a smile touched her rosebud lips.

Anthony staggered backward and raised his hands in a gesture of defeat, palms up. "Please, my lady. I'm ill- prepared for the bounty of your first smile as well as a civil conversation with you."

Faith couldn't stop the bubble of laughter that escaped at his response. "Sir Godfrey, I fear I've encounted Edward's court jester."

Anthony bestowed his most charming smile upon Faith and gave an exaggerated bow from the waist, sweeping the floor with the tips of his fingers. "I have been found out. I thought my ruse had succeeded, yet you are as wise as you are beautiful."

Faith felt her cheeks burn from his compliment and low- ered her dark lashes. "I am wise enough to know you are a rogue, sir." To regain her composure, she busied herself straightening the folds of the skirt of her loose, flowing bliaud and tucked her hands into the fichets to hide the trembling that had suddenly beset them. When she looked once more at Anthony, her eyes were once more blue ice. "And I, sir, have no time to spare on your antics. I will convey your message to my cousin. Now, good eventide to you."

Faith turned and made a regal exit from the solar, leaving Anthony staring openmouthed and wondering what he had done wrong.

"Damn," he muttered, and strode from the room. He stamped down the stairs and across the great hall to the long table that held the large keg of ale. Drawing himself a tan- kard, he drained it in one long gulp and then wiped his mouth with the back of his hand. His actions reflected his disgust. In the past hour he'd gained far more from the Lady Faith than he had ever expected. Her smile in itself had been a miracle, much less the gentle laughter that had so briefly filled the solar. However, something had gone wrong. It was as if she was afraid to enjoy his company or she suddenly remembered she loathed him. Whatever it was, it had brought back the ice maiden he detested after seeing what Lady Faith could really be like.

Anthony refilled his tankard and settled his lean frame in a high-backed chair with intricately carved arms and legs. The soft leather squeaked under his weight as he shifted to a comfortable position and stretched out his long legs, crossing them at the ankles.

Resting the cool tankard against his hard middle, he stared into the fireplace, watching the leaping flames devour the five-foot logs. It was spring and the weather was warm, yet inside the stone walls of the keep, a fire was needed to chase away the chill even on such a pleasant night.

Anthony didn't consider the weather; his thoughts were with the fair Lady Faith. She was a mystery to him, one he was determined to solve before he returned to Raven's Keep to report his findings to Richard and Justin.

In her chamber, Faith pressed her back against the iron-bound door and breathed in a deep breath to try to quell her racing heart. She didn't know what on earth had possessed her to let down her guard where any man was concerned, much less one like the charming rogue Sir Godfrey.

Faith squeezed her eyes tightly closed and silently renewed her vow to keep all men at a safe distance. She could never allow herself to be so vulnerable again, even if Sir Godfrey wasn't like Mallory. He was a man, and they all wanted only one thing from a woman and nothing more. She had to remember that, no matter how much Sir Godfrey's charm managed to make her forget. It was for her own protection so she would never be hurt again. Yet even as Faith reaffirmed her feelings about men, she couldn't stop herself from remembering Anthony's boyish smile or the gentle light that had appeared in his eyes when he'd apologized.

Unnerved by her own veering emotions, Faith gave herself a sharp mental shake and strode across the chamber to stare out the cross-slit window at the dark landscape beyond. It was time to put Anthony Godfrey from her thoughts. She had far more important things to occupy her mind than girlish musings over the way Anthony's smile made her insides feel.

Faith balled her fists against the cool stonework of the window ledge and peered into the moon-drenched night, searching for any sign of her wayward cousin.

"Megan, if you're worrying me for no reason, I swear, once you're home and hear what I have to say about your behavior, you'll wish something had happened to you," she muttered ominously even as her heart constricted at the thought of her cousin lying hurt or dead somewhere along a dusty roadway.

Faith glanced up at the star-studded sky and sent a prayer toward the heavens. "God, in all Your wisdom and mercy, please take care of Megan. As You already know, she does only what she has to do for all of us here at Dragon's Lair."

At that moment Megan sat stiff and aching by the fire Sandy had built while their new companion cleaned the rabbit he'd killed for their evening meal.

"Sandy, you have to go back to Dragon's Liar to let Faith know I'm all right. By now she's probably standing on her head with worry over my disappearance," Megan whispered. She cast an anxious glance in Royce's direction to confirm he hadn't overheard their conversation.

Sandy shook his wheat-colored head and also looked in the reaver's direction before turning once more to Megan. "Nay. I'll not leave ye here at the mercy of a thief. I'll stay with ye until ye can travel, and then we'll both return to Dragon's Lair.''

Megan drew in a long, exasperated breath. Sometimes Sandy could be so bullheaded, she wanted to scream out in vexation. Instead of giving in to her desire, she eyed her bailiff sternly, and when she spoke, her voice held no room for any dissension on his part. "I've given you an order and expect it to be obeyed. Should Faith give in to her worry and confide her fears to the wrong person about our escapades, it could mean my life as well as your own if they report it to the sheriff at Nottingham.''

Sandy looked chastened as he nodded. "I'll obey, but 'tis not to my liking. We know nothing of this man called Royce beyond what he has told us. How do you know he isn't in the service of the sheriff and is only trying to use us to learn who the others are?''

"That's ridiculous. There are no others, and I told him so when he thought we were members of the band of thieves who've been robbing the wool pack trains.''

Sandy's gaze rested suspiciously upon the man who sat with his back to them, skinning the rabbit. He mused aloud, "So, he is interested in the stolen wool?''

"Nay, he only thought we were part of the band from hearing the sergeant's accusation last night.''

"I'm not as sure as ye seem to be, Maggie,'' Sandy said, running a hand thoughtfully over his beard-stubbled chin. He looked once more at Megan and shrugged a wide shoulder. "But until I can prove he's not what he says, I'll have to accept him as is.''

"He's one of us, Sandy. His actions of last night have proven it. He saved my life.''

Sandy nodded begrudgingly. "Aye, I owe him that much. And because of it, I'll reserve me judgment. But should he harm one hair on yer head, he'll not live a minute longer.''

Megan reached across the space separating her from her

bailiff and squeezed Sandy's work-roughened hand. "I'm proud to have you as my companion, Sandy McTavis. Few people can claim a friend as loyal and brave as you are in their entire lifetime."

Embarrassed by her compliment, Sandy flushed a deep red and shifted his gaze away from the blue eyes that were mirrors to Megan's soul. "Ye have a tendency to overlook the faults of those ye care about, Meggie. I just hope ye won't be blind when it comes to the rogue." He cocked his head in Royce's direction. "And heed me words, he's not all he seems, no matter what he says or does."

"Are any of us here exactly what we seem?" Megan said, and gave Sandy a mischievous grin.

He chuckled low and shook his head, seeing her point of view. "Nay, Meggie, but keep up yer guard. Ye have to be wary of Royce McFarland. He has a way about him that could make a young, inexperienced girl lose her heart."

Megan's lips quivered and she had to fight to contain the laughter bubbling up in her throat at Sandy's assessment of Royce. She had to admit the scar-faced, one-eyed bandit was handsome in an intriguing sort of way, yet she couldn't imagine losing her heart to him. He could serve only one purpose, and that was to help line her pockets with the gold she desperately needed for Dragon's Lair's coffers. There would be no other relationship with Royce.

Megan wiped at her glistening eyes with the back of her hand. "If that is what is worrying you, old friend, then you can set your mind to rest. At this point in my life, I'm not interested in giving my heart to anyone, much less a reaver. My duty is to Dragon's Lair and nothing else."

"Aye, 'tis yer duty, Meggie. Yet we can't make our hearts always follow the direction of our heads, no matter what we say."

"You are forgetting I'm not free to love. Even if my ruse frightened away Richard St. Claire's envoy and the wedding is called off, I'm still Edward's pawn. Someday he'll find one of his courtiers so desperate to please, he'll take me, disguise and all. Then I'll be forced to marry. The game I've played has given me only a short time to try to make Dragon's Lair what it was before Mallory paupered the estate with his gambling and wenching. If I succeed, it will be the only chance I have to evade another arranged marriage."

Sandy considered Megan. She spoke with conviction, but she was still young. She had as yet to know the thrill of a passion that could make every inch of skin tingle with anticipation of a lover's presence. She had as yet to feel her blood race hot and fast through her veins when her lover took her into his arms and pressed his mouth against hers in an intoxicating kiss. She had as yet to feel the heady excitement of a lover's hands upon her beautiful body, rousing her to the peaks of ecstasy. She had as yet to learn that love between a man and a woman could make her forget all her duties and all logical reasoning.

But Sandy knew he could not explain those things to Megan now. She would have to experience love for herself to learn it was something unexpected and often unwanted, and that it couldn't be denied, no matter what your mind told you. Love wasn't prejudiced. Rogue or gentlemen, it didn't matter once the sparks began to ignite the fires of passion.

"But ye will heed my warning, Meggie?" Sandy asked, still unable to leave her in Royce McFarland's care until he was sure she understood his fears since he would not be there to guard against what might happen.

"I will heed your warning," Megan finally said, to speed his leave. Yet she secretly chuckled at the humor of Sandy even thinking she could lose her heart to Royce McFarland.

Satisfied at last, Sandy released a long breath. "Then I'll go back to Dragon's Lair and tell Lady Faith what has happened."

"What are the two of you conspiring?" Royce said, spitting the rabbit on a green stick above the campfire.

" 'Tis nothing to concern you," Megan said, and frowned from the pain her movement caused when she'd turned to look at her new companion in crime. "Sandy is going to Nottingham to see if he can hear anything that might indicate Lord Ashby's men are still looking for us."

Richard stretched his lean frame out beside the fire and propped his head in his hand. A smile curved up the corners of his sensuous mouth. " 'Tis a good idea, but shouldn't I be the one to go into Nottingham? Ashby's men might recognize Sandy."

Megan cast an uncertain glance at her bailiff. Royce's logic had completely shredded her excuse for Sandy's departure. She opened her mouth to speak, but Sandy intervened before she could say anything.

"Nay, 'tis best I go. I know Nottingham like the back of me hand, and me friends will tell me if we're being sought without my having to be seen."

Richard shrugged and prodded the rabbit with a stick until it turned on the spit. "So be it. I merely wanted to insure we would be three instead of two the next time we ventured onto the roads."

" 'Tis best this way," Megan said with relief. Had Royce insisted he go to Nottingham, then she didn't know exactly what she would have done. In her present condition, she was unable to fend for herself and couldn't be left alone, nor could she allow Faith to keep worrying if she was alive or dead.

"Then 'tis settled. I'll leave at dawn," Sandy said.

Taking respite from digging dandelion root, Faith straightened and wiped the sweat from her brow. A movement at the edge of the woods caught her attention and she squinted against the bright sunlight as she tried to discern the figure striding toward her from across the meadow. As he drew nearer, she immediately recognized the brawny build of Dragon's Lair's bailiff. A wave of relief swept over her, yet it was only a momentary reaction. Sandy was alone.

Anxiously she searched the shady woods behind him for Megan, but the only thing she saw was a hare scurrying into the tall grass out of Sandy's path.

Faith cast a furtive glance in the direction of the keep before returning to her chore. No matter how much she wanted to drop everything and run to Sandy to learn Megan's whereabouts, she refused to give in to her desires. She didn't want anyone who might be observing them from the castle to think Sandy's presence was anything out of the ordinary.

When Sandy came abreast of her, she paused to wipe her hands on the old gunna she wore when collecting herbs, and innocently said, "Good day to you, McTravis. How is your family?"

"My lady, me family has been ill but is now doing well. You shouldn't worry on their behalf. They are being well cared for, and all should return to normal in a few days," Sandy answered, fully understanding Faith's meaning.

Faith glanced once more at the castle and lowered her voice. "Then Megan is all right?"

"Aye, Meggie is fine. She received a slight wound, and it's made it difficult for her to move about, but she's in no danger. She sent me to tell you not to worry and to ask if Sir Richard's men are still quartered at Dragon's Lair?"

"Aye, they are here. You must tell Meggie Sir Godfrey will not leave Dragon's Lair until he has spoken with her about the estate books. I don't know how much longer he's going to believe my lies that she's in seclusion and refuses to see anyone."

"I'll give her yer message, my lady, but I fear in her present condition there will be little she can do about Sir Godfrey. She'll be unable to ride for at least a week."

Contrite, Faith colored a deep rose. She was being selfish. She'd been thinking only of protecting Megan's secret and Dragon's Lair when in truth she should have been more concerned about something more important: Megan's life. Placing her hand on Sandy's arm, she looked up at him with eyes that were great pools of distress. "Tell Megan not to be concerned about things here. I'll take care of everything. She should only worry about getting better and coming home. I only wish I could go with you and nurse her back to health."

"You'll do her more good here, Lady Faith. She's worked too hard to lose everything now."

"You're right, Sandy, yet I can't help but be concerned. She is all the family I have left and I love her."

"We all love Meggie, Lady Faith, and because of our love, I'll not let anything happen to her. Ye can be assured of that."

Faith squeezed Sandy's arm. "Bring her home safe, Sandy. 'Tis all I ask."

"Aye, my lady," Sandy said, and turned once more toward the woods from which he'd just come. He was thirsty and tired, but he wouldn't consider taking the time to refresh himself with a tankard of cool ale from Dragon's Lair's cellars. Megan had already been alone with Royce McFarland far too long as it was. Sandy'd give the rogue no more time to work his wiles on Meggie than he already had. He'd be back at the campsite before dusk.

Observing Faith from the window in the solar, Anthony saw the man come striding from the woods. He watched the stranger stop and speak with Faith and then turn once more in the direction he'd come a few moments earlier. There was something furtive in the way Faith kept glancing toward the keep. She acted as if she didn't want anyone to know of the man's visit.

Anthony frowned and scratched his head. What purpose

could be served by keeping a villein's presence a secret? He couldn't answer his own question, and up until that moment he hadn't thought anything was unusual about Dragon's Lair beyond its mistress. However, Lady Faith and her mysterious visitor had roused his curiosity. He already wanted to learn all he could about the beautiful Lady Faith, and now he added the stranger to his list of riddles to be solved. There was something strange going on at Dragon's Lair, and he meant to get to the bottom of it.

Chapter 7

In order to avoid pursuit, Megan, Royce, and Sandy had separated soon after waylaying the travelers along the road to Nottingham. Nearly light-headed from the excitement of the robbery and the wild race back to their campsite, Megan strode to the blazing fire and hoisted the bag of coins above her head triumphantly. She threw back her head and let laughter spill into the night. Tonight she had gained enough to pay for the seeds Sandy had purchased last week.

"We can settle our debts, old friend," Megan said, giving the area a quick survey to assure herself Royce hadn't arrived back at the campsite.

"Aye, now maybe we can put an end to this charade," Sandy grumbled. His somber face was lined with worry, his shoulders hunched as he sat before the fire.

Megan frowned at Sandy. "What do you mean?"

"Exactly what I said, Meggie. We have gold for the seed. 'Tis time to put an end to all this thievery before we end up with a noose about our necks again."

Megan hunkered down at Sandy's side and placed the bag of coins in his hand. "We have enough to pay for the seeds, yet I want to insure Dragon's Lair's survival until the crops come in."

88

" 'Tis not all ye want, Meggie," Sandy said.

Megan sat back on her heels and turned her gaze toward the leaping flames to avoid looking at her friend. "I don't know what you're talking about."

"Methinks ye know far more than yer letting on."

"Damn it, Sandy. Say what you mean and stop talking in riddles."

"All right. I'll say what I mean. Ye don't want to give up reaving because ye can't stand the thought of leaving yer one-eyed bandit. Ye've ignored yer responsibilities these last weeks because of him."

"How dare you to say such a thing. The reason I'm here now is because of my responsibilities," Megan snapped. Disturbed by Sandy's accusation, she pushed herself to her feet and turned her back to the fire. "All I feel for Royce McFarland is gratitude."

" 'Tis true, he's helped us gain what we wanted. Yet I fear ye've lost far more."

"Damn it, Sandy, that's enough. I haven't lost anything to Royce McFarland," Megan ground out even as she felt her heart give a sudden lurch at the thought of leaving Royce and going back to her rightful place as the chatelaine of Dragon's Lair. "And that's all I have to say about it."

"But it is not all *I* have to say on the matter," Sandy said. Coming to his feet, he faced Megan. The firelight emphasized his flushed features. "I've obeyed ye at times when I knew I shouldn't, but on this, I'm going to speak me mind."

"Then speak your mind and be done with it before Royce returns," Megan said, keeping a tight rein on her own temper.

"I've watched ye, Meggie. Yer different when he's around. Yer not taking to the roads now for Dragon's Lair. It's yer fascination with that rogue which keeps ye coming back each night."

Guiltily, Megan glanced away from Sandy and shook her

head. "You're wrong, Sandy. My only concern is for Dragon's Lair."

"What are the two of you arguing about? Surely tonight's take was large enough to share," Royce said, leading his horse out of the darkness and into the glow of firelight surrounding Megan and Sandy.

" 'Twas a fair night," Megan said, and felt her spirits lift at the sight of Royce McFarland. She grinned and tossed the bag of coins to him.

His gaze never wavered from Megan's animated features as he caught the pouch in midair and absently weighed it in his hand. During the past few weeks he'd found there was something about this girl bandit that lifted his spirits and made his heart want to sing. Perhaps it was her joy of life and the indomitable courage she displayed each time they set out on another venture. He wasn't exactly sure what it was about her, but she had begun to inch her way into his life in a way he wasn't sure he even understood. One thing he knew for certain was he'd miss Meggie once he'd accomplished his mission for the king.

The thought of Edward brought Richard back to the moment. He gave Megan a disarming smile and tossed her the bag of coins before turning his gaze to Sandy. His grin deepened as he delved into his pocket and retrieved a jeweled necklace and brooch encrusted with diamonds and emeralds. They were the only valuable pieces of jewelry he'd come across in the last few weeks, and he intended to use them to get the information he needed for Edward.

"These should bring a hefty price from your friends in Nottingham," he said, looking Sandy directly in the eye.

"Aye," Sandy mumbled, still annoyed with Megan. "They could also cost us our lives."

Richard arched a dark brow at Sandy. "Am I to believe you've suddenly taken a dislike to reaving, McTavis? Or has your courage deserted you?"

Sandy faced Richard, a mulish expression playing across his features. After his conversation with Megan, he was in no mood to overlook anything the reaver said or did. "McFarland, ye've hinted I lack courage for the last time. I've done me part, and ye've no right to accuse me of being a coward."

Standing with feet splayed wide, Richard tossed the necklace to Megan and folded his arms across his wide chest. Through narrowed eyes he regarded Sandy thoughtfully for a long, tense moment and then nodded. " 'Tis true, McTavis. I had no right to say it. You've done your share."

Sandy stared at Richard, bewildered. He'd been prepared to fight the man, but he'd not expected Royce to acknowledge he had erred. Sandy glanced uncertainly at Megan and saw her triumphant smile. Her expression spoke volumes and made him want to squirm. In the blue depths of her eyes he read, I told you so, so loudly that he could have sworn she'd voiced the words at the top of her lungs.

During the past weeks on the road with Royce McFarland, she'd told him several times the reaver wasn't a bad sort. And until now he had disagreed with her assessment of their companion in crime. Now he was beginning to understand what Megan saw in the man. He was a thief in the first degree, yet he had a sense of honor about him that was rare for someone in his profession. Since the three had ridden together, McFarland had made no attempt to cheat them, nor had he tried to seduce Megan, as Sandy had feared. Begrudgingly, the bailiff also admitted he had come to respect Royce McFarland even if he didn't necessarily like him.

Sandy relaxed and glanced once more at Megan. "The hour grows late as we stand here arguing over nothing."

"Aye," Richard said, glancing up at the midnight sky. " 'Tis time to ride if we expect to meet your friend before morning."

Sandy shook his head. "Me friend won't do business if

yer along. He don't know ye and he won't do business with strangers.''

"Then it is time he changed his way of doing business. We are in this together, and I'll meet your friend or he'll not have the jewels," Richard said with determination. It was time to start putting an end to the charade he'd been living. Things weren't going quite as he'd expected when he'd set out to do Edward's bidding to infiltrate the band of thieves. For one thing, he hadn't counted on finding a young, beautiful reaver. Nor would he have ever imagined he'd begin to be concerned about her safety each time they took to the roads. Yes, Richard reflected cynically. It was time to put this ruse to an end. He had his family's welfare to think about and couldn't be worried about one young girl with indigo eyes and a laugh that made his skin tingle. He had to learn who was behind the theft of Edward's precious wool, and once this deed was accomplished, then maybe he'd be free to live his life as he saw fit.

Megan glanced at Sandy and shrugged. They couldn't deny Royce's request. He had earned the right to be present when the jewels were sold.

'' 'Tis too late to pay me friend a visit tonight. Meet me here tomorrow night,'' Sandy said.

"I'll keep these safe until then," Richard said, retrieving the necklace and brooch from Megan's hand before she had time to pocket them. He trusted Meggie and Sandy to a certain degree, but he wasn't fool enough to allow them to keep a small fortune in jewels. It might be far more temptation than they could resist.

Richard turned to his mount, secure he was finally beginning to make progress in the right direction. Hopefully by tomorrow night he would have a contact who knew the man behind the theft of the wool.

Grasping the pommel to hoist himself into the saddle, Richard paused as a sound in the dark woods caught his attention. Cocking his head to one side, he listened. The hair on the nape of his neck rose, and without waiting to explain, he pulled himself into the saddle. He called out a warning to Sandy at the same time he gave the horse a sharp kick in the side. He leaned from the saddle and caught Megan about the waist, lifting her off her feet and drawing her up in front of him as the animal responded, leaping forward—its great hooves sending clots of dirt into the air behind them.

Royce's warning gave Sandy only enough time to reach his own mount before the sheriff's men came charging into the camp. He caught a glimpse of the men they had robbed earlier in the evening as he spurred his horse into the darkened woods. However, in his haste, he didn't see in which direction Royce and Megan escaped.

Knowing instinctively Royce would protect Megan, Sandy centered his whole being on his own effort to elude the sheriff's men. Driving his mount hard, he rode through the maze of trees. Even as he sought to escape, he found some satisfaction in the occasional loud grunt and sound of impact as one of the sheriff's men was knocked from the saddle by a tree limb.

When Sandy reached the open fields, the distance between his mount and the sheriff's men began to widen. He spurred the animal onward until he blended into the shadowy forest alongside the cleared land. Reining his winded horse in beneath a stand of oaks, Sandy sat still and quiet as the rumble of horses' hooves passed him. Wiping away the sweat beading his brow, he breathed a sigh of relief at his close encounter with the sheriff's men. He had been fortunate to make good his escape, and he prayed that Megan and her one-eyed bandit had also done the same. For now all he could do was wait for her return to Dragon's Lair. If she didn't come home by dawn, he would know her fate.

At the disturbing thought, Sandy shifted uneasily in the saddle and then quietly urged his mount out of the shelter of oaks. He glanced in the direction the riders had taken before setting out for Dragon's Lair. Until he saw Megan come through the Judas gate, he'd not be able to rest.

Megan curled her body into Royce's to avoid the tree branches slapping at them from all directions as they raced through the dark forest. The destrier, surefooted and well trained, heeded the simple commands from his master and outdistanced their pursuers until they dropped from sight, and soon the only sound to be heard was the steady rhythm of Royce's heartbeat beneath her cheek.

The danger was past, but Megan did not move from within Royce's protective embrace. She was content to remain in the cradle of his strong, muscular arms forever if she could continue to feel as secure as she did at that moment. For the first time in years, she allowed someone else to bear the responsibility for her welfare, and she marveled at the sudden feeling of freedom it gave her.

Megan glanced up at Royce's night-shadowed features. She couldn't stop herself from wondering what life would be with a man like Royce at her side. Strong and resolute, he would know how to handle the legion of problems that arose daily on an estate such as Dragon's Lair. It would be wonderful to have such a man to share the burdens that weighed so heavily upon her shoulders. And in her mind's eye she could envision them together, walking through the fields, discussing whether to plant or to let the land lay fallow.

Megan squeezed her eyes closed and fought to rid her mind of the imagery. Such thoughts only made her more discontent with the life she was born to lead. She wasn't free to do as she pleased, despite her actions of the past few months. Her destiny had been planned for her by none other than the king of England himself. And a reaver like Royce McFarland could never fit into Edward's plan. Beyond what they shared now, there could never be anything between herself and Royce.

A sinking sensation settled in the pit of Megan's belly, and she unconsciously wrapped her arms about Royce's lean waist. Royce McFarland intrigued her, and she didn't want to go back to the sedate role of mistress of Dragon's Lair. There was excitement riding with her one-eyed bandit; it was as intoxicating to her as a good wine. And each night she could barely wait until darkness fell so that she could once more join him upon the roads.

"We're safe now, Meggie," Royce whispered against her dark hair, believing she clung to him out of fear. He reined his destrier to a halt near a still pond and dropped the reins as he set Megan away from him and slipped from the saddle. He held up his arms to her, and she came into them, eagerly.

As she slid her feet to the ground, neither expected the sudden burst of emotion that assaulted them when their bodies touched. In the instant soft yielding flesh met hard, bulging muscle, the smoldering coals of dormant passion ignited, flaming the embers of desire until both stood still and breathless—poised on the brink of decision.

Awed by the stunning rush of feeling sweeping over her, Megan gazed up at Royce, her eyes wide pools of wonder, her lips slightly parted, her hands resting upon his shoulders.

"Meggie," Richard murmured, his tone reflecting the same wonder as he looked down into eyes darkened with desire. Stunned by the revelation in the indigo depths, he slowly lowered his mouth to hers in a gentle, questing kiss until he felt her begin to respond in kind.

Richard's heart leaped within his chest and then began to pound against his ribs in a rapid tattoo. He swelled with need when her small tongue followed his and tasted of him as he had done of her a moment earlier. A low groan of pleasure escaped him. He pulled her into his arms and cupped her head in the palm of his hand to prevent her escape as he devoured the sweetness of her mouth.

Instinctively Megan responded to Royce's heady touch. She wrapped her arms about his neck and pressed her body against the length of him. She reveled in the feel of his sinewy muscles beneath her hands, and her blood caught fire when their hips came into contact. Her breathing grew rapid as the kiss deepened, and her insides gave a quivering response when Royce moved his hand down along her back and pressed her closer to his tumescent body. An unexplainable yearning burst into life at the very core of her being, and her knees felt as if they had turned to jelly beneath her. She clung to Royce for support, and her head fell back to allow him access to her soft throat.

Greedily Richard covered the ivory column with kisses as he lowered Megan to the leaf-strewn ground. He swiftly worked loose the lacing of her tunic to expose the white mounds tipped with rose-colored nipples. He tasted of their sweetness, suckling each in turn and making Megan moan with the new sensations his lips and tongue created within her. He enjoyed the bounty of her breasts with his mouth while he explored her sleek limbs with his hands and sought out the moist, secret places where ecstasy dwelled.

Experience made his task easy as he divested Megan and himself of their clothing and cast them aside. Gently he slid a questing hand between her thighs and teased the tiny bud until her legs opened voluntarily to his seeking fingers. He delved into her warmth and was momentarily surprised to find that Meggie still possessed her maidenhead.

A thrill of excitement shot through Richard at finding his beautiful bandit a virgin. With the life-style she led, he had thought many things of her, with one exception. Because of the close bond they shared and their reluctance to discuss where they went each night, he had assumed McTavis was her lover.

"Ah, my Meggie," Richard murmured against her soft breasts, and felt the heat of his ardor rise a degree higher. He would be her first lover, and he felt honored she should bestow such a treasure upon him.

Unable to contain his own passion much longer, Richard enticed Megan with his fingers until she moved her hips against his hand, wanting him to put an end to the sweet torment. Moving between her legs, he raised himself above her and looked down into her passion-glazed eyes. He could not take what his throbbing body craved before he knew Meggie understood she could never reclaim her loss after he made love to her.

"Meggie, I want you, but I'll not take you until I hear you say you want me. There can be no turning back afterwards. All will be changed, and I don't want you to have any regrets."

"I want you, Royce, and I'll have no regrets," Megan said, smiling up at him with lips slightly swollen from his kisses. She had spoken truthfully, she realized, as she reached up and caressed Royce's scarred cheek. She would have no remorse about this night. Society could condemn her for loving the handsome reaver, but she'd not deny herself this moment of happiness. It might be all she'd ever have. Edward had decided her future once she returned to Dragon's Lair; however, for now, she would savor her time with the man she loved.

There was a sinking sensation in the pit of her belly as Megan openly admitted her true feelings for Royce. She had so little time left before she would put aside her life as a reaver and return to Dragon's Lair. Every moment of time with him must be spent building memories to last her a lifetime. Sliding her arms about his neck, Megan drew Royce down to her.

Megan's answer made Richard want to laugh aloud with relief. He had restrained himself until his entire being ached with the need of her. He recaptured her mouth with a moan of pure pleasure and thrust into the wet, dark depths of her, sinking deep and tearing away her maidenhead in one swift motion.

Megan didn't cry out or react as the other virgins Richard had bedded in the past. She stiffened momentarily and drew in a quick breath until the stinging sensation subsided. Then she wrapped her arms tightly about his neck and began to move against him, urging him on.

Richard surrendered to her demands. He took his fill of the tight, warm flesh surrounding the satiny length of him. The muscles beneath his tanned flesh rippled as he moved above her, thrusting to the cadence in his blood. His movements were music, and together they executed the dance of love, arching, dipping, swirling ever upward toward a fiery sunburst of feeling. When it exploded, nothing existed in the universe except the ecstasy they shared.

Perspiration dewed their bodies as they lay together, savoring the sweet afterglow of lovemaking. No words passed between them. None were needed. Without reservations or promises, Megan and Richard had given a part of each other, and a bond had been formed between them that could not easily be broken.

Turning on his side, Richard raised himself on one elbow and propped his tousled head in the palm of his hand while he traced Megan's profile with the tip of one long, shapely finger. He marveled at the perfection of her features and wondered how he had managed to keep his desire in control for as long as he had. Now that his passion had been momentarily quenched, he could admit he had wanted Meggie far longer than he'd realized. She had begun to creep into his blood soon after he'd rescued her from Lord Ashby's men. She was unlike any other woman he'd ever met, and to his regret, she could never be anything more to him than his mistress. Edward wouldn't look kindly upon him turning his back on the noble ladies of the court to marry a common wench who took to the roads to make her living.

Marry! Where on earth had that thought come from? Richard wondered. Disturbed, he pushed himself upright and reached for his chausses. There was only one woman he had ever wanted to marry, and she had already been claimed by his brother.

No. He had no intention of marrying anyone—not the fetching Meggie nor the ugly lady Edward had chosen for him at Dragon's Lair. Wasn't this the reason he was here now instead of at Raven's Keep with his family?

Richard jerked on his chausses and then ran a hand through his tousled curls. Tonight had been special. He would never forget Meggie for as long as he lived, but when the time came, he'd have to leave her.

Sated, Megan stretched her arms over her head and smiled. In her wildest imaginings she hadn't dreamed lovemaking could be so pleasurable. Honestly, though, she'd had little time in the past few years to consider what it was like at all. Mallory's abuse and Dragon's Lair had kept her mind directed in other areas, draining her emotionally and physically.

Megan's smile dimmed. She didn't want thoughts of her responsibilities to intrude upon her moment of happiness. For a little while she wanted to be free to love the reaver who had stolen her heart. This night might be the only time in her life she could put all her obligations aside and think of no one but herself.

Oh, Royce, she thought, watching him as he buckled the wide leather belt about his lean waist. Were I responsible for only myself, I'd gladly turn my back on society to remain at your side.

A sad little sigh escaped Megan. To her regret, she knew such a thing would never come to pass. There were too many

people depending upon her to allow herself the luxury of
love.

Megan sat up and began to pull on her chausses. Reality
had intruded. It was time to end her magical interlude with
Royce and return to her duties.

Megan glanced at Royce. She knew she should never see
him again. Her heart lurched once more at the prospect. She
had enough gold now to give up her nightly excursions, but
she didn't believe she had the strength to deny herself a brief
time with the man she loved before she was sentenced to a
life of unhappiness.

Chapter 8

Dawn was already greying the sky when Megan left a relieved Sandy at the Judas gate and stealthily crept into the keep. She glanced warily at the yeoman who lay snoring loudly on the rushes at the foot of the stairs before she tiptoed rapidly up to her bedchamber. She eased the iron-hinged door open, silently praying it would not squeak loud enough to awaken the household. To her relief, it opened easily. Slipping inside, she quietly closed it behind her. She had just released the breath she'd been holding when a voice came from behind her.

"Megan, this has to stop. I cannot go on wondering nightly if you're alive or dead."

Megan jumped with a start of surprise and swung around to face her cousin, her hand going to her thumping heart. "Faith, you nearly frightened me to death."

"Frightened *you* to death?" Faith challenged with an unusual show of spirit. "How do you think I feel every time you don't come home until dawn?"

Annoyed, Megan didn't answer. Faith's words nearly echoed the same thing Sandy had said only a short while ago. After hugging her exuberantly and muttering his thanks to

God, he had given her another lecture about ending their reaving.

Megan tossed the bag of gold onto the bed and, without looking at her cousin, began to untie the strings to the peasant's coif covering her dark hair. Already torn between her love for Royce and her responsibilities to her people, she'd had about all of the advice, no matter how well intentioned, she could take for one night. Megan's hair fell about her shoulders, and she absently ruffled it before stripping off her chausses and jerkin. She slipped on her tattered robe and crossed the chamber in her bare feet. Sinking down onto a small stool in front of the fire, she began to braid her heavy mane of hair.

"The spring planting is complete, Megan. The villeins finished it today. Now there's no reason for you to continue the reaving," Faith said, undeterred by her cousin's silence. Others in the household might be intimidated by Megan's moods, but Faith had known her too long and too well.

When Megan finally turned to look at her cousin, her eyes held a haunted expression. "Faith, I now have another reason to go back. My heart."

Faith stared blankly at Megan as if she hadn't understood what her cousin had said.

Megan's smile was wistful. "It's true. I'm in love."

"In love?" Faith finally managed to say. "Megan, you can't mean what you're saying. Sandy McTavis is your bailiff."

Megan's soft laughter spilled through the chamber. "I'm not in love with Sandy. I'm in love with Royce McFarland."

"Megan, that's even more preposterous. The man is a thief."

Megan shrugged. "So am I."

"You know what I mean," Faith said. "Nothing can come of your feelings. You're already betrothed to Richard St. Claire."

Sadly Megan nodded and turned back to the fire. Her face reflected her inner turmoil as she once more picked up the heavy skeins of shining hair.

Megan's heart-wrenching expression tore at Faith's tender heart. She forgot her annoyance with her headstrong cousin and quickly crossed to the woman's side. Kneeling, she put her arms about Megan and hugged her close. "I know it's unfair, but 'tis something we can't change."

"And love is something else we can't change," Megan said softly, her voice cracking. Her eyes were glassy with unshed tears as she turned to look at her cousin. "Until to-night, I never imagined what it would be like."

"My God!" Faith said, shocked at the implications of what her cousin had said. "Surely you didn't give yourself to that rogue? What will your husband say when he learns you've had a lover?"

"Stop it, Faith," Megan said, coming to her feet with arms folded across her chest, her face set with determination. She glared down at her cousin. "I won't allow you or anyone to place a shadow on the only happiness I might ever know. I love Royce and I'll be with him for as long as I'm allowed. I know better than anyone our love is doomed and I must put my happiness aside for the welfare of my people. But I intend to savor the time I have with him, and I'll not let you, Sandy, or anyone deny me a small bit of paradise."

"Megan, please. You're only going to bring more heart-break upon yourself if you continue. Please reconsider your decision and end this affair before it goes any further. Rich-ard St. Claire is a powerful man and he can make your life miserable if you should become pregnant with the reaver's babe."

Megan's chin came up in the air. "Our love may be for-bidden because of society, but I would welcome his child. Then I would have something of Royce to love and hold."

"Be reasonable, Megan. You're thinking with your heart

and not your head. What would Edward do should he learn what has transpired? You could lose Dragon's Lair. Then where would you be? Would your reaver be able to take care of you after you've given up everything for him? Has he even told you that he loves you and wants you to be his wife?''

The breath stilled in Megan's throat and she turned away, unable to face Faith. No words of love had passed between herself and Royce even at the height of their passion. Nor had Royce spoken of his feelings when they rode back to the campsite to fetch her horse. He had given her a brief kiss and sent her on her way, his only concern being their contact the following night with Sandy's friend in Nottingham.

'' 'Tis none of your concern, Faith. 'Tis my life to live as I see fit,'' she said at last. She wouldn't allow herself to even think she might have made a mistake by giving her heart to Royce. ''Now if you will excuse me. I've had a long night.''

''Megan, I don't want to hurt you, nor do I want to see you hurt. I just want what is best,'' Faith said.

''I know you do and I understand your feelings. Now I bid you good night,'' Megan said, her sharp tone cutting into Faith like a knife.

Faith, hurt from her cousin's curt dismissal, ran from the room and down the corridor toward her own chamber. Fighting against the blinding tears filling her eyes, she turned a corner and collided with a hard masculine form.

''Excuse me,'' she murmured. Assuming she had run into the night watchman, she tried to step past without looking up.

''My lady, is something wrong?'' Anthony Godfrey asked, taking her by the arms and turning her toward the rush light. When Faith had come charging around the corner, he'd just stepped from his own chamber, intent upon using the excuse of an early morning hunt to leave Dragon's Lair without rousing anyone's suspicions. He'd received a message from Richard last eve asking him to meet him at dawn.

Faith looked away. Her lower lip quivered as she drew in a shuddering breath. "Sir Godfrey, there is nothing wrong. Please allow me to go to my chamber."

Anthony shook his head. "Nay, Faith. You look as if you could use a friend, and I would help if you'd allow me the privilege."

The combination of worry, hurt, and Anthony's kindness weakened Faith's resolutions to keep her distance from him. His offer of friendship was like a beacon to a ship on a stormy night. Great tears spilled over her thick lashes as she instinctively leaned toward him, desperately craving solace for her battered feelings.

Faith's expression rent Anthony's heart. Automatically his arms came about her, cradling her like a baby, smoothing the heavy mane of golden hair cascading down her back. "Hush, love. 'Tis far too early in the morning for tears."

His softly spoken words broke the dam of her reserve, and for the first time in her adult life she gave way to a torrent of tears. She sobbed like a small child against his chest, completely unaware of the protective and tender feelings her actions aroused within Anthony.

Gently Anthony tipped her chin up and, with the tip of his finger, brushed away the crystal droplets that were making their slow path down her pale cheeks. He had no intention of kissing her until she raised her eyes and looked at him from beneath dewed lashes. In that moment, all else was forgotten except his need to wash away the misery he saw shining in the crystalline depths. Lowering his head, he placed his mouth lightly against hers in a tender kiss of friendship.

A moment later, he found her arms encircling his neck and her lips opening to him. Surprise and delight mingled within Anthony from her intense response to his kiss. Anthony tightened his arms about Faith, drawing her closer to his hard body. The sudden rush of desire made him forget he'd meant only to comfort her in a time of need.

The morning sun streaked in through the cross-slit window to fall blindingly upon the two lovers. The sudden brightness jerked Faith from the rapture of Anthony's kiss and back to her senses. She struggled to be free, and when his arms fell from her, she backed away from him. Wiping her mouth with the back of her hand, she eyed him as if he'd suddenly turned into a repulsive dung beetle.

"How dare you!" she exploded, and then turned and fled to her chamber. The sound of the door slamming echoed eerily through the stone corridors of the keep.

Stunned by the sudden transformation of the cuddly little kitten into a spitting wildcat, Anthony made no move to follow her. Faith bewildered him, Faith excited him, and Faith intrigued him far more than any woman he'd ever met. And after experiencing a brief moment of the lady's passion, he intended to have her. With a merry tune upon his lips and a jaunty gait to his steps, Anthony made his way down to the stables.

From her window Megan watched Sir Godfrey cross the bailey and enter the stables. She released a tired, disgusted breath. That man seemed determined to take up residence at Dragon's Lair. She knew he would still not take his leave until he met with her about the estate books. All of her refusals hadn't put him off.

Megan covered a yawn with her hand and turned away from the window. She'd been foolish not to have already dealt with Sir Godfrey. But she had hoped her refusals to meet with him and her seclusion from the rest of her household would be taken as a sign of madness. Unfortunately, her plan hadn't had the desired effect. He hadn't ridden away to tell her future husband of what he'd found at Dragon's Lair. Instead he had stayed to wait her out, and if she didn't do something soon, he would become a permanent fixture at Dragon's Lair.

"If he wants to see the ugly old hag again, so be it," Megan grumbled, letting her robe slip to the floor at her feet. She crawled into the large bed her mother and father had shared and where she had been born. At least her appearance would solve one of her lesser problems. She'd act the idiot when she went over the books with Sir Godfrey. Maybe then he would be satisfied the discrepancies he'd found were of the making of an idiot, and all was right at Dragon's Lair after all.

Smiling smugly to herself, Megan curled into a ball and hugged her pillow. She pushed all thoughts of Anthony Godfrey and Dragon's Lair from her mind. Dreamily she went back to her moments with her one-eyed bandit and again felt pleasure curl her insides at the exquisite memory of their lovemaking.

She was honest enough to admit Faith had been right when she'd urged her to put an end to her relationship with Royce. But the happiness she'd found in his arms made it impossible to deny herself the pleasure again. Her thoughts on the night to come, Megan drifted off to sleep.

"Ho, Anthony," Richard called from beneath a gnarl-limbed oak whose crooked branches draped to the ground and hid his presence from passersby.

"Damn you, Richard," Anthony said, reining his mount to a halt and slipping agilely to the ground. He dropped the reins and strode across to where his friend stood in the shade. "I should flay you alive for deserting me at Dragon's Lair. If you only knew what I've been through just trying to get your future wife to go over the books with me."

Richard feigned ignorance. "How do you find my bride, Anthony? Is she beautiful or was Mallory's judgment correct?"

"Didn't you come to Dragon's Lair as you'd planned?" Anthony asked, uneasily.

Richard shook his head and hid his grin at his friend's obvious discomfort.

Anthony looked up at the tree limbs overhead, to the horses, down at the ground, anywhere but at Richard. How could he tell Richard that Edward had betrothed him to an ugly hag who was also dim-witted?

"Richard," Anthony began, "I don't know exactly how to explain your betrothed. She's—well—ah—different from any woman I've ever had the opportunity to meet."

"Then you think she's acceptable?" Richard said gruffly, trying not to laugh at his friend's discomfort.

"I wouldn't . . . Oh, damn it to hell," Anthony said. "I can't lie. There is no easy way to tell you but straight out. Mallory didn't lie. His sister is as ugly as he said."

Richard could no longer refrain from giving in to his mirth. He threw back his head and roared with laughter.

Feeling the butt of a jest he didn't quite understand, Anthony glared at his friend. "Damn it, Richard. How can you laugh? It's no laughing matter to be saddled with such a bride."

Richard managed to get control of himself and wiped at his mirth-misted eyes with the back of his hand. Sniffing, he cleared his throat. "Friend, my mirth comes from you and not the thought of marrying the Dragon Lady."

Anthony flushed, realizing he'd made a fool of himself. "Damn you, Richard. You already knew what Lady Wakefield looked like, didn't you?"

"Aye," Richard said, a roguish grin curving up the corners of his mouth. "I've known since she came down the stairs to greet you on the first night of your visit to Dragon's Lair."

Anthony frowned. "Then why in God's name didn't you just come out and say it instead of watching me try to find an easy way to tell you your future bride was nothing but a rotten-toothed, greasy-haired, simpering hag?''

''I just wanted to see how you'd handle the situation,'' Richard said, choking back another laugh. From the look on Anthony's face, he doubted if his friend appreciated his humor.

''You could have spared me,'' Anthony said, still unappeased.

''Forgive me, Anthony. You've been a good friend and I shouldn't use you for sport, no matter how entertaining I find it,'' Richard said, slapping Anthony companionably on the back, even as another grin tugged at the corners of his shapely mouth.

''Entertaining, you say? I'll show you what's entertaining, you rogue,'' Anthony said, his own good humor reinstating itself. He grabbed Richard and they scuffled like two young pups. Both ended up on the ground, flat on their backs, breathing heavily and chuckling over their few moments of boyish play.

''Anthony, I swear we must be getting old,'' Richard said, his voice breathless.

''Aye, time doesn't stand still for any of us,'' Anthony agreed, pushing himself into a sitting position and looking disgusted at the dirt and grass clinging to his favorite green hunting jerkin.

''Do you ever stop to think our lives are passing us by?''

Anthony frowned down at his friend. ''What has brought on all this introspection? I thought you were quite satisfied with your life the way it is.''

Richard pushed himself up and plucked a long-stemmed piece of grass. He chewed on it thoughtfully for a moment before he looked once more at Anthony. ''I don't really know what brought it on, but lately I've been thinking how it would feel to marry the woman you love and have children.''

''Damn, that is unusual for you, especially in your situation,'' Anthony said, dusting off his sleeve before turning his attention to the suede front of his jerkin.

"Damn it, Anthony. Life can be unfair,'' Richard said, coming to his feet. Placing a hand on a thick limb, he stared out through the green oak leaves to the landscape beyond.

"Friend, no one ever said life was fair,'' Anthony said. He'd never seen his friend in such a mood. Richard was always the carefree St. Claire. He let life take him where it chose without worrying over it. The first time he'd really ever seen him upset was when Edward's message had come ordering him to marry.

Anthony reflected upon those last days at Raven's Keep. Perhaps Richard had already begun to change and he hadn't noticed it. He knew Richard had always loved Jamelyn. He himself wasn't immune to the effect Justin's wife had upon men. He'd fallen in love with her for a while several years ago, and he guessed he would always be just a little bit in love with his friend's beautiful auburn-haired wife. He admired Jamelyn's spirit, though he'd come to realize of late that he wasn't the same type of man that Justin was. When he married, he'd look for a woman with strength and courage but not with Jamelyn's volatile temperament. He preferred a more gentle woman like Lady Faith.

Anthony shook his head and forced his thoughts away from the fair-haired beauty he'd kissed earlier. It did no good to muse over something that would never come to pass if Lady Faith had her way. She hated everything about him.

"Richard, I've never seen you in such a mood.''

"I don't believe I've ever been in this mood before,'' Richard admitted.

"Is there a woman involved?'' Anthony asked, suddenly seeing the longing in the distant look on his friend's face.

Richard glanced over his shoulder at Anthony and grinned. "Aye, there's a woman, but it's not what you think.''

"Then you're not in love with her?''

Richard glanced away from Anthony and shook his head. "No, I've only loved one woman in my life and have no need to encumber myself with such an emotion again."

Anthony pushed himself to his feet and crossed to his friend. Placing a hand on Richard's wide shoulder, he stood quietly at his side, giving him the companionship and support he knew Richard needed. He would not delve into Richard's secret feelings about his brother's wife. Richard was a man of honor, and he would never do anything to come between Justin and Jamelyn. He loved them both too much. Yet it saddened Anthony for his friend. Richard needed to find another woman to love, but after seeing the hag Edward had chosen for him, Anthony feared his young friend was doomed never to know the same happiness that his brother had found in marriage.

Richard glanced at Anthony and shook off his melancholy mood. There were other important matters he had to discuss with his friend beyond his love life. "Anthony, when will you be leaving Dragon's Lair?"

Anthony shrugged. "For the life of me, I don't know. Lady Wakefield refuses to show herself, and I can't get to the bottom of the discrepancies in the account books until I've spoken with her."

"What kinds of discrepancies?" Richard asked, his brows knitting into a frown.

"Nothing makes sense. If the books are right, then Dragon's Lair is in far worse financial shape than we'd first believed. But that's the problem. If the books are right, how have they survived these past months?"

It was Richard's time to shrug. "I don't know, and hopefully I won't have to find out. If I succeed in getting the information Edward wants, then I have hope he'll forget about forcing me to marry the Dragon Lady. And that's where you come in, my friend."

Anthony arched a curious brow but said nothing.

Richard understood his friend was waiting for a long overdue explanation. He nodded. "I know, and I'll tell you everything."

"From the beginning?" Anthony said, smiling.

"Aye, from the beginning." Richard launched into his tale of Edward's scheme to catch the wool thieves as well as his return to reaving with the beautiful female bandit. By the time he'd finished, Anthony was staring at him in amazement.

"My God, Richard. You've been a busy fellow since we last saw each other. And I should have known there was a woman involved somewhere. You St. Claire brothers have the luck of the devil in finding willing young beauties to take to your bed."

"As I recall, you don't have such bad luck yourself," Richard teased.

"My luck has deserted me," Anthony said, raising his hands in a helpless gesture. "Lady Faith loathes the very sight of me, and she's the only female at Dragon's Lair who I would even consider bedding. I need to return to London, where I'm appreciated, before I lose confidence in my own abilities to woo the fairer sex."

Richard chuckled. "And that's exactly what I want you to do."

Again Anthony arched a brow at Richard.

"By returning to court you can keep your ears and eyes open for any clue that might lead us to the ringleader behind the wool robberies. Edward is certain it is someone at court, but I've made little progress in that area. I can do nothing until I meet the thieves responsible for the robberies. Hopefully tonight will set me on the right course."

"So you want me to play the spy?" Anthony asked, liking the idea and the intrigue. After weeks of biding his time at Dragon's Lair, he was ready for some excitement, no matter how dangerous it might be.

"Aye. Should you learn anything, send a message to Justin. I'll keep in touch through him."

"I'll leave for London as soon as I've spoken with Lady Wakefield about the estate books."

"Don't worry about the books now. With any luck, you'll be able to get the information I need and there will never be a reason for me to know anything about Dragon's Lair."

"Then I'll leave immediately. I'm sure my departure will please Lady Faith."

"It seems, my friend, you're smitten with the fair lady."

Anthony shook his head. "She intrigues me is all."

Richard gave Anthony a knowing smile. "Beware, Anthony. You may find yourself shackled to the fair maid by your curiosity. Many a man has lost his freedom by trying to solve the mystery behind a beautiful woman."

"You don't have to be concerned about my falling into a trap. When I bind myself to a woman, she will at least like me." Anthony chuckled. "And that's the one thing I doubt Lady Faith will ever do."

"Then I'll bid you farewell and good hunting at court," Richard said, extending his hand to Anthony.

Anthony clasped it fondly. "I will do my best to glean the information you need, for I'd hate to see you saddled with your Dragon Lady for life. It is even more punishment than I would wish upon my worst enemy."

The two friends parted company, each going his own way to find the man responsible for the theft of Edward's wool.

Megan watched the St. Claire standard disappear from view and breathed a sigh of relief. It was finally over. Just when she'd been about to give in to his demands to see her, Sir Godfrey had sent word he couldn't wait any longer for their meeting, he had urgent business elsewhere.

Megan glanced over her shoulder at her cousin. Faith stood quietly staring in the direction Sir Godfrey had just traveled.

The wistful expression on the other woman's lovely face made Megan take pause. In all the years her cousin had lived at Dragon's Lair, Megan had never seen Faith display such longing.

"You love him, don't you?" Megan asked softly.

Faith seemed to shake herself out of the trancelike state that gripped her as she watched Anthony ride out of her life. "What did you say, Megan?"

"I said, you love him, don't you?"

Faith flashed Megan a puzzled look. "I don't know what you're talking about."

"I think you know exactly what I'm talking about," Megan said, refusing to change the subject.

"And I'm just as sure I don't," Faith snapped, and made to turn away, but Megan's hand on her arm stopped her.

"Faith, you're in love with Sir Godfrey," Megan said, undeterred.

Faith shook Megan's hand from her arm. "Don't be ridiculous. I'm not in love with anyone, much less Sir Godfrey. I don't even like the man. He's crude and vulgar and—"

"And handsome and charming and gentle," Megan finished.

"Stop it, Megan." Faith said, her tone sharp, her face flushing a deep rose. "You don't know what you're talking about. Of late you've been so tied up with your reaver, you don't know anything about how I feel."

"I know from the look I saw in your eyes a moment ago your feelings for Sir Godfrey go far deeper than you're willing to admit."

"What I feel is none of your affair," Faith snapped.

"Aye, 'tis none of my business, but I want to see you happy."

"Then just leave me alone," Faith said. She turned and fled, her heart and head warring, the conflicting emotions viciously tearing at her insides. After the brutal treatment

she'd received from Mallory, she'd vowed never to feel anything for a man. But then Anthony Godfrey had come into
her life, a blond giant with flashing blue eyes and a smile
that made her bones seem to melt.

"What on earth is happening to us?" Megan asked, staring after her cousin, dumbfounded. It was the second time
within twenty-four hours that she and Faith had had words.
In all the years they had lived together, seldom had an angry
word passed between them. Megan knew much of the credit
for their relationship wasn't due to her own temperament. It
was Faith's quiet nature and her easy way of accepting what
life had to give her that had kept them from each other's
throats.

A frown creased Megan's brow as she turned back to the
window and thoughtfully stared out across the newly planted
fields. She suspected Faith's confusion about her feelings for
Sir Godfrey had been the cause for her strong reaction, and
until she was willing to admit she loved him, there was nothing Megan could do.

Oddly enough, Sir Godfrey was the first man to attract her
cousin's attention. When they were young girls, they had
shared dreams of knights in shining armor sweeping them
off their feet and carrying them away to their enchanted castles. But later, Faith had changed. There had been no more
talk of marriage and children, no more hopes a handsome
young man was just waiting for the right moment to ride into
her life. Her dreams seemed to have died when she reached
sixteen.

Megan's frown deepened. It was odd that she could nearly
pinpoint the time when Faith had changed. She was still as
loving and gentle as she'd always been with her family, but
there was an air of aloofness about her when she dealt with
others, especially men. It was as if she had erected an invis-
ible wall about herself and kept fortifying it to keep anyone
from breaking through her defenses.

Megan looked in the direction Anthony Godfrey and his men had ridden earlier. Perhaps some good had come out of Sir Godfrey's visit after all. Faith's emotions, no matter how she denied it, had been touched by the handsome knight. And when he returned, hopefully her cousin would admit her feelings for him.

The thought of Sir Godfrey's return to Dragon's Lair made Megan hesitate. She wanted him to come back for Faith, but for herself, she would be just as happy if she never set eyes on the man again. For when he returned, she didn't doubt Edward's lackey, Richard St. Claire, would also be in attendance to claim his bride.

Megan gave a snort of disgust and turned away from the window. After what she had shared with Royce, the very thought of making love . . . Megan paused. She couldn't use the words *making love* in the same sentence with Richard St. Claire, for it would never be love between them. Her heart belonged to Royce. She might have to surrender her body to her husband's will, but never her heart. The idea of being touched and used by Richard St. Claire made her stomach churn with nausea.

"If there is any way I can prevent it, no other man will ever touch me," Megan vowed. She picked up the coarse woolen chausses and leather jerkin from the pile of discarded clothing at the foot of her bed. The bag of gold clinked upon the rough wooden floor at her feet. She'd been so caught up in her earlier musings, she'd failed to put it away.

Megan bent and retrieved the small leather pouch, weighing it in her hand. Gold was the only way to insure her freedom. It would enable her to reman Dragon's Lair and provide Edward with the strong defenses he needed without shackling herself to Richard St. Claire.

Tucking the pouch away in the strongbox she kept hidden under her bed, Megan stepped into the chausses and pulled them up over her softly rounded hips. She tightened the laces about her small waist and tied them securely before slipping the jerkin over her head. Retrieving the peasant's coif from where she'd dropped it that morning, she pulled it on and hurriedly stuffed her hair once more beneath it.

The hour was growing late, and Royce would be awaiting them in their regular meeting place. A thrill of excitement raced over Megan. The thought of seeing the man she loved made her skin tingle and her stomach quiver with anticipation.

Turning to the polished steel mirror, she gazed at her altered appearance and smiled. It seemed like a lifetime ago when she had wanted to gain enough gold to quit her nightly excursions into the countryside. Now the very thought of ending her reaving was too painful to contemplate. It would mean she would have to give up Royce. Pushing all thoughts of the future aside and concentrating on the evening to come, Megan made her way down the narrow steps that led past the kitchen to the outside.

She breathed a sigh of relief once she made her way clear of the keep and out of the Judas gate behind the stables. Fortunately in all the weeks she'd disguised herself and slipped away from Dragon's Lair, no one except her cousin knew of her actions each night. It was best for all concerned that her activities remain a secret.

When Megan reached the cave where Sandy kept the horses hidden, the evening sky had already turned lavender and the clouds were bathed in shimmering gold. The deepening shadows obscured the bailiff's presence from her until she stepped through the craggy entrance of the cave and called his name.

"I'm here, Meggie," Sandy said, stepping into view with the two saddled horses.

"Are you ready to ride? Royce will be waiting for us at our usual meeting place by the stream. He's anxious to meet your friends in Nottingham and sell the jewels from last night's raid."

"Meggie, I wish you'd reconsider taking to the roads again. I have a bad feeling about all this. Last night was far too close for my peace of mind. We could now be at the end of a rope."

"You already know my feelings on the matter," Megan said, taking the reins to her mount. Climbing into the saddle, she flashed Sandy an annoyed look. "I've made my decision, but if you don't agree with it, you have my permission to remain here."

Sandy gripped the reins to her mount and looked up at her, his eyes pleading for her understanding. "Meggie, yer like me own sister. I feel closer to ye than me own blood kin, and I don't want to see ye hurt."

"I know you're only trying to do what you think is best for me, but you have to realize there are things in my life I alone can decide. No matter how much you care or object, it is my choice, and I alone will pay the price if I've made the wrong decision."

Neither Megan nor Sandy voiced the name of the man at the center of their conversation, but each knew from the look on the other's face exactly who they were discussing.

Releasing a resigned breath, Sandy stepped back and let Megan pass before turning to his own mount. He climbed into the saddle and watched Megan ride away into the dusky night.

"Aye, 'tis yer decision, Meggie," he muttered to himself as she disappeared from sight. "But I will be the one to pick up the pieces when yer reaver is done with ye."

Giving a disgusted snort, Sandy kicked his mount in the side and followed in Megan's wake. He didn't approve of what she was so set to do, but he'd not desert her. He loved her too much.

Chapter 9

Megan smiled with pleasure. The easy motion of the horse,
the silvered beauty of the moonlit night, combined with the
fact she was riding companionably at the side of the man she
loved, made the night perfect. Releasing a sigh of contentment, she glanced at Royce and wondered again at the beauty
of his intriguing face.

The black patch he wore and the white scar that marked
one side of his face from brow to cheek created a mysterious
aura. Yet his flawed features only served to emphasize the
perfection of the unscarred side, giving the impression that
two beings dwelled within one man. The imagery of the combination of devil and angel excited Megan, and she didn't
doubt Royce's intriguing looks had the same effect upon most
women who met the handsome reaver.

At the thought of another woman in Royce's life, Megan
shifted uneasily in the saddle and tried to ignore the birth of
her jealousy. Her head told her it was only natural for a man
like Royce to have experience with other women, but her
heart raged against the idea. Royce was the man she loved,
and she couldn't bear the thought of him caring for another
woman.

Sensing Meggie's gaze upon him, Richard glanced at his

lovely companion and smiled when he caught her eye. She blushed and quickly shifted her gaze back to the road. Richard chuckled to himself at the look of embarrassment he'd seen flicker across her face before she'd looked away. Like many women in the past, he'd caught her staring at his face. Oddly, he'd found his scarred features had not hindered him where women were concerned. Women of all walks of life and ages seemed to find his face fascinating. He didn't understand the attraction, nor did he worry about it. If they liked scarred, one-eyed men, it was their choice, and he was more than willing to accept the favors they offered.

Richard glanced once more at Megan and felt his own pulse quicken from the knowledge that she, too, found him attractive. A tiny, perplexed frown creased his brow as he drew his gaze away from her and thoughtfully looked up at the star-studded sky. He didn't understand why Meggie's response made him feel differently. In the past he hadn't truly cared one way or the other about how women viewed him.

Gazing once more at Megan's moon-silvered profile, Richard felt a wave of confusion ripple over him. Of late it seemed that many things about his life had been altered. He'd even begun to think of Jamelyn in a different light. He knew he still loved her, but it wasn't the passion-filled emotion that had claimed him since their first meeting over four years before. Oddly, he found his feelings for her were those for a cherished sister instead of the woman with whom he had wanted to share his life.

Richard's confusion deepened with his frown, and he flashed Meggie an accusatory look before turning his attention back to the road in front of him. Something had changed in him during the past few weeks. Somehow Meggie had managed to work her way into his life far deeper than anyone else had ever managed to do. Even Jamelyn hadn't had the power to lift his spirits and make his pulse quicken just with her smile. He wouldn't say he loved Meggie, but he was beginning to realize he couldn't give her up as easily as he'd once believed.

Especially after last night, Richard mused, casting a surreptitious look at Megan. Be damned to Edward's schemes and threats, I should take her and flee to the highlands.

Richard's eyes widened in shock at his own wayward musings. What in God's name am I thinking? He could not endanger his family because of one beautiful young woman, even if he had been her first lover. He had a mission to fulfill and must concentrate all his efforts upon it.

Resolutely, Richard turned his thoughts away from the woman at his side and glanced at the man riding several paces ahead. McTavis had spoken only a few words all night, and Richard suspected the reaver was still disgruntled about having to give in to Royce's demand to meet the man who bought Sandy's stolen goods.

Richard gave a mental shrug. It didn't matter how McTavis or anyone else felt about the situation. It was necessary to use any means at his disposal to glean the information he needed for Edward.

Through the trees ahead, Richard caught a glimpse of the moon-silvered Trent meandering through the countryside and knew they were near the outskirts of Nottingham. The events in this city seven years ago had made Richard and all of England aware that Edward was not a weakling king like his father, Edward II. Nor was he a pawn for those who sought to rule England through him. He had shown his strength and cunning by catching his mother, Queen Isabella, with her lover Roger Mortimer, the Earl of March, at Nottingham Castle—the royal residence.

In one ingenious move Edward had managed to seal his power as the monarch of England as well as put an end to the civil wars Mortimer so frequently stirred up. Edward had the Earl of March taken prisoner to the Tower in London, where he remained until late November, when he was sent to Tyburn to be hanged and quartered on a common thief's gallows.

Edward was a shrewd politician who maintained a close eye on his kingdom and allowed no one, friend or foe, to jeopardize what he had built from the ruins of his father's reign. In the past years he had proved he'd brook no disloyalty or disobedience to his orders. Richard's own recent experience was proof of that.

In the distance the dark shape of Nottingham Castle came into Richard's view. Nottingham had been a turning point for Edward, and if Richard found the clues he needed, it would also benefit him.

The soft thud of the horses' hooves changed to a clatter upon the narrow cobbled streets when Megan, Richard, and Sandy entered the city. They maneuvered their mounts around the piles of cinders which had been thrown out into the streets from the bell foundry and iron workshops that had made Nottingham a wealthy and thriving borough. Following Sandy's lead, they traveled past the dark, timbered buildings where the shopkeepers worked, and turned toward the waterfront on an uncobbled street. The horses' hooves mired in the mud created by the drainage running from the more prosperous section of the city toward the river. Entrails from the butcher's shop, stale fish from the fishmongers' yard, feathers from the poulterers, and household excrements clogged the gutters, spilling into the street before the stream reached its destination and was washed away by the Trent. The stench rising from the filth filled the air and made it difficult to breathe.

Nearly gagging on the odor, Megan raised a hand to cover her nose and mouth and fought to retain the few bites of bread and cheese she'd eaten before leaving Dragon's Lair. This was her first visit to Nottingham, and she determined if all cities were as foul as Nottingham, she had no desire to visit others.

" 'Tis not much farther to the waterfront," Sandy said, glancing back over his shoulder at Megan. He understood her feelings. The stench had also made him sick when he'd first come to deal with the man who called himself the Rook. It still made him queasy if he didn't force himself to concentrate on other things while traveling through the muddy street to the Rook's hideout. Even after all these months he still couldn't understand why any man would choose to live in such a foul place. Yet the Rook seemed happy in his rat's hole near the docks.

The scent of offal lessened somewhat when they reached the river and reined their horses to a halt behind a large, dilapidated building. Its timbers sagged from damp rot, and like a stooped old man withered with age, it leaned precariously toward the water's edge.

"Rook lives here," Sandy said. Dismounting, he cast a cautious glance about the area. The waterfront wasn't a place for Megan, even with him and McFarland to protect her. It was far too dangerous an area at night. All of the human vultures crept from their hiding places to prey upon anyone weaker than themselves. Roving gangs of cutthroats and thieves scoured the city, seeking anything of value. In the past they had even ventured into the country, raiding estates whose owners were not prepared to fight off their attack. At times they had seized and held estates until their owners ransomed them. The thieves also plundered manor houses, raping the women and often murdering any man who tried to oppose them.

"Then let's get this over with," Megan said, anxious to be gone from the vile atmosphere. Slipping from the saddle, she made a disgusted face when her boots stuck in the odorous mud. Gingerly she followed Sandy onto the narrow planks that led into the decaying structure. The hair at the nape of her neck stood on end at the loud squeal of protest emitted by the rusty hinges when Sandy pulled the heavy door open and stepped into the black cavern beyond. Megan paused uncertainly upon the threshold to the Rook's nest. Every instinct she possessed screamed for her to call Sandy back before it was too late.

"You've nothing to fear, Meggie. I'll let nothing harm you," Royce said close behind her.

His presence helped her feel somewhat better but didn't completely rid her of the feeling she was walking into danger. Swallowing back the lump of fear clogging her throat, she glanced over her shoulder and gave him a wobbly little smile before nodding. Drawing in a deep breath, she followed in Sandy's wake.

To her relief, it wasn't as totally dark as she'd first thought. A tiny glimmer of light could be seen filtering from the crack around the door at the end of the short passageway. Hurrying to catch up with Sandy, she nearly collided with him as he raised his hand to knock. At the sound of the prearranged signal, the door swung open to reveal a large man wearing a red rag tied about his bald pate. His heavy features were marked by a surly expression, and he grunted, stepping aside to allow them to enter the inner sanctions of the Rook's nest.

The light surrounding them momentarily blinded Megan until she was able to adjust to the bright glow of hundreds of candles. She raised a hand to shield her eyes as she stepped into the chamber, heavily scented with burning tallow. She squinted in amazement. She'd never seen so many candles lit in one place before. Dozens of wall sconces and candelabras illuminated the room nearly as bright as day. Surveying the unusual display, her gaze came to rest on the man lounging negligently at the large table in the center of the room. He wore a long robe of white velvet beaded with gold about the sleeves and neck. He tapped the long nails of one blue-veined hand against the scarred surface of the table while he regarded them through narrowed, emotionless dark eyes which looked like shards of cold onyx. Thin lips above a grey, pointed beard pursed, and the nostrils of his hooked nose flared with irritation. Slowly he uncoiled his lean frame from the leather monk's chair and stood. His unmerciful gaze rested on Sandy. "McTavis, how dare ye bring anyone here without me permission."

Sandy didn't flinch under the man's fury. " 'Twas the only way if ye want the goods that have come into me friend's possession."

Rook's cynical expression didn't change. "What kind of goods do ye have?"

"These," Richard said, stepping around Sandy and holding the brooch and necklace in the air. "But if you're not interested, then we will go elsewhere."

Rook's greedy gaze took in the expensive jewels, and his entire demeanor seemed to alter. He licked his lips and smiled ingratiatingly up at Richard, looking more like a kindly old grandfather than the hard, angry man of a moment before. "Perhaps I was a little hasty. Ye can never have too many friends, can ye?"

"I don't want to be your friend," Richard answered coolly. "I just want the money you'll pay for these." Richard opened his hand. The emeralds and diamonds sparkled temptingly.

Nonplussed by Richard's contemptuous remark, Rook curled a long-nailed finger at Richard, urging him forward. "Let me have a closer look."

Richard placed the jewels on the table and then laid his hand on the hilt of his sword, the gesture silently warning the man not to let the temptation to steal the jewels override his better judgment.

Rook picked up the necklace and inspected each stone. A multitude of colors flashed over his hollowed-cheeked features when the diamonds reflected their icy brilliance upon him. A gasp of pleasure slipped unconsciously from his thin lips as he realized the perfection of the jewels in his hand. At last he looked back at Richard.

"I'll give ye fifty pounds fer the lot."

One corner of Richard's mouth curled in a cynical little smile. "Rook, don't try to play me for a fool. I know the value of the jewels. They are worth at least two hundred pounds in London."

Rook nodded rapidly. "Aye, they are worth a high price in London, but we're in Nottingham, and I'm not a wealthy man. I can't give ye a pence more than I've offered."

" 'Tis a shame," Richard said, closing his hand over the gems in one fluid motion. "I thought we might be able to do business." He pocketed the jewels and turned to leave.

"Don't be in such haste," Rook said, wringing his hands. "Perhaps I can raise the money you require if you'll give me a little time to arrange matters."

Richard flashed Rook a skeptical look.

Rook gestured with his hands and grinned sheepishly as he shrugged. " 'Tis not safe to keep that kind of money here. Give me just a short while and I'll have Oakes collect what you need."

Richard sensed something wasn't quite right about the Rook's behavior. His instincts warned him not to remain a moment longer in the thieves' den, yet he pushed the uneasy feeling aside. He'd come too far to go away without answers to his questions. "I'll give you an hour and I'll take no less than a hundred and fifty pounds."

"Agreed," Rook said, smiling with relief. Retrieving a piece of yellowed paper from the pocket of his velvet robe, he scribbled a few words and then handed it to the silent, grim-faced man standing guard at his side. "Give this to our friend and tell him 'tis urgent."

Oakes stuffed the paper into his pocket and left without a look at Richard or his companions.

"Now, friends. Won't you join me for a dram or two while we wait for Oakes to return with the money. I've been fortunate of late to have come into possession of one of France's finest wines." He bent, withdrawing a bottle from a straw-filled box beneath the table and then opening it. Like a connoisseur of fine wines, he sniffed the cork and smiled. "It has the sweetest bouquet of any I've ever tasted."

Richard smiled to himself as he settled his lean frame at the table and watched Rook fill several goblets with his ill-gotten gains. The French wine was all the evidence he needed to assure him he'd come to the right place for the information. Rook would know who smuggled in the wine as well as who smuggled out England's wool to the lowland cloth manufacturers. As middleman, Rook would also know the identities of the wool thieves.

Richard lifted a goblet to his lips and pretended to drink. Wise to the ways of men like the Rook, he took no chance on the wine being drugged. Nor would he allow the Rook to steal the jewels by getting him intoxicated.

Glancing down the table at his two silent companions, he surmised they'd had the same thoughts about the Rook's hospitality. Neither made a move to taste the wine.

Rook regarded his visitors' hesitation, and chuckled. "Yer wise to be wary, but I wouldn't waste a fine wine such as this by drugging it. McTavis, if ye don't want it, then me and yer friend here will drink yer share. 'Tis too fine to waste."

Demonstrating his point, he filled his own goblet and downed the contents in one gulp. A small dribble of the burgundy liquid ran from the corner of his mouth into his pointed, grey beard. He wiped it away with the back of his hand, smacked his lips, and belched heartily.

" 'Tis a fine wine," Rook repeated, refilling his goblet.

"Aye, 'tis a fine wine," Richard agreed, eyeing the Rook curiously. "You are a fortunate man. Few are able to enjoy such quality since our good king has seen fit to quarrel with France."

"Aye," Rook said. "The fool thinks his embargo against

trading with France and the lowlands will stop us from enjoying such as this.'' He raised his goblet.

Richard pretended to take another sip of his wine and then gave the Rook a roguish grin. "He doesn't realize his foolishness will make us rich."

Richard and the Rook laughed companionably while Megan and Sandy sat listening, bewildered by the sudden comradery that had sprung up between the two men.

"More's the fool. No embargo will stop the trade. The wool will keep going to Flanders, and the gold will keep coming back into my hands to buy fine wine"—Rook gestured around—"and candles."

"Perhaps we could make a new deal, Rook," Richard said, leaning forward. "I might consider letting you have the jewels for a hundred pounds if you would be willing to help me."

Rook sat up and eyed Richard cautiously. "What kind of help?"

Richard glanced toward Megan and Sandy. "I've grown tired of the pittance we earn on the roads. I want to get into a far more profitable trade."

The Rook relaxed and leaned back in his chair. He smiled knowingly. "Ye want to join up with the smugglers?"

"Aye," Richard said, and heard Megan's sharp intake of breath.

"Perhaps I can arrange something for you, but I'll have to talk with me friends first. Come back tomorrow night at the same time and I'll have me friends here to meet ye."

Not wanting to arouse the Rook's suspicions, Richard nodded and schooled his expression to hide his elation. He had to keep a tight rein on the urge to laugh aloud at how easily he had worked his way into the Rook's confidence. By tomorrow night he would have managed to infiltrate the band of thieves, and from that point it would be easy to learn the identity of the ringleader.

Richard glanced once more at his silent companions. He

frowned when he saw Sandy's flushed, angry expression, yet it was the look in Meggie's bright eyes that tore at him. His heart seemed to stop at the pain lacing her misty gaze before she turned away and focused her full attention on the goblet sitting on the table in front of her. He ached to explain why he had to leave her, yet he did nothing. Anything he said would only serve to make their parting more painful for both of them. It was best to leave things as they were, severing their relationship now before it could develop further.

Oakes lumbered into the room and crossed to Rook. He placed a bag of coins on the table and handed the old man a piece of paper before he turned and shuffled back to the door.

Rook scanned the note and then tucked it away in his robe before opening the bag. Gold coins spilled into a pile on the scarred table. Lovingly he stacked them into neat rows, counting each piece until he was satisfied all was as he'd requested. Glancing up at Oakes, he nodded his approval and then turned his attention back to Richard. Oakes grinned and left the room.

"I believe it is all here. Now if you will turn over the jewels, our business for tonight will be concluded."

Richard placed the necklace and brooch on the table beside the coins.

A long, assessing look passed between the two men before each moved to collect his property. A confident smile curved Richard's sensuous lips as he scooped up the coins and put them back into the leather pouch. He tucked them safely away and then pushed back his chair and stood. "Then I'll bid you farewell until tomorrow night."

Feeling betrayed and hurt by Royce's decision to join the smugglers, Megan rose from her chair so swiftly that it tumbled over backward. It crashed loudly to the rough wooden floor and drew all eyes to her as she fled the room. Blinded by the rush of tears filling her eyes, she stumbled along the dark passageway and out into the night. Ruled by her shattering heart, she couldn't bear to remain in Royce's company and know what they had shared the previous night had meant nothing to him. Intent upon reaching her horse and getting as far away from him as possible, she failed to notice a movement in the shadows as she crossed the narrow planks to her mount. However, before she could put her foot in the stirrup and hoist herself into the saddle, a blow to the back of the head sent her into oblivion.

"Meggie," Sandy called, but received no answer. He flashed Royce a contemptuous look and hurried in her wake. He'd nearly been able to feel Megan's pain when McFarland had revealed his decision to leave them for the more profitable venture of smuggling. He had warned Megan not to get involved with the reaver, but from the expression he'd seen in her eyes, she had not just gotten involved, she'd fallen head over heels in love with the rogue.

Sandy gritted his teeth and stepped through the sagging doorway, intent upon only one thing—comforting Megan. He realized too late the danger awaiting him. He saw a flicker in the shadows, but he didn't have time to cry out a warning before a cudgel knocked him unconscious and he fell face-down in the fetid mud.

Hearing the commotion outside, Richard glanced at Rook. There was no surprise written on the man's hollow-cheeked face, only a look of satisfaction. Richard realized all of his instincts had been right and he had played the fool by not heeding their warning. Without being told, he knew the message the Rook had sent had been to Nottingham's sheriff.

"You little bastard," Richard growled, withdrawing his sword from its scabbard so swiftly, the air seemed to sing. Regarding the Rook menacingly through the red haze of fury, he pinned the smaller man against the wall with the needle-sharp point of his blade, pricking the Rook's throat beneath his pointed beard. "You won't live to enjoy the money you've been paid to betray us."

Eyes bulging with fright, Rook tried to shake his head in denial, but the movement only increased his pain. He lifted his hands beseechingly, palms upward, and whispered hoarsely, "They made me do it. I had to send them word when the necklace and brooch were brought to me or I'd have been hanged in your stead."

Richard was sickened by the betrayal. Rook was like any scavenger living off its host, sucking it to death, and then when a richer meal came along, sacrificing the one who had kept him alive.

Richard pressed the blade home, ending Rook's life. The little man's eyes widened momentarily and a deep gurgle emerged from his gaping mouth before he sank to the floor and lay staring at the ceiling. It was not Richard St. Claire who had robbed Rook of his life and stood gazing down at the scarlet stain spreading over the front of the white velvet robe. At that moment he was again Royce the Reaver, a man who killed his enemies to insure his own survival.

A sound behind Richard alerted him. He turned, a bloody-tipped blade in hand, to find himself outnumbered by the sheriff's men. He made no move to surrender.

"Damn me, if we ain't caught all three of the bastards who caused me so much trouble," one man said, smiling at Richard.

It took a moment for Richard to recall where he'd seen the man before. He'd been the sergeant-at-arms when he'd rescued Meggie and Sandy from hanging.

"So we meet again," Richard said, still on guard.

"Aye, ye bastard, and this time I intend to let Lord Ashby deal with ye himself since I'm no longer in his service because of ye."

Richard smiled. "Don't get your hopes too high, Sergeant."

The ex–sergeant-at-arms smiled, revealing broken stubs of teeth. "Ye ain't getting away. One way or the other, I'm

sending ye back to Ashby Keep. It don't really matter to me
if yer alive or dead.''

Richard tensed to defend himself against an imminent attack from the sheriff's men. ''I don't doubt your intentions,
Sergeant, but it doesn't mean you'll succeed.''

''It's yer decision, vermin. Ye can fight, but yer outnumbered and ye'll die. Yer two friends are already trussed up
like Christmas geese. Even without ye, they'll be prize
enough to allay Lord Ashby's anger with me. He'll enjoy
putting the noose around their necks himself.''

Richard's heart stilled as he realized Meggie and Sandy's
lives lay in his hands. He was Richard St. Claire and he
would not be hanged as a common thief; Edward had assured
that with the amnesty paper hidden in Richard's boot. It was
to be shown in the event of his capture. However, his friends
were a different matter. Without his influence they would
once more end up on the gibbet after Robert Ashby satisfied
the mean streak that ran through the man like a fouled river.

Richard felt a sinking sensation in the pit of his belly at
the thought of Meggie's fate at Ashby's hand. The man's
reputation for cruelty was well known at court, as was his
sadistic treatment of women. When he learned the youngest
reaver was not a boy but a beautiful and desirable woman
who had no protection of name or birth, Meggie would be
at his mercy, a mercy that would not be given.

Richard let his sword fall to the floor. He had no choice
but to surrender. His deception would be shattered when he
came before Ashby and was recognized, but it was a cheap
price to pay to protect Meggie. Richard didn't stop to wonder
why he was willing to jeopardize his future and his mission
for the fate of one young woman.

Megan moaned and raised a hand to her bruised head. She
blinked several times but found herself staring into total
darkness. The first thought to enter her mind was that she

was blind. However, after several moments, the darkness above her began to take on different shapes and she could make out the form of a man. Raising a tentative, exploring hand, she touched the warmth of living flesh.

"Sandy?" she whispered, her dry mouth making it hard to speak.

The dark shape moved and Megan heard a rumble through the leather jerkin as the person cleared his throat, and she realized she was resting against his chest. She felt the man's arms tighten about her possessively.

"Meggie, thank God," Richard said, coming fully awake at the sound of her voice. He hadn't meant to fall asleep, but his weary body had finally succumbed to its need for rest.

"Where are we? Where is Sandy?" Megan asked. Disoriented, she shook her head to clear her mind of the haze that kept her from thinking coherently. The movement made an excruciating pain shoot up from the base of her skull. Like an arrow circling her head with twine, it tightened about her temples and made her feel as if the top of her head would explode. Cringing against the agony, she groaned again and pressed her face against Richard's chest.

"We're in the dungeons of Ashby Keep, and Sandy's been taken up for questioning," Richard said softly. Splaying his fingers through her hair, he began to gently massage her aching head. He knew from the lump he'd found while examining her earlier, she had one hell of a headache from the blow she'd received.

Megan relaxed under Richard's gentle ministrations. She lay with her cheek against his chest, listening to the strong beat of his heart. Contentment filled her as his fingers worked their magic. The pain gradually began to abate and her thoughts cleared. Megan frowned at the recollection of the scene between Royce and Rook.

"Am I hurting you?" Richard asked, feeling her tense beneath his fingers.

Suffering from the onslaught of the new pain centering in her heart and finding it far greater than any she suffered physically, Megan forgot about her aching head. At that moment all she wanted was to put as much distance between herself and Royce as their small, damp cell would allow. She didn't want to be near him knowing he would already have left her had not the sheriff's men intervened.

Unable to speak without bursting into tears, she pushed herself upright and moved to the other side of the cell. Heedless to the slime coating the cold stones, she braced her back against the wall and tucked her knees up against her chest. She didn't feel the moisture seeping through her coarse woolen jerkin as she buried her face in her arms and tried to shut out the pain in her heart.

"Meggie, what's wrong? Did I hurt you?" Richard asked, puzzled by her sudden actions.

No answer came.

"Damn it, Meggie, answer me. Did I hurt you?"

"No, you didn't hurt me, nor will you ever hurt me," Megan spat, her voice raspy with unshed tears.

Perplexed by her angry tone, Richard frowned. "Then if you're not hurt, what's wrong?"

Megan's dark hair tumbled into her face when she lifted her head and peered at Royce's dark shape. Her bark of sarcastic laughter echoed eerily off the stone walls and sent chills up Richard's spine.

"Should anything be wrong when I awake to find myself in a dungeon and don't know if Sandy is alive or dead?"

"Meggie, you don't have to worry. I won't allow anyone to hurt you or Sandy," Richard said, fearing she was becoming hysterical. He closed the short space separating them and reached to take her into his arms.

"Don't touch me," Megan ordered, cringing away from him. "I don't want you to ever touch me again."

Convinced now the ordeal of being bashed on the head and then awakening in the dark cell had shaken her wits, Richard soothed, "Meggie, I just want to hold you."

Battling to keep herself from succumbing to the temptation, Megan ground out between clinched teeth, "No. I made the mistake of letting you hold me last night, but I'll not be so foolish again."

Richard paused—finally comprehending the reason for her anger. "I understand your feelings, but now is no time for us to become enemies."

Megan gave another harsh laugh. "We are not enemies, Royce. We are nothing to each other."

Richard reached out a hand and traced her soft cheek in the darkness. "I never meant to hurt you."

Richard's touch made Megan feel as if her heart were splitting asunder. She wanted nothing more than to throw herself into his arms and accept the comfort he offered. Instead she drew in a shaky breath and said, "By all that's holy, leave me alone. I don't need your pity nor your assurances."

"Meggie, you have to trust me when I say I'll always treasure the moments we shared. I wish I could make things as they were, but I can't change the fate awaiting us. Just believe me when I say I've never met another woman like you and you'll always be special to me."

Unable to fight the call of her heart any longer, Megan squeezed her eyes closed and surrendered to her feelings. She had known from the beginning her love for Royce was doomed and had vowed to enjoy what little time they had together. There had been no pledges or vows spoken between them, and she had no right to condemn him for ending their relationship when she would have soon had to do the same because of her responsibilities to the people of Dragon's Lair.

Suddenly struck by their precarious situation, she realized nothing mattered now but her feelings for Royce. In a short time they would face Lord Ashby's judgment, and she would not go to her death with her love for Royce unappeased. There was no time left for anger, nor any feelings of betrayal. She loved Royce, and no matter how he felt about her, she would spend the last hours God granted her in his arms.

"Love me, Royce," Megan said, throwing herself into Richard's arms. Molding her body to his, she wound her arms about his neck and pulled his head down for her desperate kiss.

Richard's arms automatically tightened about Megan. His mind told him to put her away, to deny himself his need to feel her against him once more, to know again the satiny warmth of her surrounding the hard length of him. He'd already hurt her enough without adding more pain by succumbing to the hot rush of desire streaking through him. The heat of it settled achingly in his loins, throbbing there with an intensity that made every muscle in his lean body grow tense until he felt as if he were being stretched upon the rack.

Richard ground his teeth together and fought against the passion raging within him even as her small tongue darted into his mouth, raking his teeth and teasing him with its sensual movement. His will to fight evaporated. All coherent and reasonable thoughts vanished under a fiery storm of desire. His heart turned into Thor's hammer, thundering in his chest, and his breathing grew ragged.

Her beauty obscured from his view by the darkness surrounding them, Richard's other senses became his eyes. The feel of her soft flesh beneath his fingertips made him see the creamy richness of her flawless skin as he cupped the sweet curve of her cheek and deepened their kiss. His tongue played an erotic game with hers—sucking and thrusting as he moved his hand down to stroke the slender column of her throat before gliding slowly onward to the swelling mounds hidden beneath her jerkin. He left her mouth to bury his face in the curve of her neck, his nostrils flaring as he drew in her sweet woman's scent. His lips teased her flesh and he savored her smell as he worked loose the lacings of her garments and slipped his hand inside the soft material to fondle her breasts.

Megan moaned her pleasure and arched to give him access to the rose-colored nipples peeking from beneath her linen chainse. She gasped at the sensation his lips aroused within her when he closed his mouth over the hardened bud and flicked it with his tongue. He moaned and pressed his face to her, sucking greedily. Her fingers curled into the leather of his jerkin and kneaded the flesh beneath as she felt his hands move down to her waist and untie the lacing there. She raised her hips to assist him in freeing her from her chausses and eagerly spread her legs to receive him.

Hot and throbbing, she wrapped her legs high about his waist and took him deep within her. They moved together, completely unaware that they were still half-clothed as they surrendered to the pleasure rippling through their bodies. Nothing existed for them beyond the sweet agony of the passion they shared. Greedily they savored each uniting of hips, each thrust taking them higher into the glorious realm, soaring upward and away from the ugly darkness of Ashby's dungeon to the fiery land made of sunbursts and stardust.

Ecstacy streaked through Megan and she arched against Royce, drawing him deeper within her as her cry of rapture echoed against the cold stone walls. The muscles on his corded neck stood taut and he bared his teeth as he thrust to the woman's core of her, his seed mingling with hers in the rich womb of life.

"My Meggie," Richard whispered before tasting once more of the sweetness of her passion-bruised mouth.

Still intimately united with Royce, Megan wrapped her arms about his neck and held him close. She knew if her world ended within the hour, she would die happy.

Chapter 10

The sound of voices forced Megan and Richard back to re-
ality. Reluctantly they left each other's arms and righted their
clothing only moments before the heavy cell door was thrust
open. Torchlight shattered the darkness as four burly guards
entered the cell and, without preamble, grabbed them by the
arms and roughly hauled them into the passageway. The
guards holding Richard led him away first. The sound of their
footsteps had already died away before Megan's guards began to lead her toward the stairs. Megan stumbled, her small
size making it impossible for her to keep in step with the
large guards.

Annoyed by the delay, a guard cuffed Megan on the side
of the head. The blow momentarily staggered her senses and
sent the peasant's coif she'd hurriedly pulled on to hide her
hair, sliding down her back. Her hair tumbled free, falling
over her face as she sagged between the two men.

"Damn!" the guard named Hurd exclaimed, shocked to
find what he'd thought to be a youth was in fact a woman.

His partner chuckled and flashed him a sly look. "I've a
feeling we're going to enjoy ourselves tonight. After Ashby's
through with her, he won't mind if we have a little taste of
his leftovers."

Hurd nodded. "Aye, 'tis only right we get something for all our time and trouble." Jerking Megan back to her feet, he held the torch close and roughly tipped her chin to get a better look. What he saw made him smack his lips with satisfaction. "Looks like we got us a real beauty here."

"Aye, I'd like a piece of her before Ashby gets a chance to ruin her."

Hurd frowned. He didn't like the thought of taking Ashby's leavings. He'd lived a hard, cruel life himself, but he'd never seen anyone enjoy hurting another living thing the way Lord Ashby did. He'd seen the man whip a servant to death just for serving food he considered too cool for his taste. The women he used fared little better. They came away from the man's bed scarred and bruised and with haunted eyes that looked more dead than alive. No, Hurd thought. He didn't want to take Ashby's leavings. It would be like making love to a dead woman when the man finished with her.

"Come on, wench," the second guard ordered, dragging her toward the stairs. "We ain't got all day. Lord Ashby is waiting to render his sentence for the crimes ye've committed. After that's done, then we can have a little fun before he hangs ye."

A chill of terror rippled down Megan's spine as she looked from one hard face to the other. She swallowed back the bile rising in her throat at the thought of the fate she knew would await her when she was returned to the dungeons. The guards had made their intentions clear, and she knew she would be raped. Sickened by the very thought of being touched by any man after having known the beauty and wonder of Royce's love, Megan silently vowed she'd fight to her death before she allowed it to happen.

White-faced and resolute, Megan stumbled up the stairs between her guards and was led along a corridor paneled in dark, rich walnut and tiled in beautiful marble. At their approach, two wide, intricately carved double doors swung open to reveal a huge, vaulted chamber where Robert Ashby held court. Sitting upon a raised dais like a king in his high-backed velvet chair, he regarded Megan through narrowed lids as she was pushed forward.

At the cold expression in the man's eyes, a shiver of dread raced up Megan's spine, yet she thrust out her chin defiantly. From what her guards had said, she knew she'd receive no mercy at Ashby's hand, and she was determined he'd not see her cower in fear. She'd meet her fate bravely.

Flashing Ashby a look that clearly bespoke her desire to see him join his counterpart in hell, she regally turned her attention to the many faces in the room, scanning each for the one she loved. She found him standing to one side with a goblet of wine in his hand as if he belonged in the luxurious surroundings. His guards were nowhere to be seen.

Megan frowned when Royce smiled reassuringly at her and raised his goblet in a silent greeting. Glimpsing Sandy standing behind him, she wondered at the odd expression on his face as well as the strange way the two men were acting. Like herself, they had been brought here to be convicted of their crimes and sentenced to death, yet they didn't look at all concerned.

A hush fell over the room when Ashby sat up and leaned forward. He glanced at Richard and arched an inquisitive brow. "I was under the impression your friends were both male. Why wasn't I told you had a female working with you, Richard?"

Richard set his goblet aside and stepped forward. "My lord, I assumed you already knew."

"How was I to know when I've only just learned about you, Richard? Edward should have made me aware your mission here was to catch the men smuggling in wine from France. Had I known, I would have gladly offered my services," Ashby said, turning his attention back to Megan. His cold gaze raked over her from head to toe before coming to rest on the sweet curve of her lips.

" 'Tis of little consequence now since you understand why I had to actually steal Rowena's jewels. Had I not played the part of a thief, I would never have gained access to the Rook."

Tearing his gaze away from the soft fullness of Megan's mouth and his thoughts away from the pleasure such luscious lips could give him, Ashby looked once more at Richard. "I fully understand, but I fear your mission has failed. My household is now aware you are Richard St. Claire, so your secret is no longer. The news will be spread all over the estate before dark. Servants' gossip travels faster than lightning."

Stunned, Megan gaped up at Richard, unable to believe what she'd just heard. Royce McFarland, the man she'd given her heart and soul, was in truth Richard St. Claire, the man King Edward had chosen to be her husband.

Rage, like the lightning of which Lord Ashby had just spoken, swept over her with such force, Megan was nearly blinded by it. She could see nothing but a sea of red as she looked at Richard. Two scarlet spots colored her cheeks, and her eyes snapped with blue fire. She'd felt betrayed when Royce—or Richard, or whatever his name was—wanted to join the smugglers. Yet that feeling was nothing compared to the virulent emotions sweeping over her. Hate, rage, bitterness, and pain all mingled to obliterate any residue left by their lovemaking.

Megan drew in a deep breath and clenched her fists at her sides in an effort to control the urge to tear out Richard St. Claire's eyes. Livid at having been used and tossed aside like an old wet rag, she forgot her own duplicity, focusing her ire on Richard's. He had only used her to gain access to the Rook and the smugglers. He had lied to her from the beginning, and like the great, great fool she was, she'd placed her trust in him, giving him her heart. And the blackhearted, greedy bastard had taken her love to appease his own selfish desires without any consideration for her feelings.

Reflecting upon her orders from Edward, this revelation about Richard St. Claire only confirmed what she'd suspected from the beginning. Then why does it hurt so much? she asked herself, and swallowed against the rush of tears clogging her throat and making it difficult for her to breathe.

"Meggie," Richard said, watching the different expressions flickering across her face. "I wanted to tell you the truth earlier. I didn't do this to hurt you. Edward forced me into this situation. It was the only way I could get out of the marriage he'd arranged for me."

Richard's explanation only increased the ache in Megan's heart. She couldn't look at him. If she did, she couldn't be responsible for her own actions. Forcing a calm into her voice, she stared straight ahead and pretended to ignore him as she asked, "Are we free to go, Lord Ashby?"

"Since you have been granted amnesty by the king for your crimes, I see no reason to detain you further," Ashby said, wondering at the sudden tension he sensed between Richard and the beautiful girl.

"Thank you, Lord Ashby," Megan said. Intent only upon making good her escape from Richard St. Claire, she executed a perfect curtsy and then turned and strode from the chamber with head held high.

Stunned by her display of gracious manners, Richard made no move to follow Meggie. The woman he'd just glimpsed was not the girl he'd known for the past weeks. She was a lady of breeding. Richard frowned and shook his head. That was impossible. He knew Meggie, and she was far from nobility. She was too much the gamine for anyone to make into a lady.

Richard wasn't the only man who watched Megan walk regally from the chamber. Robert Ashby could not take his eyes away from the shapely pair of chausses emphasizing her long legs or the feminine sway of hips he could glimpse beneath the hem of the large woolen jerkin. His mouth went dry with a longing to run his hands up the slender legs and delve into the moist warmth hidden at the apex of her thighs. He imagined hearing her shrieks of pain as he used her until she bled. Licking his lips at the thought, he swallowed and shifted on the velvet seat to ease the uncomfortable swelling against his tight-fitting chausses. Someday, he vowed silently, the wench would again fall into his hands, but he'd not be as lenient as he'd been today. Had it not been for Richard St. Claire's position with Edward, she'd now be in his bedchamber awaiting his desires.

Sandy noted the look on both men's faces and, without drawing any attention to himself, quietly made his way from the room and to the stable to collect his mount. After the revelation of Royce's real identity, he already knew Megan's destination, and followed in her wake.

When he passed through the gates of Ashby Keep, he cast one brief glance back at the walled castle and wondered what now lay in Megan's future. The man she'd fallen in love with was the man she was to marry, but he feared after today there would never be any peace between the two Edward had chosen to unite. He'd seen Megan's reaction when she'd learned the truth. His own reaction had been similar. He'd felt betrayed. However, there was a difference between their feelings about Richard St. Claire. His heart was not involved, but Megan's was. She had fallen in love with Royce only to learn everything about him had been a lie.

Sandy realized such knowledge would not be easy for anyone to forgive, but it would be even harder for Megan after her experiences with a brother like Mallory O'Roarke. He'd made her wise to the ways of liars and cheats, and she would not allow anyone a second chance. She'd learned one lesson in dealing with Mallory over the years—you placed your faith in a person until he betrayed your trust, then you cut him out of your life without looking back. It was a sad lesson, but it was one that had saved her much heartbreak through the terrible years when Mallory ruled Dragon's Lair.

Resigned to picking up the pieces left by Richard St. Claire, Sandy urged his mount in the direction of Dragon's Lair. He knew he would find Megan there, licking her wounds. As she'd done for so many years of her life, she'd pretend to the world she didn't hurt. And as he'd always done in the past, he'd go along with her pretense until she turned to him for comfort.

Gazing toward the horizon where the sun slowly sank behind Sherwood Forest, Richard ran a long-fingered hand through his hair in exasperation. He'd searched high and low for Meggie and Sandy but could find no trace of them. He'd been told they had left Ashby Keep, but no one knew in which direction they'd traveled. He knew Meggie was furious about his deception, but he had thought after all they had shared, she would have allowed him to try to explain the situation.

You're a damned fool if you believe that, his conscience chided. He had seen her hurt when she learned of his lies, and he knew Meggie well enough to know she wouldn't easily forgive him.

"I shouldn't have allowed her out of my sight until I made her listen to my explanation," Richard muttered to himself, and again ran his hand through tousled ebony curls.

You've no one to blame but yourself, his conscience challenged. Had you the willpower to resist your own lust, you'd have told her the truth before she learned it from Ashby. It's your fault if you never see her again.

Richard's heart gave a sudden lurch at the thought. He'd known from the beginning he'd have to leave Meggie behind when his mission for Edward was complete, but now, to his amazement he found it more disturbing than he would have ever believed possible. He suddenly felt as if he'd lost a portion of himself somewhere along the way.

Richard frowned and turned back to his horse. Clasping the pommel, he put his foot in the stirrup and hauled himself into the saddle. His mood was bleak. He had no way of finding Meggie. In all the weeks they'd worked together, he'd never taken the time to learn where she went when they separated each night. He'd been too concerned with succeeding with his mission for Edward to worry about Meggie's life when she wasn't with him. He'd taken her help and her love without question, and now, to all appearances, she'd disappeared from the face of the earth.

"Damn me if I let her get away that easily," he muttered, and kicked his horse in the side. He'd scour every hamlet from Nottingham to London before he gave up the search. Meggie was his, and he'd be damned if he wouldn't find her and make her realize that truth.

Exhausted, Richard crossed his arms over the saddle pommel and looked up at the great walls of Windsor, the birthplace of the man he'd come to see. Comprised of three wards and resting on a chalk outcrop rising a hundred feet above the Thames and commanding distant views, Windsor—its walls and round towers built of silver-gray stone quarried nearby from the heathlands near Bagshot—had withstood many sieges during the past centuries. Until his succession to the throne, the king had been known as Edward of Windsor.

Spying the royal standard with its three golden lions waving in the wind, Richard admitted the title had been an accurate one. Edward loved Windsor and kept most of the masons and carpenters throughout the whole of England working to complete the plans of William of Wykeham. The king was determined to make Windsor the most glorious castle in all the world.

Richard drew in a long breath and urged his horse forward. He could sit reflecting upon Windsor's magnificence all night, but in the end he would still have to face Edward and admit he'd failed to uncover the culprits responsible for stealing the wool. He would also have to explain the reason he'd not come directly to Windsor to tell his monarch his plans had been ruined by Robert Ashby's interference.

A frown knit Richard's brows over his slender nose as his thoughts drifted to the reason behind his delay: Meggie. He had searched every village, questioning everyone he encountered about the beautiful dark-haired, blue-eyed girl. Regrettably, he'd learned nothing to aid him in finding her, and he was beginning to believe she'd disappeared off the face of the earth.

"Where are you, Meggie?" Richard muttered for what seemed like the millionth time since his incarceration at Ashby Keep. But as usual, he had no answer to solve his problems about the beautiful reaver.

The guards recognized Richard and saluted him respectfully as they set the well-greased portcullis into motion. Richard returned the gesture as he passed beneath the arched gateway between the two towers and into the bailey, which was far more like the main thoroughfare of a small town than of a castle. He turned his horse in the direction of the royal hall and apartments, which flanked the northern side of the Lower Ward. There he knew he'd find Edward enjoying himself planning his war against France or dallying with one of his women. For he was as relentless in the pursuit of his physical pleasure as he was as a warrior. And he was at his happiest when he could have both.

Without a glance at the young liveried man who rushed forward to assist him, Richard tossed the groom the reins to his mount and strode up the wide stone steps to the massive double doors guarded by two men-at-arms, who stood stiff and straight at their post. Drawing in a fortifying breath,

Richard entered the long, tiled corridor that separated the state apartments from those of the royal family. The dark wood paneling of the walls was intricately carved, and gleamed richly in the soft light from the large chandeliers hanging from the massive carved beams overhead. Tapestries depicting the feats of Edward's ancestors in battle, as well as the king's standards, swayed gently in the cool draft flowing through the great rooms of Windsor.

Richard paused briefly at the foot of the winding stairs leading up to the royal apartments. He paid no heed to the beauty surrounding him; his thoughts were centered upon his audience with England's monarch.

"Richard," Anthony called upon seeing his friend posed hesitantly at the bottom of the staircase.

Richard turned to greet his friend, clasping Anthony's extended hand. " 'Tis good to see you, Anthony."

Godfrey frowned, hearing the note of exhaustion in his friend's voice as he warmly shook Richard's hand. He glanced about their surroundings to insure their privacy. Seeing a guard near the entrance, he drew Richard toward the antechamber and closed the doors behind them. "It's about time you showed up. It's been nearly two months since I last saw you."

"Aye, 'tis been far longer than I planned."

"I had begun to believe you'd decided to run off with your beautiful reaver and take up life on the roads again."

"I had thought of it," Richard said, giving Anthony a wry grin.

" 'Tis glad I am you've changed your mind. I'd hate to see Edward have you hanged and quartered," Anthony chuckled.

"I fear our good monarch may still have that option. 'Twas my misfortune to be caught by Robert Ashby's men and my ruse exposed."

"Damn me, Edward will be displeased if you haven't

gleaned any information about his culprit. I've spoken with him, and he had high hopes on your ability to root out those responsible. He's itching to hang someone for putting him in such a position with his creditors. The financial houses in Florence have already sent representatives to demand payment.''

Richard's shoulders seemed to sag from the burden of his failure. ''I've done my best.' 'Tis over now, and I can do nothing more about it. Everyone in Robert Ashby's household was aware of my true identity, and Ashby made no secret of my intentions to anyone. He plainly announced it to the entire assembly when I was brought before him.''

Anthony frowned. '' 'Tis strange indeed. If the man is as loyal as he pretends, then why would he expose your identity?''

Stunned by the sudden revelation flashing through his mind, Richard stared at Anthony as if he'd never seen him before, his mouth falling slightly agape in wonder. He'd been so involved in finding Meggie, he'd not stopped to ponder the motives behind Ashby's actions. Since their first meeting years ago, he'd never liked the cruel little man. He'd reminded Richard too much of Mallory O'Roake. However, he was tolerated because of his loyalty to Edward and England. Now Richard questioned the man's devotion. Could there have been a reason behind Ashby's seemingly stupid way of allowing his retainers to know Richard's identity?

''What is it, Richard? Did I say something wrong?'' Anthony asked, puzzled by the strange expressions flickering over his friend's face.

Richard absently touched the scar running from beneath his eye patch to his jawline and shook his head. ''Nay, what you said only makes me realize what a fool I've been for not suspecting it before.''

''What are you talking about? You're as bad as Justin, talking in riddles,'' Anthony said, baffled.

"I'm sorry, Anthony. I was just considering what you said, and now I think I've found our culprit. However, we must have proof of his guilt before I go to Edward."

"You mean Ashby? You think he's behind the wool theft?" Richard nodded. "Aye, it's what I believe. Have you learned anything to the contrary since you've been at court?"

"Nay, I've seen nor heard nothing that would be of help."

"Then I will have to keep my ears and eyes open if Edward allows me to keep them long enough. After what you've said, I don't know if Edward will be in any mood to let me continue to root out the culprits." Again, a wry grin tugged up the corners of Richard's sensuous mouth.

"He'll understand if you explain you were detained by a beautiful reaver," Anthony laughed, slapping his friend companionably on the back and giving him a roguish wink. "Edward enjoys the sport too much to think ill of one of his subjects for falling prey to the call of his loins."

The smile wavered on Richard's lips. "I fear when he hears the real reason for my delay, he'll not think so highly of such things—now or in the future."

"Truly you jest. I've never known you to let any woman come between you and your responsibilities before."

"Aye, I've never known it to happen either," Richard said, shrugging.

"Could it be you've finally fallen in love after all these years of mooning after something you could not have?"

Richard flashed Anthony a censuring look, silently telling his friend he was trespassing upon dangerous ground. "Nay, I've not fallen in love. 'Tis only my need to explain that I didn't mean to hurt her with my lies."

"That in itself is unusual, my friend. I've known you to take your pleasure where you found it without ever a thought to the woman you left behind."

"Aye, but they were different from Meggie. They knew exactly what they were getting when they offered themselves to me. Meggie was innocent of the ways of men until she met me, and I can't forget it. I owe her at least an explanation.''

''Meggie? Is that the girl's name?'' Anthony asked, his eyes lighting with humor.

Richard nodded.

'' 'Tis also what Lady Faith calls your future bride. It seems you're destined to be plagued by the name, one way or the other,'' Anthony said.

Richard gave Anthony an irritated look. At his friend's obvious annoyance, Anthony couldn't control his mirth a moment longer. He threw back his head and burst into laughter, his action gaining him another black glare from Richard.

''I see nothing humorous in my situation,'' Richard growled. ''The ugly hag at Dragon's Lair might have the same name as Meggie, but that is where the resemblance ends. My Meggie has eyes as dark blue as the lochs of Scotland, and hair like midnight, and her skin is like silk beneath my hand.'' Richard drifted into silence and he released a long, tired breath. A wistful expression touched his scarred features as his thoughts turned once more to the woman he'd sought during the past months.

Anthony sobered at the look upon Richard's face and the tone of his voice. His friend might deny it, but he'd fallen deeply in love with the beautiful reaver who had ridden with him in the night. Sadly Anthony reflected that this love of Richard's was as doomed as his first with Jamelyn. Edward would never allow one of his valuable courtiers to marry a woman who could bring no benefit to her husband or the crown.

''Richard, from what you've said, your Meggie has disappeared, so I suggest you put her out of your mind. You know nothing can come of it.'' Anthony placed a comforting hand on his friend's shoulder.

Richard's eyes were haggard as he looked at Anthony. ''I

can't put her from my thoughts. You may not understand how I feel, but she has a part of me I need to reclaim before I can go on with my life.''

"Friend, you may deny it to yourself, but you've fallen in love with this girl called Meggie.''

"Nay, Anthony. I've known love, and this is different from what I felt then. 'Tis something I can't even explain to myself, much less to you.'' Richard gave Anthony a sad smile. "But have heart, friend. I will manage to work everything out eventually, and then I can put the past months behind me.''

"I pray you will. 'Tis only asking for trouble if you continue with this folly. Edward will not allow it.''

Richard crossed to the window overlooking the courtyard. For a long reflective moment he watched several workmen lug a large timber toward the site of Edward's latest renovation project before glancing over his shoulder at his friend. "I'm aware of my duties to my family and my king, and I will do them.''

Richard turned once more to the window and sought to resign his heart to his role as a St. Claire. It wasn't going to be an easy task, but he had no other choice. Anthony was right about Edward's reaction. He'd never accept an unbred chit with no money or land as Richard's wife. It was best for all concerned to let things stay as they were instead of finding Meggie. Because if he did find her, he feared he'd not be strong enough to let her go again, no matter what his king ordered.

A movement in the garden below drew his attention away from his predicament over his beautiful reaver. Two men stood huddled in the shadow of a large hedge. They glanced about to insure they were not observed by anyone passing by. His curiosity pricked by their furtive actions, Richard watched until they moved apart. When the tall, skinny man dressed in a velvet cotehardie stepped out of the shadows and into the sunlight, Richard immediately recognized him as one of Robert Ashby's henchman. But the other man's features remained obscured from view by the shadows of the hedge.

"Look here, Anthony," Richard said, calling his friend to his side with the wave of his hand. "I think from their clandestine actions, these two don't want their meeting known."

"Aye," Anthony agreed, upon spying the two men below. " 'Twould seem they are hatching up some mischief. I wonder who they are."

"The tall, skinny man is Ashby's, but I don't know the other." As the words left Richard's mouth, the man moved from the shadow. Richard frowned. The man was familiar to him, but he couldn't place where he'd seen him before.

When the two men shook hands a moment later and the workman extended a hand possessing only four fingers, Richard gasped in surprise.

"No Thumbs! What the devil?" he muttered, finally recognizing the man as one of the ringleaders of the London underworld.

"No Thumbs?" Anthony said, noticing the deformity for the first time.

"Aye. His thumbs were cut off for picking pockets when he was a child. That's how he gained his name." Richard also knew he could identify the man by the red rope scar beneath the dirty rag tied about his neck. No Thumbs had been hanged and left for dead at Tyburn. Pitying the woman weeping at his feet and believing the man dead, Richard cut him down only to find he still breathed. To this day No Thumbs's voice was only a croaking whisper.

"What is Ashby's man doing consorting with the likes of him?"

"I suspect you already know the answer to your own question, Anthony. It's as we suspected."

"Then we must tell Edward of our suspicions. It will go much easier on you if we do."

"Nay, I need more proof. Seeing two men talking in a garden is not enough evidence to convict Robert Ashby."

"Then what will you do, Richard?"

"I intend to follow No Thumbs when he leaves Windsor."

"But what of your audience with the king?"

Richard patted Anthony on the shoulder. " 'Tis the reason we have friends."

Anthony shook his blond head rapidly from side to side. "Nay, I'll not bring Edward's wrath down on my head because you won't take the time to tell him your suspicions."

"Edward will not be angry with you. Just tell him I've gone to find his thieves, and he'll be satisfied."

"I seriously doubt he'll be happy, but I'll do it anyway," Anthony said, made miserable by the prospect of facing Edward alone. The St. Claire brothers had a knack for putting him in the middle of difficult situations.

Richard clasped Anthony's hand fondly and gave him a roguish grin. "I'll repay the favor. Now I must be on my way or I'll lose No Thumbs before he makes contact with the thieves."

"Godspeed, Richard," Anthony said, and gave his friend a hug.

The cool night air wove the mist into an eerie grey shroud that rolled off the Thames to blanket London's streets. It made Richard's task of following No Thumbs nearly impossible, for he could see only a few feet in any direction. Fortunately his previous experience as a reaver again held him in good stead. He knew London's underbelly like his own hand and could follow No Thumbs blindfolded if necessary.

Moving stealthily through the damp night, the soft leather soles of his boots making little sound upon the cobbles, Rich-

ard stopped and listened intermittently for any sound to indicate the thief was aware he was being stalked.

Oddly, since leaving Windsor, No Thumbs hadn't veered
from his course. Richard smiled. The man's arrogance would
be his downfall. He was so confident his visit to Windsor
hadn't been noted, he hadn't taken the precautions necessary
for every thief who wanted to keep his neck out of the noose.

The sound of ribald laughter spilled out into the night and
a flash of light briefly turned the grey shroud into a golden
mantle as No Thumbs pulled open a heavy portal and entered
the Bear and Bull Tavern. Knowing the place well, Richard
eased from his hiding place, pulled his coarse woolen coif
over the unscarred side of his face to shadow his features,
and then followed No Thumbs into the verminous den of
London's underworld.

The Bear and Bull was the meeting room for cutthroats,
pickpockets, thieves, and assassins. It was also the perfect
place for No Thumbs to relay his information about the time
of shipment and destination of the wool pack trains. There'd
be no questions asked nor answers given. In the Bull and
Bear, anyone who wanted to keep his life didn't probe into
another man's business.

Spying No Thumbs sitting alone drinking a tankard of ale
in a shadowy corner at the rear of the tavern, Richard sank
down on a roughhewn bench to await the arrival of No
Thumbs's contact. He ordered a dram of ale and smiled at
the way the bosomy barmaid took one look at his scarred
features and quickly turned her attention to her other custom-
ers.

Richard gave a mental shrug and chuckled to himself as
he took a deep sip of the dark, foamy liquid. Every man
needed to be brought down a notch or two now and then.
Even if the woman doing it was a barmaid who had the look
of the pox about her. It kept things in perspective and prevented him from becoming arrogant.

Turning his attention back to No Thumbs, Richard frowned, squinting through the smoky blue haze that lay over the room. He knew No Thumbs had come to meet his accomplice, but no one had approached the man since he'd entered the Bull and Bear. Richard took another long sip of his ale, thoughtfully considering No Thumbs over the rim of his tankard.

Richard tensed when No Thumbs shoved back his stool and stood up. He scratched his bearded chin and then his belly before tossing the barmaid a coin for the ale. His gaze rested for a fraction of a second on a skinny, pock-faced man sitting at the table to his right before he maneuvered his heavy frame through the forest of legs and chairs to the tavern door and then slipped out into the night. A moment later the pock-faced man followed in his wake.

Richard smiled his satisfaction. No Thumbs had made his assignation without a word being spoken. The man was far smarter than Richard had assumed after all. Giving a shrug at how his own wits had dulled since he'd become Richard St. Claire, he tossed the barmaid a piece of silver for the ale and quickly followed No Thumbs and his accomplice.

Unable to see the direction the two men had traveled only a few moments before, Richard paused to listen. The quiet murmur of voices in the alleyway between the dilapidated buildings drew his attention. Moving stealthily, he hugged the wall with his back and eased toward the sound. Richard paused when the voices became distinct enough for him to overhear the thieves' conversation.

"Do ye have me instructions?"

"Aye. Yer to meet in Nottingham. Ye'll wait at the White Hare Tavern until ye hear from 'im."

"I don't like all this waiting around just to please 'im. 'Tis too risky. Me contacts in Flanders says they wants the wool now."

"Let the swine wait. They'll get it in good time," No

Thumbs growled. "I just do what I'm told, and if yer wise, ye'll do the same. If ye don't, ye might find yerself hanging from a limb of a tree some dark night, and it won't be the sheriff's men who hung ye there."

"I'll do what I'm told. Just ye make sure ye get the information to me in time to alert the rest of the men or 'im won't get his wool to sell to the lowlanders."

"Ye'll get it, ye weasely little bastard, and ye'd best make sure the wool gets to the right place. Now I've given ye the orders given to me, and it's all I have to say to ye. So get goin'."

"Fer someone who just works fer 'im like me, ye sure do like to give out yer orders. One of these days we're going to have to see just who gives and takes the orders, No Thumbs."

"Titus, ye little pitted-faced bastard, I'll look forward to that meeting. Just ye let me know when yer ready."

Listening to the two men quarrel, Richard smiled his satisfaction. Dissension among Ashby's troops could well be to his advantage. One shaky stone could make the whole castle crumble if he gave it the right push. Richard pressed himself deeper into his ebony hiding place as the two men passed. They split up when they reached the street. No Thumbs headed back to the Bear and Bull while the pock-faced man No Thumbs had called Titus turned in the opposite direction.

Every instinct Richard possessed was attuned to his fog-shrouded surrounding. With the grace of a stalking wolf he eased from his hiding place and warily followed Titus. After all these months he had finally found the man to lead him to the wool thieves and their ringleader.

Chapter 11

Megan scrambled from the bed, her insides roiling with nausea. Blanching white, she stumbled across the chamber and managed to reach the chamber pot before her stomach gave up the few bites of food she'd managed to choke down earlier.

With a trembling hand she wiped away the sweat that beaded her brow and leaned weakly against the cold stone wall. It had been the same every morning for the past week. Faith had always nursed the sick at Dragon's Lair, but Megan was beginning to question her cousin's ability to diagnose her illness. Faith had assured her there was nothing seriously wrong—her ailment was probably the result of eating something that hadn't agreed with her, perhaps tainted meat. However, no one else in the household had been affected by it.

Megan poured a goblet of water and washed out her mouth before she staggered back to the bed and collapsed facedown across it. Burying her head in her arms, she considered Faith's diagnosis. She desperately wanted to believe her cousin, but deep in her heart she knew the real reason she couldn't keep down any food in the morning. She carried Royce Mc-

Farland's child. Megan ground her teeth together and clenched her fists. Her nails bit into the palms of her hands.

No, damn it, she swore silently. He was Richard St. Claire. Royce McFarland had never existed, nor had the gentle lover whom she'd given her heart. It had all been lies.

Megan felt her insides cringe at the thought. In the past two months she'd done her best to keep so busy, she wouldn't have time to think of Richard St. Claire and his deviousness. She had nearly driven everyone at Dragon's Lair mad with her effort. She'd involved herself in even the most minor things concerning the estate as well as usurping some of Faith's duties in the kitchen and smokehouse, which didn't please her cousin. However, none of her efforts had been successful in making her forget, and now she carried a permanent reminder of him beneath her heart.

Megan gave a half laugh, a half-strangled sob. How she had bragged to Faith about how proud she would be to have Royce's child.

Megan rolled onto her back. A frown marked her brow as she stared pensively up at the dark-timbered ceiling and considered the irony of her situation. Unconsciously, she laid a protective hand over the small mound of her abdomen. She'd fallen in love with the man England's monarch had chosen to husband her and had already conceived his child. Yet she could never marry him after what he'd told her at Ashby Keep. He wanted no part of the mistress of Dragon's Lair and had been willing to agree to anything Edward commanded in an effort to persuade the king to change his mind about their marriage.

At the thought, Megan again felt her stomach churn. A look of misery flickered across her face and she bolted upright. Clamping a hand over her mouth, she scrambled from the bed and dashed toward the chamber pot. All color drained from her face as she doubled over and gagged. A shudder shook her and her nostrils flared as she drew in a steadying breath. The muscles in her legs trembled as she turned and stumbled across the chamber to the small stool in front of the fireplace. Weakly she sank down upon it.

"I have to get control of myself," she muttered resolutely. It did no good to rehash everything that had transpired between herself and Richard St. Claire. She'd made a fool of herself by giving so freely of her love, but it would never happen again. The lesson she'd learned from Richard St. Claire had been a hard one, but she had learned it well. In the future she'd be wary of all men.

Megan hugged her arms about her small waist. Her morose expression reflected her feelings as she stared into the grey ashes in the fire pit. Her experience with Mallory should have prepared her to face the reality of life, yet until she met Richard St. Claire, she hadn't lumped all men into the same pile with her cruel brother. Sandy was the only exception, in her view. His loyalty had never wavered and he'd done his best to protect her from harm even at the expense of his own safety. But for the rest of the male population, she wasn't at all certain they didn't belong in Mallory's maggot heap. For all she knew, they could all be just as cruel and selfish as Mallory and Richard. They certainly hadn't cared for anything beyond their own gratification and had given no thought to her feelings.

Ruefully, Megan realized how innocent she'd been where men were concerned. Even after suffering Mallory's abuse, she'd kept her dream alive. Her naïveté had made her like an autumn apple waiting to fall when the right warm breeze came along to stir it from its innocent haven. Then it fell hard.

She'd thought herself so mature, the responsibilities of Dragon's Lair convincing her she could handle any situation. However, she'd not been prepared to deal with the blossoming of her own sensuality nor the strong call of her lonely heart. She had been a child playing at a woman's game until

Richard St. Claire's duplicity opened her eyes and made her grow up. And after her experience with him, she'd never allow herself to be vulnerable again.

Megan lifted her bowed head and jutted her chin out at a pugnacious angle. Her eyes flashed with blue fire as she resolutely repeated the vow she'd made on the day she'd received the king's edict for her to marry. "Never will I allow myself to be used by any man again."

"Did you say something, Megan?" Faith asked, quietly closing the door behind her. She'd knocked but, receiving no answer, had grown concerned since Megan hadn't felt well the past days. She had peeked into the chamber to assure herself her cousin was all right before going about her own business.

Drawn from her reveries by her cousin's entrance, Megan turned and smiled up at Faith as she gracefully crossed the chamber. "Nay, Faith. 'Twas nothing of importance."

"Meggie, I'm worried about you. Of late if you're not working yourself to death in the kitchen or gardens, you spend all of your time locked away up here."

"I haven't felt well," Megan said, lowering her gaze to the hands she had clasped tightly in her lap. She wondered how she would be able to break the news of her pregnancy to Faith. Her cousin hadn't taken the news of Royce McFarland's true identity well. She'd been anxious and upset for days after Megan's return to Dragon's Lair.

"I know you've not felt well, but 'tis not like you to keep to yourself so much."

"I've had much on my mind of late," Megan answered, shifting uneasily on the stool.

Sensing her cousin's disquiet, Faith asked, "What is wrong, Meggie? Have you had word from the king about your marriage to Richard St. Claire?"

"Nay. I wish it was that simple," Megan said, looking

directly at her cousin for the first time, their blue eyes locking. "You see, Faith, my trouble lies within me alone."

Faith frowned down at Megan. "I don't have the slightest idea of what you're talking about. Your riddles don't explain why you've been acting so odd."

"Faith," Megan said, and gave her innocent cousin a reassuring smile. "I'm going to have Richard St. Claire's baby."

Faith blanched and abruptly sat down in a nearby chair. Great tears of sympathy brimmed in her pale blue eyes as she sadly shook her head. "Oh, Meggie, I'm so sorry."

"There's no need to be sorry. I will love my child, no matter who sired him. He's not responsible for my error in judgment, nor his father's devious nature."

"Will you send word to Sir Richard of his impending fatherhood?" Faith asked, fidgeting nervously with the fabric of her gown as she struggled to keep her own horror-filled memories at bay.

Megan rapidly shook her head. "Nay, this child belongs to me—alone."

"But Sir Richard is the man King Edward has chosen for you to wed, and it is only right he should recognize his own child. It is his heir," Faith argued, her voice strained. Megan's news had resurrected the demons of her own tormented past, and the memories flashed hauntingly through her mind.

" 'Twas his seed that created my babe, but he doesn't deserve the right to call himself its sire. His lies have made him unworthy to hold the title. If I have my way, my child will never know his sire was such a dishonorable man," Megan said, firmly and successfully ignoring her own duplicity.

"What will you do if Sir Richard comes here to fulfill the marriage contract after all? I know you believe Edward will agree to let him out of the marriage, but what if you're wrong? He may still be your husband whether you say yea or nay, and you can't live in your horrible disguise forever. Sooner or later he'll know the truth about you and the child you're carrying. It is one thing you can't keep hidden for very long.'' Faith's voice trembled slightly.

"Should that happen, I don't know what I'll do,'' Megan answered honestly. Coming to her feet, she turned her back to Faith and stared at the distant wall without seeing its cold grey stone. Her voice reflected all her inner turmoil when she said, "And I pray I'll never have to find out. After the way he used me, the very thought of being shackled by marriage to a man like Richard St. Claire sickens me to my soul. He's just like Mallory. He thinks of no one but himself, and I'd rather die than suffer a fate such as that again.''

Understanding Megan's plight far more than her cousin realized, Faith's heart went out to her. She came to her feet and crossed the short space to where Megan stood with her head bowed. Hugging her close, blond head resting against ebony, she sympathized, "Oh, my dear Meggie, I didn't ever want you to know such pain. I would have spared you of it had it been in my power.''

Absorbed in her own troubles, Megan failed to hear the pain in Faith's voice. Nor was she aware of the memories assaulting her cousin or the faraway look entering Faith's eyes as she drew away. "I know you would, but nothing could have saved me from my own foolish heart.''

"Nay, I could have warned you. 'Tis my fault you now suffer. I should have told you what men are like,'' Faith said as her thoughts turned to the babe she had lost because of Mallory's cruelty. As long as she lived she'd never forget the blood and the pain. After he'd learned she carried his child, he had viciously turned on her like a rabid animal. She had tried to flee but had not succeeded. He'd caught her at the top of the stairs, and with an unholy smile spreading his lips, he'd thrown her down them. Mallory had saved himself the problem of seeing his bastard running around Dragon's Lair.

Incredulous, Megan gaped at her cousin, unable to understand why Faith held herself responsible for her folly. "You can't blame yourself for my ignorance, cousin. 'Tis not right to condemn yourself when you're as innocent of the ways of men as I once was."

"You're wrong, Meggie," Faith said, turning on Megan with hands balled into fists at her side and a wild light gleaming in her eyes. "I know from experience exactly what all men are like. I've known for years they're all selfish, cruel beasts who can give nothing to a woman but pain." The tight rein Faith had kept upon her horrid secret slipped a degree with each word that passed her lips.

Completely bemused by Faith's outburst, Megan stared at her cousin. Faith, to her knowledge, had never been involved with any man. At age sixteen, she'd turned away from men as if she'd contract the plague if she gave them a kind word.

Seeing the question in Megan's eyes, Faith dug her fingers into her golden hair, all her self-control vanishing like the mist upon a spring morn. She shook her head rapidly from side to side and a moan of despair escaped her as she sank back into the chair and rocked to and fro. Tears of remorse slid unheeded down her ashen cheeks as she raised haunted eyes to Megan.

"Please forgive me, Meggie. I didn't ever want you to go through what I endured. It was wrong not to tell you what they were like, but I didn't want my feelings to turn you against men before you had a chance to find love. I had hoped someday you'd be lucky enough to have the husband and family I've always dreamed of. I wanted you to have what I could not." Faith convulsed as if she had been struck by a large fist in her stomach and she pressed her hand over her trembling lips to stifle a strangled sob.

"Faith, I don't understand. You will have a husband and family someday. Are you forgetting about Sir Godfrey?" Megan said in an effort to soothe her frenzied cousin.

"Nay, I've forgotten nothing. I'll never have a family of my own," Faith said through clenched teeth. "I lost my chance the night Mallory raped me."

"My God," Megan breathed, and then fell silent, struck dumb by the revelation. She stared down at Faith's bowed head. Her cousin's words kept screaming through her brain, torturing her with the knowledge of the terrible secret Faith had carried for so many years. Her own troubles shrank as she realized Faith's agony.

"Oh, Faith. By all that's holy, what you have endured" was Megan's tortured cry as she sank down on her knees in front of her cousin and embraced the still, unyielding body. Her own tears ran freely down her cheeks as she hugged her cousin close and wept.

Guiltily she felt a sense of relief when she reflected upon her own experience with Richard St. Claire. It could not compare to what Faith had suffered at Mallory's hand. Unlike Richard, Mallory hadn't given her cousin a choice. She'd not been allowed to experience the sweetness of knowing the height of her femininity or the wonder of lying sated in a gentle lover's arms.

Sadistically cruel as was his wont, Mallory had taken Faith's virginity by force, using her to satisfy his animalistic lust and debasing her by making her realize she was his chattel and had no recourse but to submit to him. He ruled Dragon's Lair and had the power to cast her out at any time if she didn't please him.

Megan squeezed her eyes closed and her face screwed up as a wave of suspicion roiled into her mind like a black, ominous cloud. She knew her cousin well. Faith would not meekly submit to Mallory without him forcing her to his will by using threats against someone she loved. Megan drew in a shuddering breath. Though Faith had not admitted anything, Megan suspected her cousin had protected her from far more than just the knowledge of men's cruelty. By submitting, she had kept Mallory from using his own sister as a vessel in which to spill his lust.

By all that's holy! Megan swore silently. If you were not already dead and in hell, Mallory, I would kill you myself. Aloud she said, "Faith, can you ever forgive me for not realizing what you were enduring?"

Faith drew in a shuddering breath. She sat back and wiped at her eyes as she fought to regain her composure. Her chin quivered as she gave Megan a wobbly, sad little smile. "Meggie, there is nothing to forgive. You were only fourteen years old when Mallory raped me. Even if you had known, you could have done nothing to stop him from using me as he wished. He was the master of Dragon's Lair and I was merely a woman, and in my position without a protector or inheritance, I was little more than a serf. In the eyes of the church and law, I could be treated in a similar manner as the serf who toils in your fields. They can't defend their honor against their overlord, no more than I."

Megan came to her feet and began to pace the room to vent her frustration. Faith was right. A man had the power to do what he willed, and no one could say him nay. He could beat his wife to death, and if he could prove he was in the right to take such action, he might pay only a minimum fine and then be free to go about his business.

" 'Tis unfair Mallory is dead. He died without paying for his crimes. I would like to skewer him like the vermin he was," Megan grumbled.

"Meggie, 'tis over. Mallory can never hurt me again. We must put it from our minds or go mad," Faith said, once more in control of her emotions. She wouldn't allow herself to think of the child Megan now carried. It reminded her too much of her own lost babe.

"You can say we must put it from our thoughts, but it's always there to haunt you. That's the reason you didn't encourage Sir Godfrey's suit, isn't it? Mallory is dead, but you're not free of him. His memory is still here to taint our lives.

"You're wrong, Meggie. Mallory is in the past and I'm happy with my life as it is now," Faith said, lowering her lashes to hide her feelings from her perceptive cousin.

"We both know you are lying to yourself," Megan snapped. "You forget I was at your side when we used to wish upon falling stars for handsome knights to come and sweep us off our feet and carry us away to their fairy-tale castles."

Faith shifted uneasily, keeping her eyes glued to her tightly clasped hands. "We were only children when we wished those things, Meggie. It was a long time ago and we have changed from those gangly-limbed girls. We are now grown women."

"Aye, we are women, not girls, but our dreams have not changed. They've only been altered by a course of events beyond our control."

"You can still have your dream, Meggie. Sir Richard will marry you if you will only tell him of his child."

Megan shook her head. "That was not my dream nor yours. If you will remember, we wanted our knights in shining armor to marry us for love and not out of duty."

"Aye, but you have the child to think about now, Meggie. Life is not a dream and we must accept things as they are and try to make the best of it."

Megan stamped her foot. "Damn it, Faith. I don't want to make the best out of a bad situation. And I won't accept things as they are, and neither should you."

"I have no other choice. Mallory assured it."

"You *do* have choices. Don't accept what life dishes out to you. Don't let Mallory defeat you even in death. You still have life, and as long as you have breath, there is always hope," Megan said. Sinking down on her knees in front of her cousin, she grabbed Faith by the arms and shook her.

"You have to believe you are worthy of life before you can face it. If you want Sir Godfrey, then go after him."

Faith shook her head. "Sir Godfrey would not want Mallory's leavings. No man would."

"Then he is not worthy of you, Faith. You are a wonderful, loving woman who any man should be proud to claim as his wife and the mother of his children."

The blood slowly drained from Faith's face and she swallowed back the sudden lump of agony rising in her throat. How could she explain to Megan no man would ever want her because she could never give him children? The midwife had told her after she lost her child that she'd been torn inside and it was doubtful if she could ever conceive again.

Drawing in a deep, steadying breath and with a supreme effort, Faith smiled at Megan. "I'll remember everything you've said."

"I love you, Faith. You're like a sister to me and I would see you happy in spite of your beliefs," Megan said, hugging her cousin before sitting back on her heels. She had given Faith sound advice and prayed her cousin would consider it. Now if only she could advise herself on her own problems and find a way to solve them. However, from her vantage point, there didn't look to be a way out of her present situation for at least seven months. A rueful little smile touched Megan's lips and she released a long, resigned breath.

"I love you, Meggie. I know it matters little, but remember I'll always be here for you. I wish I could be of more help," Faith said, noting the way Megan unconsciously rested her hand on her slightly rounding abdomen.

"I've always known that, Faith. You've stood with me through all the bad times and I love you for it. But I'm afraid in this no one can help me. Nature takes its course, and nothing can stop it. All I can do now is to pray Richard never learns I carry his child."

Megan drew in a deep, fortifying breath and resolutely

shook off her melancholy mood. She smiled up at her cousin. "Enough of this gloom. There is no use worrying about something that may never come to pass. Now, what was the real reason you came up here to see me?"

Faith smiled, falling easily into the game. In the past years she'd become an expert at pretending all was well at Dragon's Lair and no dark cloud loomed on the horizon of their futures. "I came up to see how you were feeling and to tell you the gossip I overheard in the kitchen this morning."

" 'Tis unlike you to listen to the servants' gossip, Faith," Megan chided, giving her cousin a wry grin.

"I don't usually listen to their chatter," Faith answered haughtily, and raised her chin at an imperious angle, letting her cousin know the taunt didn't affect her. "And I only did it this time because I thought you'd find it amusing."

Megan arched a curious brow and nodded for Faith to proceed with her tale.

Without any hesitation and ignoring the twinkle in Megan's eyes, Faith eagerly repeated what she'd heard in the kitchen. After retelling the misadventures of several villagers, one of whom had gotten his oxen and himself mired so deeply in mud, it took his entire family to pull him out, she concluded with "Mary said the villagers believe Robin Hood and his band of thieves are still alive and living in Sherwood Forest."

"That's impossible," Megan said, wondering at the incredulous story being bandied around about the legendary thief who had gained his reputation by robbing the rich to give to the poor. "Even if he did exist and had managed after all these years to escape the hangman's noose, he'd be too old to mount a horse, much less waylay travelers for their gold. The legend says he was an adherent to Thomas of Lancaster and lived in Edward Second's reign, not Edward Third's."

"I remember the tales your father told us as well, but don't you see the point?'' Faith asked, her eyes dancing with glee. ''The villagers are talking about you and Sandy. It wasn't until you took to the roads that the tales began to spread about Robin Hood's return.''

''Surely you jest. They couldn't believe we are Robin Hood. We haven't robbed the rich to give to the poor. The gold went into our own coffers to support Dragon's Lair.''

''Nay, I do not jest. This isn't the first time I've heard Mary mention Robin Hood. And you didn't have to give to the poor to bring the old legend back to life. The people want to believe in Robin Hood even if they haven't received any benefit from it except an exciting story.''

Her gloomy mood returning, Megan shook her head, bewildered that her exploits were a topic of conversation. Had she heard the tales about Robin Hood's return before she knew the truth about Richard, she would have found it amusing. Now it was only a sad reminder of the happiest moments in her life—a time that would never come again.

''Megan, I thought Mary's tales would lighten your mood instead of making you sad,'' Faith said, sobering at Megan's expression.

''I'm sorry. It is amusing to know I'm now Robin Hood,'' Megan said. The smile she forced to her lips didn't reach her eyes as she looked at Faith and sadly shook her head. ''We are a pair, aren't we? Here we sit discussing servants' gossip when our worlds have been shattered.''

''I've found 'tis better than crying,'' Faith said, giving Megan a reassuring smile.

Megan gazed at her cousin in wonder. In all the years they had lived under the same roof, she'd always considered herself the stronger of the two. Now she realized she had misconstrued her cousin's gentleness for weakness when, in truth, Faith possessed a quiet strength far stronger than her own. She knew it took more courage to suffer in silence and choose to sacrifice your own future to save those you loved.

Megan's eyes misted with tears. She prayed that in time she, too, would gain the courage to accept what life had dealt her. Megan knew her cousin still hurt, yet she didn't cry and rage to the world. She held her head high and bore it with quiet dignity. In essence, Faith was the true lady of Dragon's Lair, and Megan knew she owed her more than she could ever repay if she lived a hundred years.

Chapter 12

A jester danced by, wearing striped hose of red and green, a tunic with dark green upper sleeves and orange forearms, and a multicolored pointed cap. The small bells on the tips of his red, pointy-toed boots jingled merrily and mingled with the sound of the larger bells he carried above his head on a long pole. Spying the tall, one-eyed man who stood with arms folded across his broad chest, he gave an extravagant bow, sweeping the hard-packed earth with the tip of his cap before dancing off down the crowded thoroughfare, where giggling children and yapping dogs followed in his wake.

Several gaily dressed youths, inebriated from their day-long sojourn in the striped ale tent, staggered outside. Upon hearing the jester's tinkling bells, they set off in the same direction. With arms looped over each other's shoulders and grinning from ear to ear like simpletons, they bellowed a bawdy song at the tops of their lungs. Their raucous croaking soon drowned out the merry sound of the jester's tin bells.

From his vantage point in the shade of the cloth vender's stall, Richard smiled and shook his head, recalling his own youthful misadventures. It was all a part of Fair Day as well as growing up. Young men wanted to prove their masculinity to their companions by too much wenching, too much drinking, too much gambling, and too much fighting. Nothing ever changed. He'd done the same thing and had had more headaches from his wild adventures than he cared to remember. The same held true for the women he'd bedded in his youth. There had been too many faces and too many bodies for him to recall any one in particular.

Richard paused, thoughtfully considering those days gone by. He couldn't remember the women from his days as a wild, eager young man, and he wished the same held true today. He wanted to forget the one he'd sought but failed to find.

Annoyed with himself for letting his thoughts drift once more to Meggie, Richard shifted position. He had to forget her, to put her completely from his mind. He had to realize she was out of his life for good, and he needed to concentrate on finding the wool thieves for Edward. Once the deed was done, he could put the past months behind him. He could take himself back to his family at Raven's Keep and go about setting his life back to rights.

Forcing his mind away from the sudden feeling of desolation filling his chest, he turned his attention back to the daub and wattle building which housed the White Hare Tavern across the way. Built on the outskirts of Nottingham, it was home to those who lived outside of society. Like the Bear and Bull Tavern of London's waterfront, at any given time of day or night, there could be found within its walls the dregs of humanity, the scavengers of man—those who preyed upon others for their own survival. From his own experience he knew there was many a good thief who wouldn't soil his reputation by associating with those who patronized the White Hare.

Casting a surreptitious glance along the crowded lane, Richard ambled toward the White Hare, where he knew he'd find Titus ensconced at the makeshift table in the rear corner of the tavern. Every day for the past week Richard had followed the thief to the White Hare, where he ordered several tankards of ale and then departed without speaking to anyone except the barmaid who served him.

To his exasperation, Richard had gleaned nothing for his efforts and was beginning to believe his expectations of putting a quick end to his mission for Edward had been far too high. From the way things were turning out, it looked as if he'd become a permanent fixture at the White Hare before Titus met with the men he'd come to Nottingham to see.

Glimpsing a familiar face before it blended into the throngs crowding the street, Richard hesitated. A frown knit his brow over the bridge of his narrow nose as he surveyed the stalls where spices, jewelry, meat, vegetables, velvet, and lace, as well as a sundry other items, were offered for sale by the farmers and merchants who hawked their wares, claiming to have the cheapest and the best goods anyone could wish to buy.

The glimpse of Sandy McTavis's face instantly made Richard forget the man in the tavern. He turned and began to push his way through the mass of people. His heart beat rapidly within his chest from the prospect of at last finding a clue that might lead him to Meggie. He scanned each face he passed, yet when he reached the stall where he'd seen Sandy, the man had completely vanished.

Releasing a long breath of disgust and feeling a great fool as his hopes of finding Meggie again faded, Richard stood searching the crowd for any sign of McTavis. A dull ache engulfed his chest, and his shoulders sagged, as he turned once more toward the White Hare Tavern. His desire to find Meggie was beginning to make him see things that did not exist beyond his imagination. He had only deluded himself into seeing McTavis's face in the crowd.

Unable to give up hope completely, Richard paused at the door of the White Hare and cast one last glance in the direction he'd just come. In that moment the crowd parted enough for him to see Sandy talking to the herb vender. McTavis lifted an open vial, sniffed it, and then made a moue of disgust as he nodded and dug a coin from his pocket and handed it to the vender. Restoppering the vial, Sandy tucked it away in a leather pouch he carried slung over one wide shoulder. He made his way toward the end of the street, where an ingenious soul had improvised a stable of sorts from thick hemp for those fairgoers who, for a pence, could hire a boy to assure their horses would be secure while they enjoyed themselves.

Richard followed close upon Sandy's heels yet kept enough distance between them so as not to reveal his presence. Only when McTavis had mounted and headed south on the road to London did Richard let him out of his sight long enough to rush back to where his own mount was tethered behind the cloth vender's stall. Breathing heavily, Richard leaped into the saddle, and heedless to the curses and shrieks of fright he roused as he passed, he galloped at full speed in the direction McTavis had traveled only a short while before.

Richard didn't slow his pace until he rounded a bend in the road and saw McTavis's horse ambling along, its rider seemingly unaware of any pursuit.

Richard relaxed and settled himself comfortably in the saddle. Eyeing the distant rider, he felt his spirits lift.

"Soon we'll meet again, my dear Meggie," he murmured to himself, and smiled with satisfaction. After he found the beautiful reaver and assured himself she was all right, there was going to be hell to pay for all the worry she'd caused him by disappearing without a word of explanation. Ignoring the fact that his own duplicity was behind her disappearance and thinking only of his own feelings during the exasperating months he'd spent searching for her, Richard contemplated his sweet revenge. His body responded to the images his mind created and he shifted in the saddle to ease his discomfort.

Twilight had darkened the shadows to ebony when Sandy veered from the main thoroughfare and onto a narrow track leading through the dense forest bordering each side of the road. Cautious and alert, Richard drew his horse to a halt. Using only the pressure of his knees, Richard nudged his horse off the road and into the dark woods before reining him once more. Poised and wary, he sat for a long moment listening intently. When he heard the soft, steady drum of hooves in the distance, he breathed a sigh of relief. McTavis was still unaware that he was being followed, and his mount's increased gate meant he was anxious to reach his destination.

Instinctively sensing he was near the end of his quest, Richard flicked the reins, urging his horse forward. Soon he'd be able to solve the mystery of Meggie's whereabouts.

A short while later, Richard sat bewildered below Dragon's Lair's granite walls. He folded his arms over the saddle pommel and stared up at the keep, unable to fathom McTavis's reason for coming back to the place he'd previously robbed.

Perplexed by the ease with which the reaver had entered Dragon's Lair, especially so late in the evening, Richard scratched his head. As bold as you please, the man had ridden through the gates with no questions asked from the guards stationed above the portcullis.

Recalling the chiding he'd taken from McTavis about his own hasty departure from Dragon's Lair, Richard's frown deepened. The reaver had bragged he'd come away with full pockets at the expense of those who resided within the granite keep. Now he rode into that very same keep as if he belonged there.

Suspicion clamped angry, jagged-toothed jaws down on his insides. Something wasn't right. No thief, no matter how brave or foolish, would intentionally put his neck in a noose by returning to the scene of a crime.

The mystery mounting, Richard eyed the granite walls through narrowed lids. Before he left Dragon's Lair, he would know exactly who and what Sandy McTavis was.

Swinging himself agilely from the saddle, Richard reached into the leather roll behind the cantle to retrieve his cloak. Glancing up at the clear night sky, he turned and strode to a large, gnarl-limbed oak. The weather was fair, and the leathery-leaved tree would provide enough shelter for the night.

He stretched out upon the mossy ground and shifted onto his side to make himself more comfortable. Pulling the mantle about him to ward off the night's chill, he made a pillow from one folded arm and relaxed, but sleep did not come. His gaze kept wandering back to the granite-walled keep, and his thoughts turned to the following morning.

Richard's sensuous lips curved into a cunning smile. When the sun crept over the horizon, he'd be waiting at the gates of Dragon's Lair, once more disguised as the minstrel begging for a morsel of food. After he gained entry to the Dragon Lady's lair, he'd learn why McTavis acted as if the keep was his home.

Slowly Richard's thick lashes drifted downward and he slept. His dreams were filled with visions of Meggie with her raven hair and laughing blue eyes. Needing to feel her warmth against him, he reached out to draw her into his arms, but the woman who filled his embrace was not his beautiful reaver but the rotten-toothed hag from Dragon's Lair. Her high-pitched giggle sounded like a screech of an owl and raised the hair on the nape of his neck as she brought up a dirty-nailed hand to caress his scarred cheek.

"No!" he cried, jerking away from her hand in disgust.

Richard bolted upright. Sweat ran in rivulets down his face, and the hand he raised to wipe it away trembled from the horror of his vivid dream. His heart pounded against his ribs, and his gaze darted about like a frightened mouse, seeking through the grey light of dawn the ugly specter who terrorized his dreams.

Annoyed with himself when he realized he was alone in the still glade, he muttered, "Get hold of yourself, you fool. Quit acting the child. 'Twas only a dream."

Richard drew in a long, shaky breath and tossed away the mantle tangled about his legs. Pushing himself to his feet, he stared up at Dragon's Lair. The hag of his dreams resided within its granite walls, waiting like a vulture for the man Edward had chosen to sacrifice to her. Richard shivered with revulsion. He loved his home and country, yet he would never marry the Dragon Lady, no matter what happened in the future.

The rumble beneath his ribs reminded Richard he'd not eaten in nearly a day. Pulling up the peasant's coif and tying it securely beneath his chin, he set out in the direction of the castle gate. Even from the distance, he could hear the first stirring from within. The servants were already at work to provide their ugly mistress with her morning meal.

"Well, O'll be," Mary said with a smile of recognition spreading her full-lipped mouth when she spied the tall man standing in the shadows near the entrance to the kitchen. Cocking her head saucily to the side, she braced her hands on her wide hips and eyed Richard with interest. "If it ain't the minstrel back again. 'Tis far too early in the day for ye to be of any use here."

One side of Richard's sensuous mouth quirked up in a roguish grin as he boldly slid his gaze over the serving maid, exploring her charms from the top of her tousled head to the tip of the worn work boots peeking from beneath the hem of her coarse woolen gown. Remaining in the shadows, he casually braced a shoulder against the doorframe and folded his arms over his chest. "Aye, 'tis I, sweet Mary. Would ye be generous enough to give me a few bites to ease me hungry stomach? 'Tis about to eat me ribs.''

Flustered by his look, her rosy cheeks deepening in color, Mary glanced nervously about and shook her head. Her voice was filled with regret when she finally answered. ''Nay, 'tis not me place to give to beggars. Only Lady Megan or Lady Faith can do that.''

''Ah, be a good girl, Mary. I'm near famished, I am. I'll sing ye another song for only a wee piece of bread and a bite of meat to stop me belly from growling like a wolf on the prowl.''

Mary glanced once more toward the kitchen table laden with fresh loaves of bread. ''I cannot. The cook would see me whipped should I disobey the rules. But if ye can wait till me lady awakes, I'll ask her if I can give to ye.''

Richard shrugged, not wanting to get the serving girl into trouble with the Dragon Lady. ''I guess I'll have to await your lady's awakening. I just pray she isn't like many noble ladies, who lie abed all day. I might starve to death if so.''

''Nay,'' Mary said, rapidly shaking her head. ''Me lady has always been an early riser.'' She hesitated uncertainly, a frown of worry creasing her smooth young brow. ''That is, until recently. Now things have changed. She's not herself of late.''

Curiosity pricked Richard and he arched a brow. ''How so, sweet Mary?''

Again Mary glanced uncertainly toward the servants busily preparing the large household's morning meal. She had been dying to tell someone of her suspicions but had been afraid to say anything to anyone at Dragon's Lair out of fear of being sent back into the fields. '' 'Tis not me place to say. I could lose me position here if anyone heard me talking about things that's none of me affair.''

''Pretty Mary,'' Richard cajoled. ''Never let it be said I have ever revealed anything told to me. 'Tis ungallant to use a lady's trust in such a way, so say what you will and it will remain with me until my dying breath.''

Unable to resist her need to gossip even to this stranger, Mary leaned forward and said in a loud whisper, " 'Tis the way me lady's been behaving.''

" 'Tis nothing unusual with lords and ladies. They're not like the rest of us,'' Richard said, recalling the way the Dragon Lady had simpered and giggled. He didn't know what Mary's mistress could further do to make the maid think her behavior odd. Perhaps she'd begun to act normal instead of like a simpleton, Richard thought cruelly.

"Nay, 'tis more than that. I fear me lady is—'' Mary paused and glanced once more around the kitchen to make sure no one could overhear her conversation.

"What do you fear, Mary?'' Richard asked, wondering at the girl's stricken expression.

"Me lady—ah—I do love her and she's been so ill and I've been so worried but too afraid to say anything to anyone.''

Richard frowned. "Your lady has been ill?''

"Aye, every morning of late, and she keeps to her chamber when she's not working herself into the ground.''

"Do you know why your lady has been ill?''

Mary nodded and lowered her eyes as she divulged the secret she'd been carrying for well over a week. "I fear me lady is with child.''

Richard stiffened at the unexpected flash of anger that shot through him. It singed every nerve. The bitch! he swore silently. Edward had not only chosen him an ugly hag to wed but a rutting whore who had hoped to pawn off her by-blow when they were wed. Had Richard accepted Edward's edict without question, he would now be expecting some swine's bastard as his heir.

Realizing his narrow escape from the hag and seeing a silver lining behind the dark cloud that had shadowed his horizon for so many months, Richard drew in a deep breath.

Trying to sound normal, he asked, "Are you positive she is with child?"

Mary nodded sadly. "I fear 'tis so. 'Tis the only ailment I know that won't let ye keep down yer morning meal."

His anger passing and his spirits soaring with his sudden feeling of freedom, Richard grinned down at Mary. " 'Tis not your worry, sweet Mary. 'Tis the lady's and her lover's. They will work things out between them in time."

"But me lady doesn't have a lover," Mary blurted out.

Richard shook his head and stifled the urge to burst out laughing at the girl's shocked expression. "Surely you're not so innocent? Your lady can't be with child without a lover."

Mary's young face screwed up thoughtfully as she concluded that she had been wrong in her assumption. She brightened. "Nay, I know how women get with child, and I also know me lady has never taken a lover."

Poor, ignorant child, Richard mused as he looked down into Mary's wide-eyed face. The girl might think she knew everything that went on at Dragon's Lair, yet she wouldn't know when her mistress crept out to bed one of the stable-boys or men-at-arms.

"Mary," a soft, well-cultured feminine voice called from the passageway leading to the main hall of the keep. "Would you ask Sandy if he found the herbs I asked him to buy for me?"

"Aye, me lady. I'll look fer him immediately," Mary said, silently praying Lady Faith wouldn't scold her too soundly for taking time off from her duties to talk with the handsome minstrel.

Richard pressed farther into the shadows to conceal his presence as Faith emerged from the passageway. She didn't glance in his direction as she glided past Mary and began giving orders to the cook. He couldn't stop himself from admiring Faith's grace and beauty as she moved about the smoky chamber to oversee the daily preparations of food.

Nor could he stop himself from wondering what McTavis was doing buying herbs for the lady when he had stolen from her and her guests only a few months ago.

"I have to go and find Mr. McTavis for Lady Faith," Mary whispered, easing from the chamber without notice. "When I come back, I'll ask if I can give ye a few bites of food."

"Mary," Richard asked, taking the serving maid by the arm and drawing her into the shadows with him. "Who is Sandy?"

"Mr—Mc—Tavis—" Mary said, her tongue stumbling over the words. The close proximity of his hard, lean frame next to hers was making Mary giddy. She leaned into him, molding her body to his as she breathlessly answered. "He's—the bai—liff here."

Without realizing it, Richard tensed his fingers about Mary's arms, making her wince with pain.

"Ouch, ye don't have to be so rough. I answered yer questions," Mary whined.

"I'm sorry, sweet Mary," Richard said, setting her away from him. "You'd better go about your duties before your mistress sees you tarrying here with me."

Mary rubbed at her arm as she eyed Richard, thrusting out her lower lip. "I thought ye liked me."

"I do, Mary, but I don't want to see you get into trouble. Be a good girl and go about your duties now, and when you return, I'll sing a song just for you."

Only slightly appeased, Mary nodded and then pushed open the heavy iron-bound door leading out into the bailey. The sunlight made her tousled hair sparkle with highlights as she flashed Richard a timid smile and then was gone.

Richard breathed a sigh of relief. Mary was a sweet girl, but he was glad to be rid of her. He could now turn his attention to solving the riddle of Sandy McTavis. However, Richard had no time to decide his next move before Sandy entered the kitchen from the hall in the company of a rotund, balding man dressed in a monk's robe. Richard sank farther into the shadows of the passageway to watch and listen, hopefully putting an end to the mystery of the reaver-turned-bailiff.

"Sandy, I had just sent Mary to find you," Faith said as she turned to greet the two men. "Did you buy the herbs I need?"

"I was bringing 'em to ye when Mary found me with Father Rupert at the well. He's come to bless the new babe born to the crofter Williams," Sandy said, handing the vial he'd purchased in Nottingham to Faith.

"It's good of you to come so far, Father," Faith said, turning her attention to the monk as she secreted the vial away in the fichet of her gown. "Will you stay to break the fast with us?"

"Aye, my lady," Father Rupert answered, his face lighting up with joy. He'd hoped to be invited to partake of Dragon's Lair's hospitality. It was the reason he'd veered from the shortest route to the crofter's cottage. Dragon's Lair wasn't a rich estate, yet he always could expect to be served their best upon his visits.

"I am honored by your kindness," Father Rupert continued absently as his gaze feasted upon the loaves of freshly baked bread. He inhaled the sweet fragrance of the crusty brown loaves and his mouth watered. His stomach rumbled at being denied the feast his eyes enjoyed.

"Father, you know you are always welcome at Dragon's Lair," Faith said, watching the rotund priest eye the food. Her lips twitched suspiciously and her eyes glowed with mirth, yet she managed to keep a straight face. Everyone at Dragon's Lair knew the man's appetite matched his girth in size.

"Aye, now I am, but there was a time when Lady Wakefield's brother would not have any of the clergy on his land."

"Fortunately for the people of Dragon's Lair, that time has passed," Faith said, her voice reflecting her conviction.

Father Rupert nodded solemnly, though silently he thanked God for Mallory O'Roarke's demise. Immediately after the risqué thought, his round, bulbous-eyed, double-chinned face flushed with guilt and he quickly made the sign of the cross and asked forgiveness from the Holy Father for his transgression. Even as he sent the prayer forward, he suspected God didn't hold it against him for his feelings against someone as evil as Mallory O'Roarke.

"And how is the fair lady Megan?" Father Rupert asked as he stepped over the bench and settled his large frame down at the kitchen table. " 'Tis been some time since I've had the pleasure of seeing her." The monk reached for a piece of warm bread and began to spread it with a large dollop of fresh-churned butter.

Faith glanced uneasily at Sandy. "My cousin has been ill recently, but I'm sure she'll visit you soon with the tithes for the church."

Biting into the crusty brown bread, Father Rupert nodded. At the present moment he was far more concerned with filling his belly than with filling his tithe boxes. Savoring the succulent taste, he rolled his eyes toward the soot-blackened ceiling and momentarily felt as though he'd already died and gone to heaven.

"If you'll excuse me, Father, I'll see to my duties," Faith said. "Please enjoy your meal."

Father Rupert nodded as he lifted the tankard of warm milk a serving maid had set before him and raised it to his lips. He gulped down the entire contents without taking a breath.

Seeing the priest well served, Faith gathered the tray she'd ordered the cook to prepare for Megan and hurried from the kitchen. Hopefully the food, along with the herbs Sandy had bought, would help ease her cousin's morning sickness.

From his vantage point in the shadows, Richard watched Faith retreat down the passageway toward the main hall. Her expression when asked about her cousin reminded him of Mary's suspicions. Deciding to ascertain if the fair lady Megan, as the priest had called the Dragon Lady, was carrying another man's child, he cast one quick glance at the assembly about the huge fireplace and worktables to make certain his passage went unnoticed and then set off in Faith's wake. He treaded quietly down the passageway and slipped up the stairs toward the sleeping chambers. The soft murmur of voices drew him in the direction of Megan's bedchamber.

Bracing his back against the cool stone wall, he edged along until he was near the doorway. The door to the chamber had been left open upon Faith's arrival, and he could easily hear the two women conversing.

Richard frowned as he listened to the sweet, feminine voices. Again he experienced the same feeling he'd had when he'd seen Sandy go through the gates unhindered. There was something not quite right about the cultured voices.

Suddenly Richard's eyes widened with realization. There was something wrong about the way at least one of the women in the room spoke. Lady Megan's words lacked the simpering, high-pitched tone she'd used when he'd seen her greet Anthony Godfrey. Also, there was something oddly familiar about her voice. Its soft, sultry tone pricked at his memory as well as his heart.

"Meggie," he breathed, easing closer to the open portal and peering around the corner. His heart pounded dangerously loud with anticipation. It thundered in his ears like the hooves of a hundred battle horses charging the enemy. His gaze came to rest on Lady Faith, sitting upon a low wooden stool, her lovely face turned toward the woman who stood with her back to the door.

Richard felt as if a band of iron bound his chest as he took in the glorious mane of blue-black hair cascading down the woman's back to the waist of her tattered velvet robe. Without having to see her sweetly curved chin or her laughing blue eyes, he knew he had found the beautiful reaver he'd sought for so long. Stunned by the revelation, Richard pressed himself back against the wall and gulped in several long breaths to still the frantic pace his heart had set. He stared up at the dark-beamed ceiling and felt his blood race with excitement. He had finally found his beautiful reaver, yet his mind refused to reconcile the Meggie he had known with the Lady of Dragon's Lair. Even knowing they were one and the same, Richard could not immediately wipe out the animosity he'd harbored since receiving Edward's order to marry.

Confusion ripped through him, tearing him asunder with conflicting emotions. Anger reared its red-eyed visage and chomped with yellowed fangs at his insides. He felt the full force of it explode in his brain and wanted nothing more than to march into the room and extract the full measure of revenge for her duplicity. Even as he tensed to move toward the door, his thoughts veered wildly in a different direction. One moment he wanted to strangle her to death and in the next he wanted to throw her upon the bed and make love to her until she cried out with esctacy.

Unable to get a rein on his emotions, Richard quietly retraced his path down to the kitchen and slipped away from Dragon's Lair. He made his way back to the copse of trees where his mount was tethered, and stood for a long moment with his face pressed against the animal's warm, muscular neck. Desperately he sought to sort out the confusion gripping him. He failed.

In one agile movement, Richard gripped the pommel and swung himself up into the saddle. He didn't look back at the granite keep standing sentinel over the green valley but urged his mount in the direction of the town of Stamford. It possessed the nearest tavern, where he could drink himself into oblivion.

He wanted to numb his rioting emotions and forget for just a short while the young woman who had played him for a fool and had managed to turn his world upside down. Hopefully if he ever came back to his senses, he'd find his life once more in kilter.

Before the evening sun had reached its zenith, Richard sat peering drunkenly through the haze of a smoky tavern. Propped with one elbow on the roughhewn table and chin resting in the palm of his hand, he gave the bosomy barmaid who placed another full tankard in front of him what he considered his most charming smile. In his befogged state he was completely unaware the gesture came out as a leering, lopsided grin. The barmaid turned up her nose at him with a sniff of disdain and sauntered across the crowded room to a less drunk and less villainous-looking man.

"Go to hell, bitch," Richard muttered, his words slurred, his mood blackened with thoughts of Megan. He swayed slowly from side to side as he straightened to drink. Lifting the tankard to his lips, he gulped down the dark, foamy brew. He ignored the protest his taste buds made against the bitterness of the cheap ale. As long as it numbed him of all feeling, he didn't care how it tasted.

Giving a loud belch, Richard slammed the empty tankard back down on the table and wiped his upper lip free of the foam. A moment later, his eyes rolled back in his head and he slumped forward. His head landed against the table with a loud thump, and a snore escaped his slack lips before the sound had completely died away.

Richard groaned and raised a tentative hand to see if his head was still attached to his body. The excruciating pain made him feel as if it had been trampled beneath iron-shod hooves. When he moved, he realized with mounting distress that his stomach wasn't in much better condition. It revolted, churning wildly to expel the bitter, cheap ale he'd forced into it the previous night.

With another agonized groan, he bolted upright, his eyes nearly bulging from their sockets from the movement. Taking in the crude, dilapidated room, its floorboards rotting from dampness, its rough-timbered ceiling sagging from age, Richard had no time to wonder where he was and how he'd gotten there. His stomach's momentary needs overcame any curiosity the strange surroundings might have roused and he quickly crawled from the straw pallet toward the hole gapping in the wall. Leaning heavily against the rotting wood of the opening, he surrendered to his nausea.

Wiping his foul-tasting mouth with the back of his hand, every muscle in his lean body trembling with weakness, Richard knew he was surely going to die. His chest rising and falling rapidly, his heart pounding against his ribs, he finally managed to regain control of his limbs enough to creep back to the damp straw ticking and collapse.

"Let me die soon so I'll not have to suffer more of this," he murmured, feeling another wave of nausea roil his insides.

The high-pitched squeal of rusty hinges sent agony racing through Richard's skull and he buried his head in his arms to shut out some of his misery.

"I thought I heard ye moving about out here," a gruff masculine voice said from the doorway.

Slowly Richard peered up at the man who stood in an excruciating beam of sunlight. He squeezed his eyes closed and drew in several deep breaths to quell his rioting stomach.

"Where am I?" he asked, his voice hoarse, his throat burning.

"Yer in the Goose and Gander. And ye owe me a night's lodging as well as fer the drink ye had last eve," the man answered without any sign of sympathy for Richard's condition. "I suggest ye pay what ye owe and then be about yer business or I'll send fer the sheriff."

"Never fear you'll get your due; now, just get out and leave me to die in peace," Richard muttered, disgruntled at the man's lack of feeling for his last minutes on earth.

The man threw back his head and the sound of his laughter reverberated through the small room and Richard's head. It ricocheted off his brain like arrows off steel. "Ye ain't a-dying, ye fool. No matter what ye believe right now, ye'll feel better after ye've had a nice tankard of ale to help ease yer plight."

At the thought of more ale Richard felt his gorge rise again and he rapidly shook his head. Jerking upright, he lunged once more for the hole in the wall. His entire body heaved and he wondered briefly if he would soon be spitting out his toes. He felt as if he'd been turned wrong side out. Every muscle he possessed was sore from the effort it took to rid himself of the last remnants of his night's binge.

"Never again," he mumbled as he sat back, white-faced. He leaned weakly against the wall and slowly shook his head as he repeated, "Never again."

"Many a man has made that vow," the stranger said with a knowing smirk.

Disgusted and feeling no generosity toward the man or his advice, Richard dug into his pocket and tossed him a gold piece. "Hopefully this will pay what I owe and I'll be free to suffer in silence."

The man bit down on the coin with yellowed teeth, tucked it away in his pocket, and nodded before closing the door behind him to leave Richard alone once more.

Grateful for the small reprieve, Richard let out a long breath. If the man had stayed much longer and had he been able, Richard would have been forced to take his sword to him so he could suffer in peace.

Resting his head back against the rough wall planking,

Richard closed his eyes with the hope it would ease his pounding head. He'd been a fool to imbibe so freely of the cheap ale. It had served no purpose. Nothing had changed. His Meggie was still the Dragon Lady and she carried his child.

At the thought, the breath stilled in Richard's throat. He'd been so confused emotionally at finding Meggie at Dragon's Lair, he'd failed to consider what Mary's suspicions meant to him. Lady Megan Wakefield carried his heir.

"And she thinks to keep my child away from me! I'll be damned and in hell before I allow that to happen," Richard growled, coming to his feet with hands clenched tightly at his side. He seethed through every sinew of his lean body, his fury obliterating the headache and the nausea in its path. Pale, the scars marking his face contrasting starkly with the ashen hue of his skin, Richard crossed the small room in two strides and jerked the door open.

The sun momentarily blinded him, but his pace didn't falter. He marched across the yard to the dilapidated lean-to which served as a stable. Spying his mount munching fresh hay, he breathed a sigh of relief, grateful someone had been kind enough to see to the animal when he didn't have his wits about him.

" 'Im's a mighty fine beast," a young, dirty-faced boy said, climbing from a pile of new-mown hay.

"Aye," Richard said. "The Raven has served me well."

"Someday I'll ride a destrier," the boy said confidently, stroking the huge black horse's muscular neck. "And the king will make me a knight."

Richard smiled at the boy's boast. What dreams youth possessed. From the looks of the young imp, he doubted if he'd ever have a chance in his lifetime to travel more than a few miles from the Goose and Gander. Most peasants spent their lives within a few miles of where they were born.

"Aye, the king could do far worse," Richard said, not wanting to shatter the boy's dreams.

The boy seemed to swell with pride at the compliment. "I saw to yer mount, sir. He's been fed and watered."

Richard glanced down at his coarse woolen jerkin before eyeing the boy curiously. "Why do you call me sir, lad? I'm dressed much like yourself."

"Aye, but yer a sir, all right. No peasant or villein has ever owned an animal as fine as this 'un. That I know fer sure. I know me animals if I know anything."

"What's yer name, boy?" Richard asked, surprised to find himself interested in the towheaded youth. There was something about the boy that tugged at memories long past and reminded him of how Thomas McFarland had taken him in about the same age and raised him as his own.

The young stableboy hesitated before jutting out his small chin and staring Richard directly in the eye. "Most call me little bastard. But me mum called me Travis before she died."

"Then ye have no family?"

"Nay, me mum was all I had. Though she said me father was of the gentry, I never knew him."

Touched by the boy's story, the question sprang from Richard so unexpectedly, it shocked him. "Travis, would you be interested in entering my service?"

"Ye want me to serve ye?" Travis's eyes widened in wonder.

"Aye, if it is your want."

"I'd—be—honored—sir," Travis said, stumbling over the words in excitement.

"Then saddle the Raven and we'll be off. I've several important matters to attend in London. When we reach Windsor, I'll have you sent to stay with my brother and his wife until my affairs are settled."

"Oh sir. I'm ever so grateful," Travis said, lugging the

huge saddle from the stall. He staggered backward under its weight but finally managed to regain his balance.

Richard moved to help the boy but thought better of it when Travis jutted out his chin at a determined angle and agilely swung his body around like an ancient Greek discus thrower. Unbelievably, he managed to place the saddle upon the tall destrier's back. He fastened the cinch and turned to Richard with a smile of satisfaction spreading his dirt-smudged cheeks.

"Yer mount is saddled, sir."

"Then gather yer belongings and we'll be off."

"I have nothing but what's on me back, and if I tell old potbellied Swain I'm leaving his service to go with ye, he'll take even that from me."

Richard nodded and climbed into the saddle. He gave Travis a hand up behind him and then turned his mount south. Once he had the stableboy on his way to Raven's Keep, he'd make sure the Lady Megan Wakefield didn't keep his child from him.

Richard smiled. Edward was going to be in for the shock of his life when he heard Richard's plans for his own future.

Chapter 13

"Did I understand you right?" Edward asked, eyeing Richard as if he'd lost all of his wits.

"Aye, Majesty. I failed to find the culprits behind the theft of your wool and I'm now willing to accept the fact I must do as you first bid me and marry Lady Megan."

Edward leaned back in the high-backed leather chair and thoughtfully cocked his head to one side, studying the younger St. Claire suspiciously through narrowed lids. " 'Tis the right word coming from your lips, Richard, yet I feel there is more here than meets the eye or the ear. 'Tis odd, your sudden capitulation to my orders."

Richard had the grace to blush. "Sire, I know this all sounds strange since I protested so vigorously when you first bid me to marry Lady Megan. However, I've come to see the merits of being lord of a demesne such as Dragon's Lair."

"I had hoped you'd see the benefits to your family from such an allegiance. Since you are the younger son with few prospects, my order for you to marry was, what I thought at the time, a show of my gratitude for your loyalty during the past four years," Edward said, recognizing the look on Richard's face. He smiled. "You've served me well, Richard, and I'm grateful, but I fear our acquaintance has also allowed me to come to know you far better than you believe. Even if you say you now are willing to accept my edict, I can tell by your expression there is something else afoot here. What has happened to change your mind?''

Richard hesitated and then admitted the true reason behind his sudden change of heart. "The lady carries my child.''

"Your child?" Edward said, his good humor fading as his ire rose. "For a man who had no interest in marrying the lady, you certainly have taken much onto yourself. How dare you seduce a lady under my protection when you had no intention of making her your wife.''

Helplessly Richard looked up at England's monarch. He couldn't defend himself without tarnishing Megan's reputation. How could he tell the king his first sighting of the woman carrying his babe was with a hangman's noose about her neck for highway robbery? And even if he told Edward where he'd first met the Lady of Dragon's Lair, there was no guarantee the king would believe such a wild story. Ladies of the realm didn't ride the roads at night nor steal to survive. Even after all the lies between them, he didn't doubt that was the one truth Meggie had told him when they'd first met. She robbed to survive because of the financial situation her brother had left her in upon his death. Richard only wished everything else about Meggie had been as true.

"Don't you even have an excuse for your behavior?" Edward asked, shattering Richard's reverie with a voice laced with icy steel.

"Nay, Sire. I can't and won't deny the child she carries is mine. Nor can I deny your right to be angry with me for my behavior. I would make amends to you and Lady Megan by marrying her.''

"Make amends!" Edward exploded, coming to his feet in one angry motion. "Would you now be asking for the lady's hand had she not found herself with child?''

Richard's flush deepened.

Noting it, Edward glared down at Richard through narrowed lids. "I thought not. You trespass, ruining my chances to find the girl another husband, and then think to go about your merry way without paying any penalty. By all that's holy, I should have you whipped for your insolence!"

"Sire, 'twas not like that. I've come to love Lady Megan," Richard said, and to his own surprise, realized the truth of his words. He did love Meggie. Therein lay the essence of his troubles from the beginning of his adventures with the beautiful reaver. He'd thought never to care for another woman like he had Jamelyn, but now he knew he'd begun to love Meggie long before he'd made love to her. Her spirit and beauty had charmed his affections away from his brother's auburn-haired wife without him even realizing it.

"I do love her," Richard said, more to himself than to the handsome golden-haired monarch with the pointed beard and long, drooping mustache.

Edward stared at Richard and shook his head, unable to stay angry with him in the face of this newest revelation. He couldn't have asked for anything more. Richard would marry Lady Megan, and then the defenses along the heavily traveled wool routes would be safe.

Always ready to take advantage of any situation beneficial to him or England, Edward smiled and repeated his motto, "It is as it is. And since you've confessed your feelings for Lady Megan, I will forget about your trespasses. You may marry the lady with my blessings."

"Thank you, Sire," Richard said, and released a breath of relief.

"But remember this, St. Claire. I will still expect you to find the culprits behind the theft of my wool. I placed the mission in your hands and expect you to fulfill it. I'll not tolerate less."

"I will do my best, Sire. Now, if I may ask a favor of you?"

Edward cocked a golden brow. "What need do you have?"

"Would you bid the Lady Megan to marry me? I fear she's as against our union as I was at first."

Edward rolled his eyes toward the intricately molded ceiling and spoke as if to his creator. "What is it about my friends, the St. Claires, which brings this about? Women fall all over themselves trying to get into their beds, but then the women they choose to wed can't abide the sight of them."

Edward chuckled as he looked once more at Richard. "I'll send a message by Sir Godfrey to notify the lady of my decision. It should give her time to prepare for your imminent arrival and your marriage. Does that meet with your approval?"

"Aye, Majesty," Richard said, and bowed.

"Now be gone with you." Edward gave a flick of his bejeweled hand. "I have other important business which has need of my attention, and she awaits in my chamber."

Richard smiled, knowing Edward's insatiable appetite for the fairer sex. He was a relentless womanizer, yet Richard honestly believed he loved Queen Phillipa. His affairs were always kept private. The king didn't flaunt his mistresses in the queen's face and seemed the perfect husband when she wasn't confined away from court awaiting the birth of another child. The queen had already given him five children; his heir—Edward of Woodstock—was now seven years old.

Giving another graceful bow, Richard backed from the chamber. Relief and trepidation mingled as one when the audience chamber's intricately carved double doors closed behind him. He was relieved to have Edward's help, yet he dreaded Meggie's reaction to the news since she was firmly set against their union. He didn't doubt there would be a storm of protests from her when Anthony arrived at Dragon's Lair with the king's order for her to prepare for a wedding.

Striding down the newly marble-tiled corridor of Windsor, Richard spied a small, dirty face peeping around the door to the alcove off the private sitting room. He glanced about to ascertain no guards had seen the young imp and then raised one hand and motioned him forward with a curled finger.

Travis immediately scurried from his hiding place, his be-grimed face breaking into a welcoming grin as he sped toward Richard on bare feet.

"Young man, I thought I told you to wait in the stables," Richard scolded.

Travis nodded. "Ye did, sir, but I thought I might be of some help to ye in some way."

"The best way you can help me is to do as I bid you. Is that understood?"

"Aye, sir. I'll do as ye bid me," Travis said, his smile fading at the angry light in Richard's sapphire gaze. Ashamed of his behavior, he lowered his head and stared down at his grimy feet.

"It is all I expect, Travis. I know it's hard for young boys to do everything they're ordered, yet 'tis often for their own good. Had you been caught slipping around in the palace corridors, the guards would have acted first and asked questions later. You'd have been tossed into Newgate, and I wouldn't have ever seen you again. Is that what you want?"

"Nay. I just want to be of service to ye," Travis said, rapidly shaking his towhead from side to side.

Richard ruffled his hair. "I know you do. Now get yourself back to the stable and stay there. I'm sending you to my brother in Scotland for the time being. You'll be welcome there and can work in the Raven's Keep's stables. If all goes well and you do as you're bid, I'll have you brought to Dragon's Lair. Then we'll see if you can be trained for something far more suited to a young man with the ambition to be a knight in Edward's service."

Travis's face brightened. "Oh, sir. I'll do exactly as ye say."

"I'm glad to hear it," Richard said, and smiled. "Now,

off with you before a guard finds you creeping about like a little mouse after a piece of cheese. Instead of throwing you into Newgate, he might decide to squash you under his boot.''

''He'll have to be fast to catch me,'' Travis said with an impish grin before dashing back in the direction he'd come moments earlier.

Richard shook his head and chuckled, wondering what he'd gotten himself into by taking on the responsibility of the little imp. Giving another shake of his head, he turned and strode back down the corridor, his mind turning back to Dragon's Lair and the surprise Anthony would find there.

Unaware of the sounds that roused her, Megan awoke from her afternoon nap. Of late she didn't seem to be able to keep her eyes open for more than a few hours at a time. It seemed she slept the greater part of each day, only awakening for meals. At the thought, her stomach responded with a hungry rumble.

''Sleep and eat, that's all I do,'' she mumbled, and then hid a yawn behind her hand before sitting up. She slid her feet from the bed and stood, her toes curling against the cool floor. Turning toward the polished steel mirror which hung on the opposite side of the chamber, she critically surveyed her naked, slender form. The only evidence of her pregnancy was her rounding belly.

''But my slimness won't last much longer if I can't quit cramming food into my mouth.'' Even as the words left her lips, the aroma drifting up from the kitchen drew her thoughts to the haunch of venison the cook was roasting for the evening meal.

Forcing herself to ignore the mouth-watering smell, Megan pulled on a soft linen undergown and then a cyclas made of fustian. She smoothed the material down over her hips, remembering the time when her mother had ordered the cotton fabric from Germany. At the memory, she sighed with regret. At this point in her life she needed her mother more than ever. She needed her advice about the baby as well as her feelings about its father.

Shaking off the melancholy mood, Megan lifted her heavy mane of hair off her shoulders and began to braid it. Her fingers worked swiftly with the raven strands, and she'd just secured it with a riband when a rapid knocking sounded on the door.

"Come in," Megan said, and with a light toss, sent the thick braid cascading down her back.

"Megan," Faith said, bursting into the room, her face ashen, her eyes round with distress.

Megan came to her feet, her own heart thudding uncomfortably against her ribs at the stricken expression on her cousin's face. "Faith, what is it? Has something happened?"

"Aye," Faith said, nodding rapidly. " 'Tis Sir Godfrey."

Megan felt a chill of premonition race up her spine. "Sir Godfrey's here—at Dragon's Lair?"

"Aye, he's just returned and demands to see you immediately."

Megan closed her eyes and drew in a deep breath to still her racing heart. There could be only one reason for Sir Godfrey's return to Dragon's Lair. The king had decided it was time to enforce his order for her to marry.

"This can't be," was her broken whisper as she slowly sank down on the bed.

"I fear it is, and Sir Godfrey said he'd accept no excuse for your absence from the hall at the evening meal. He has brought a message from the king."

Tears brimmed in Megan's eyes even as she raised her chin in the air. "Then he shall not be disappointed. Have Mary fetch the lard and soot."

" 'Tis ridiculous, Megan, and I won't participate in aiding you again. You carry Sir Richard's child, and he is the man chosen for you to marry. It is the answer to all of your problems.''

''The answer to my problems? Nay, I think not, Faith. Sir Richard wants no part of me or Dragon's Lair.''

''It doesn't matter what he wants. You have to think of the child you carry. The babe deserves its birthright even if you hate its father, which I think you do not.''

Megan turned away. ''It would seem from Sir Godfrey's arrival, neither Richard nor I will have anything to say on the matter. Our lives are in Edward's hands.''

''Then you will accept the king's edict and marry Sir Richard?''

Megan looked back at her cousin. Her eyes held a haunted look and her tone reflected her heartbreak as she said, ''It would seem I have no choice.''

''Then I will tell Sir Godfrey you will join him for the evening meal.''

Megan nodded, unable to find a way out of this final act of the tragedy her life had become. Tired of the battle, she accepted her fate. But even as she realized the decree of England's monarch, her spirit wouldn't allow her to accept total defeat. She would be forced to marry a man who didn't want her; however, she would never humiliate herself by letting him know how much it hurt to be close to him. She would do as the king bid, but she'd never surrender her pride. It was all she had left.

Perspiration beaded Anthony's forehead as he sat waiting before the blazing fire. Yet the moisture that gleamed on his wide brow had nothing to do with the heat filling the great hall. It was roused from his dread of again having to face Richard's future bride. He'd seen her only once, but it had been enough to last him a lifetime.

Casting an uneasy glance toward the stairs, he sipped at the tankard of ale he held in one white-knuckled hand and wished every plague known to man down upon Richard's head for putting him in this situation again. A rueful smile tugged the corners of his mouth as he looked back into the leaping flames. His wish was already in the process of coming true. The Lady of Dragon's Lair was enough misery for any man's life.

The firelight made Anthony's blond hair gleam with golden highlights as he absently shook his head. He didn't know what had come over Richard. After all he'd done to stay out of the trap Edward had set for him, now he was running headfirst into it without one word of protest.

"Something must have addled his wits, or he's only marrying the chit for Jamelyn's sake. Nothing else could have forced Richard to change his mind," Anthony mused, unaware he had spoken aloud, or of the beautiful woman who stood quietly listening to his ramblings.

"Sir Godfrey," Megan said after swallowing several times to force her throat to work enough to speak. She now knew the reason behind Richard's distaste for their union. He was in love with another woman—a woman named Jamelyn.

Anthony jumped with a start and came to his feet so swiftly that his ale spilled onto the stones at his feet. He thought nothing of the mishap as he turned to the woman who had spoken his name. His mouth fell open and his eyes grew round with wonder as he stared at Megan.

"My lady?" he said after a long, bemused moment.

Megan extended her hand to him and smiled warmly, though the gesture wasn't reflected in the blue depths of her eyes. "Again I bid you welcome to Dragon's Lair."

"It is my pleasure, my lady," Anthony said, still uncertain to whom he spoke. Taking her hand, he bent and placed his lips courteously against it. There was something oddly familiar about her, but he'd have known if he'd ever met her before. No man alive could forget such a ravishing beauty, whose thick-fringed eyes reminded him of a deep lake at twilight.

"How may I be of service to you, Sir Godfrey?" Megan asked, withdrawing the hand he still held. "My cousin told me you wished to see me this eve."

Anthony frowned. For the life of him, he didn't know what she was talking about. Upon his arrival he'd spoken with only Lady Faith about dining with her ugly cousin. Clearing his throat, he said, "My lady, I fear I'm at a loss. Have we met previously?"

"I would think you would remember me well," Megan said, perversely enjoying Sir Godfrey's confusion.

"Forgive me, my lady. I fear I do not recall our meeting."

"We met on your first visit to Dragon's Lair," Megan said, hiding her smile with an effort as she watched Anthony's face screw up in a puzzled frown.

Anthony searched his memory for any clue to the lady's identity. Nothing surfaced. He shook his head. "I'm afraid I'm at a loss."

"Sir," Megan said, her eyes glittering with mirth. "Surely you recall the lady with whom you dined the first night."

Anthony gaped at Megan, dumbfounded. He'd dined with a greasy-haired, black-toothed hag whose nails were lined with dirt. As he assessed her features and stripped away the disguise, the crease across Anthony's brow deepened and his face grew flushed as he suddenly comprehended he'd been played for a fool. His nostrils flared and his lips firmed into a thin line of ire. His tone was cold when he spoke. "Lady Wakefield, I presume?"

Megan dipped into a graceful curtsy. "May I again bid you welcome to Dragon's Lair, Sir Godfrey?"

"It would seem, my lady, your previous welcome was as false as your appearance. Should I now trust you because you've revealed your true self to me?"

"Sir Godfrey, let us not play any more games. You know

exactly why I disguised my appearance, for I was not the only one at Dragon's Lair that night who pretended to be something they were not. I'm sure you will recall Sir Richard visiting the keep disguised as a minstrel. He came dressed as such because he feels the same as I do about our union."

Blushing under her censure, Anthony failed to wonder how she knew of Richard's disguise when he alone had been privy to his friend's actions. "I fear there have been too many deceptions here, and I apologize for the part I've played in them. Shall we begin again, Lady Megan? You are to be the wife of one of my closest friends, and I would not have you as an enemy."

"Nor do I want you as an enemy, Sir Godfrey, but if I have my way, I will not become Lady St. Claire."

"I fear it is the reason I've returned to Dragon's Lair. King Edward has instructed me to inform you Sir Richard will arrive within the week and you should prepare yourself for your marriage."

Megan's breath grew short and her knees became weak beneath her. She slowly sank down in the high-backed chair nearest her. She had known the reason for Sir Anthony's mission the moment Faith had told her of his return to Dragon's Lair, yet she had held on to the fragile hope she was wrong.

Seeing Megan's sudden pallor, Anthony grew concerned. He knelt in front of her, taking her hand into his own. "Lady Megan, are you all right? Shall I call your cousin or a servant to assist you?"

Megan gave Anthony a weak smile and slowly shook her head. "I'm all right. 'Twas only hearing my worst fears finally put into words which has shaken me. For you already know I do not want this marriage."

" 'Tis Edward's wish," Anthony said, patting her hand to comfort her.

Megan nodded. "Aye. I know 'tis the king's wish, but I

want no part of Sir Richard or anyone Edward chooses for me. If the king would only give me a chance, I could hold the demesne as well as any man.''

Anthony smiled, remembering another young woman who had fought to hold what she considered hers. ''I doubt it not. Richard's brother's wife, Jamelyn, felt much the same way when she was ordered to marry Justin. However, things have gone well in their marriage, and perhaps it will be the same with yours and Sir Richard's.''

His mention of the name she'd heard him murmur only a short time earlier drew Megan's thoughts away from her own conflicting emotions. ''Then I am not the only woman Edward has used to gain his wants.''

Much as it had done four years previously with the auburn-haired Scottish beauty, Anthony's heart went out to the enchanting woman sitting so forlornly before him. ''Nay. Lady Jamelyn's marriage to Justin came about in much the same manner. Edward needed her fief secured by marriage to insure the peace in the lowlands, much like he needs Dragon's Lair to protect the wool route from York. Both marriages benefit England's welfare, and he chose two of his most favored knights as well as two of his strongest to fulfill the duty.''

''If it is true, I don't see how Lady Jamelyn's marriage can have gone as well as you say. I may have to obey Edward's command, but I know no happiness can come out of such a travesty.''

'' 'Tis a long story and much has happened, but you must believe me when I say that Lady Jamelyn is now happy with Lord St. Claire. 'Twas at her urging Richard agreed to come to Dragon's Lair in the first place.''

Jealousy streaked through Megan with such force she trembled, and she quickly lowered her eyes to hide her feelings from Anthony. Richard might have jumped to do Jamelyn's bidding, but because of his feeling for her, he'd already made up his mind to dislike what he saw before he ever set foot within Dragon's Lair's walls. Even had she not looked so wretched in her disguise, he would not have been willing to marry her. His heart was held by his brother's wife.

Brother's wife! Megan thought with contempt. That was even more disgusting. Richard lusted after a woman out of his reach, so he used any female who crossed his path as a surrogate for the one he truly loved. Megan's eyes flashed blue fire when she looked once more at Anthony. "Then I pray she'll urge him to refuse the king's order immediately."

Anthony shifted uneasily and stood. "Lady Megan, Richard can't refuse to do Edward's bidding any more than you can. His family would suffer the consequences."

From the uncomfortable expression on Anthony's face, Megan knew there was only one person Richard St. Claire wanted to protect by agreeing to a marriage he so vehemently detested. And that person was his brother's wife.

Megan clenched her fists in the folds of her cyclas and gritted her teeth to control the burst of fury sweeping over her. How dare Richard use her in such a manner? And how dare Lady Jamelyn interfere in her life! What gave her the right to send Richard to Dragon's Lair to inspect his future bride as if she were nothing more than a piece of meat on the butcher's block?

"My lady, Richard has asked me to present you with this ring," Anthony said, unable to bring himself to say "a token of his affection" after their conversation. Digging into his pocket and retrieving the small velvet bag which contained the diamond and sapphire betrothal ring, he emptied it into his hand and held it out to Megan.

Megan stared down at the glittering gems but made no move to accept the gift sent to the ugly crone he believed the Lady of Dragon's Lair to be. If only it had been meant for Meggie, the woman he'd loved beneath the stars, she might have reconsidered. However, she'd heard his feelings about this marriage from his own lips, and she could never place his ring upon her finger. This was only a marriage of convenience to Richard so he could protect the woman he truly loved. And Megan could never let herself forget that fact. Even after he learned the Lady of Dragon's Lair was Meggie the reaver.

Megan shook her head. "Nay. I am forced into this marriage, but I will not wear his gift to proclaim my subjugation. I'll obey Edward's wishes; however, I do have some pride and I'll never accept anything from Sir Richard beyond what I need to survive. And it does not include his jewels. This marriage will benefit the crown but not the two people who have been bound together because Edward needs Dragon's Lair to defend the wool route from York."

Megan rose from her chair and bravely faced Sir Godfrey. "Now if you will excuse me, I need time alone to prepare for my wedding. Good eve, Sir Godfrey."

Graciously Anthony nodded his consent, unable to say more. He felt at fault for Megan's rejection of Richard's gift. He'd let his wayward tongue have free reign, letting it run on, wild and untamed, until he revealed things best kept between those who understood the relationship between Jamelyn and Richard. He'd meant only to make Megan understand marriages of convenience could turn out well if given the chance, but it seemed he'd only made things more difficult. The only thing he hadn't done to make the situation worse was mention the affection between Richard and his sister-in-law. Had he been foolish enough to reveal that, Lady Megan might have refused to obey Edward's order to marry Richard altogether. No woman, not even one who was forced into a marriage, wanted to know the man she was marrying had once deeply loved another.

From the resolute set of the Lady Megan's small chin and the regal way she'd walked from the hall, Anthony suspected she wasn't a woman easily ruled, nor was she one who would overlook a husband's first love. She had too much pride to accept being second in anything, especially her husband's life. She was a female version of Richard, strong and determined as well as stubborn.

Richard, Anthony mused sadly to himself. *You have a hard path ahead of you with this one. If at all possible, she's even more stubborn than you.*

"Hawks and Falcons," Anthony muttered aloud. Mentally throwing up his hands in despair, he marched across the hall to the keg of ale. Drawing another full tankard, he gulped it down. Refilling the vessel, he returned to his seat before the fire. Slumping into the soft leather monk's chair, he crossed his legs at the ankles and stared moodily into the flames.

If Richard had thought Anthony could handle a woman like Lady Megan, he'd made a tremendous mistake by sending him on this mission. His friend needed a diplomat like his brother, Justin, if he wanted to gain favor in the lady's eyes and change her opinion about their match.

"Instead of sending me here, why in the hell didn't he get Justin and Jamelyn to visit Lady Megan?" Anthony muttered before taking another long swallow of ale. No one stood a chance between the two of them. They could outtalk and outcharm the stubbornnest of souls, as Richard should well know.

Disgusted with the way he'd mishandled the situation, Anthony irritably pushed himself from the chair and strode from the hall. Like Lady Megan, he needed time to be alone and rehash what had been said between them. He also needed time to prepare himself for his next encounter with the beautiful mistress of Dragon's Lair. He had to figure out a way to repair the damage he'd done before Richard arrived at the end of the week. Hopefully he could manage to make Megan see the benefits of her union to such a powerful family as the St. Claires.

Taking the narrow flight of steps, Anthony made his way up to the parapet walk overlooking the green fields. A frown marked his brow and he held his lips in a pensive line as he thoughtfully stared out across the softly rolling landscape of Dragon's Lair.

Folding his arms upon the cool granite crenellation, he rested his chin upon velvet sleeves like a small boy daydreaming of his future. He remained in a comtemplative position until the full moon rose high in the sky, its light illuminating his attractive face, flawed only by a bemused expression.

Completely unaware of Anthony's presence, Faith strolled along the parapet walk, enjoying the solitude and beauty of the quiet summer evening. Next to her gardens, this place was her favorite at Dragon's Lair. Here she could think and dream as if nothing in her past had ruined all of her chances for happiness. Here she could return to being the young girl who had searched the heavens at night for falling stars to wish upon. And here she could reflect upon the problems that seemed to beset her family daily.

Worried over Megan's impending marriage and her cousin's reaction, she needed the peace and solitude to soothe her troubled mind. Megan had said she would accept the king's edict, but she was so high-spirited, her words did little to relieve Faith's mind. One never knew what Megan might do when she was pushed into a corner. Usually she came out with claws bared and ready for a fight.

Her mind lingering upon her cousin, Faith nearly collided with Anthony before she became aware of him standing so quietly in the moonlight. She abruptly halted and began to turn back in the direction in which she'd just come when something about his still, reflective expression made her pause. In a moment she saw past the suave exterior the handsome English knight presented to the world. The look on his face told her that behind the facade resided a man of much more depth than was exposed by all his swaggering and banter. Now, surrounded by the quiet night and unaware he was no longer alone, his expression revealed the tender side of his nature.

Startled by the revelation, Faith realized she was looking upon a rare man. For tenderness was considered a weakness, not an asset. If a man possessed such feelings at all, he kept them harbored and well hidden until they were forced out of existence. There were few men such as Anthony Godfrey, who still possessed a gentle side to his nature. Most were ruled not by the heart but by their greed for power.

The soft sound made by the soles of Faith's slippers upon the stone walkway drew Anthony from his reveries. He glanced in her direction and found his breath caught in his throat at the sight of Faith drenched in moonlight, her pale hair shimmering like spun silver, her thick lashes shadowing her cornflower eyes just enough to add a seductive element to her alluring features.

"Lady Faith," Anthony breathed softly, not raising his voice above a whisper out of fear he'd frighten her away and she'd vanish into the night like a silver fairy.

"I'm sorry, Sir Godfrey. I didn't mean to intrude," Faith said, unaware she had taken a step closer to Anthony.

"You're not intruding. After my meeting with your cousin I came up here for a breath of fresh air as well as to ponder the strange twists of fate."

"Then I'll leave you to your privacy," Faith said, her heart racing from their close proximity. Oddly disturbed, she started to turn and retrace her steps to the keep.

Reaching out even before he was aware of his own actions, Anthony caught her by the arm and turned her once more to face him. His softly spoken words reflected the man she'd glimpsed a moment before. "Faith, please don't go."

Faith glanced up at Anthony uncertainly. The plea in the blue depths of his eyes cried out to her, drawing her inexorably toward him. She struggled to deny the message sent out by her heart but failed. No matter how she felt about men, this man needed her, and it wasn't in her power to refuse.

Awed by her beauty, Anthony raised a hand and caressed her moon-silvered cheek. "You are the loveliest creature I've ever seen."

"Sir Godfrey, please. You must not say such things," Faith said, her mouth suddenly going dry, her insides trembling like a wild thing snared in a trap as she felt herself drowning in his gaze.

"Why should I not say what I've wanted to say since I first set eyes on you?"

" 'Tis unseemly, Sir Godfrey," Faith replied, falling back on the rules of etiquette as a means of self-preservation. There was something about Anthony that dashed her fears and shattered her willpower. If she allowed herself to succumb to the feelings he aroused within her, she knew she'd find herself doing his bidding like a dewy-eyed maid who knew nothing of life.

Sensing her withdrawal and fully understanding her ploy, Anthony let his hand fall to his side and nodded. "Forgive me, Lady Faith. I took too much upon myself. I'll not overstep the boundaries again."

Anthony turned away, leaving Faith suddenly bereft. She wanted to reach out to him, but even as she raised her hand in the air, her mind rebelled. She let her hand fall back to her side.

"Sir Godfrey, I—" Faith paused, unable to explain her feelings without revealing too much of the secret only she and Megan now shared.

Anthony glanced back and gave her a tender smile. "I understand. You've made your feelings clear to me since the first moment we met. I'm only sorry we couldn't become friends."

"Sir Godfrey, you don't understand," Faith said, her misery mounting.

"I fear I do. However, I would know if you only dislike me, or is it all men?"

Faith drew in an unsteady breath, and a tear slipped from beneath her lashes when she pressed her eyes closed. Her knuckles grew white as she clenched her hands together in front of her. "No. You don't understand. 'Tis no fault of yours I feel this way."

Sensing far more to Faith's words than she'd divulged, Anthony frowned. Something terrible had happened to make this beautiful creature become nearly an ice maiden. Yet some inner voice told him she had not slipped completely beyond the need to be loved. He sensed that within her fragile body still lay smoldering coals just waiting for the right man to ignite them into blazing flames of passion. Anthony knew he was the right man. However, he couldn't force her to recognize the woman just waiting to burst forth, nor could he pry from her the secret that had nearly frozen her heart against all feelings. She had to freely give up her secrets or nothing would be salvaged.

Turning once more to Faith, he took her by the arm and peered down into her stricken face. "I would give my shoulder for comfort should you need it."

Reacting on instinct alone, Faith succumbed to her needs. Tears streamed down her face as she threw herself into Anthony's arms and wept against the shoulder he had offered.

It had been so long since she'd had anyone to hold her and tell her everything would be all right. The problems in Megan's life forestalled her talking over her own troubles with her cousin. Megan had taken on enough burdens without Faith adding to them by baring her soul.

"Oh, sweet Faith," Anthony murmured against her moon-silvered hair. "How I wish I could take your pain as my own."

His words a balm to her battered emotions, Faith wept harder. Her tears dampened the soft fabric of his jerkin, but when her weeping was spent she didn't move out of Anthony's strong, comforting embrace. For the first time since her parents died, she felt she'd found a home. When they were alive, Megan's mother and father had always been good to her and had given her what she needed physically. Yet until that moment with Anthony Godfrey, she'd never felt as if she truly belonged. Snuggling closer to his hard, lean body, Faith tucked her head beneath his chin and listened to the steady rhythm of his heartbeat. A tender smile curled her lips at the corners as a burst of warm security rippled along every nerve in her body. She had finally found her place in the world, and it was in Anthony Godfrey's arms.

Anthony drew in an unsteady breath, swallowed hard, and set his jaw resolutely. No matter how much he desired the beautiful woman in his arms, he refused to give way to his needs and take her innocence. He was determined to keep his baser thoughts at bay. He'd just hold and comfort her and ignore the searing heat scalding every sinew of his flesh. Even as he made his resolution, he could feel his wayward body betray him, his hard length throbbing painfully against the tightness of his chausses.

"Faith," Anthony murmured hoarsely, struggling against the urge to lift her into his arms and carry her to his chamber, where he would make mad, passionate love to every inch of her tantalizing body. Had it been any other woman besides the one in his arms, he wouldn't have given it a second thought. She would already be spread beneath him.

"I—I—" Anthony's words stumbled to a halt over his thick tongue. Swallowing hard once more, he took her firmly by the shoulders and set her away. He knew himself too well to remain in such close proximity to his desire. It was best to put temptation out of reach.

Running an unsteady hand through his blond hair, he gazed

down into Faith's glistening eyes. "Faith, I want you more than any woman I've every known, yet I won't take your innocence until you are sure it is also what you want. I know you've been hurt, and I want everything to be perfect between us before you take a step which could change your life."

"Thank you, Anthony," Faith murmured, and wondered why he couldn't hear her heart shattering. He believed her innocent of a man's touch. Once he found out she had been tainted by Mallory O'Roarke, Anthony would want nothing else to do with her.

Faith felt as if the entire world were crumbling about her. An evil man cruelly rapes her, robbing her of her innocence and forcing her into his bed, while the one man she wants to take her to his bed refuses to do so because of an innocence that doesn't exist. She would have laughed at the irony of her situation had she been able to force her frozen features into a smile. For years her past had fostered a hatred for all men so deep that it had stopped her even considering marriage or family. Now she'd found the man who could make her heart come alive again, but she still couldn't have him.

Before Anthony could say a word to halt her, Faith turned and fled back down the narrow stone steps and across the bailey to the keep. She had to get safely into her chamber before she threw herself from the parapets to end the misery her life had become.

Anthony made no attempt to follow Faith. He had shocked her by openly telling her of his feelings, and he'd have to give her time to consider what he'd said. Hopefully she'd come to return his love. Suddenly feeling much better than when he'd first arrived at Dragon's Lair, Anthony smiled and looked up at the indigo sky. Perhaps some good would come out of his visit after all.

Chapter 14

A chill of dread rippled down Megan's spine as she stood transfixed upon the parapet walk, her eyes glued to the riders approaching Dragon's Lair. Even from the distance she could make out the figure at the head of the column of men. Richard St. Claire sat straight and tall in the saddle, his family's red and black gonfalon flapping in the breeze over his dark head.

Megan felt sick. Her stomach roiled with nausea from the war being waged within her. Her emotions were pitched into a wrestling match. Her heart struggled valiantly against her mind, urging her to rush down the narrow granite steps and throw herself into Richard's arms when he rode through the gates of Dragon's Lair. However, her mind kept her frozen in place, reminding her the destiny now riding forth upon his black destrier looked as dark as his mount's shining coat. Richard St. Claire was again entering her life, but he did not come as the willing bridegroom nor the gentle lover. He came only because the king commanded it.

"I don't know if I have the strength left to go through with this farce," Megan murmured, unaware she was no longer alone.

"Ye've never failed to have the strength before, Meggie,"

Sandy said, crossing to her side and placing a rough, callused hand over her small one lying on the cool granite merlon.

Megan flashed Sandy a grateful look. "I fear you're wrong about me this time, old friend."

"Nay, I know ye, Meggie. Ye won't let Richard St. Claire defeat ye when yer own brother couldn't. Yer just uncertain because yer heart's involved this time."

Sandy's encouraging words were the life-giving force Megan's flagging spirits needed. Over the past weeks she had lacked the willpower required to fortify her own defenses. Nostrils flaring, she drew in a deep breath and made an effort to shore up her faltering courage. Feeling it begin to come back to life, she inched her chin up in the air, stiffened her spine, and squared her shoulders. She held herself regally poised, and only those who knew her well could see the flicker of uncertainty still lingering in the shining depths of her eyes.

"Aye, you're right, Sandy. I'll not let Richard St. Claire make me into a sniveling coward, nor will I allow him the upper hand at Dragon's Lair. By Edward's edict he may be its new lord, but he's not mine."

Megan took in the landscape before her with a wide sweep of her hand. "Dragon's Lair is my heritage and has been my responsibility far too long for me to relinquish it to the first man to lay claim to it."

Sandy smiled. " 'Tis been a while since I've seen that kind of spirit from you, Meggie."

Megan nodded. "Aye, 'tis been a while since I've felt it. In the past weeks I've had so many things on my mind, I seem to have allowed myself to surrender to defeat before the battle was even waged."

" 'Tis the babe which worries you?" Sandy asked, quietly.

Megan blinked up at him. "How did you know of my babe?"

"I'm yer bailiff, Meggie, and I hear servants' gossip, especially from the serving wench, Mary. She chatters so much about other people's affairs, she should be called Magpie instead of Mary."

"The servants are aware of my pregnancy?" Megan asked, aghast. And there was no explanation she could make to anyone about her condition. She couldn't tell them she'd already met her future husband or she'd have to explain how she'd gained the money to buy the seed for the spring planting. Without an explanation the rumors would soon spread that she'd really pulled the wool over Richard St. Claire's eyes by foisting off another man's child upon him.

Megan paled. She hadn't considered the true extent of the lies she'd begun to weave so many months before. They had far-reaching consequences if she didn't find some way to stop the rumors about her child's parentage. In the future it could even mean her child might be ruled a bastard and lose his rightful heritage.

Megan opened her mouth to tell Sandy she had to set things to right before her world turned upside down but quickly snapped it shut when she spied Sir Godfrey strolling toward them from the stairs.

"Lady Megan," Anthony Godfrey said, crossing to her. "Would you give me the pleasure of your company when I greet Sir Richard?"

Megan shook her head. At the present moment she was in no state to be the gracious lady of the keep. She had far more important matters on her mind—her child's future. "Nay. When Sir Richard arrives please bid him to attend me in the privacy of the solar. There is much we must discuss before the ceremony takes place."

"Surely it would be best if you greeted him as you would any guest seeking your hospitality. It would make things far easier to meet your first time amid other members of your household."

Megan turned misty, pain-filled eyes upon Anthony. "Nothing will make this marriage easier, Sir Godfrey. Now if you will excuse me." Megan turned her back to Anthony.

Slightly vexed by her abrupt dismissal, Anthony bowed and turned to the steps. There was nothing more for him to say. Regrettably, she had made up her mind against this marriage, and there was nothing he could do to change her feelings before Richard arrived. He had done his duty to the best of his ability, but when Richard rode through the gates of Dragon's Lair, it would be his responsibility to handle the irascible Lady Megan. The course was set, and in the future he would be nothing more than an observer.

The thought made Anthony smile. In a short while he would be relieved of the duty Richard had placed upon him. His sudden feeling of relief was so great, Anthony felt as if he'd just taken off a heavy coat of mail.

"I must be getting old," he mused to himself as he descended the narrow stone steps to the bailey. "I used to find pleasure bedeviling my friends, but now all I want is to tend to my own affairs."

His thoughts turning once more to the gentle cousin of the firebrand he'd just left on the parapet, Anthony quickened his pace. The sooner Richard was in charge of Dragon's Lair and its mistress, the sooner he could turn his full attention to wooing the lovely Lady Faith.

A tender smile curving his full lips, Anthony crossed the bailey and entered the keep in search of the woman of his thoughts. He found her sitting calmly before the fire, her head bent over the tapestry frame, her fingers busily drawing the needle and thread through the fabric to create a rich, vibrant collage of Dragon's Lair's history.

The breath stilled in Anthony's throat as he took in her beauty like a man starved. He'd never seen anything as lovely. She was the perfect picture of innocence, her flawless features reflecting her gentle nature.

In that moment Anthony reaffirmed what he already suspected. He'd found the woman he wanted to share his life. Richard and Justin could have their beautiful, high-spirited wives. At one time he would have envied them their good fortune. However, he'd mellowed over the past years and he didn't want the turmoil such fire created in his friends' lives. It might be exciting, but when he married, he wanted a woman whose gentleness was her strength.

Ah, Faith. You are the woman, and now all I have to do is make you realize I'm also the man for you, Anthony mused as he crossed the hall to tell Faith of Richard's impending arrival.

"So, my lady, we meet again," Richard said from the doorway to the solar. His voice was laced with annoyance and his face was drawn and haggard. The day had been long and tiring for man and beast. Anxious to see Megan again, he'd had his men in the saddle at first light, and they'd ridden without stopping to rest until they reached Dragon's Lair. Then Anthony had greeted him with Megan's order to have him meet with her in the solar as if he were some lackey instead of the man she intended to marry within a few hours. His patience and temper were sorely being tested to the limit.

Megan spun around, her face draining of color as she stared up into the scarred features of the man who had stolen her heart. She moistened her suddenly dry lips and cleared her throat. She was too unnerved to wonder at his calm acceptance at finding her in the stead of the ugly crone he'd seen on his previous visit to Dragon's Lair.

"Aye, we meet again, Sir Richard," she said, setting her chin at a haughty angle to hide her raging emotions.

"Since it is our wedding day, I think you would have had the courtesy to greet me upon my arrival to your home."

"Sir Richard, I see no reason to perpetuate the pretense."

Richard folded his arms over his wide chest and propped

one shoulder against the doorframe. His gaze raked over Megan from head to toe and then came to rest on her slightly rounding abdomen. A muscle twitched in his scarred cheek and he arched a dark brow when he once more looked her directly in the eyes.

"Pretense, my lady? I doubt you know of little else since you are Mallory O'Roarke's sister. It seems liars run in your family."

"How dare you compare me to Mallory," Megan said, her temper flaming. "He was only my half-brother, but if I was to compare him to anyone, it would be you, Sir Richard. You're well versed in the art of deceit if memory serves me."

Richard showed no outward sign her barbed words affected him, though his stomach gave a slight lurch at her attack. "My lady, if memory serves *me*, you are the one who blackened your teeth and greased your hair to disguise your appearance when you knew of my impending visit to your home."

"Aye, and I'd do it again if I knew it would save me from marriage to the sneaking man who crept into my home in the guise of a traveling minstrel."

Richard saw the sudden humor in their situation; a corner of his mouth twitched and he fought to suppress his smile. Here they were, chewing each other to bits over something of which they were both guilty. Richard chuckled and shook his head as he uncoiled his lean frame from his position at the door and crossed the chamber to where Megan stood with back stiff and chin squared for battle.

"Meggie, it would seem we are both at fault in this situation. Let us put it behind us by admitting our duplicity. Then, hopefully, we can go on from here."

"Go on? How can we go on when neither of us wants this marriage the king seems determined to foster upon us?"

Richard flinched. Megan's words were razor-sharp, cutting him to the quick. Deep within his heart he'd hoped she would have changed her feelings toward their union. However, he now knew she was still set against it, though she carried his child.

Richard's expression hardened, his earlier annoyance returning in full force. He'd tried to put the past aside and start anew with Megan, but if she was so determined to make no effort to do the same, then so be it. He had already resolved to have the child she carried, no matter how she felt about him. He'd not let her nor anyone else deny him his own flesh and blood. The king had commanded they marry, and he was damned well determined to obey the order even if he had to drag Megan to the altar kicking and screaming.

"How can we not go on, Meggie, especially since you now carry my child?" Richard asked, his voice laced with sarcasm.

Megan turned a deathly white and slowly sank down into the chair she'd vacated when Richard entered the solar. "How did you find out?"

"The same way I found out the ugly crone was the beautiful reaver who I thought had vanished off the face of the earth. But how I found out I was to be a father doesn't matter. What does matter is the fact you never intended to tell me of my child."

"Then the babe is why you're now willing to marry?"

"That and other reasons. If you will recall, it is Edward's wish to have us wed to keep up Dragon's Lair's defenses."

A sharp pain stabbed Megan's heart and she quickly looked away to keep Richard from seeing the agony his words caused her. Fool that she was, she'd wanted him to say he loved her and when he'd learned of their child, he'd begged Edward to let them wed.

Megan lowered her gaze to the hands she had clasped tightly in her lap. But her wishes were not to be. No matter how hard she wanted them to come true, nothing would change his feelings, she reminded herself. Richard already loved another—his brother's wife.

The thought stirred jealousy and resentment to life. It boiled to the surface to overshadow her pain, and when she looked once more at Richard, her eyes were icy with contempt. Her voice was equally cold as she finally managed to compose herself enough to speak.

"Since we now find ourselves thrown into a mutually distasteful situation, I suggest we think only of the child I carry. 'Tis your heir, and in the future I want no stigma to touch him which might deny him his right. However, our situation does pose a problem since we are supposed to have only met for the first time this afternoon. My servants are already aware of my condition."

Richard's nostrils flared as he drew in a deep breath and sought to compose himself enough to speak normally over the constriction in his throat. Megan's apparent hostility made him feel as if a cold, gauntleted hand gripped his heart and squeezed with all its might.

He ached to reach out and take her into his arms, to cradle her against him and to know the small mound between them was a child they had created from their love. Yet he made no move to succumb to his needs. He'd not willingly open himself up for more rejection and pain. He'd never allow her to know how much he hurt, nor how much he loved her. He'd satisfy his need of her with the child she bore him, and nothing, not even the woman he loved, would ever take his child away from him. It would be all he had besides his memories of the sweet love affair with his beautiful, spirited reaver.

"I agree we should think of our child, but how do you propose to waylay the gossip? I fear it is widespread by now."

Megan regarded Richard cynically. "Surely between the two of us, we can find a plausible story."

Richard nodded, no longer seeing any humor in their situation. "Aye. We are both experienced in creating stories to suit our own end. This should be no different."

"It will be the same. Having our child recognized as your true, legitimate heir and not a bastard serves us both."

"Then, my lady, I suggest the first thing for us to do is to summon the priest. It should begin to waylay a few wagging tongues."

Megan drew in a deep breath and moistened her dry lips nervously. Her fingernails marred the smooth surface of the chair's wooden armrests as she gripped it in a death hold. She had now come to the point of no return. Once the priest was summoned and the vows were spoken, she would forever be bound to Richard St. Claire. Her wayward heart rejoiced, yet her mind tortured her with taunts of his reasons behind their marriage. Her eyes burned with the need to cry out her frustrations and pain as she searched Richard's scarred features for any sign of tenderness. She found none.

Swallowing back her tears, she nodded. "I'll have Sandy fetch him from the village."

"Then I'll leave you until it is time for the ceremony. I have need of a few hours rest before the priest arrives. It's been a long day," Richard said, and turned toward the door.

"Sir Richard," Megan called before he made good his exit from the solar. "I would know one thing before you go."

Richard paused and arched a curious brow as he glanced over his shoulder.

"Why didn't you question the paternity of my child? 'Twould have been a simple way to force Edward to reconsider his decision for us to marry should I carry another man's child."

"I do not doubt the child is mine, Meggie. You were innocent until we made love."

Megan's breath caught in her throat at the tender tone in

Richard's voice. "But how can you be sure I didn't take other lovers after you?"

A weary smile touched Richard's shapely lips. "You may lie about everything else, but I know the child belongs to me for one reason alone."

Megan frowned up at Richard, perplexed.

"From the way you feel about our marriage. Had the babe belonged to another, you would have been shouting it from the top of the towers to let the world know."

Megan had the grace to blush. Richard knew her well. Had Royce and Richard not been the same man and the king had forced her to wed the latter, she would have done that very thing. "I, too, know your feeling about our union, and you have my thanks for your willingness to protect my babe's future."

"There is no need for your gratitude. You should remember, 'tis my child as well, my lady. In time you will learn I'll let no man or woman keep me from what is mine. And I protect what I hold, be it child or beast." Richard paused and looked Megan in the eyes. "Or wife."

"You still have my gratitude," Megan said, lowering her eyes away from Richard's disturbing gaze.

"Then I accept it as it is given, my lady," Richard said, struggling to suppress the urge to cross the room and drag the unwilling Megan into his arms so he could refresh his memory with the taste of her luscious lips. Swallowing hard, Richard cleared his throat and then bowed gracefully. "Until this eve, my lady."

Megan nodded regally and schooled her features not to respond to Richard's innate charm. During the past weeks she had allowed herself to forget the power he possessed to stir her senses with only his smile. Now, ruefully, she realized the danger she was in by being married to Richard. He was the man who already claimed her heart, and she feared if she didn't keep up her guard at all times, he could make her betray all the vows she'd made.

Father Rupert downed the tankard of ale and extended his hand to Richard. "Congratulations, my lord. Lady Megan will make you a fine wife indeed. I've watched her grow from a stick-thin girl into a lovely young woman whose heart is filled with warmth and tenderness for those she loves. You are a fortunate man. Yes, indeed, you are."

"Thank you, Father," Richard said, glancing at the woman of whom they spoke. She sat on a padded low bench in front of the fireplace, quitely speaking with Lady Faith. Only those who knew her well could detect the air of tension and the mark of strain the last few minutes had left upon her lovely features. But Richard saw them. He easily noted the tightness about her lovely lips and the flicker of something akin to fear in the depths of her indigo eyes.

"Sir, I would have a word with ye," Sandy McTavis said close at Richard's side.

Sandy had watched the ceremony from behind the tapestry covering the passageway to the kitchens and he'd seen the look upon Megan's face when the priest had placed her hand into Richard's and pronounced them man and wife. His heart had gone out to Meggie. The expression in her eyes revealed her feelings more clearly than if they had been spoken aloud. She was vulnerable to the man at her side, having no weapons to defend herself against her own heart. She loved Richard St. Claire, and Sandy was determined to see he never used her feelings to hurt her. Sandy had intruded upon the nuptial celebration to insure that fact. Megan had been hurt enough by her brother, and Sandy would not allow another man to take up where Mallory left off.

"McTavis, I wondered where you've been. Why weren't you here to celebrate my marriage to Lady Megan?" Richard asked, smiling down at the stocky man.

"I'm yer bailiff, sir. 'Tis not fitting for me to be present at the ceremony," Sandy said, slightly taken aback at Richard's reaction to his presence in the main hall.

"You're my lady's friend, McTavis, and should have been present." Richard drew Sandy a tankard of ale and handed it to him.

A puzzled frown marred Sandy's wide forehead as he glanced from the tankard in his hand back to the man at his side. He didn't know what to think of Richard's actions. They were no longer partners in crime, but lord and servant, and he was acting as if nothing had changed between them.

"Now, what did you want to speak to me about?" Richard asked, glancing once more in Megan's direction. Since Father Rupert had pronounced them man and wife, he couldn't take his eyes off of her for more than a few seconds at a time. Something within him was afraid she would vanish as she had done on the fateful day at Ashby's Keep.

" 'Tis about—Meg—Lady Megan," Sandy said. Unused to using her proper title, he stumbled over Megan's name.

Richard drew his gaze away from Megan and arched a brow at Sandy. "What about Meggie?"

Suddenly unsure of himself under Richard's scrutinizing gaze, Sandy shifted uneasily. "I would speak in private."

"So be it," Richard said, setting aside his tankard and excusing himself from Father Rupert's company. "I think the solar should afford us the privacy you require."

Sandy nodded and followed Richard up the stairs to the solar. He waited patiently as Richard closed the door behind them and strode across the chamber to the fireplace. Eyeing the man standing with hands folded over his wide chest, his expression curious yet wary, Sandy drew in a deep, steadying breath to quell the chill of apprehension racing up his spine. This man was no one to trifle with. And he doubted if Sir Richard would take kindly to what he had to say. Yet he had to speak, no matter what the consequences were to himself. Megan's happiness was at stake.

"Now, what is it you would tell me about my wife, McTavis?" Richard asked, arching one dark brow in question. "What mischief has she gotten herself into since we last saw each other?"

"I would see her happy," Sandy blurted out, ignoring Richard's bantering.

Richard frowned. "Is this the only reason you asked to speak with me in private?"

"Nay, I wanted you to know I've loved Meggie like a sister for most of her life and I'll not see her mistreated again. She suffered enough at her brother's hand, and I won't allow any man to hurt her."

Richard's frown deepened. He'd known what a bastard Mallory O'Roarke was from his own experience, so it had come as no surprise to learn he'd squandered Megan's inheritance. He had also heard the rumors of Mallory's attempt to auction her off to his friends with the stipulation she be used as a servant. But because of his own chivalric vows to protect and cherish the opposite sex, he'd foolishly not realized the true depths of Mallory's vicious nature. Beyond his mental abuse, he had also physically abused Megan. That bit of information solved another mystery about the woman he loved, but he couldn't let McTavis give him orders about how to treat his own wife. "McTavis, you overstep your bounds. Lady Megan is my wife and I am now the Lord of Dragon's Lair. I rule this demesne and all upon it as I see fit."

Braving Richard's wrath, Sandy stood his ground. "I'll not stand by and see her mistreated again. She deserves far more happiness out of life than she's received in the past years. For one so young she's already had too many burdens placed upon her shoulders. Since her parents' death, she's been responsible for Dragon's Lair and those who depend upon her for their livelihoods. Her sacrifices have been great and her rewards few, and you may be my lord, but I'll not abide seeing her suffer at your hand.''

Through narrowed lids, Richard regarded Dragon's Lair's bailiff. Each word he'd spoken had added to his esteem of McTavis. His loyalty to Megan ran deep and true, and Richard could ask for nothing more. At least he would always know she would be protected if it was in the bailiff's power to do so. But again he couldn't allow McTavis to dictate to him, no matter how much he liked the man and his courage.

"McTavis, it seems you're unaware we are both set to serve the same purpose. I don't seek to harm Megan nor hurt her in any way. She is now my wife and carries my child. I can appreciate your concern, but 'tis none of your affair about what transpires between myself and my wife. However, from your honesty and your loyalty, I will try to set your mind to rest on one account. You have nothing to fear for Megan. I would also see her happy if given the chance."

"I don't understand," Sandy said, perplexed. From what Meggie had told him, Richard hadn't wanted this marriage.

" 'Tis not for you to understand. It is a matter between myself and my wife. 'Tis our life and we will work it out in time between us and without any interference from anyone, and that includes you."

A glimmer of suspicion inched its way past Sandy's distrust, and he eyed Richard assessingly for a long, thoughtful moment before he spoke. "Ye've fallen in love with Meggie, haven't ye?"

"As I've said, McTavis. 'Tis none of your affair what goes on between myself and my wife, and I'll not repeat it again."

Sandy smiled for the first time since entering the solar. He nodded. Sir Richard was right. It was none of his business what went on between Meggie and her new husband. But he suspected that if they were left alone, things would work out for the best. Meggie loved Sir Richard, and though the man refused to answer his question, he suspected her feelings were returned in full. Satisfied, Sandy said, "Sir Richard, 'tis your affair, and I'll not meddle again unless I feel Meggie has been hurt."

Richard chuckled and shook his head at the man's audacity. "McTavis, I appreciate you allowing me to handle my own affairs. Hopefully I won't be such a failure as you seem to believe."

Sandy's face flushed a deep red at Richard's chiding. He knew he'd far overstepped the bounds of his position at Dragon's Lair and he was fortunate not to find himself in shackles for his presumption. However, something good had come from his boldness. He'd learned there was far more to Sir Richard's feelings for Megan than even she realized, and hopefully in time the two strong-willed people would recognize their love.

"Now it's time I return to my bride and the feast I've ordered prepared to celebrate our marriage," Richard said, striding toward the door.

"Aye, sir," Sandy said, bowing.

Richard paused with his hand on the latch and regarded Sandy curiously. He'd made no move to follow. "Are you not going to join in the celebration, McTavis?"

Sandy blinked at Richard. "Ye want me to take my repast in the great hall, sir?"

"You are a friend of the bride, are you not?"

Sandy bobbed his head up and down. "Aye, sir. Since we were wee babes. Me father was bailiff and me mother was cook here in the keep."

"Then you will join us tonight. I want Meggie to feel the warmth of her family about her until she accepts our marriage." Richard turned and strode from the room without a backward glance at the bailiff he'd left standing dumbfounded by the strange turn of events.

It took Sandy a moment to collect his wits and follow Richard. He'd expected many things from St. Claire, but not this. Still bemused, Sandy descended the stairs to join the wedding party at the long table which had been set with Dragon's Lair's finest linen. Sadly there was no silver left to grace the table. It had been sold long ago to support Mallory's gaming.

Father Rupert sucked the last piece of meat from the bone and tossed it beneath the table for the hounds. Angry growls emerged over the morsel before his foot sent the mongrels scurrying to safer grounds. A wide, sated smile spread his heavy jowls as he leaned back in his chair and gazed at the newlyweds.

" 'Tis growing late, Sir Richard," he mused aloud, and did not have to feign the yawn he hid behind his pudgy-fingered hand. " 'Tis time for the bride and groom to be escorted to their chamber for the bedding."

Megan snapped alert at Father Rupert's mention of the bedding. She blinked at the priest, wondering if she had correctly understood what he'd said. Since the beginning of the wedding feast, she'd done her best to keep her attention centered upon the food on her trencher and ignore the ribald comments being made about her wedding night by Richard's friends. She'd pretended to enjoy the delicately browned capon, the juicy peacock which had been extravagantly re-plumed in its own feathers, the pink-meated salmon swimming in wine sauce, and the sundry of vegetables which had been prepared with the spices and fresh herbs from Faith's garden.

In all, Megan had to admit her wedding feast was fit for a king. But the knowledge she was now irrefutably bound to Richard St. Claire made every bite she took leave a bad taste in her mouth.

She was grateful for only one thing on her wedding day, and that was the absence of Richard's family, especially his sister-in-law, the Lady Jamelyn. Fortunately, they did not receive the news of Richard's plan to obey his king's edict and marry until a few days ago, so it was impossible to travel the distance between Scotland and Dragon's Lair in time to be present at her wedding.

"I couldn't agree with you more, Father," Richard said, turning his intriguing sapphire gaze upon Megan. Seeing her stricken expression, he smiled. " 'Tis time to retire, Meggie. 'Tis expected of us."

Megan swallowed hard and tore her gaze away from her husband's and back to the food on her trencher. " 'Tis still early, my lord. What would our guests think of us should we leave them now?"

Her comment brought forth several loud guffaws from Richard's men, and Megan flushed a deep scarlet.

Richard placed a comforting hand over Megan's tightly clenched fist and bent close. His voice was firm as he said, " 'Tis time, my lady."

Megan's lower lip quivered as she drew in a deep breath and nodded. She had no other choice but to obey.

But God, how can I go through with this night when I know he doesn't love or want me? 'Tis all for the child and nothing more, Megan agonized silently as she scanned the eager faces watching her from down the length of the long table. They knew nothing of the reason for her marriage to Richard St. Claire, and it was her responsibility to insure they never suspected the truth. She reminded herself she was only thinking of her child and his future when she did as her husband bid her by making all appear normal.

Spurred on by the thought, Megan resolutely pushed back her chair and stood. She took the arm Richard proffered and gracefully walked at his side up the stairs to her chamber. Father Rupert followed in their wake to bless their union while the guests crowded the stairs behind him, laughing and making more risqué comments about the ecstasy to be had once the priest left them to enjoy the pleasures of the flesh.

At the door to their chamber, Megan turned misty, pleading eyes upon her husband. Her trembling voice reflected her distress as she said, "Please allow me to have my cousin help me undress in private."

Understanding her plight, Richard tipped up her chin with his thumb and forefinger and gently lowered his lips to hers in a gentle kiss, to the merriment of the crowd in the hallway behind him. When the kiss ended, he peered down into her indigo eyes and smiled. " 'Tis not too much to ask. I'll wait here until you are ready."

"Thank you," Megan breathed before quickly slipping into the room and closing the door behind her. She leaned back against the heavy portal and her eyes filled with tears as she looked at Faith, who stood holding the shimmering silk kirtle which Richard had brought for her to wear on their wedding night.

A silent message passed between herself and her cousin, and Megan slowly nodded. She understood what Faith wanted to tell her. She would be brave. The face she presented to the world would reflect what everyone expected of a new bride. She would fulfill her obligations to still the wagging tongues that could hurt her child's future, but when she was alone with Richard behind closed doors, she'd never submit to him again. Her marriage was necessary, but she'd never be used as a surrogate for the woman he truly loved.

Bravely she inched up her chin, wiped her eyes with the back of her hand, and gave Faith a wobbly smile. " 'Tis a lovely fabric."

"Aye, Sir Richard chose well for you. The blue matches your eyes," Faith said as she came forward to undress Megan.

" 'Tis the hardest thing I've ever had to do," Megan said, unable to avoid the subject of her wedding night completely with inane chitchat.

"I know," Faith murmured softly, her heart going out to

her cousin. "But 'tis the right path you've chosen to follow. It isn't easy for you, but you must think of your child."

"Aye, 'tis the only reason either of us agreed to this match."

"Meggie, I wish there was something I could say or do to make things easier," Faith said as she undid the laces of Megan's bliaud and let it fall to the floor. She slipped the sheer silk gown down over Megan's head and let it fall about her rounding curves.

"As I told Sir Anthony, 'tis nothing anyone can say or do to make this marriage easier. 'Tis left to Richard and me to work things out between us."

"Then you have accepted this marriage and are going to forgive him for his deception?"

"I've accepted our marriage, but I'm afraid 'tis not the deception which I can't forgive, Faith. 'Tis his feeling for another woman."

"But you're now Sir Richard's wife and you carry his child."

"Aye, but it means nothing. How many men have wives they don't love yet still have children? 'Tis Richard's heart I want and I'll settle for nothing less before I become his wife in truth."

Faith gaped at her cousin. "Surely you don't mean to deny him his rights as your husband, Meggie? 'Twill earn you a beating or worse."

"Nay, Faith. Richard is not like Mallory. He'll not beat me. He might get angry enough to strangle me at times, but he'll never lay a hand on me in anger," Megan said, speaking from her heart. She also knew she could never love a man like her brother.

"I pray you're right, cousin. Or 'twill be too late before you learn you're wrong," Faith said, turning back the covers of the bed for Megan to crawl beneath before her husband entered the room in the company of the priest and his drunken companions.

Megan slid into the bed and pulled the covers up about her chin. ''Now 'tis time for you to stop worrying about me and concern yourself with your own affairs. Sir Anthony couldn't take his eyes off you at dinner.''

Faith shook her head. ''Nay, Meggie. Sir Anthony is kind, but he's not for me. 'Tis best I stay as far away from him as possible.''

Before Megan could answer, Faith crossed to the door and swung it open. To Megan's embarrassment the doorway filled instantly with eager spectators. Richard himself had been undressed, and, with much laughter, he was roughly carried into the chamber and dropped onto the bed by Anthony and, to Megan's amazement, Sandy McTavis. Amused by the ritualistic bedding, he sat naked and grinning like a buffoon as the priest, rosary in hand, made the sign of the cross and prayed for their union to be blessed with children.

Richard felt Megan shift uneasily and glanced at his wife. For the first time since entering the chamber, he noted she was scarlet from embarrassment. Realizing her distress and feeling like an ass for allowing himself to fall in with the merriment of his inebriated friends, Richard let the priest finish his prayers before clambering from the bed and ushering him out the crowded doorway. Before anyone could object, he forcibly closed and locked the door against the merrymakers.

Eager to once more be in bed with his wife, he turned and, in less than three strides, landed back in the middle of the down-filled mattress. When he found himself alone, his surprise and vexation were evident by the expression on his face.

''What in hell,'' Richard growled, turning to find his bride standing with hands braced on her hips and chin thrust out at a pugnacious angle. At the sight of Megan standing bathed in the golden glow of the firelight, the sheer silk gown turning transparent, his mind didn't register her hostile stance. His breath caught in his throat and his heart began to hammer against his ribs as his blood caught fire. A pleased grin quirked one side of his sensuous mouth.

Completely unaware of her tantalizing display, Megan regarded her husband calmly. "Surely you didn't expect to share my bed, Sir Richard?"

Richard drew his gaze away from Megan's luscious curves draped in shimmering silk and blinked up at her. He drew in a long breath, gave her a roguish smile, and relaxed back on the bed, stretching out his lean, muscular body like a lazy cat. Propped on one elbow, he eyed Megan. "Should I expect anything less, Lady St. Claire? This is our wedding night."

"Expect what you will, sir, but be aware your expectations are not what is going to take place, now or ever."

Richard's smile faded and his sinewy muscles tensed, though his expressions didn't alter to reveal the anger simmering to the surface.

"My lady, you are now my wife and I have the right to take you when and where I please."

"Aye, you have the right, but you'll not use it."

Richard arched a dark brow. "Why so, madam?"

"Because if you lay one hand on me, I'll scratch out your eyes and hand them back to you on a platter."

Richard sat up, all amusement gone. His sapphire gaze was ice. "Megan, if you think your threats will stay me, then think again, dear wife."

Richard came to his feet, naked and angry, the angelical side of his face altering to match the scars as the devil in him took over. He strode forward, his lean muscles rippling beneath bronzed, sinewy flesh; his hands balled into fists at his side. He moved so swiftly, Megan didn't have time to escape the hands that captured her shoulders. His fingers bit into her upper arms as he drew her slowly, inexorably against him.

"I have already warned you, Meggie, no man or woman will keep me from what is mine," he growled as he lowered his mouth to hers. His lips pressed hers open and his tongue plunged inside her mouth to plunder the bounty found there.

Megan brought up both hands and pounded against his chest, but he was unrelenting. He captured the back of her head in the palm of his hand, holding her prisoner so he could taste her sweet lips to his fill.

Megan moaned her protest, desperate to escape his embrace. His mouth was bringing back too many feelings—feelings she didn't want, feelings that made her stomach quiver with anticipation and her hips move of their own volition against his hard flesh.

No, her mind cried even as her tongue sought out his and her arms inched their way up his wide chest to curl about his corded neck. Stop it, you fool, her mind ordered, but her heart paid no heed. She molded herself to Richard and gave one last moan of protest before she surrendered to the fire his touch ignited within her.

Richard swept one arm down the length of her thinly clad body and scooped her up in his arms, quickly laying her upon the bed. His gaze devoured each inch of her curvacious body as he stripped away the silk gown and tossed it to the floor. A moan of pleasure escaped his lips as he buried his face in the valley between her breasts and drew in her arousing fragrance.

Of all the women he'd bedded in his life, only Meggie's scent made him feel like a stag in rut. The mere smell of her sent desire rushing through him in a fiery current, making him react on instinct alone. Meggie was his and he had to have her.

Fondling one passion-swollen, rose-tipped mound, Richard took its twin into his mouth, teasing the nipple with his tongue and feeling it grow into a hard little bud before he suckled like a man starved. Eager to know all of the woman he loved, he began to explore her satiny-limbed body, his fingers seeking out the secret places before his lips followed to erotically tantalize each inch he discovered.

Megan moaned her pleasure and thrust her hips up to meet his probing tongue. Her dark hair fanned across the pillow as she arched her back and savored the ultimate caress. It was unlike anything she had ever experienced before, and she felt herself begin to melt. The muscles in her belly quivered violently as a wave of pure, undiluted lust took control. Like her ancestors, the Celts, whose women were equal to their men in all ways, in one lithe movement she changed positions with Richard. Her raven hair spilled about her ivory body in a silken web as she came on top of him with a sensuous, animalistic growl. Straddling him, her taut-peaked breasts brushed against his furred chest as she bent and captured his lips in a demanding, possessive kiss. She shifted her hips temptingly against him, yet when he moved to bring her down on top of his hard, passion-swollen member, she denied him. She tossed her head and smiled provocatively.

"Nay, 'tis my time to enjoy you," Megan said, her eyes and hands already exploring his sinewy flesh as he had done to hers only moments before. She brushed her breasts against his chest and smiled at the look of pleasure that crossed his face. Feeling a surge of power, she inched her body down, keeping flesh to flesh as she moved toward the object of her desire.

For one heart-stopping moment she raised herself above him, teasing him with the tips of her fingers as her eyes sought his. She moistened her lips with the tip of her tongue and gave him a smile that made the breath freeze in his throat. He swallowed hard as she lowered her head and loved him as he had done her. A groan of pure pleasure escaped Richard as he moved to the music she created with her mouth.

"By all that's holy," Richard groaned. Unable to stand the sweet torment a moment longer, he captured Megan by the arms and drew her up. He tasted himself upon her lips as he flipped her onto her back and sought the moist haven between her beckoning thighs. Thrusting deep within her, he claimed her as his wife and as the woman he loved.

Together they soared—tasting, savoring the glory of their union and of their love. Their cries of rapture mingled as one through the still chamber as their passion exploded.

"Meggie," Richard breathed at last, collapsing over her and burying his face in the curve of her shoulder. " 'Twas worth the cost of marrying to know such passion."

Richard's words sent Megan abruptly spiraling from the peaks of esctasy back toward the hard, cold truth of the real world. Like ice water upon a flame, his words killed her passion until there was nothing left but cold grey ash. Gone was her wild need to possess him and be possessed in turn. His words had reminded her that she could have his lust but not his heart.

Blinking back hot tears, she squirmed from beneath Richard and sat up. Her voice was cold when she spoke. "I have fulfilled my obligation as your wife. Now will you be good enough to leave my chamber, Sir Richard?"

Dumbfounded by the abrupt change, Richard stared at the bare back turned to him. His soft, sated expression faded as he narrowed his eyes and pressed his sensuous lips into a thin, angry line. "Nay. I will share this chamber with you, dear wife. 'Twould seem odd for me to leave your bed so soon after the vows were spoken, and if you will remember, we must make everyone believe our child was conceived on our wedding night."

Megan hung her head, surrendering without argument to the trap she'd laid for herself by agreeing to marry Richard for the sake of their child. She begrudgingly admitted he was right. They must stay together if they wanted people to believe their lies.

Glancing over her shoulder, she regarded Richard for a

long moment before she said, "We may fool everyone by staying in the same room, yet Father Rupert will expect to see the sign of my virginity upon the sheets in the morn."

"It can easily be taken care of," Richard said. Rising from the bed, he crossed to the pile of clothes his friends had tossed at the foot of the bed earlier. The muscles rippled beneath his bronzed skin as he bent and took his dirk from its sheath. He pricked his finger and pressed it until it beaded red. A sarcastic little smile tugged at his lips as he bent and smeared his blood upon the sheet.

Glancing once more at his wife, he shrugged. "See, madam. Your virginity cannot be questioned. After this evidence everyone will believe our child was conceived tonight from love and in the sight of God and England's law."

"How I wish it were true," Megan murmured so softly Richard failed to hear her heart-wrenching words.

"Did you say something?" Richard asked, his brows knitting in puzzlement.

"I said, good night," Megan lied. Biting her lip, she lay down and pulled the covers up to shield her nakedness. She had made her own prison and now must accept the sentence her gaoler meted out.

I do this only for the sake of my babe, Megan mused silently in an effort to bolster her flagging spirits. However, deep inside she knew the real reason she didn't protest his demands. No matter what she said and did, she still loved Richard St. Claire with all her heart.

Chapter 15

Richard tossed the dice and then swore when he lost to Anthony. Chuckling at his friend's run of bad luck, an impish grin curling the corners of his shapely lips, Anthony said, "Of late your luck seems to have changed, Richard."

Vexed with himself, Richard ran his fingers through his hair and pushed himself to his feet. He looked down at his fair-haired friend kneeling by the bone game pieces and shook his head. " 'Tis fair to say, my luck in all things has changed of late."

Anthony glanced toward the two women sitting before the embroidery frames on the far side of the hall. " 'Tis often the way of things, especially when hawks and falcons mingle."

Richard frowned. "Damn me, Anthony. I've about had enough of this hawks and falcons you keep muttering about. Since I arrived at Dragon's Lair, it's all I've heard from you, but you never have the courtesy to explain yourself."

Anthony collected the dice and pocketed them before standing. He looked at Richard and smiled. "You and your lovely bride remind me of hawks and falcons 'tis all."

"I don't see the resemblance," Richard said, unappeased by his explanation.

"I see it well. Hawks and falcons are birds of a kind, fierce and strong. The only difference is in their size; one is small and the other is large."

"I still don't see the comparison," Richard muttered, turning his gaze to look upon his wife. They had now been married for nearly six months and she was nearing her term, though nothing had changed between them since their wedding night. Their lives had settled into a pattern. Like the metal mirror in their chamber, they acted like the newlyweds they were supposed to be, a content if not overly loving couple in front of household retainers and his men. However, things changed drastically when their chamber door closed behind them to shut out prying eyes and ears. They became strangers. A distance that seemed to stretch miles was always between them, though at times Megan was only inches away from him in the large bed they shared each night.

Richard clenched his teeth and a muscle worked in his jaw. He didn't know how much more of this strange arrangement he could take. Every nerve in his body was as taut as a longbow string, and his temper was so frayed, it took every ounce of his willpower to keep it under control. Out of fear of finding themselves the object of his ire, the servants and his own men had begun to avoid his company.

Richard's gaze swept over Megan's round figure and he swallowed hard. It had been agony sharing the same bed with her and never being able to reach out and touch Megan except when she was so deeply asleep she was unaware of his actions. There had been many nights when he had lain awake just to hold her in his arms once she was soundly asleep. He'd cradled her next to him and placed his hand on her swollen abdomen to feel the movement of his child within her. Those moments had been the hardest to bear. He'd wanted to laugh his joy aloud, to let the entire world know the thrill it gave him to feel the life he had sired, but he'd managed to control himself. He'd kept his secret well during the past months. For he knew if Megan ever suspected his actions, she'd make her bed on the floor to avoid his touch.

Richard swore again under his breath and turned away. He'd endured the torment of wanting Megan for months, and he'd continue to endure it until she turned to him. Never again would he plant his hopes in the sandy loam of her capriciousness and then watch them take root before withering from her wintery rebuffs.

Refilling his tankard with ale, Richard hoped the brew would help ease his frustration for a brief time. He knew most men would have already chosen some likely young maid to share their bed, and he had considered it since he'd been denied his wife's affections. But oddly enough, and to his dismay, he hadn't found any of the women of his acquaintance desirable since he'd spoken his wedding vows. There was only one woman he wanted to bed, and it was Megan St. Claire, his wife.

Seeing his friend's misery, Anthony placed a comforting hand on Richard's shoulder. His words came from the heart of a man who understood everything Richard was feeling. " 'Tis hard to love someone and then not have the love returned."

Richard glanced over his shoulder at Anthony and gave him a commiserating look. "Then 'tis safe to say, you've had no luck wooing your fair lady?"

"Luck? 'Twould take Lady Fortune herself to change Faith's feelings about me. I've done everything within my power to charm her, but she refuses to give me the slightest chance. The times I find her alone, she quickly finds something urgent which has need of her attention and then flees as if I'd set the hounds upon her heels. Sadly, if given the choice, she avoids me completely. I've come to believe I've finally found one woman who honestly can't stand the sight of me."

"Aye, it does seem we have found the only two women in

England who can resist us," Richard said, his lips curling into a rueful grin. He glanced thoughtfully at Megan and Faith for a long, considering moment before he looked once more at Anthony. A mischievous expression crossed his intriguing face. "Perhaps we should make our fair ladies realize we aren't without charm to others of our acquaintance."

"What are you scheming, Richard?"

"I thought only to bring our ladies' attention to us," Richard answered innocently.

"If you will recall, your schemes in the past haven't been successful, so why do you think they'll succeed now?"

Richard grinned. "Because there will be another beautiful woman under the same roof with our vixens."

"Who do you propose to invite to Dragon's Lair? There are no women at Edward's court who can rival Megan and Faith."

"She's not at Edward's court. She resides at Raven's Keep."

"Jamelyn! Justin will never allow Jamelyn to participate in one of your outrageous schemes, especially after the earful he received from Edward about your last one."

"Justin is now in Flanders as Edward's emissary. He's to appear as if he's there to persuade the lowlanders to align themselves with England when Edward goes to war with France. But in truth he's there to try to solve the mystery about the wool thieves. Since I've failed to learn anything here, the king thought it might be possible for Justin to learn more in Flanders."

"Even with Justin in Flanders, how do you propose to get Jamelyn to come to Dragon's Lair? I know she loves you like a brother, but I fear she'll not go along with you on this. She knows how it is when a husband brings another woman into his home. If you will recall, it is how Anne came to visit Raven's Keep."

"Aye, I know Jamelyn well, but what she doesn't know won't hurt her."

Anthony shook his head. "I think, friend, you have lost your wits. You already have one firebrand on your hands, and now you're planning to invite another to come to Dragon's Lair. I warn you. You could be risking your life."

Richard chuckled. "The risk is small if you reap the rewards of love, Anthony."

Anthony again shook his head and turned to pour himself another tankard of ale. He caught a glimpse of Megan hurrying from the hall. Her expression made him pause. White-faced and eyes bright with unshed tears, she fled up the stairs to her chamber. He momentarily wondered what had caused her tears but immediately assumed they stemmed from her pregnancy. Pregnant women often acted oddly.

Satisfied with his conclusion, he turned his attention to the woman who sat by the embroidery frames. His heart stilled and a shiver raced down his spine at the look of loathing she flashed at him before huffily rising from her seat and marching from the hall with back stiff and head held high.

Anthony scratched his head as he turned to Richard. "Now, I wonder what I've done to deserve that."

Richard glanced at the stiff-backed figure ascending the stairs and shook his head. "I fear I'm not the one to ask when it comes to dealing with the women of Dragon's Lair. Hopefully when Jamelyn arrives, she'll be able to help us understand the women we love."

"If Jamelyn can solve this one problem for us, then perhaps your scheme has merit after all," Anthony said, glancing once more toward the stairs. "Aye, 'twould be well worth it."

Megan pressed her back against the rough surface of the door and gulped in a shuddering breath. Her eyes burned with tears, but she refused to allow them to fall. She'd shed enough tears in the past six months to last her a lifetime. It seemed as if everything and everyone at Dragon's Lair had conspired against her. Her people had accepted Richard as their overlord without complaint, and even Sandy seemed to have deserted her. She'd always been able to count upon his support in everything she did, but of late, he seemed to align himself with the enemy, her husband. When she made any remark about Richard and his actions at Dragon's Lair, Sandy refused to comment one way or the other. He kept his own council, and if he saw anything that displeased him, he certainly hadn't let her know anything about it. From the way he looked at her sometimes, she sensed he felt she was in the wrong to complain about the grand Sir Richard St. Claire.

"But he doesn't know him like I do. Sandy isn't aware of his plans to invite the woman he loves to Dragon's Lair," she ground out between clenched teeth. Swiping at her burning eyes, she crossed the chamber to stare out into the dark evening. Unlike the emotions running rampant through her, the night was still and quiet.

If only my life could be as peaceful, Megan mused, her eyes again filling with tears and her thoughts turning once more to the bit of conversation she'd overheard between her husband and Sir Godfrey.

She'd heard only a few words of Anthony's warning before her husband's words made her realize nothing had changed over the past months. Her hope that the uneasy relationship between herself and Richard would change when the babe was born had been shattered tonight when he'd said any risk was small as long as you gained love. She knew Richard didn't care who he had to hurt to be with his brother's wife.

"The bastard," Megan muttered before gasping in surprise. Her eyes widened as she looked down at her swollen stomach, and something akin to bewilderment crossed her lovely features at the feel of the muscles contracting across her abdomen.

Again the muscles tightened and the nagging ache that had begun in her lower back earlier in the afternoon returned in full force. Paling, Megan placed a hand against her taut belly and drew in a deep breath, bracing against the pressure that was slowly building into another contraction.

Megan gasped again and made her way across the chamber to the bed. She sank down on it and moistened her lips with the tip of her tongue. She wanted to deny it, but now she accepted what she'd refused to recognize earlier in the day: her labor had begun. She'd experienced a few twinges in the afternoon but had not been greatly concerned. However, to-night she'd thought to tell Richard in the event their babe decided it was time to enter the world. She'd hoped to choose a time when he was enjoying himself with his friend so he'd be in a much better mood to accept her news. That was what had taken her across the hall to where the men had been playing at dice and savoring their ale. A moment later their conversation had completely sidetracked her from her pur-pose until nature decided to reassert itself in force.

Another contraction gripped Megan and she moved with it, bending over and wrapping her arms about her middle. She held her breath, but nothing helped allay the magnifying pain. When the spasm ended of its own accord, sweat beaded her brow.

Breathing heavily, she pushed herself upright and eased her heavy body from the bed. She had to get to the stairs and call for help or she could end up having her child alone. The thick stone walls that gave her the privacy she had always treasured would now make it nearly impossible for anyone in the hall to hear her cry.

"I shouldn't have sent Mary to the kitchens," Megan mut-tered, disgusted with herself for not realizing she would have need of the serving maid later in the evening. But Mary's incessant chatter had tired her to the bone, and she might have been tempted to cut the serving maid's tongue out to quiet her if she hadn't sent her away.

Now, due to her not having the forethought to wonder at the strange feelings she'd experienced since early in the afternoon, she had to reach the stairs and call for Faith to help. The thought paramount in her mind, she stood upright. Megan's eyes widened in shock as a hot stream of liquid drenched her clothing and puddled at her feet. Before she had time to react to the breaking of her water, another far more intense pain took her into its grip. She moaned and doubled over, clutching her belly. She sank back onto the bed and lay there, face buried against the pillows, breathing rapidly and praying for the contraction to subside.

Megan's moan greeted Richard when he entered the bedchamber. Fear trickled down his spine like a stream of melting snow and dread settled a rock-hard fist in his stomach as he viewed his wife's awkward position on the bed.

"Megan, what's wrong?" he asked, and felt like a fool for asking a question for which he already knew the answer.

Megan shifted her weight and spread her hand over her taut belly. Her eyes were misty with tears as she looked up at her husband and gave him a wobbly little smile. " 'Twould seem your son has decided 'tis time to venture into the world, Sir Richard."

A thrill shot through him and he felt like laughing aloud. Not only was his child to be born, but Megan had said "your son," not "my son," the term she'd continued to use since their wedding day.

"Meggie, you should have had Mary call me," Richard said, forgetting he would be the last person she'd want to help her. In a glance he noted the maid's absence and questioned, "Where in hell is the wench? You shouldn't have been left alone."

A flicker of pain crossed Megan's ashen features and she automatically reached out for the succor of Richard's hand.

When the pain eased, she ran her tongue across her dry lips and drew in a fortifying breath. "Unaware my time was so near, I sent Mary away in order to enjoy a little peace. And our son hasn't given me a chance to call anyone since he decided he'd wait no longer to join us."

She flinched again as a new spasm gripped her belly. Megan arched her back against it and her fingernails bit into Richard's hand, drawing blood.

"By all that's holy," Richard breathed, suddenly realizing the true extent of her agony. He held her hand until her pain eased and then gently lay it on her swollen belly before he ran from the chamber, calling for assistance at the top of his lungs. A few minutes passed before he was back with Faith following quickly upon his heels, carrying sharp-bladed scissors and white linen.

"Meggie," Faith said, laying a hand upon Megan's swollen belly to feel the contractions. As if on cue, Megan's responded, the pressure increasing as she curled forward and drew her legs up. When the pains eased once more, her hair was damp and her lips were swollen and ridden with teeth marks.

Faith flashed Richard a look urging him to leave them alone so they could do what nature intended. Yet he made no move as she silently bid him. He returned to Megan's bedside and knelt. Taking her hand once more into his own callused palm, he placed his lips against it and looked into the indigo depths of Megan's pain-glazed eyes. "Hold on to me, Meggie. Let me help you bring our son into the world."

"Sir Richard," Faith said, dumbfounded by Richard's actions. " 'Tis best you leave us. 'Tis no place for a man at a birthing."

"I'll decide where I should be when my child is born, Lady Faith," Richard said, turning his sapphire gaze upon Faith.

Faith took a step back. The expression on Richard's face

sent a chill down her spine. From the resolute look, she knew she didn't have the courage to ask him to leave Megan again. She feared no man or woman had enough strength to oust him from his wife's side at this time. The thought made Faith take pause. Her cousin believed Sir Richard loved another woman, but from his actions, Faith had to wonder at Megan's assumption. For Sir Richard was now acting like a man deeply in love with his own wife.

Faith's gaze rested on the dark head bent close to Megan's. When Megan had fled the hall earlier, ashen and teary-eyed, without a word of explanation, she'd suspected Richard had again hurt her cousin. Now she wondered if the onset of Megan's labor had been the cause and not her husband's actions.

Megan's cry broke through Faith's reverie and she quickly tied the linen straps about the posts of the bed to give Megan handholds when the labor grew worse. She then stripped away the covers and placed fresh linen beneath Megan's hips. Seeing there was nothing more she could do to help her cousin until it was time for the babe's delivery, she turned her attention to building a fire in the cold grate. The mother as well as the babe would need the warmth.

"Meggie," Richard murmured softly, feeling helplessly inadequate in this situation. But he wouldn't leave Megan's side until he knew she would survive the birth of the child he'd placed within her. Gently he brushed several damp curls away from her sweat-beaded brow. "God, I didn't know it would hurt you so much."

Megan's nostrils flared as she drew in a deep breath and then began to pant. She wanted to tell Richard all women suffered during childbirth, but the pains were coming too fast now to think coherently, much less speak.

She bucked up and then curled against the terrible pressure. Her body was no longer hers as she drew her knees to her chest and growled like a lion. She went with the pain and pushed down.

"Faith!" Richard cried, ignoring the tiny rivulets of his own blood running down the back of his hand where Megan's nails had bitten into his flesh. " 'Tis the babe."

"Everything is going smoothly, Sir Richard," Faith said, moving to the side of the bed, where she could assist Megan when the babe slipped into the world. Having helped in the birthing of several villeins' children, she calmly took charge.

"Smoothly! By all that's holy, Lady! She's suffering," Richard swore, his voice tinged with panic.

"Aye. 'Tis the way of things. No one comes into this world without suffering, Sir Richard. 'Tis why I wanted you to leave us. Men can't understand this side of the begetting of children."

"Isn't there anything you can do for her?" Richard said, suddenly sick to his stomach. He'd been so proud Megan carried his child, but he'd never thought of the agony she'd have to go through to bring his heir into the world. Richard swallowed back the bile rising in his throat. Megan's suffering was his fault. Cold sweat beaded his brow and his face was as white as his wife's ashen features. He looked down into her lovely face, contorted into an agonized grimace as another contraction took hold of her beautiful, young body.

Megan's scream rent the still chamber and echoed off the stone walls as the last contraction gripped her in its final throes. She bit through her lower lip as she clasped her knees and strained to push her babe into the world. A moment later a tiny dark head emerged and then a pink, screwed-up little face before its small body slipped easily into Faith's awaiting hands. She quickly tied and cut the umbilical cord before swatting Richard's son on his tiny bottom. His angry wail filled the chamber as Faith looked up into his father's bemused face and handed him to Richard. "Your heir, Sir Richard. A fine healthy boy."

Richard looked down at his son—bloody, screaming, arms and legs flailing the air. He was the most beautiful thing Richard had ever seen. A crooked, foolish grin curved up the corners of his sensuous mouth as he inspected the tiny being in his hands from head to toe, counting all the babe's limbs, as well as fingers and toes, eyes, ears, and nose. He nodded, satisfied all was in order, before he glanced once more at the woman who had given him the greatest treasure on earth. His throat constricted with emotion as he knelt and held out their child for her to see.

"He's a fine lad, Meggie, and I thank you for giving him to me," Richard murmured, unable to voice all the things dwelling in his heart for this woman who had endured such agony for him.

Megan reached out a tentative hand and stroked the black down upon her babe's pate. A tender, loving smile briefly touched her bruised lips before her hand fell to her side and her eyes closed from exhaustion.

Richard panicked until he saw Faith shake her head and smile. " 'Tis normal. She's endured much and now must regain her strength. She'll sleep for a long while." Faith reached for the babe, but Richard drew back, refusing to relinquish the tiny life he'd been given.

" 'Tis necessary I take him now, Sir Richard. He needs his fingers and toes worked to chase away the evil humors and then he must be cleaned with honey and salt before he's ready to be wrapped in the silk swaddling Megan has prepared for him."

Reluctantly Richard handed his son to Faith. "Take good care of my heir, Lady Faith, for his mother paid dearly to bring him into the world."

Faith cradled the babe in her arms, but the questions filling her mind made her hesitate to turn her full attention to the infant. "You love Megan, don't you, Sir Richard?"

Richard, his heart exposed and made vulnerable by the birth of his son, merely nodded.

Faith smiled and turned away. She was satisfied. In time she knew Megan and Richard would finally admit their feelings to each other, and the child in her arms could only help them down the path to their happiness.

Chapter 16

Richard stood quietly by the fireplace, sipping a glass of wine and enjoying the sight of his son suckling at his wife's breast. Megan's contented sigh was like a caress to him, for it mirrored his own feelings—feelings that had emerged since the birth of their son. Gone was his wild need to lay claim to all of Megan's emotions. He was now happy to share her affections with the tiny being she held tenderly within her arms. He was satisfied watching Megan with their child; his feeling overshadowed any doubts that still lingered about his lovely wife. Although outwardly things had changed little between Megan and himself, his heart told him that in time he would have all he desired. He'd seen the gentle looks she'd cast in his direction when they were alone and she thought herself unobserved. The birth of their son had wrought many changes, and hopefully the love they shared for the child would weave its web about them and they could again find each other.

Drawing his gaze away from the hungry babe, Richard took in Megan's lovely features one by one, memorizing each in turn and feeling the desire for her simmer anew through his veins. He savored her beauty, and when his gaze came to rest upon her mouth, he knew an unbearable craving to again taste the sweetness beyond her soft lips. His fingers itched to caress her flawless skin, which the firelight had gently burnished with warm gold. He longed to peer into the mysterious blue of the eyes hidden beneath her thick lashes as she gazed down at their child.

Giving their son nourishment, she reminded him of a painting of the Madonna he'd seen in Westminster Abbey. Like the Madonna, her loving spirit seemed to halo her in radiance. But unlike the virginal mother of Christ, Megan stirred within him less than holy feelings. He wanted her to the core of his being, and in all honesty he didn't know how much longer he could sustain his self-imposed celibacy. Every fiber of his being seemed to ache with need, yet there was only one woman he wanted to give him ease.

Instinct guided Richard's actions. He set aside his wine and crossed to the bed, where Megan sat holding their son. Gently he caressed the small head where the dark down had already begun to thicken into curls much like his own. His gaze locked with Megan's.

"Meggie, our son is growing into a strapping lad. In no time at all he'll be challenging my men to joust," Richard said, his voice husky with pent-up emotion.

"Aye, he's like his father," Megan answered softly, her smile reflecting the feelings she'd desperately tried to keep hidden from her husband during the past months. It was growing harder with each day to live with Richard and not show her love for him. The birth of their son had been the catalyst to obliterate the hostility between herself and her husband and had allowed her to feel the love she'd sought to deny since learning of Richard's true identity.

Unaware of his own actions, Richard had also helped ease her misgivings about him. His devotion to their child had again shown her the gentle lover she knew before their capture at Ashby Keep. He no longer spent his evenings gaming and drinking in the hall with Anthony and his men, but sought out their chamber in order to watch her feed and care for their son.

Suddenly becoming aware of her need to know Richard's love again, Megan blushed a becoming rose as she eased from the bed and crossed to the cradle. Ever aware of protecting her son from harm, she had placed it close enough to the fire to gain the warmth given off by the logs but far enough away to keep her babe from the danger of popping sparks. Laying her plump, well-fed, sleeping son down upon the soft linen, she covered him snugly with a fur-lined blanket to ward off the chill before turning to face her husband once more.

The breath stilled in her throat at the look of pure, raw desire upon Richard's scarred features. Her heart responded to the look—fluttering wildly against her ribs like a bird snared in a cage. She moistened her suddenly dry lips and swallowed hard, fighting the urge to rush across the chamber and fling herself into his arms.

"Megan," was all Richard said, yet the one husky word was a heart-wrenching plea as he raised a bronze, long-fingered hand, palm upward toward her.

Hesitantly Megan drew her eyes away from Richard's burning gaze and looked at the hand he held out. Again she swallowed. How she longed to go to him and surrender to her heart's demands. She wanted nothing more from life than to know the feel of his arms about her, holding her close to his hard, lean body as his mouth captured hers in a searing kiss. She ached to experience again the rapture that would cool the desire burning deep in the pit of her belly.

Briefly Megan sought escape from the trap her emotions were setting for her, but she couldn't flee swiftly enough to avoid capture. Her eyes again locked with Richard's and she knew the bittersweet feeling of defeat. Her heart had finally forsaken the vows she'd made to keep Richard at bay. Ruled by it, her feet moved toward him of their own accord, taking her to the man she loved.

Sensing her surrender and unable to wait for her to cross the few feet separating them, Richard met her halfway. He wrapped her in his arms, pressing her tightly against his aching flesh as he took her lips in a desperate, demanding kiss. A groan of pure, undiluted pleasure escaped him as he devoured the sweetness he'd craved for many months.

Megan gave herself up to Richard's kiss, clasping her arms about his corded neck and entwining her fingers in the dark curls that touched his wide shoulders. Freely she admitted the battle was over. It was much easier and much more pleasurable to enjoy her husband's caresses.

Richard tore his mouth free of hers and buried his face in the curve of her neck. He drew in a ragged breath and a tremor shook his strong body as he tightened his embrace about her. "God! How I've wanted to feel you in my arms. Every muscle, every bone, and every inch of my body aches with the need to love you. You don't know how many nights I've lain awake at your side longing to pull you into my arms and make love to you until you cried out with ecstacy."

"I know, my darling," Megan whispered, her fingers gently stroking his head.

Richard raised his head and peered down at Megan. "You know?"

"Aye. I know. I haven't forgotten how it feels to be held in your arms."

"God! The time we've so foolishly wasted!" Richard said, his voice a mixture of exasperation and laughter. His face showed his joy as he bent and swept Megan into his arms. In less than two strides he fell with her upon the down-filled mattress and made swift work of freeing her from the thin kirtle she wore when feeding their son. Giving her no time to think, he captured her mouth, plunging his tongue past her lips to ignite the banked embers of their passion until it flamed white-hot.

Stroking and fondling gently, Richard explored her silken flesh, relearning each inch of Megan's lithe body until he could no longer resist the dark glean at the apex of her thighs. There he delved into her rich warmth as he left her lips and slowly worked his way along her smooth cheek to the alabaster column of her throat. Then he moved to savor the bounty of her full breasts. He tasted the sweetness that gave his son sustenance but resisted the temptation to fulfill his own need to suckle the milk meant for his child.

A moan passed his lips as he buried his face between the heavy mounds and fondled the moist, hot folds which hid the satiny sheath he longed to surround the hard length of him. Megan thrust her hips up, beckoning his hand to know more of her—arching her back as she opened to him. Unable to bear the torment of his need a moment longer, Richard sought the dark, wet haven—burying himself deep within her.

Together they soared, moving in the motions of love, seeking—mouth to mouth—thigh to thigh—hip to hip—the ultimate glory only those who love can receive. It came. Like a searing whirlwind it took them, spiraling ever upward, drenching their hot bodies in liquid diamonds as they moved amid the exploding stars of rapture. Tremor after tremor rippled as they gripped each other, and their voices rose in unison as they cried out their ecstasy.

Breathing heavily, Megan clung to Richard's wide shoulders, unable to release him out of fear everything she'd just experienced would turn out to be only a dream.

"God, you're wonderful," Richard murmured, raising himself on his elbows above her and framing her sated features in the palms of his wide hands. "I've been such a fool. I never should have allowed us to waste the past months.

When I think of the nights I lay at your side, needing and wanting you until my teeth ached, I could kick myself."

Megan smiled up at Richard. " 'Tis not all your fault, my lord. If you will recall, I had something to do with the decision."

"Aye, you did, and that makes you just as foolish as I," Richard said, grinning down at her. "Just think of all the pleasure we've missed because of your fit of temper."

"Fit of temper, my lord? Your memory serves you ill if you fail to recall what brought about our arrangement. True, I was angry, but—" Richard's finger against her lips stayed her next words.

"Shush, love. I don't want to argue. I know why and what caused our arrangement, and I don't want it to come between us again. We were both at fault, but it is all in the past, where it belongs. We have a beautiful child and 'tis time for us to look toward our future. Tonight we've been given a second chance to make a life together, and there is no reason anything should stop us if we leave things where they belong— in the past."

Megan placed her hand against Richard's scarred cheek and gently brushed his lower lip with the pad of her thumb as she gazed up into his intriguing face. God, how she longed to let the past go, to give way to the callings of her heart. She wanted nothing more from life than to be a wife to Richard in all ways. But how could she do that when she didn't have his love?

By just doing it, you fool, her heart cried. Do as he asks and let the past go. He is your husband and the father of your child. Forget everything else and enjoy what you've been given.

Again Megan tasted bittersweet defeat as she surrendered to her heart's urgings. If she gave in now, hopefully in time she would gain more than just the pleasure of his body. In time, she prayed, she would also have his love.

Megan nodded. "Aye, 'tis time to put the past behind us if for nothing else but the sake of our son. 'Tis not good to raise a child on a battlefield. He needs not to be torn between us like a prize of victory. He needs the security of his family if he is to grow into a man worthy of ruling Dragon's Lair."

Megan's answer was not the one Richard desired. He wanted to hear her say she loved him. However, for now he'd be content. He'd managed to gain far more tonight than he would have dreamed only a few short hours ago, and in time he'd also gain her love and hear the words his heart craved.

"Aye, Meggie. Young Richard needs two parents," Richard said aloud. He smiled down at Megan as he thought, As much as we need each other, my beautiful reaver. And given time, I'll make you realize that, sweet wife, indeed I will.

"I agree," Megan said. Her thoughts running along the same lines as her husband's, she smiled provocatively up at him.

Unable to resist the temptation a moment longer, Richard swooped down, capturing her mouth and plunging his tongue past her kiss-bruised lips as he devoured her sweetness like a man starved. All thoughts fled as his body took control with a resurgence of passion. He hardened against her flat belly and chuckled his pleasure when she moved her hips in response to his passionate display.

"My wonderful Meggie," Richard breathed before he was lost once more in the sensations of making love to his wife.

Megan let her hand come to rest against the gleaming threads of the brightly colored tapestry she'd been weaving. For a long, reflective moment she looked about the great hall as if seeing it for the first time. It was odd to realize actually nothing had changed within the keep during the past weeks when she felt as if everything about her life had been altered. Had anyone asked her, she would have sworn Dragon's Lair had become an enchanted castle where Prince Charming

wooed his lady each night until she lay breathless with ecstasy.

A tiny, secretive smile curled the corners of Megan's mouth
as she turned her attention back to the work at hand. The
past weeks had been the most wonderful of her life. Richard
had become the perfect husband, father, and lover, and there
was nothing upon the horizon of her future to mar the happiness she had found with him.

"Megan, you're doing it again," Faith said, smiling from
where she sat on the pallet at her cousin's feet, cradling young
Richard in her arms. As had become her habit since the
weather warmed, Faith spent the evenings playing with her
youngest cousin while the rest of the household entertained
themselves in other ways.

"Doing what?" Megan asked, pausing to give Faith a
bewildered look.

"Daydreaming and grinning like a buffoon," Faith answered as she tickled young Richard's round little belly until
he giggled his delight.

"Don't be ridiculous. I was only thinking of the things I
need to attend."

Faith lifted the baby above her head and peered up into
his chubby little face. She cocked one golden brow. "I suspect 'tis far more than Mother's duties on her mind, young
man. Methinks she is so besotted with your father, she does
little else than sit and daydream about him. I don't know if
you've noticed the change which has come over her of late,
but I, for one, have. My dear cousin never used to enjoy
sitting quietly doing needlework, nor any of the ordinary
things which now seem to hold her interest. 'Twas too wifely
and unexciting for the Meggie I knew before your father came
to Dragon's Lair."

"Now you are jesting, Faith. I've changed little since
Richard's arrival at Dragon's Lair. As far as my needlework
and my other duties, blame the change on the young man in

your arms. He demands too much of my time to turn my sights to the pursuits I used to enjoy before he came to claim my attention.''

"The impetuous Meggie I knew before Sir Richard arrived wouldn't let her son hinder her pursuits. She'd bundle him up and take him with her. 'Tis love which I think keeps you bound."

Megan threw up her hands. "I surrender. I'll argue no more with you. I will admit I've been happy to act the obedient wife and attend my duties as chatelaine during the past weeks."

"Do you also admit 'tis Sir Richard who has caused this miraculous transformation from lady rogue to lady of the manor?"

Megan flashed her cousin a brilliant smile and nodded. "I now see a much brighter future than I first imagined when I wed Richard, and I want to make everything perfect in his household."

"I'm so happy for you, Meggie," Faith said, placing the wiggling babe back on the pallet. "I'm so glad you and Sir Richard have finally realized how much you love each other."

Megan's smile dimmed. " 'Tis not exactly how things are between us, but I'm satisfied with what I have now."

Faith frowned. "But you've seemed so happy of late. I felt sure Sir Richard had finally told you he loved you."

Megan shook her head. "Nay. Love is not something we speak of between us. Yet someday I hope it will come to pass."

Faith reached up and caught Megan's hand, squeezing it sympathetically. "Meggie, I'm so sorry. I know how much you love him."

"Save your pity, Faith. I have no need of it. I'm satisfied with the way things stand now, and hopefully in the future Richard will come to love me as much as I love him."

"I'm sure he will in time," Faith said. She wanted to tell

Megan she knew Richard already returned her feelings, but she remained silent. Things had been gradually working themselves out between her cousin and her husband, and 'twas best she not interfere in their affairs. She would leave it to Richard to explain his love when he felt it was the right moment.

"Now, enough about me and my love life. 'Tis time you told me how you and Sir Godfrey are getting along. Has he proposed to you yet?"

Faith stiffened and turned away. She busied herself with straightening the pallet. "Nay, Meggie. That will never happen."

"Surely you realize the man is in love with you?"

Faith gave a harsh, brittle laugh. "Sir Godfrey isn't in love with me. He's in love with the idea of what he believes me to be."

Megan frowned. "I don't understand. I've seen the way Anthony looks at you—all moon-eyed with longing."

"Aye. He looks at me, but he doesn't really know me or he'd turn away in disgust."

"Disgust! How can you say such a thing? Any man would be proud to take you as his wife."

"You love me as a cousin, Meggie, and you can't see in me what others would see if they knew the truth of my past. No man would want Mallory's leavings."

"What happened to you was not of your making. 'Twas not your fault that Mallory raped you. You were defenseless against him, and no one can hold it against you."

"Aye, 'twas not of my making, but who would believe it?" Faith said, her eyes misting with misery as she lifted young Richard into her arms and got to her feet. His yawn told her it was time to put him in his cradle for the night. She turned with the intention to carry him to his bedchamber and found Anthony blocking her path at the stair landing. He stood with back rigid, one hand poised on the rail, the other clenched into a tight fist at his side. His ashen features were pinched and his eyes were blue ice. Faith froze, the blood slowly draining from her face, leaving her a deathly white.

Anthony stared at Faith, unable to say or do anything. He'd come upon the scene of the two lovely women talking quietly together, dark head bent close to gold. He had only meant to enjoy the view for a few moments when their conversation had rooted him to the floor. The more he listened, the more his fury mounted against the man who had abused the beautiful woman who had stolen his heart, and it was all he could do to keep himself from seeking out Mallory O'Roarke's grave and desecrating it to ease the burning rage which made his tongue thick with lead.

Misinterpreting Anthony's expression for one of disgust, Faith watched the muscles in his throat work for what seemed to her like an eternity and felt the last of her dreams fade into oblivion. Her heart cried out for him to understand, but her pride stayed the words on her tongue before they could be spoken. She'd not humble herself only to be rejected. She raised her chin in the air and marched past Anthony with all the dignity her battered self-esteem could muster.

Anthony drew in a long breath as he silently watched the woman he loved ascend the stairs. He'd finally learned the secrets she harbored, but he'd never dreamed they would be so horrible. His heart broke for her as he remembered the ice queen he'd first met. He now understood why she'd reacted as she had. It had been her means of self-defense, and he couldn't fault her if she disliked all men after what she'd endured. Yet even with his understanding, he didn't know what to do. His own turmoil was so great, he knew not what to say to ease Faith's pain. When she disappeared from view he cast a haggard look at Megan. His eyes pleaded with her to come to his aid.

"Go after her and tell her what's in your heart" was Megan's soft answer to his unspoken request.

Anthony glanced toward Faith's chamber. He wanted
nothing more on earth than to say those very words. He'd
been aching to tell Faith of his feelings for months, yet now
he couldn't make his feet move nor force the words past his
lips. They rose in his throat and then died before they could
reach his tongue.

Megan eyed Anthony with something akin to disgust. She
wanted to shake him until he collected his wits enough to go
after Faith and make her realize nothing had changed his
feelings.

"You're a fool, Sir Godfrey," Megan said, her voice
clipped with anger as she viciously stuck the needle into the
cloth.

Anthony nodded as he crossed to the chair opposite Megan's. He slumped down into it and buried his face in his
hands. A shudder shook his entire frame.

"Do you realize what you've just done? Don't you understand the pain you've just meted out to that gentle woman?
Faith was the victim and not the perpetrator of the crime.
She was only sixteen when Mallory forced himself upon her,
and she's lived with the horror every day since. Don't you
understand she believes she's not worthy to have a decent
man's love?" Megan raged, venting her fury freely.

Another shudder passed through Anthony before he raised
his blond head and looked at Megan. "By all that's holy, I
didn't want to add to her pain with my silence. Faith is my
heart. I love her and want her to be my wife, yet I couldn't
speak the words you asked of me."

"Coward," Megan ground out. "Your vows of love are a
fleeting thing, Sir Godfrey. You use them when it serves your
purpose, not when it would ease Faith's pain."

"Enough, Lady Megan," Anthony said, still reeling from
the shock of learning Faith's secret, as well as Megan's verbal
attack. "I need time to think."

"Think!" Megan said. Giving the tapestry frame a shove,

she came to her feet. "You men are all alike. You want love on your own terms. You expect us to be perfect when you yourselves are flawed to the core of your beings."

Megan turned on her heels and strode from the great hall in a huff. She passed her husband as he entered the keep, gave him a withering look, and squared her shoulders as she marched up the stairs.

Richard blinked and scratched his head in bewilderment, wondering what he had done to cause such a reaction. During the past weeks he'd thought things had been settled between himself and his wife.

"Anthony, what in the devil was that all about? After this fruitless day of wandering in search of evidence against Ashby, I'm in no mood to try to figure out what has riled Meggie's temper. When I left here this morning, she was in good spirits and I could not have asked for a sweeter-dispositioned wife."

" 'Tis my fault," Anthony said, turning haggard eyes upon his friend. "I just learned that Mallory raped Faith when she was sixteen, and I didn't take the news as well as Megan expected of me."

"Damn," Richard swore. "The bastard died too easily."

"Aye," Anthony said. "And like a fool, instead of giving Faith the comfort she needed, all I could do was think of my own need to kill a damned dead man. The bastard is probably laughing at me from his place in hell for adding to the hurt he's already given to Faith."

" 'Tis not too late to make amends, friend," Richard said, patting Anthony on the shoulder.

"After the way I just acted, I fear 'tis far too late for me to make Faith understand," Anthony said, running long fingers through his pale hair.

Completely unaware he was giving nearly the exact advice to Anthony that Megan had given to Faith months before, Richard smiled and shook his head. " 'Tis never too late unless you're dead. As long as there is a breath in your body, you have a chance to right your mistakes."

"If only I could believe it."

"Believe it, old friend. At one time I felt it might have been too late to right things between myself and Meggie, but look how it has turned out. And someday I hope she'll come to love me as much as I love her. Go to Faith and be honest with her, Anthony. Tell her you love her and let her decide. If she still turns away from you, then it was meant to be no matter what you learned of her past."

"Shouldn't you take your own advice?" Anthony said, cocking a golden brow at his friend and eyeing him through narrowed, assessing eyes.

Richard shifted uneasily. His words had been thrust back at him like barbed lances, pinning him to the spot. Resignedly he nodded. "Aye. 'Tis time I took my own advice and told Meggie of my feelings."

Richard ran a hand through his dark hair, straightened his tunic, and squared his shoulders before turning toward the stairs. Tonight would be the night he opened his heart to his wife, and he prayed she'd be gentle with it and not crush it beneath her small heel as if it were a piece of vermin.

"Then I shall also take your advice," Anthony said. Flawlessly mimicking Richard's preparations, he followed his friend up the stairs. They exchanged encouraging smiles before each turned to separate chambers.

Richard pushed open the portal and cast a nervous glance about the room. His heart drummed against his ribs when he saw Megan standing pensively by the window, staring out into the balmy summer night. Quietly he crossed to his wife. "Meggie, we need to talk."

Megan did not stir but gave a tiny, nearly imperceptible nod.

"Look at me, Meggie," Richard said, taking his wife by the shoulders and turning her to face him. He tipped up her chin with his forefinger and momentarily found himself drowning in the dark slate pools of her eyes before he managed to get a grip on himself. "There are matters between us that we need to discuss."

Again came the nearly imperceptible nod.

"Blast it, Meggie. Can't you say something?" Richard asked, his voice gruff with the annoyance he was determined to keep under control. It was no time to let his temper have free reign.

"What is it you want me to say, Richard? Tell me and I will say it like any dutiful wife should."

Richard rolled his eyes toward the ceiling. This wasn't going exactly as he'd imagined. He'd thought she'd instinctively understand what he wanted to say and know it was not the time for verbal sparring.

"In truth I don't really know the words I want you to say. No—damn it—" Richard said, pausing to draw in a deep breath. "I do know what I want you to say, but it's something I can't demand. It has to be given freely."

Megan stilled, but her heart flew on peregrine wings, its swift flight making her breathless with anticipation. Yet she was afraid to hope her dreams were finally about to come true. "I don't know what you're talking about."

"Don't you, Meggie?" Richard asked softly, his gaze holding hers riveted to his.

Megan swallowed back the burst of hope rising in her throat and moistened her suddenly dry lips with the tip of her tongue. "Richard, I—" Her words faltered to a halt.

" 'Tis something that has waited far too long to be said, and I'm determined to end the wait tonight." Richard smiled provocatively down at his young wife before he surrendered to the overwhelming need to taste her slightly parted lips. Enfolding her unresisting body within his arms, he lowered his head to savor the sweetness of her mouth for a long, heart-stopping kiss.

At last he managed to drag his lips away from Megan's and draw in a cooling breath. He smiled and shook his head. "Meggie, you have the damnest effect upon me. You have the power to drive all sane thoughts from my mind when there are important matters that need to be settled between us once and for all. Things just can't go on the way they have without us being honest about our feelings."

Warily Megan regarded Richard. She wanted to believe the gods of love had granted her a reprieve and Richard was going to confess his undying love for her, but doubt, lying coiled and ready to strike, chased away such reasoning and made her misread the meaning of his words as well as the look in his eyes. Her heart froze within her breast. Hope lowered its head, hunched its shoulders, and crawled back into the dark dungeon where it had been imprisoned until a few moments ago.

Again Megan moistened her lips and nodded as she stiffened her back and raised her chin. She'd bravely face whatever Richard had to say. She'd never allow him to suspect the agony she was enduring. "I agree. 'Tis time for us to talk."

Richard relaxed. After tasting the sweetness of Megan's luscious lips, it would be easy to admit his love of her. Every inch of him throbbed with need, but he'd wait until he had said the words in his heart before he fulfilled his desire to love her with his body. "Megan, I—"

Richard's words faltered to a halt at the loud squeal of the castle gates screeching open. A moment later the clatter of horses' hooves sounded on the cobbles below. Instantly alert and on guard, Richard gently set Megan away from him and moved to the cross-slit window to see their late night visitors. He peered down at the torchlit yard below and a perplexed frown marred his brow at the sight of his brother's standard waving in the evening breeze.

" 'Tis Justin's men below," he murmured, sensing trouble. "We'll continue this conversation later." The warrior asserted himself over the gentle lover as he turned his thoughts away from his personal affairs and strode toward the chamber door. Something was amiss or Justin's men would not have arrived at such an hour. From the looks of their mounts, they'd been in the saddle all day.

Richard met Anthony at the top of the stairs and saw by his friend's concerned expression that he, too, had similar suspicions. They exchanged worried glances as they descended the stairs two at a time.

"There must be trouble at Raven's Keep or Justin's men would have arrived before nightfall," Richard said as they reached the landing. "By the looks of them, they've traveled hard and fast."

"Aye. 'Tis odd for them to travel at night," Anthony agreed as he kept pace with his friend and crossed the great hall. They had just reached the iron-bound, heavy-timbered doors that led out to the bailey when the barriers swung wide and in strode a small figure dressed in a long-hooded cloak and chausses which clung to shapely legs like a second skin. A glint of auburn hair peeked from beneath the edge of the hood while laughing emerald eyes halted the two men in their tracks.

"Jamelyn? By all that's holy! Where is my brother? Has something happened to Justin—to Raven's Keep? Is Justin ill? Do you need my help? Where is little Kat?"

"Slow down, Richard," Jamelyn laughed, tossing back her hood. "Canna you welcome me to your home without putting me through such interrogation?"

"Where's my brother? Is he all right?" Richard asked, ignoring Jamelyn's question.

"Aye, Justin is all right, but 'tis the least you could do to welcome me with a bit more warmth when I've come so far to visit you and your family, Richard." Untying the laces at her throat, she tossed the cloak to the serving girl who hovered just in the shadows beyond the torchlight. She ran her fingers through her mane of auburn hair and shook her head to let it spill freely about her shoulders in a cascade of curls. She glanced at Anthony and chided, "You could at least act as if you're glad to see me even if my brother-in-law is not."

Richard released a long, exasperated breath and nodded. "You're always welcome in my home, as you well know, Jamelyn. Now will you be good enough to tell me what in the devil brings you to Dragon's Lair without sending word of your arrival?"

"Justin's message from Flanders," Jamelyn answered, and then reached behind her to drag a young, towheaded boy into the light. "And this."

Travis grinned up at Richard, thrilled to once more be in the company of the man he idolized. His grin faded when Richard ignored him, centering his attention on his sister-in-law.

Jamelyn held up a hand to silence another round of Richard's questions. "I know I should have sent word, but I only received Justin's message a few days ago and thought it would be more expedient for me to deliver it myself. And delivering this young rascal and Justin's message also gave me an excuse to come to meet my new sister-in-law as well as my new nephew."

"Then I bid you welcome to Dragon's Lair," Richard said, his voice filled with relief to find all was well. Courteously he proffered his arm to his sister-in-law and gave her a bewitching smile. "Will you allow me to escort you to the solar, where we can have refreshments and privacy for you to tell me the news from my brother?"

"I'd be honored, sir, but first I want to see this young man settled and out of trouble's way. He seems to have a knack for being in the wrong place at the wrong time. He has stayed under my men's feet since he arrived at Raven's Keep, and at times I've feared they'd trample him," Jamelyn said, smiling up into Richard's beloved face as she placed a graceful hand upon his sleeve.

Richard glanced at Anthony. "Would you see Travis has a pallet for the night? Tomorrow I'll decide what I should do with the young imp."

"Yer said ye'd make me into a knight," Travis said in a tight voice. He eyed Richard mutinously to hide the hurt Richard's cool reception caused him. He suddenly felt as if he were no more than a mongrel waiting for a bone to be tossed his way by the lord of the manor. He'd been so happy when Lady St. Claire had told him she was taking him to Dragon's Lair to be with Sir Richard. Now it seemed as if Sir Richard didn't even remember him, nor the promises he'd made.

"If you recall, I never promised to make you a knight. I only told you I'd give you a chance to train with my men. It will be up to you to use what you learn to the best of your abilities, and then someday you may receive your wish to enter Edward's service."

Travis's young face brightened. "Then ye still mean to let me serve ye?"

"Aye. Now 'tis time for you to be abed. Sir Godfrey will show you where to sleep tonight, and then tomorrow I'll find a position for you at Dragon's Lair."

"Oh, thank you, Sir Richard. I'll not let ye down. No, sir. Never, sir. I'll do as ye bid me, sir," Travis said, bobbing his towhead up and down. He felt like jumping with glee but held a tight rein on the urge. He'd not give Sir Richard cause to find fault with him again. Nor would he ever question his word again. He'd keep his vow to serve Sir Richard and he'd do everything within his power to imitate the knight until he, too, was a great man.

"Then be off with you. I've business to attend."

Travis bobbed his head once more and turned to follow Anthony through the great hall and into the warmth of the kitchen. His mouth watered at the smell of freshly baked bread, and when he closed his eyes to savor its sweetness, he felt as if he'd died and gone to heaven.

Aye, Travis mused to himself as Anthony instructed a serving maid to pour him a cup of milk, Dragon's Lair was heaven and Sir Richard was his god.

Richard seated Jamelyn before the fire and ordered wine and a platter of food before he turned his attention to the matters at hand. He waved the serving maid out of the solar and closed the door behind her to afford them the privacy they needed to talk freely about Justin's message.

"Now, 'tis time to tell me exactly what Justin wanted me to know," Richard said, propping one elbow on the carved stone mantel.

Jamelyn took a long sip of the refreshing burgundy. " 'Tis as you suspected. Justin has found Ashby's lowland contacts, but he said you would need to find the stolen wool to prove the man's guilt."

"Aye," Richard said. "Ashby isn't a man who one would accuse of such a crime. His wealth enables him to have friends at court who have Edward's ear. And with a few well-placed bribes, Edward would never believe it was a friend who had been stealing from him. Especially after Ashby's search for reavers along his borders and on his estate."

Richard shook his head in admiration. "The man plays the game well. He's given the illusion of someone who believes in upholding the law of the land. My own capture is evidence in his favor." Thoughtfully he worried his lower lip with strong, even white teeth. His brow furrowed as he narrowed his eyes speculatively. "Justin is right. Finding evidence of his crimes is the only way, but it is far easier said than done. I've stayed in the saddle day in and day out during the past weeks, and I've uncovered nothing to help us. Ashby is as wily as a fox and far more clever. Beyond what Justin has learned, the only evidence I have against him is seeing his man talking with No Thumbs.''

''Justin said you should watch the Wash near Holbeach, whatever that means.''

''The Wash,'' Richard said, slapping his forehead with the palm of his hand as if to knock some sense there. ''Damn me, I should have thought of it myself. I've scoured the countryside but never looked to find where the smugglers would have to ship out the goods to the lowlands. Tomorrow Anthony and I will search the entire coastline if necessary until we find what we need.''

''Perhaps Sir Richard has lost more of Royce than he ever imagined.''

Richard arched a dark brow at Jamelyn. ''And pray tell, what does that mean, dear sister-in-law?''

''Royce is fading away and giving Sir Richard his rightful place.''

Richard grinned. ''You could be right.''

''I know I'm right. I can see it in your every action.''

Richard released a long breath. ''Is it obvious?''

''Aye. The air of contentment about you since you've wed and become a father was never in Royce. He always felt the need for adventure.''

''That side of me must now forever remain in the past. There are certain things expected of Richard St. Claire— obligations as the Lord of Dragon's Lair. This estate is now my son's heritage, and I must protect it and leave the wild adventures to younger men.''

''I understand your feelings. I feel much the same way where Katherine is concerned. I've put the old me away to be a better mother to her. I now accept the fact Justin is the Lord of Raven's Keep and my place is at his side as chatelaine to his home,'' Jamelyn said with an understanding nod.

'' 'Tis the hardest thing you've ever done, isn't it, Jamie?''

''Aye. And like you, I'll do anything for the benefit of my

child. For Kat's future, I've even managed to hide my hostility toward Edward when we are at court,'' Jamelyn said, smiling with all the love she felt for the small replica of herself.

A mischievous grin curled the corners of Richard's mouth. '' 'Tis true I have to think of my son, but it doesn't mean Royce can't escape at times. I miss the freedom of the life I lived before finding I was Justin's brother. My time reaving with Meggie was the happiest I've spent since our days together.''

"Meggie, reaving?" Jamelyn asked, suppressing the smile tugging at her lips.

"Aye, 'tis how I met my tempestuous wife, but 'tis too long a story to go into tonight. However, I will say this much. She reminds me much of you, Jamelyn.''

Jamelyn acknowledged the compliment with a slight nod and smiled her happiness. She knew her friend was satisfied with the marriage Edward had arranged for him. Now she could set her mind to rest. From the little Richard had already revealed, he'd found a woman his equal, one who had captured his heart.

Nearly able to read Jamelyn's thoughts, Richard grinned down at her. "You know me far to well, Jamie. That's why I love you.''

Enjoying their easy companionship and conversation, Richard and Jamelyn didn't hear the door ease open. Nor were they aware their conversation had been overheard until an audible gasp came from the other side of the portal.

Suspecting a traitor in their midst and determined their plans would not be discovered, Richard, his hand on the hilt of his dagger, silently moved toward the door. In a flash he jerked it open with such force, Megan spilled into the room. She stumbled forward and would have fallen had not Richard saved her from the embarrassment.

"Meggie! By all that's holy! Why are you lurking around in the halls?" Richard asked.

"I'm not lurking, my lord. I thought it my duty to come and greet our guest since you failed to have the good manners to have my maid summon me to the hall upon her arrival," Megan said, struggling for some semblance of dignity in front of the beautiful auburn-haired woman.

"I'm sorry. I should have requested you join us, but Jamelyn brought news from my brother in Flanders that I was anxious to hear," Richard said, suppressing a smile. The heated look of doubt Megan flashed told him far more of her feelings than any words. His heart leaped within his breast. His wife must care after all if she disliked the thought of him being alone with another beautiful woman. "I'm glad you've come down, because I would like to present my sister-in-law, Lady St. Claire."

"Jamelyn," Jamelyn said cordially, coming to her feet and extending her hand to Megan. A warm smiled played upon Jamelyn's lips as she took in Richard's lovely bride. A sense of relief swept over her as she realized Richard was finally free of his infatuation with her. He was deeply in love with Megan.

Keeping her expression bland, Megan stiffly took Jamelyn's hand and dropped into a formal curtsy. "I'm honored to meet you, my lady. I've heard much about you from my husband, and I welcome you into our home."

Jamelyn's smile faded. Richard's wife said the right words, but female instinct told her there was much more behind the polite welcome than met the eye. There was no denying the air of tension and hostility her sister-in-law exuded from every pore.

"Thank you for your welcome, Lady Megan. I fear I should have warned you of my visit, but I thought it best to deliver Justin's message without delay. I hope you will forgive my rudeness."

"As a member of Richard's family, you are welcome any time, my lady. Now if you will excuse me, I will see your chamber is prepared." Megan's welcoming words nearly choked her when in truth all she wanted to do was scratch out the beautiful emerald eyes of the woman standing before her. She was finally face-to-face with the woman her husband loved, and she felt her own world crumbling. She'd been deluding herself if she ever believed she could capture her husband's feelings away from the auburned-haired beauty. Jamelyn St. Claire's arrival had sealed the coffin upon those dreams.

Unable to bear the thought, Megan turned and fled the solar, leaving Jamelyn and Richard staring after her, bewildered.

Richard looked from the empty doorway back to his sister-in-law and shrugged one wide shoulder. "We've been married for nearly a year now, and I still haven't the slightest idea of how Meggie's mind words. One minute she's the loving wife and in the next she's the vixen, ready to tear off my head."

"If you will recall, I reacted much in the same manner before Justin and I realized the true extent of our love for each other. Could your wife not know you love her when I can see it written all over your face?"

"Aye, she knows nothing of what I feel, but I had been trying to correct that matter when you arrived."

"Oh, Richard," Jamelyn apologized as she crossed to her friend's side. "I'm sorry my arrival interrupted you. But 'tis still not too late. I suspect right about now your lovely young wife could use the comfort of your words as well as your arms."

Richard glanced toward the doorway and ran a hand through his already tousled hair. "I suspect you're right, but I doubt Meggie will think so after what she overheard."

"Take my advice, Richard, and don't waste the time God

has given you together. Don't be as foolish as Justin and I were. We nearly lost everything by letting our pride rule us and by not being honest about our feelings for each other. Don't chance it, Richard. Love is too precious and you might not be as fortunate as we were.''

Richard hugged Jamelyn close, but there was nothing in the gesture beyond friendship. ''I'm already a fortunate man to have such a wise friend as you, Jamie.''

''We've been friends for a long time, and I hope it never changes,'' Jamelyn said, resting her cheek companionably against Richard's chest.

Richard wound a gleaming copper curl about his fingers as he'd often done in the past when he'd given Jamelyn comfort. ''Have no fear, Jamie. We've shared too much for anything to ever come between us. You'll always have a special place in my heart.''

''I know and I'm grateful for the honor, but I'm also glad you've found someone with whom you can share your life. The moment I saw you look at Megan I knew she was the one who had stolen your heart away from me.''

Richard leaned from Jamelyn and peered down at her, a quizzical frown marking his brow. ''And it makes you happy?''

''Aye. 'Tis what I've longed for. My life with Justin is wonderful and I've wanted to see you find the same happiness. And you have with Meggie.''

''Make no hasty judgments, Jamelyn. 'Tis still a long road I have to travel to gain the same kind of happiness you and my brother share. Meggie and I are just venturing upon the first league of the journey, and I fear there are many obstacles we still have to cross before we can gain the love you speak of.''

Jamelyn smiled a superior female smile. He'd have to find the answers for himself.

"All right, I'll go and try to finish what I started earlier."
He let his hands fall to his sides.

"St. Claire men are stubborn, but never let it be said they
are stupid. Good night, Richard, and good luck."

Richard paused at the door and looked back at Jamelyn.
"Thank you."

Jamelyn nodded, understanding his gratitude, and blew
him a kiss. "Be happy. 'Tis all I want for those I love."

"I'm going to do my damnedest" was all Richard said
before striding from the solar and down the long corridor to
the bedchamber, where he knew his wife awaited him.

Chapter 17

Jealousy oozing from every pore, Megan stood staring down into the dying embers of the fire with arms folded over her chest, dry, sparkling eyes narrowed, lips pressed into a thin, angry line, and foot tapping against the thick-timbered floor. Anger had at last asserted itself over the shock of seeing her rival for the first time, and jealousy fueled it into white-hot flames.

How dare Richard have the nerve to bring that woman to Dragon's Lair? It had been hard enough to live with the knowledge of his love for his sister-in-law, but it was nearly intolerable to have her under the same roof, where she was a constant reminder of Megan's failure to woo her husband's affections.

Megan's frown deepened. She had given him a bright, healthy son, yet it hadn't changed Richard's feelings. She knew that now for a certainty. Hadn't she heard him say he loved Jamie from his own lips?

At the thought, a bolt of rage sizzled through Megan with such force, she trembled. "Damn him. I'll not be used as her surrogate any longer. He can have one of us but not both."

A little voice told Megan she might be making a mistake

by forcing Richard to choose between herself and Jamelyn, but she shrugged the doubt away. There had been too much between them in the last weeks for her to accept less than all of her husband.

The words had barely left her lips when the door latch rattled. Megan stared at it but didn't move. She knew who was on the other side and she'd be damned if he'd share her chamber until he chose which woman he wanted.

For a long, reflective moment Richard stared at the iron-bound portal separating him from his wife. A mere three inches of wood kept him from the woman he loved. Eager to close the distance between them, he reached out and tried to turn the latch. It would not move. Thinking the latch stuck, he rattled it several times. It squeaked under the pressure but remained steadfast.

"Megan, open this damned door," Richard swore when it finally dawned on him his wife had locked him out of his own bedchamber. The heavy force of a balled fist against the sturdy panel emphasized his demand. No sound came from inside.

"Megan, do you hear me? I said open this damned door before I break it down."

"Be gone with you. Find somewhere else to sleep tonight because you're not going to share my chamber. Perhaps your guest would be willing to share hers."

"Megan, by all that's holy! You are slowly but surely testing my patience to the limit. Now, open this damned door! 'Tis my bedchamber you have confiscated."

Megan eyed the portal for a fraction of a moment longer before she quickly crossed to the bed and jerked off the velvet counterpane covering the soft linen sheets. Striding to the chest where Richard kept his clothing and personal effects, she flipped back the lid and delved into the neatly folded jerkins, chausses, and a sundry other things. She came up with arms full and turned once more to the bed. Scattering clothing in her wake, she strode back across the chamber and dumped the clothes in a pile. She quickly gathered the four corners of the sheet together and tied them into a knot. She finished her task at the same moment another heavy-handed knock sounded.

"Megan, this is my last warning. By damned if I let you get by with this fit of temper."

Before the words were completely out of his mouth, Richard heard the latch slide back. He couldn't stop the superior, self-satisfied grin from tugging at the corners of his sensuous mouth. Megan was finally coming to her senses by realizing he was the master of Dragon's Lair and all beneath its slate roof. The thought had no more than flickered through his mind when the door opened and a voluminous white ball hit him squarely in the face, along with Megan's words. " 'Tis my chamber and my bed, and you'll share neither."

Richard staggered backward several paces. He drew in a furious breath, but before he could say a word, the door was once more slammed in his face. Stupefied, Richard stood holding the sheet, which contained all of his clothing. It took only a fraction of a second for his fury to override his momentary bewilderment. Tossing the makeshift ball down the corridor with such force it rolled to the top of the stairs, he drew back his foot and kicked the latch, shattering the wood surrounding it. The door slammed back against the cold stone wall. His face flushed with rage, the white of his scars contrasting starkly, and blue fire blazing in his sapphire gaze, he strode toward Megan. His expression boded no good.

Hands braced on her hips, her chin raised at an imperious angle, Megan stood her ground. She wasn't afraid of Richard St. Claire or any man. Her experience with her brother had driven any fear of punishment out of her years ago. She might suffer a beating, but she'd do her damnedest to give as good as she got.

Richard's hand snaked out and captured Megan before she

could avoid it. He jerked her against him and glared down at her. "Woman, you deserve a beating for such childish behavior. You are a woman grown with a child of your own, so isn't it about time you desisted in such displays of ill temper? Have you no consideration for yourself or what your guests will think?"

"Don't you mean your guests, Richard? I don't recall inviting your sister-in-law to come to visit."

"Megan, what's come over you? When I left Dragon's Lair this morning, you were in good spirits. What's happened to change you into a termagant?"

Megan eyed Richard coolly. "That you even have to ask the question shows you'd never understand."

"Blast it, Meggie! Understand what?" Richard said, his exasperation mounting by the moment.

"I'm your wife," Megan spat, and jerked her arm free of his hand. She turned away and stalked to the cross-slit window. Keeping her back to Richard, she said, "Now, if you will leave, I will retire for the night."

"Damn it! I'm not going anywhere until we get this thing settled."

"You are the one who has to settle things, Richard. I have nothing to do with it."

Richard crossed the room in three strides and took Megan by the shoulders, turning her to face him once more. He peered into her indigo eyes, reading in their shining depths her resolution not to give in to the callings of her heart. Understanding flickered through him. He'd seen a brief glimpse of Megan's jealousy a short while before, and he now sensed everything revolved around the same problem.

"Megan, you have nothing to fear from Jamelyn. She's my brother's wife and they love each other dearly."

Megan tilted her head back and held Richard's gaze. "But it doesn't stop your feelings, does it?"

Richard's fingers tightened upon Megan's shoulders. He

shook his head. "There is nothing now, nor has there ever been, anything between Jamelyn and myself."

"Then why is she here?"

"I explained that to you in the solar. She came to bring me a message from Justin."

Megan eyed Richard cynically. "Since you have the message, there is no reason for her to remain at Dragon's Lair."

Richard frowned. "If you think I'll turn Jamelyn out of my home, then you are mistaken. Jamelyn is my sister-in-law as well as my friend."

"Then you choose her over me?" Megan said, her throat clogged with pieces of her shattered heart.

"I don't choose her over you, Megan. You are my wife and the mother of my child, but there is a bond between Jamelyn and myself that can never be broken, so don't ask it of me."

"I ask nothing of you, Richard, but to be left alone. Please leave me."

Richard let his hands fall to his sides. His gaze sparkled with renewed annoyance. "Then damn it to hell, sleep by yourself and wonder where I'll spend my night. If you aren't willing to share my bed, I believe I should be able to find someone who is, and she won't have a tongue so sharp each word cuts out part of a man's soul."

"Then go to her with my blessing," Megan snapped, the new pain fueling her own anger to a higher degree. "Maybe she won't care she's being used as a surrogate for your brother's wife!" Megan turned away.

Richard felt his head would leave his shoulders, and for the first time in his life he had the urge to strike a woman. Clenching his fists tightly, he turned and stalked from the chamber before trying to beat some sense into his wife's beautiful head. He slammed the door behind him and listened with a measure of satisfaction when he heard Megan begin to cry.

The feeling was only a fleeting thing as he stood outside the door to his bedchamber hearing his wife's misery. His heart ached to go to her and give her the comfort she needed, but his pride rebelled. Megan was at fault in this. He'd done nothing to deserve her fit of temper. He loved his wife but couldn't do as she asked where Jamelyn was concerned. Like Justin had done, Meggie would have to realize the bond between himself and Jamie had been forged in the fire of their adventures, and like tempered steel, it was not easily broken.

Turning away before he gave in to the urging of his heart, Richard picked up the bundle of clothes and strode down the corridor to the stairs. He paused briefly at the landing to consider where he would make his bed for the night. All the bedchambers were taken unless he wanted to share with Anthony. In his present state of mind the thought didn't appeal to him. He was in no mood to answer his friend's questions nor give Anthony advice about his own love life. That left only the stables. His decision made, Richard strode down the stairs, out of the keep, and toward the stables. The Raven wouldn't begrudge sharing his stall.

"It'll only be for one night," Richard muttered as he crossed the bailey. "By damned if I'll let Meggie lock me out again. This thing will be settled once and for all after I've returned from Holbeach tomorrow."

Megan lay on her stomach, chin propped on her folded arms, brooding over Richard's threat to find someone else to share his bed. The thought was agony in itself, and her burning eyes were evidence of the emotional toll his threat had taken upon her.

"Fool," she chided herself beneath her breath. "You're so strongheaded, you've sent your husband into the arms of another woman." Disgusted with herself, Megan gave a slight shake of her head. Her tempestuous actions had brought about the very thing she'd wanted most in her life to prevent.

Richard was her husband, and she couldn't stand the thought of him making love to another woman, be it Jamelyn St. Claire or a serving maid.

"What did I expect when I sent him away?" Megan mused aloud as she flipped over on her side and lay looking at the pillow where Richard's dark head would now be resting had they not quarreled.

"But it's his fault I acted that way," she muttered in her own defense as she ran a hand across Richard's pillow. "Out of respect for me he shouldn't have brought that woman into my home."

"But he doesn't know you have any idea of his feelings. You've never told him of what you overheard Anthony say that night, nor is he aware you overheard what he said tonight in the solar," Megan said, trying to see both sides of the situation.

She bolted upright, disgusted with the direction her thoughts were traveling. If she kept thinking like this, she'd finally succumb to her need of Richard and allow him to do anything he wanted, no matter how he trampled her pride.

"No! I'll not be his plaything while his heart belongs to his brother's wife. 'Tis best I leave things as they are, no matter how much it hurts."

The sound of the knock upon her chamber door set Megan's heart to racing against her ribs. Her hopes Richard had come to apologize rushed past all her resolutions of the moment before, and she didn't take time to consider her own actions. She scrambled from the bed and ran to the door.

"Richard," she breathed as she swung it open. Megan's features fell at the sight of the woman who was at the root of all the dissension between herself and her husband.

"What do you want?" Megan said, her voice icy. She made no move to invite Jamelyn into her chamber.

"You disappoint me," Jamelyn replied, stepping past Megan into the room without invitation. She cast a quick glance about the chamber before she turned once more to the young woman who still stood holding the door open. "Close the door, Megan. We have much to discuss, and I think this is something neither of us wants bandied about in the kitchens in the morning."

Keeping her eyes on the beautiful Lady St. Claire, Megan slowly closed the door and leaned back against it. "What do we have to discuss, my lady? Isn't your chamber to your liking, or is there something more you require? Surely one of my serving maids would have been able to assist you, and it would have saved you the trouble of seeking me out so late at night."

"Megan, cease this game of Lady of the Manor caring for her guest's comfort. I know exactly how you feel about me. Had I not sensed your feelings earlier in the solar, then the ruckus a short while ago between you and Richard would surely have made me aware of them."

Megan had the grace to blush but stood her ground. She was face-to-face with her enemy, and her future happiness was at stake in this game they played. "All right, my lady. The game is over. You know how I feel, so why did you come here? Did you think to gloat over your success of keeping my husband's heart away from his wife?"

"Don't be a little fool, Megan. I came here to tell you you don't have anything to worry about where I'm concerned. Richard loves you, not me."

Megan drew in a deep breath and swallowed hard. "There is no need for lies, my lady. I heard for myself exactly how my husband feels about you. 'Tis only out of fear for your safety he wed me in the first place."

Sidetracked by Megan's statement, Jamelyn frowned. "What are you talking about? Richard married you because he loves you."

"You jest, my lady. Surely you don't believe that? Richard

married me because of Edward's threats to you and your family. 'Tis the only reason he decided in favor of our union.''

"Again you disappoint, Megan. You don't truly know your husband at all. Richard isn't a man Edward can force to do anything if he sets his mind against it."

"I care little if I disappoint you, Lady St. Claire. And if you've said what you came to say, I will bid you good night."

"Damn it, Megan. Canna ye see your husband loves you?" Jamelyn said, her exasperation with the younger woman making her Scottish brogue more apparent. "I've known Richard for more than five years and I've never seen him so happy. He's a different man from the one who left Raven's Keep to come south to do the king's bidding by marrying the mistress of Dragon's Lair."

"Cease this prattle," Megan snapped, her temper exploding. "I heard with my own ears. Richard said he loved you."

"Aye, ye heard the words, but ye didn't understand the meaning," Jamelyn said, her own temper flaming over Megan's stubbornness.

"I heard enough to know I'll never be able to have his love as I had hoped during the past weeks."

"Had you stayed, you would have heard Richard tell me how happy he's been since you wed. But no, ye canna wait to make your hasty decision. You're too afraid to listen with your heart instead of your ears."

"I listened long enough," Megan spat, and turned her back on Jamelyn.

"Foolish child. You're much like I was when Justin and I first married. You won't let go of your pride long enough to gain what you really want: your husband's love. You hide behind something that can't hold you in its arms nor whisper tender words of love in your ears when you desperately need comfort."

"You don't know what you're talking about," Megan said, a tremble in her voice.

"I know well of what I speak. I have experienced everything you're going through right now. Even the thought of my husband being in love with another woman as well as having the woman under my roof."

Megan looked over her shoulder at Jamelyn. "You are only telling me that to allay my suspicions about Richard's feelings for you."

"Nay, Megan," Jamelyn said with an understanding smile. "I speak only the truth." Seating herself in the monk's chair by the dying fire, Jamelyn patted the seat at her side. "Come and I'll tell you how Richard's brother and I came to marry and the things that nearly separated us before we ever acknowledged we loved each other."

Curiosity pricking every fiber of her being, Megan crossed the chamber and took the chair Jamelyn offered. She sat still and quiet as Jamelyn told the story of her adventures with Richard as well as her turbulent relationship with his brother. She left out nothing, and when she finished her tale, Megan sat with mouth agape in wonder.

"I feel much the fool for my behavior, Jamelyn. Can you ever forgive me?"

Jamelyn reached out and placed a comforting hand over Megan's. Her smile was warm and reassuring. " 'Tis nothing to forgive. I acted much in the same manner, and I don't blame you for your feelings. You love Richard, and it hurts when you believe your love isn't returned. I just hope what I've told you about my friendship with Richard makes you realize he loves me like a sister and it can never be anything more, especially since you've stolen his heart."

"I understand and I'm grateful to you for coming to me. I hope we can be friends now that I've managed to get my jealousy under control."

"I welcome your friendship, Meggie. We are much alike in temperament, as are our husbands, and it will be pleasant to have an ally in the family when it comes to the St. Claire brothers. They have a tendency toward stubbornness, if you haven't already noticed.''

Megan and Jamelyn burst into laughter, sharing the first of many confidences about the men they loved. When their mirth subsided, Megan sobered and her eyes went round with worry as she looked at her newfound friend.

''Oh, Jamelyn. What have I done? I must find Richard and apologize.''

Jamelyn shook her head. ''Nay. Let Richard simmer in his own juices for tonight. It will do him good. It always does Justin.''

''But what if he does decide to find some comely wench to share his bed? I forced him into it and I have to stop it before it's too late,'' Megan argued.

Again Jamelyn shook her head. ''The only comely wench Richard will find is one of Dragon's Lair's mares. I saw him from my window as he made his way to the stables. I doubt he'll see anything to his taste there.''

Both women again broke into laughter.

''Then I'll tell him first thing in the morning,'' Megan said, feeling suddenly as if the weight of the world had been lifted from her shoulders, and completely unaware of Richard's plans to be far away from Dragon's Lair by the time the sun rose.

Megan awoke to the sound of horses in the bailey. Dragging her weary self out of bed, she tiptoed across the cold floor to the window and hugged herself to ward off the morning chill as she squinted down at the mounted riders. It took only a moment for her to realize her husband had planned an early expedition for his men, and they were in the process of leaving Dragon's Lair. Megan moved rapidly, hoping to speak with Richard before he left. Throwing on her clothing, she sped down the stairs and out into the bailey. She arrived too late. The last of Richard's men were riding through the gates.

Disgruntled, her toes curling from the icy cobbles under her bare feet, she turned back to the large double doors she'd left ajar in her rush to stop her husband. She'd wanted to tell Richard what a fool she'd been. Now it would have to wait till his return, whenever that might be.

Catching sight of a movement from the corner of her eye, Megan paused, her hand resting on the thick iron-ringed latch of the heavy-timbered door. Turning to get a better view, she frowned at the sight of a young boy, no more than ten years old, following rapidly in her husband's wake and riding one of Dragon's Lair's fillies.

"Who in the devil is he?" she wondered aloud as she watched him ride out of sight and into the half light of dawn. She knew every crofter and villein as well as their wives and children, and the towheaded lad was new to Dragon's Lair.

"Perhaps he's a member of Jamelyn's household," she mused aloud, and then smiled with satisfaction at her assumption. She'd solved the riddle of his identity.

"But why is he following Richard?" she asked herself before putting the matter from her mind. Rubbing her chilly arms, she entered the hall and quickly strode toward the stairs. Her feet felt like ice, and the thought of her warm bed drew her like a lodestone to a magnet. It was far too early to be about, and she wanted to be well rested when she saw Richard again.

Richard peered down at the men busily hauling the bags of wool out of the oxen cart. "Justin was right, Anthony. This is the point where Ashby ships out his ill-gotten goods."

Anthony nodded. "Aye. We've found the smugglers, yet we still don't have the man behind the scheme."

"Now that we have his men, 'tis only a matter of time and

the right persuasion until we have Ashby as well. Are the men ready?''

''Aye. They're ready, but I wish we had more than a handful to deal with this vermin.''

''More men couldn't be spared. The keep is undermanned as is, and until reinforcements arrive from Raven's Keep, the few left will have to guard Dragon's Lair's defenses. I won't leave the keep and my family vulnerable to attack from Ashby or anyone else.''

'' 'Tis a wise decision and I'm grateful for your forethought in seeing to the welfare of those residing within Dragon's Lair's walls. I would see them all safe.''

Richard smiled knowingly and placed a companionable hand on Anthony's shoulders. ''Have you told your lady you love her?''

'' 'Twas no time before Jamie's arrival interrupted us. But I plan to correct the situation just as soon as I get back to Dragon's Lair tonight.'' Anthony smiled up at his friend. ''Did you take your own advice?''

''Like you, old friend, my time will come this eve, and not even the arrival of the king, queen, and their entire brood of children can stay my intentions. I'll not sleep in the stables again.''

Anthony arched a brow curiously at Richard and saw him grin wryly and shake his head.

'' 'Tis another story for another time. Now we must put an end to Edward's wool thieves so we can turn our full attention to the more pleasant tasks of wooing our ladies.''

Richard and Anthony quietly slipped back to where their men awaited them. After bestowing orders to stealthily move down along the beach and surround the smugglers, giving no chance of escape, the two friends mounted their own horses and led the pursuit.

All seemed to go as the two friends planned. The smugglers surrendered without a fight. However, their actions puzzled Richard. He'd known many a thief in his time, and few were loyal to anything beyond their own skins. Most would at least make an effort to escape, especially if a noose awaited them.

Richard felt the hair at the nape of his neck rise in warning, but before he could react to his instincts, archers swarmed from behind rocks and dunes. Their arrows gave no reprieve from death to his men-at-arms. They felled the entire troop in their tracks, leaving only their leader and his friend unscathed. Standing back to back with swords drawn, Richard and Anthony awaited their own death.

"My, my. It does seem we have a habit of running into each other at the oddest times, Richard," Robert Ashby said as he casually strolled from the shadows of the trees.

"I see nothing odd about seeing you here, Ashby. I've suspected your part in the theft of the wool for some time now. This only confirms my suspicions."

"That's what I suspected when we chanced to catch you and your lady reaver at the Rook's. I knew then my time in England was limited, though you told a very convincing story about searching for wine smugglers."

"Then you're a fool, Ashby. If you knew I suspected you, you should have fled the country when you had the chance. Now you'll be hunted down and hanged and quartered at Tyburn for your deeds against the crown."

"Such dire predictions, Richard. But I fear they won't come true. Once I'm paid for this shipment, I need only a few days to finish up my affairs and then I'm off to France. Philip is a very generous lord and he's guaranteed I shall be well paid for my help in ruining Edward and England's finances."

"You traitorous bastard," Richard swore.

Ashby released an exasperated sigh. "Richard, I'm disappointed in you. As a thief yourself, I thought you'd appreciate my little plan."

"You jest," Richard spat, eyeing Ashby with contempt. "A good thief wouldn't waste his spit upon you—a traitor to your own country. I'll relish watching you hang."

"You get ahead of yourself," Ashby said, his voice laced with venom. "I fear you'll see nothing after I've gained your ransom."

"Then that's your plan? I knew you didn't stay our execution out of the goodness of your evil heart," Richard said.

"Aye. You and Sir Godfrey are both from fine families, and I'm sure they will pay handsomely to get you back all in one piece." Ashby smiled derisively at Richard and Anthony. "Aren't I generous to guarantee them that much? 'Tis a pity they won't also get you back alive."

"You bastard," Richard growled, and took a threatening step toward Ashby. It was the last thing he remembered. A heavy blow to the back of his skull sent him whirling into oblivion. A moment later, Anthony joined him in the dark void of unconsciousness.

Ashby dusted his hands together and smiled contemptuously down at the two men at his feet. With the gold St. Claire and Sir Godfrey brought and his profits from Edward's wool, he'd be able to live like the king of France himself once he settled into the chateau just outside of Paris that Philip had promised. "Take them back to the keep and throw them into the dungeon."

It took several of Ashby's best men to drag the limp bodies to the oxcart, where they were roughly tossed onto the burlap sacking that covered the stolen bags of wool.

Ashby, caught up in his own plans, didn't hear the shocked gasp from the small, towheaded figure who ducked behind a thick clump of tall sea grass. An arrogant smile curved Ashby's thin lips as he turned to his own mount. Due to the stupidity of men like St. Claire and Godfrey, he had managed to outwit the king of England. He hated Edward to the core of his being for not giving him the power he craved by making him a minister.

Ashby paid no heed to the rattle of dry leaves as Travis scurried toward the safety of the gnarled underbrush like a frightened hare. Climbing into the saddle, Ashby turned his mount in the direction of Ashby Keep. "Soon, dear Edward, I will come to these shores again as your conqueror. Then I'll have no need of your favors."

Breathing heavily, his young face pale with fright and worry, Travis slipped quietly back to where he'd tethered the filly. He glanced once more toward the beach and felt bile rise in his throat. He'd shown himself to be a coward today. The thought burned into his young soul. Any knight of the realm would have gone to his friend's aid instead of hiding in the bushes. And he'd never be able to forgive himself if something happened to Sir Richard and his friend Sir Godfrey.

"I'll not let it happen," Travis swore, gracefully swinging his thin body up on the filly's sleek back. His young face resolute, he turned his mount west. His chapped lips moved in prayer that he was heading in the right direction to Dragon's Lair. He'd been so intent on keeping up with Sir Richard and his men, he didn't know if he remembered the right way.

"Come on, girl. Ye know the way home," Travis urged, bending to pat the filly's muscular neck. "Now take me there." Giving her a kick in the side, he set his mount into a gallop.

The wind ruffled his pale hair as he leaned low over the horse's neck. He'd failed Sir Richard once that day, but he'd not do it again. When he reached Dragon's Lair he'd go directly to Lady Jamelyn and tell her what he'd seen and heard. She'd know exactly what to do to save Sir Richard from the man called Ashby.

Chapter 18

A wide, callused hand clamped down on Travis's upper arm and spun him about. "What do ye think yer a doing prowling about? We don't hold with thieves at Dragon's Lair."

"I ain't no thief. I've come to see Lady St. Claire. I've news for her about Sir Richard."

"What kind of news, boy?" Sandy asked, eyeing the young ragamuffin skeptically.

" 'Tis for me lady's ears alone," Travis said, standing his ground under the bailiff's unrelenting gaze. He didn't know the man and he'd not divulge a word to anyone except Lady Jamelyn. He knew he could trust her.

"Be gone with ye, brat. Ye've no business here."

Casting a quick glance about to ascertain the bailiff was alone, Travis jerked his arm free of Sandy's hand and sped up the stairs, screeching at the top of his lungs. "Lady St. Claire. Lady St. Claire. I've news of Sir Richard."

Travis came to an abrupt halt when a beautiful dark-haired woman rushed to the stair landing and asked, "What news do you have from Sir Richard?"

Giving only a quick glimpse behind him to check the distance between himself and his pursuer, Travis vaulted the last few steps to the landing. He paused, breathless and uncertain in front of Megan. "Where's Lady St. Claire? Sir Richard needs her help."

"What has happened to Sir Richard?" Megan asked, her heart racing with fear.

"I ain't talking to no one but me Lady St. Claire."

"Blast it! I am Lady St. Claire. Now, what is it you know about my husband?" Megan demanded, her voice tinged with panic.

Bewildered, Travis scratched his head and frowned until he realized his own foolish mistake. This lady was Sir Richard's wife. At last he smiled up at Megan and gave a crude bow. "I'm honored to meet you, my lady. Me name's Travis, and I'm in yer husband's service."

Feeling as if she could shake the boy until his eyeballs rattled, Megan schooled herself to try to remain calm. She failed. "Be damned with formalities, Travis. I want to know what has happened to my husband."

Blushing under her censure, Travis cleared his throat and said, "A man called Ashby has captured Sir Richard and Sir Godfrey after killing all his men."

Megan paled. The memory of her visit to Ashby Keep was still fresh in her mind.

"Why would Lord Ashby capture my husband?" she asked, praying the boy had made a mistake.

"Sir Richard said something about Edward's wool and that Lord Ashby was responsible," Travis said, shifting uneasily at the sight of the bailiff standing just a few feet away.

"My God," Megan breathed. " 'Twas Ashby all the time, and now Richard has fallen into the man's clutches."

"I heard Lord Ashby say he's sending them to the dungeons at Ashby Keep and then he's going to ask for ransom but he'd not guarantee Sir Richard or Sir Godfrey their lives." Again Travis cast a wary glance at Sandy but found he was no longer the center of the bailiff's attention.

Megan glanced past Travis to her friend. "What shall we

do? We don't have enough men to dare a rescue, nor do we have time to send for Edward's help.''

"I don't know, Meggie. Should we try anything, 'twould be like Father Reynard told us about David and Goliath.''

"But David won the battle, if you recall," Jamelyn said, crossing the corridor. She'd heard the commotion in the hall and had come to investigate. Pausing at Megan's side, she placed a reassuring hand on her sister-in-law's arm and urged, "Come to the solar, where we may talk freely. If we remain here on the stair landing, there is too much of a chance the wrong person might overhear our plans to help Richard.''

Megan nodded as she looked once more to Travis. "I'm in your debt for all you've done. Should we manage to rescue Richard, you will be responsible because of your quick action at bringing us word of his capture.''

"I don't deserve yer kindness, my lady. I should have fought at Sir Richard's side instead of hiding in the bushes.''

Megan placed a reassuring hand on Travis's bony shoulder and gave it a gentle squeeze. "Had you fought at my husband's side, you would now be dead, and then we wouldn't know where he was until it was too late. No, Travis. If my husband comes home alive, then you are the one who saved his life, and I'm grateful. Now run along to the kitchens and tell Mary to prepare you a supper fit for the hero you are.''

Travis gave Megan and Jamelyn a sheepish grin before turning back to the stairs. He still felt as if he deserved to be punished for his cowardice, but Sir Richard's wife had helped ease his guilt to a certain degree—at least enough for him to feel the hunger gnawing at his ribs.

Faith rose from her chair by the fire when Megan, Jamelyn, and Sandy entered the solar. She knew from their worried expressions something was gravely wrong. "Meggie, what's happened?''

Eyes reflecting the anxiety chewing at her insides, Megan glanced at Jamelyn for some measure of reassurance before she looked once more to Faith. "Richard and Anthony have been captured by Robert Ashby. They have been taken to the dungeons at Ashby Keep."

Faith abruptly sat back down, her face blanching white. She knew Robert Ashby well. He'd been one of Mallory's evil cohorts. They'd enjoyed the same sport: making people suffer.

"Faith, are you all right?" Megan asked upon seeing her cousin's sudden pallor.

Faith turned haunted eyes upon Megan. "Ashby is evil, Meggie. We must free Anthony and Richard before it is too late. He'll make sport out of watching them die in as much agony as he can cause."

"Aye. We must free them, but we have no men to launch an attack upon Ashby Keep," Megan said, her voice breaking under the strain of holding back the tears that clogged her throat.

"Since we can't free them with armed forces, then we must use whatever means we have at our disposal to gain their release," Jamelyn said, her long experience as the Cregan laird standing her in good stead.

Megan arched a brow at her sister-in-law. "Do you have a plan?"

"Aye, but I warn you, it could cost our lives if we are caught."

Megan glanced from Jamelyn to Sandy and then to Faith. Each face showed resolution to do everything possible to help Richard and Anthony. "If we don't try to help, they will die. As I see it, there is no other choice."

Megan looked once more at Sandy and Faith. "Do you agree?"

Both nodded in unison.

"You could choose to remain here and send for Edward's help. In that way you'd not be risking your own lives," Jamelyn said, making sure they understood the danger they were facing if they followed through with her plan.

Faith came to her feet, her pale eyes flashing blue fire. "I will not wait until Ashby decides to send the man I love back to me in pieces upon a shield."

Megan smiled at her cousin's show of courage as well as Faith's first true acknowledgment of her feelings for Sir Godfrey. "Then 'tis settled. Now, tell us of your plan."

Jamelyn looked at her three new friends and felt honored to know them. Here they were, two young women and one man who knew nothing of warfare, yet they were willing to face an army to rescue those they loved. Few had the courage to confront such odds: odds that were severely stacked against them from the beginning.

The full moon crept over the trees, illuminating the grey stone walls of Ashby Keep. A dark-cloaked figure darted from the base of the parapets and into the deep shadows beneath the trees.

"What did you find?" Megan asked as Jamelyn paused to get her breath.

"I've reconnoitered the entire area, and there are only two ways into the keep, and they're both well guarded."

"Do ye think we can scale the walls?" Sandy asked, his voice low.

Jamelyn shook her head. "I see no way for us to get into the keep except through the main gates."

"If we managed to get through the main gates, could we then open the Judas gate for Sandy and the men?" Megan asked, eyeing Ashby Keep thoughtfully.

"Aye, but how do you propose to get through the main gates without being seen?" Jamelyn asked.

"I don't. When I ride through I want Lord Ashby to know of my presence."

" 'Tis no time to jest, Meggie," Sandy said.

"I'm not jesting. We need to get into the keep, and the only way is through the main gates."

" 'Tis insane to even consider such a mad idea. You'd be walking right into Ashby's clutches."

"That's exactly what I want. If we take the keep as Jamelyn's planned, we must get inside and dispatch the guards so you and our men-at-arms can enter."

"She's right," Jamelyn said. "If Richard's wife arrives with her maid upon Ashby's doorstep, asking his help in finding her missing husband, I'm sure he will not turn her away, especially after he's seen her. And while Megan is discussing her husband's disappearance with Ashby, her maid will slip away and open the Judas gate for you."

Sandy shook his head. " 'Tis foolish. Why would Meggie ask for Ashby's help when she already knows he's the one who has Richard locked in his dungeons?"

"Ashby doesn't know Meggie is aware he's the culprit behind Richard's disappearance. 'Tis still too soon. He's had no time to send out a letter of ransom, and he'll be caught off guard by her sudden appearance. He'll never suspect her visit is anything beyond what it seems: a frantic wife searching for her husband."

"It's our only hope, Sandy, and we're going to try it whether you approve or not. The man I love and the father of my child lies in Ashby's dungeons, and I'll not leave here without a fight."

"Nor will I leave here without Anthony at my side," Faith said. Stepping forward, she eyed her cousin. "What do you want me to do?"

"You stay here with the horses. Should we not return within the hour, you're to ride to London for help."

Faith nodded. She longed to be in on the rescue, but she realized her limits. She knew nothing of weapons and warfare and would only be a hindrance, perhaps even getting those she loved killed with her ignorance. She'd do as Megan bid and stay with the horses.

"Then 'tis settled," Megan said, glancing at Jamelyn. "Methinks it's time to pay Lord Ashby a visit."

"My Lady St. Claire, what brings you to Ashby Keep so late? Is there something wrong? My men said it was urgent that you see me," Ashby said, eyeing the beautiful woman appreciatively. He took in her lovely features framed by the hood of her cloak and found himself drowning in her slate blue eyes even as a feeling of recognition tugged at the back of his mind. There was something familiar about her. He knew he'd seen her somewhere before, but he just couldn't quite recall the time or place.

"My Lord," Megan said, dropping into a graceful curtsy and using the skills of deception she'd acquired during her reaving days. "I'm near frantic with worry. I fear something dreadful has happened."

"Please, my lady, sit down and tell me what troubles you," Ashby said, and with a sweep of his hand, indicated the chair across from his own.

"My lord, 'tis my husband," Megan said, sinking down into the seat and folding her cloak securely about her to hide the coarse woolen chausses beneath. She feigned a sniffle and again wiped at her eyes.

Jamelyn smiled at the skill with which Megan wove her web and again acknowledged her as Richard's rightful mate. They were equals in all respects, from the telling of tall tales to their valor. Secure Megan had Ashby's attention, she quietly eased from the chamber. A wary glance in all directions told her it was safe to make her way out of the main hall and to the Judas gate she'd spotted earlier in the north wall. Lifting her cloak out of her way, she sped down the corridor and out into the bailey, then turned in the direction of the gate.

A few moments later Jamelyn came to a skidding halt at

the sight of the man-at-arms on guard duty. Reacting instinctively, she sank back into the shadows and surveyed the area, hoping to find some way to remove the guard from his post without a confrontation that might draw attention. Seeing none, Jamelyn frowned.

There was only one way to draw the man away from the gate. A cunning smile tugged at the corners of her mouth as she carefully adjusted her sword to make it easily accessible beneath her cloak and then stepped brazenly from the shadows. She sauntered toward the guard, hips swinging provocatively.

"Halt! Who goes there?" the guard asked, raising his pike.

" 'Tis only me," Jamelyn said, her voice low and seductive.

The guard paused, intrigued by the sultry feminine voice. "Who is me?"

" 'Tis the one ye've been chasing about the kitchen these last weeks," Jamelyn lied sweetly, and prayed she'd used the right ploy. From long experience with Raven's Keep's men-at-arms, she knew if there was a female within miles, any normal soldier would be chasing her.

"Nellie?"

"Aye," Jamelyn said, within a few feet of the guard.

"I'm on duty now, sweetling. 'Tis the wrong time for any games. Wait fer me in the stables after me shift is over."

Jamelyn feigned a pout and turned her back on the guard. "Then 'twill always be the wrong time for ye. If ye don't want me now, I'll just set me eyes on someone who does."

The guard stepped close, anxious not to lose the chance he'd been awaiting for so many weeks.

It was the mistake Jamelyn had been counting on. She firmly gripped the base of the hilt of her sword and, using it as a cudgel, swung with all her might as she turned once more toward Ashby's man.

Taking him completely by surprise, the blow landed against the side of the guard's head. For a fraction of a moment his eyes rounded in shock, then he sank to the ground like a stone.

Jamelyn gave a sniff of disdain, smugly readjusted her cloak, and glanced warily about. Spying no one, she stepped over the unconscious guard and slid back the latch to the Judas gate. She ground her teeth together at the sound as it slowly squeaked open. Again she flashed a wary look about. Seeing no one, she stepped outside and waved. A moment later Sandy and his men slipped inside Ashby Keep.

Steathily they spread out, silently dispatching Ashby's unwary guards and locking in those who still lived in the garrison before making their way to the dungeons.

"Richard," Jamelyn called after a heavy-set guard lay at the foot of the stairs, bleeding from a gash made by Sandy's blade.

Richard struggled to his feet, unable to believe his own ears as he moved toward the thick-timbered door. "Jamie, is that you?"

"Aye, Richard," Jamelyn said. Using the ring of keys she'd confiscated from the dying guard, she unlocked the door and swung it open to reveal her dirty, beard-stubbled brother-in-law. She threw herself into his arms, thinking nothing of the filth that soiled her own cloak.

"Be damned," Anthony swore, squinting against the rushlight and grinning from ear to ear. "How did you find us?"

"That mischief-maker, Travis, told us where you'd been taken. Now we must hurry," Jamelyn said, already turning toward the stairs.

"But how did you manage to defeat Ashby's men?" Richard asked, following close upon his sister-in-law's heels.

"We didn't defeat them," Jamelyn answered, smiling up at Richard as they stepped out into the moonlit night. "We outsmarted them. Your wife now keeps Ashby entertained with her worries over your sudden disappearance.''

"What? Megan's here, and with Ashby? By all that's holy!'' Richard swore, his face paling at the thought of the dangerous position in which Megan had placed herself. He turned on Jamelyn. "I'll never forgive you if something happens to Meggie.''

Sandy stepped forward. '' 'Tis not Lady Jamelyn's fault, Sir Richard. 'Twas Meggie's idea to see Ashby. 'Twas the only way to get into Ashby Keep and rescue you.''

"I should have known,'' Richard said with a resigned shake of his dark head. Eyeing his sister-in-law, he gave her a sheepish, apologetic grin. "I said she was much like you, did I not? Forgive me, Jamie.''

Jamelyn nodded and handed her sword to Richard. "I'm sure you want to be the one to confront Ashby.''

"Aye. 'Twill be my pleasure.'' Richard gripped the intricately worked hilt and strode toward the great hall. Several of Ashby's men tried to stop him, but he quickly dispatched them to their maker.

The ring of steel against steel pierced the inner sanctums of Ashby's private quarters, where he'd sat during the last half hour enjoying himself at Megan's expense. Her tears and pleas for his help in finding her missing husband had amused him greatly. But when the commotion broke out in the corridor, the change that came over her was visibly apparent and alerted him to the fact he'd been played for a fool. Her expression told him something far more serious was afoot and she'd been used as the decoy. There was no grief or misery in the depths of her indigo eyes, only a triumphant expression as if she'd only been waiting for the moment to come to pass.

Pushing to his feet, Ashby turned on Megan, his face mottled with rage, his eyes glittering with hatred, a snarl pulling his mouth into a grotesque mask. "You scheming, lying bitch! You knew all the time your husband was here, didn't you?''

Megan came to her feet and eyed Ashby contemptuously. ''Aye. I knew you had locked him in your dungeons.''

''And you think you've won, don't you?'' Ashby asked, his voice low and silky with menace as he grasped Megan by the arm. Jerking her toward him, he drew his dirk and raised it to her throat. ''But you haven't, bitch. Richard may be free, but you'll die in his stead.''

''Let her go, Ashby. 'Tis between you and me,'' Richard ordered from the doorway.

Ashby twisted Megan about so she faced her husband. Ashby shook his head and pressed his dirk against her slender throat, making her arch her head back to avoid the sharp edge of the blade. ''Nay. I think not, St. Claire. And if you're wise you won't make any wrong moves or she's dead.''

''Let Meggie go or you're a dead man.''

''Unless I reach France, I'm already a dead man, St. Claire. So you see, I have nothing to lose by slitting her lovely throat from ear to ear.''

Richard itched to throw himself upon Ashby and kill him with his bare hands, but he suppressed the urge. He couldn't risk Megan's life. Until she was free, he'd have to do as the bastard bid.

Ashby smirked at Richard. ''I see you realize I mean what I say. Now, let us pass or you'll lose this wife you seem to care so much about.''

''Richard,'' Megan whispered, her eyes and lips telling him all that was in her heart as she was forced to move toward the door. ''I love you.''

''Meggie, I won't let anything happen to you,'' Richard breathed, his knuckles white upon the sword, his face set, and his insides churning as if they were being trampled under a herd of iron-shod war-horses.

Ashby chuckled as he backed toward the doors. ''Such

devotion, St. Claire. Now call your men and tell them to saddle my horse.''

In minutes Sandy led Ashby's horse forward and watched him force Megan at knife point to mount in front of him. He kicked out at Sandy, hitting him in the middle of his chest with his booted foot. The bailiff staggered backward gasping for breath as Ashby jerked the horse's head about and rode from the keep.

After bellowing orders for the fastest horse at Ashby Keep to be saddled for him, as well as instructions to Jamelyn and Anthony about securing Ashby's holding for Edward, Richard paced the bailey like a madman until his mount arrived. It had taken less time to saddle his mount than it had Ashby's, but to him it seemed as if an eternity had passed. Leaping into the saddle, he kicked his horse in the side, startling it into a gallop. The clatter of hooves echoed in the still night air as he crossed the wooden bridge moments later in Ashby's wake.

Ashby had taken the road toward the Wash, and Richard suspected he intended to escape by ship. Determined to thwart him, Richard urged his horse off the road and into the thick woods surrounding Ashby Keep. It was the shortest way to the Wash. Tree limbs beat at him as he raced through the dark woods, but he didn't slow his pace. His wife's life depended upon his quick actions. If he didn't arrive at the Wash before Ashby, the villain would kill Meggie.

Richard was already on the ground before his horse came to a skidding halt. Muscles tensed and ready for battle, he moved stealthily toward the beach where he'd been captured earlier in the day. Bending low, he crept from bush to rock to clump of grass until he reached the bags of wool packed high for shipment. Spying a lone smuggler on guard duty by a small fire, he eased along until he was directly behind the man. His shadow stretched out across the sandy beach as he raised the hilt of his sword and rendered the smuggler senseless. Without making a sound, the man fell facedown in the sand. It took Richard only a moment to disrobe him of the hooded mantle he wore. Slipping it over his own head, he turned his attention to the unconscious smuggler. He bound and gagged the man before dragging him into the darkness beyond the campfire.

Breathing heavily, every muscle in his body tensed for the moment he saw Ashby, Richard settled himself down to await his enemy's arrival. The villain was expecting to be met tonight, and Richard would insure he'd not be disappointed.

Richard didn't rise from his position by the small fire when Ashby, his mount flecked with foam from the hard ride, jerked his horse to a halt. He gave Megan a shove, sending her sprawling to the sand at the horse's feet, and then nearly leaped from the saddle himself. In his haste to reach the safety of the open waters, he paid no heed to the hooded smuggler, who half rose when Megan was thrown from the horse. Intent upon his own escape, he grabbed Megan and jerked her to her feet. He pressed the dirk blade once more against her skin.

"Bitch, I'm not through with you yet. Once I'm in open water, then and only then will you be free of me." Ashby chuckled, running the point of his dirk along Megan's throat. "The fish should enjoy your smooth flesh. I'd sample it myself if I had the time." Ashby glanced at Richard as he dragged Megan toward the small boat. "What are you waiting for? Row me out to the *Maiden*; she's waiting in the channel."

Richard kept his head lowered and grunted an unintelligible answer as he stepped into a small boat and moved back to the rudder, where the shadows obscured his identity. As soon as Ashby moved away from Megan, and Richard was sure she was safe, then he would be ready.

"Set out to sea," Ashby ordered as he forced Megan into the prow of the boat and tied her hands and feet. Satisfied he had her secure, and ignoring her wide-eyed expression as she stared past him, he turned to find Richard towering over him, sword in hand.

"Damn you, St. Claire. You and your bitch will both die," Ashby swore. He drew his sword and lunged at Richard. His movement tilted the boat precariously, tossing Megan near the edge, where the waves lapped to get inside.

His own footing made unsteady by the sudden shifting beneath his feet, Richard, his agile body honed to react instantly to danger, managed to evade the thrust of Ashby's blade. Countering, he brought his blade down so swiftly, Ashby didn't have time to avoid it. The gleaming steel sank into his chest, piercing Ashby's heart. A look of bewilderment flickered across the man's startled features as he fell forward, again dangerously tilting the boat on its side. Unable to balance himself with Ashby's weight making the boat shift, Richard fell toward the edge. His weight combined with Ashby's made the boat tip over.

Water rushed into the hull and closed over Megan before she had time to scream for help. She felt herself sinking and struggled valiantly against her bonds, but she was helpless to stop herself from descending into the dark, murky depths of the icy sea-water. Her lungs burned with the need to breathe, and dark shadows flickered before her watery gaze. Her head felt as if it would burst from the pressure of holding her breath until she finally surrendered and let it free. Her last conscious thought was of the man she loved and the child she would never see again.

"Meggie," Richard cried before diving beneath the moon-silvered waves into the black depths that had stolen his wife. He felt the churning water where Megan struggled, and swam toward her. His hand touched her hair, but she slipped away from his. Coming to the surface, he gulped in a quick breath before diving once more. He felt only the current tugging at him, but he wouldn't give up. He plunged deeper, preferring to die with Megan than to lose her. He felt her hair web about his face at the same moment his hands came into contact with her icy, limp body. Reacting instinctively, he grabbed her and swam to the surface. His heart felt as if it would burst when Megan didn't stir.

"Meggie, you have to live," was his agonized order as he swam toward shore with his wife. Coming to his knees in the surf, he lifted Megan in his arms and carried her to the hard-packed sand at the water's edge. Placing her facedown, he pressed on her back and lifted her arms above her head to make her take air. He pressed and pulled, yet Megan lay still.

Overwhelmed by grief Richard knelt at Megan's side and buried his face in his hands, surrendering to the misery ripping his insides apart. The sound of his sobs filled the night and drowned out the small moan that emanated from Megan as her insides rejected the seawater she'd swallowed and she vomited. She gasped for breath and coughed.

"Meggie," Richard cried as he lifted her into his arms and brushed wet hair and damp sand away from her face. He gazed down into her moon-silvered features and thanked God for the miracle he'd been granted. "You're alive. I don't believe I could have gone on living without you."

"Richard," Megan murmured, her voice filling with tears of relief. "You're safe."

"Aye, I'm safe, but 'tis not me you should concern yourself with. 'Tis yourself. I nearly lost you, my love." Richard's embrace tightened about Megan.

Megan raised a trembling hand to touch Richard's tear-drenched cheeks. A tender, loving smile played upon her trembling lips as she gazed up at him in wonder. "Do you realize that's the first time you've ever said 'love' to me, Richard?"

"I know, and I was a fool, for I've loved you far longer

than I even realized. Can you ever forgive me for wasting so much time?''

"I can forgive you anything as long as I have your love,'' Megan said, and knew in her heart it was true.

"Then for the rest of my life I can be an arrogant, insensitive scoundrel and have your pardon for my faults, because I'll love you forever, Meggie.''

"Perhaps I should reconsider, my lord?'' Megan teased, her soaring spirits making her forget that only a short while before she'd been near death.

"Nay, Meggie. Forgive me my faults and I'll forgive you yours.''

"I agree, because as long as we love each other we can face anything life has to offer.''

"Oh, Meggie,'' Richard said, his voice hoarse with emotion. "I do love you so much. You are my soul, my life. You have made me forget the past and look to the future. And I see only happiness with you there to share it with me.''

"I'll always be there for you, my darling husband, for you, too, are my soul, and without you I'm only a shadow with no existence at all.''

Megan reached up and pulled Richard's head down to hers. She took his lips in a kiss that spoke more clearly than any words man had invented. It was a kiss of passion, a kiss of love, a kiss binding them in body and soul for eternity.

Richard felt his pulse soar as her small tongue enticed his lips open and then tasted of him. He longed to lie with her on the moonlit beach and make love, but he feared he'd harm her after the ordeal. Using all the willpower he possessed, he managed to extricate himself from Megan's arms and move away from her. He shook his head. "Nay, Meggie. I have to put some distance between us or I'll not be responsible for what happens. You've just come close to drowning and you're not able to endure my attentions now. You need to rest and recuperate. Come, I'll take you home to Dragon's Lair.''

Richard held out his hand to Megan, but she shook her head and gave him a provocative smile. Her gaze never left Richard's as she slowly worked loose the lacings on her water-soaked jerkin and then eased the fabric up over her head. Her full young breasts were visible through the damp fabric of her linen chainse. She arched her back enticingly before she also pulled the undergarment over her head and tossed it away to expose the gleaming, rose-tipped ivory mounds to Richard's gaze.

Again Megan gave Richard a provocative smile and ran the tip of her tongue teasingly over her lips as she lay back on the moon-silvered sand. She held up her arms to him, and her words were as soft as the night. "Let me be the judge of how I feel, husband. I want you to love me now. To show me I am alive and haven't died and gone to heaven."

"You're very much alive," Richard said, surrendering to his wife's demands as well as his body's. "And I'll prove it to you." He moved over Megan and captured her lips in a searing, earthshaking kiss before he lowered his head to the tempting mounds and suckled greedily.

The sea, the stars, the velvety night, surrounded them, blanketing the pair in enchantment as they coupled there upon the beach, savoring their union and their love. They gave of themselves fully for the first time without fear. No longer was any part hidden as they opened their hearts completely to each other. Together they touched the sun, the moon, and the universe, and never would they forget the ecstasy they found on their first journey into love unfettered by fears and doubts.

Sated and more content than she'd ever have dreamed possible, Megan returned with her husband to Dragon's Lair. Together they entered the hall where Faith sat holding Anthony's hand, while Jamelyn and Sandy peacefully watched young Richard sleep on his pallet.

"Is this any way to welcome us home?" Richard asked, slightly annoyed by his friends' lack of concern about their welfare. Had it been any one of the four, he'd still be searching for them. Richard glanced at his wife and saw her smile. He frowned. Something was afoot here, but he couldn't place his finger on it. "I would think you'd at least show a little surprise we have returned safe and sound."

"We never doubted it," Jamelyn said at last, coming to her feet to greet them. A smile of welcome played upon her lips.

Richard arched a brow. "I wish I'd had your confidence when Ashby drew his sword in the small boat. 'Tis only by the grace of God Meggie is alive now. She nearly drowned."

"But you're alright now, aren't you, Meggie?" Faith asked.

"Aye. I'm fine, thanks to my wonderful husband," Megan said, lifting her son into her arms and nuzzling him beneath his soft double chin.

"Then all is settled, Richard?" Anthony asked, a timid smile playing about his sensuous lips.

"Aye. Edward no longer has to worry about his wool. Without Ashby to notify the thieves of the pack trains from York, they'll have little luck."

"Then do you think you can manage without me? I've decided it is high time I returned to my own family estates and took some interest in them."

Richard glanced at Megan before looking once more at his friend. "What's brought on this sudden decision? I thought you were happy to let your brother care for the estate."

"I was, until tonight," Anthony said, smiling at Faith.

"Did a spell in Ashby's dungeon rattle your brains?" Richard asked, still puzzled by his friend's decision.

"I think there is more here than they are telling us," Megan said, handing her son over to Jamelyn. She smiled at the flush that suffused Faith from head to toe. "Is there anything you would like to tell us?"

Anthony chuckled. "I was wondering how long it would take Richard to figure it out. Without your help I believe he'd still be befuddled even after the vows were spoken."

Richard's face lit up and he swore good-naturedly, "Be damned if you didn't take my advice after all. And from Lady Faith's expression, I suspect the answer was yes when you asked her to marry you."

"You're right, old friend. Now Justin can quit worrying about us. We'll both be old married men," Anthony said, his face breaking into a wide, besotted grin.

"Bring us Dragon's Lair's best wine," Richard ordered the serving maid, Mary. " 'Tis a night for celebrations. Two fools have finally come to their senses."

Laughter pealed through the great halls as the St. Claire family and friends celebrated Lady Faith's betrothal to Sir Godfrey. While Anthony and Sandy happily discussed the merits of different crops, and the women talked of the wedding, Richard detached himself from the group and poured himself another tankard of wine. As he watched his wife and friends enjoying themselves, he recalled what Anthony had once said about him and his beautiful wife when they'd first married. He'd likened them to birds of prey, muttering they were the Hawk and the Falcon: one large and one small but of the same breed and equally matched in fierce temperament.

Richard's gaze rested lovingly upon his wife. When Anthony called them Hawks and Falcons, Richard hadn't appreciated the remark. However, now upon reflection of his relationship with Megan, he had to admit he now liked the comparison. For in truth they were like the Hawk and the Falcon, and there would never be a dull minute between them. Megan would keep his life interesting.

Richard glanced toward Lady Faith. He suspected from

what he'd observed of Megan's cousin tonight, Anthony's life wouldn't have too many dull minutes in it either. Lady Faith had a quiet strength about her, but there was also a bit of Megan's fire in her cousin. He'd seen it when she looked at his friend.

Happy for himself and his friends, Richard tapped his tankard with the hilt of his dirk, drawing the attention of everyone in the hall. Raising the drinking vessel high above his head, he made a toast that drew puzzled looks from the servants and smiles from his friends.

"To the Hawks and the Falcons," he roared before downing the contents of the tankard in one gulp. He slammed the vessel down on the table, gave a loud highland yell, and crossed the hall to where his wife sat. He scooped her up into his arms and carried her up the stairs to their bedchamber. Like the Hawk, he had found his mate for life.

ABOUT THE AUTHOR

Cordia Byers was born in the small north Georgia community of Jasper and lives there still, with her husband, James. Cordia likes to think of her husband as being like one of the heroes in her novels. James swept her off her feet after their first meeting, and they were married three weeks later.

From the age of six, Cordia's creative talents had been directed toward painting. It was not until late 1975, when the ending of a book displeased her, that she considered writing. That led to her first novel, *Heather*, which was followed by *Callista*, *Nicole La Belle*, *Silk and Steel*, *Love Storm*, *Pirate Royale* (Winner of a *Romantic Times* Reviewer's Choice Award), *Star of the West*, *Ryan's Gold*, and *Lady Fortune*. Finding more satisfaction in the world of her romantic novels, Cordia has given up painting and now devotes herself to writing, researching her material at the local library, and then doing the major part of her work from 11:30 P.M. to 3:00 A.M.

A touch of romance...

from

Cordia Byers

14   TAF-61